THE ESCAPE

Greg looked at Andrea. She sat next to him, ashen, shaking badly, her hands clasped. She stared at him, her eyes wide.

He couldn't bear the tension any longer and pulled her against him in a tight embrace. She started to cry and he cried, too. "I've missed you," he mumbled between sobs.

"I've missed you, too," she murmured.

He felt her body trembling and her tears running down her face. "Pauper and beggar are together again," he said. "Remember what we did in Reno? It was crazy, but we never regretted it."

She nodded.

"I still remember the old man's words and our wedding vows."

"I remember them, too," she whispered.

He released her gently and then looked outside the car windows. They had stopped at a traffic light. It was a crazy idea, but he had to do it. It was now or never, he told himself, grabbing Andrea's hand. The light changed as he yanked the door handle. He jumped out, dragging her behind him. He heard the FBI driver shouting at him, but he didn't care. He saw the subway entrance and urged Andrea to run. They had to get away—fast, very fast. . . .

THE MOSCOW SACRAMENT

ARNALDO HERNANDEZ

ZEBRA BOOKS
KENSINGTON PUBLISHING CORP.

Also by Arnaldo Hernandez
BLIND CONSPIRACY

ZEBRA BOOKS

are published by

Kensington Publishing Corp.
475 Park Avenue South
New York, NY 10016

First printing: December, 1988

Printed in the United States of America

To my wife Barbara:
Love is eternal inspiration. . . .

Prodigious birth of love it is to me
That I must love a loathèd enemy.

Romeo and Juliet
(I.v.142-143)

CHAPTER 1

Frank Hansen shifted his not so muscular body on the hard seat of the aluminum johnboat. He glanced at his watch and shook his head; a full hour had gone by and he had not caught a single trout. Maybe the trout were on vacation, too, he thought, flycasting to another spot. He studied the new area, satisfied that the line's slack was ensuring a proper float. He rested the flyrod next to him, its tip pointing at the line, and looked around mindlessly. Daybreak had just come and he could now see the calm, mirrorlike water that stretched until it met the abrupt rim of snow-topped mountains. Hansen took a deep breath as he pushed up his rimless glasses. It was early fall, and the air was crisp and smelled of fresh greenery. The morning was beautiful and slow, exactly the way he had dreamed of it for the last three years.

The thirty-five-year-old Hansen had been working for the CIA now for seven years. With a PhD in psychology from Northeastern University in Boston, he specialized in the debriefing of defectors, and this was his first real vacation in three years. He was finally spending it doing what he liked to do most. He'd wanted to take a sporting vacation ever since his father had given him a fishing rod as a present on his seventh birthday.

He glanced at the clear water and considered pulling up anchor and moving to another location, but just then the familiar sound of an airplane engine caught his attention: it was the same float plane that had taken him to the remote fly-in Moose Lake in the Rocky Mountains in British Columbia. But he had asked the pilot to come back in ten days.

The float plane, a single-engine DCH-3 Otter, circled a couple of times, then approached the lake in a perfect landing that drew long, foamy waves in the calm water. Hansen watched the Otter's landing with dismay, sure that no trout would linger after such an inopportune interruption. Even worse, there was only one reason for the float plane's return after only one day: Langley was sending him an urgent message.

Hansen's boyish face grew anguished. He had planned the vacation for months, deliberately choosing this remote lake to avoid the quick phone call that had ended so many of his previous vacations. They would have to need him pretty badly to interrupt this vacation, he had thought when he'd rented the fly-in cabin high in the snowy Rocky Mountains. Unfortunately, CIA regulations called for leaving a point of contact when an agent was on personal leave or on vacation, and he'd left the name of the pilot and his phone number. What a mistake!

Slowly he pulled the line out of the water and rested the flyrod on the bottom of the johnboat. The Otter approached him and he started to row slowly toward it, trying to control his disappointment. There was something worse than flycasting for an hour and not catching a single trout—a float plane with a message from the CIA.

He was about fifty yards from the plane when the Otter's side door opened and a man climbed down to one of the floats, waving both hands at him. Hansen recognized the angular face of Chuck Maguire, a senior CIA operative. Hansen, now sure that his vacation was over, felt his misery increase. Langley would never have sent Maguire just to deliver a message.

A corpulent man in his mid-fifties, or so his colleagues guessed him to be, for Maguire had never revealed his age to anyone, he was a senior troubleshooter for the Special Operations Division, reporting to the Deputy Director for Operations, DDO, at the CIA. He was a shrewd, tough agent with over thirty years of field operations experience, and he often boasted that his years at the CIA had given him the extra ability to spot a KGB man a mile away. Maguire's steely eyes always gleamed at the thought of chasing KGB agents, of finding and neutralizing them—just like the glint of enjoyment in the eyes of a cat, Hansen thought, when it had trapped a mouse.

Hansen had worked with Maguire many times in the past, helping him to debrief defectors, and more than once, debriefing captured KGB agents who later disappeared without a trace. It was the type of work that Maguire enjoyed and that Hansen abhorred: assignments buried under many levels of the CIA's bureaucracy with no traceable records, no written orders, no reports, and no links to higher levels of management. They were jobs that Maguire frequently called "shaking the tree."

"Hurry up!" Maguire shouted. "We don't have much time."

"What?" Hansen asked. He was now about ten yards from the Otter.

"Get in," Maguire said, climbing back to the door of the plane, "We must take off immediately."

Hansen looked at Maguire as if not understanding his words, then glanced at the boat. "What am I going to do with the johnboat and my fishing gear?"

"I already paid the pilot to come back and pick up your gear and luggage from the cabin. Damn it! Hurry up, we're wasting time."

After dropping the small anchor into the water, Hansen climbed on the float, then into the cabin. Maguire had extended a hand to help him, but Hansen ignored him, giving his johnboat and the flyrod one last, sorrowful glance. "Did Langley approve this interruption?" he asked.

"You bet," Maguire grinned. "Besides, you're damned lucky that I'm getting you out of this remote place. If the Russkies had known you were alone here, they'd've sent a KGB wet squad to pump a pint of chemicals into your veins that would have made you sing like a happy canary. Then we'd have found you drowned in a convenient fishing accident."

Hansen shook his head and said nothing.

The two men buckled their seat belts as the pilot revved the Otter's engine. The float plane vibrated and started to move on the flat water. Moments later, the pilot took a sharp turn as the plane gained altitude. Hansen looked down through the window and saw his johnboat still bobbing in the waves made by the float plane's takeoff. He thought of the trout he was leaving behind and of the dreams of a vacation that had to wait for yet another time. He also realized that Langley had to have a very important reason to send someone for him.

He turned to Maguire. "Can you tell me what's going on?"

Maguire raised a finger to his lips, glanced at the pilot, and said, "Can't talk now. I've got a Cessna Citation waiting for us at Kelowna's airport. We must land at JFK before 3 p.m." He glanced at his watch. "We'll barely make it. I'll bring you up to date when we're in the Cessna."

Hansen sank deeper into the uncomfortable seat. The noise inside the cabin was loud and the flight was bumpy. Outside the small window he saw the snow-covered mountain peaks, the sparkling reflections of a lake, and the green vegetation that stretched out with no end in sight. Fuck! he said to himself.

The seat belt sign went off in the cabin of the Swissair Boeing 747 and Andrea Hendrick unbuckled her seat belt. She turned to the man in the pin-striped business suit and red tie sitting next to her. "Excuse me, Dmitri, I must go to the lavatory," she said politely.

He nodded silently, got up, stood in the aisle and let her pass. Andrea smiled timidly at the slightly more than six-feet-tall Dmitri Kotov. Square-shouldered and muscular, with dark hair and a pockmarked complexion, he was a man who inspired no friendships. His alert eyes studied everyone he met with fierce intensity and Andrea now avoided looking into his eyes as she walked past. She didn't know much about Dmitri. She guessed that he was a KGB agent, rather than a diplomat assigned to the Mission, and that the Center had assigned him to report to the same place she was going. Her KGB control agent in Vienna had not supplied any information except that she would be traveling with a companion.

Andrea moved down the aisle toward the lavatories. This was her second flight in a 747, and the plane still amazed her with its wide body, the many seats and passengers, the attentive stewardesses offering all types of food and drink and other services. As Andrea closed and locked the lavatory door, a fluorescent light went on, and she squinted briefly. She did not feel well. Her hands were cold and shaky, her face wet with perspiration, and a slight pain nestled in her stomach. She knew the reason for her discomfort—anxiety.

The nervous strain was one of the aftereffects of her stay in a

Moscow clinic. After her release from the clinic, she had had terrible migraines, vomiting and disorientation, then nightmares. But now only the chills and the cold sweats remained. It would take some time for them to go away, a Russian doctor had told her. But after three years she still felt the effects whenever she faced the unknown and sensed danger. Unable to bear any type of stress, she would sometimes tremble uncontrollably until a cold shower stopped the shaking.

She wet her face with cold water, pulled down a couple of paper towels, and dried her face. She studied it in the mirror and her anxiety increased. Would they recognize her? she wondered. It had been three and a half years since the swap took place, and her name had been changed. She had a passport in the name of Valeri Lisenko, a Russian specialist in linguistics. The KGB technician had dyed her hair darker and trimmed it shorter. She hated it, but she had no choice but to accept the transformation. The technicians had also tanned her face to hide her fair complexion. Thinner and wearing a formal black suit that made her look older, she sighed, satisfied with her disguise. The changes might be enough, she thought, if only I can hide the terror in my eyes. She opened her purse and took out a small plastic bottle. Cupping her hand under the lavatory tap, she poured water into it, put a pill in her mouth, and swallowed it.

Feeling slightly better, she walked back down the aisle. She had been flying for only one hour and already she had had an anxiety attack. After leaving Vienna early this morning on a connecting flight to Zurich, she had taken the 747 in a direct flight to New York. The plane's arrival time at JFK was 3 p.m., and she wished the plane would never land.

Primarily agricultural, the town of Kelowna sat on the edge of Okanagan Lake about a hundred miles north of the U.S. border. Hansen had stayed briefly in Kelowna on his way to Moose Lake and as the Otter landed he looked out the window at the city. His misery increased at the thought of his fishing gear left behind and his short-lived vacation. One day I'll stay here as long as I want, he thought. Then, there would be no more Maguires—and no more CIA.

The float plane docked at a small pier and Maguire opened the door without waiting for the pilot to shut off the engine. "Let's get our asses moving," he said.

They walked to solid ground, past a small house that served as an office and a chain-link fence. A rented Ford was waiting, and Maguire fumbled inside a pocket for the key. They stopped next to the vehicle. "Are you going to tell me what's going on?" Hansen asked, not hiding his anger.

"We've got no time to talk," Maguire said, getting in the car and turning the ignition. "I'll explain it to you when we're in the Cessna. Then we'll have plenty of time to talk."

During the short ride to the airport, Maguire broke every speed limit and Hansen wondered how Maguire would have justified the rush if a police car had stopped them. Maguire drove around the terminal, through a gate manned by a police officer, and into the airfield. The policeman recognized Maguire and waved him on. Maguire's efficiency impressed Hansen; the man planned everything so well.

The Cessna Citation's door was open and two pilots stood there waiting for them. Hansen recognized the pilots: they were often used by the CIA. Maguire parked the car, dropped the keys on the seat, and ran toward the plane. Hansen, still wearing jeans, sneakers, a fishing vest, and a Chicago Cubs baseball cap, ran behind him. I hope this thing is important enough to justify all this fuss, Hansen thought.

Maguire stopped to ask one of the pilots, an older man with sand-colored hair, "Any messages?"

The pilot nodded. "They left Zurich on time."

Maguire glanced at his watch and grimaced. "It's gonna be a race down to the wire. Let's get moving." He turned to Hansen and looked him up and down in his fishing outfit. "I've got a suit for you in the plane," he said.

After takeoff, Hansen changed into a three-piece suit that was a little too big, but considering the circumstances, he gave Maguire a passing grade in selecting it. Actually, it was even his favorite color.

Maguire sat comfortably in a plush seat and had already opened a small icebox in the rear of the plane and pulled out a bottle of scotch. He offered the weary Hansen a drink, but

Hansen shook his head. "No, thanks—I'll have one later."

Maguire shrugged and poured half a glass for himself. "Nice suit," he said. "You look good in it."

"Well, we're in the Cessna now. Aren't you going to tell me what all this fuss is about? I hope we aren't starting World War III."

Maguire smiled, looking at his glass. "Nothing like that yet," he said. "But we've got something of real interest here. Our Chief of Station in Vienna sent a message yesterday and pictures of two Russians who were flying to New York to join the Soviet Mission at the United Nations. At first we didn't pay too much attention to the message. This stuff is normally routine, but when we looked at the pictures, we realized that one of the Russians was Andrea Hendrick, the KGB spy whom we swapped back to them over three years ago." He paused to take a sip of his drink.

Hansen's eyes widened. He couldn't believe that the KGB was sending Andrea back. "It doesn't make any sense," he said.

Maguire motioned with his hand, asking Hansen to wait. "She's using a new name, Valeri Lisenko. The KGB's Hollywood technicians have changed her appearance a little, but still, she's an easy catch."

"I don't understand," Hansen said.

"Let me continue," Maguire said. "She's coming with a diplomatic passport, assigned to the Soviet Mission as a linguistics expert. The Russian traveling with her, Dmitri Kotov, is coming as a cultural attaché. Y'know, the kinda fancy title the KGB uses to cover its people." He drained the glass and poured more scotch into it. "We don't have anything on him yet."

"Why do you think Andrea is coming back?"

"Don't know. The dossier we have on her is sketchy. Right after the swap, our informers told us that the KGB put her in a clinic in Moscow." He smiled. "The kinda place that makes you go crazy. Our analysts believed that the KGB was angry because of the killing of Andrea's control agent, Boris Alexei Grishin. The KGB blamed the CIA for blowing Boris's brains out and accused Andrea of being an accomplice." He took another drink, wiped his mouth with the back of his hand, then looked at the bottle. "Good stuff."

"What happened later?" Hansen asked.

"Something very strange. The KGB released Andrea from the clinic. She recovered, and after three months, they sent her on an assignment to Havana."

"Havana?"

"Yeah. We don't know what she did there, but she reappeared two years later in Vienna. She arrived on a Czech flight from Prague to Vienna's Schwecht Airport, assigned to the Russian Embassy in Vienna."

"What could she possibly have done in Havana for two years?" Hansen pursued.

"The only information we have is that she was working as an assistant to a KGB colonel on duty in Cuba."

"It doesn't make any sense," Hansen said. "From a death clinic to an assignment to Havana."

"That's not all," Maguire interrupted. "In Vienna, she commuted often to Geneva to work as a translator with the Russian negotiation team to the Soviet-American arms control talks."

Hansen let a sigh escape. "I can see now why you are so interested in her."

"You got it, buddy. What in hell has she been doing, jumping around so much? Also, what was she doing with the Russian negotiation team in Geneva? That stuff is ultrasensitive, and now the KGB is sending her back to the U.S. It's like throwing raw meat to a bunch of hungry lions. They know that we're gonna eat her alive, and those guys ain't dumb. They wouldn't do this unless they've got something else in mind. They're sending Andrea here for a reason, and Langley wants to know why."

"Are we going to pick her up?"

Maguire shook his head brusquely. "Hell, no! We're gonna play the game for a while." He looked down at the bottle in his hand. "You sure you don't want a drink?"

"That stuff is too much for me. I'll have a beer later."

Maguire stuffed the bottle into a pocket in the back of the seat in front of him. Slowly he turned his head and faced Hansen, who was staring at him intensely. "You were Andrea's debriefing officer. You worked with her for six months until we swapped her. You know her very well. I want you to watch her as she goes through customs. We instructed the officer to ask her a lot of questions. I want you to hear the tone of her voice, to see her expression, to watch her reactions and body language. We have to see through her eyes into her mind. You're the guy who knows her best—"

"There is another person who knows her pretty well," Hansen interrupted.

"Yeah, I know. Her husband, Greg Elliot."

CHAPTER 2

Hansen glanced at his watch. "We aren't going to make it. If I'm right, we're going to land after three." They had been flying for over four hours.

Maguire glanced at his watch as if to verify Hansen's words. "I don't want to miss the Swissair flight," he said with a frown. "This is too damned important."

"Besides, I won't forgive you for interrupting my vacation for nothing," Hansen said.

"Don't start."

"I'm serious."

"You'd rather be fishing than doing something exciting, huh?"

"This is exciting?"

"Sure. You can look at it as some kinda fishing."

"Fishing?"

"Yeah, fishing for KGB sharks." Maguire let a little smile lift a corner of his lips.

"Don't like sharks."

"That's your choice."

"What do you want to do? We're going to get there late."

"Perhaps the pilot can hurry up." Maguire stood up from his seat as Hansen stepped aside to let him into the aisle. When they reached the small cockpit and the two Cessna pilots, the older man with sand-colored hair turned to face them.

"Tom, what's the arrival time?" Maguire asked.

"We don't know exactly, sir," the pilot said. "Right now it looks as if we'll land at 3:10 p.m."

"That ain't good enough, Tom," Maguire said.

"I know, sir."

"Can you go faster?"

"I've advanced the throttle as far as I can."

Maguire bent down close to the pilot. "Call Kennedy and ask for the supervisor of the traffic controller in charge of our plane. I want Swissair Flight 180 put in a holding pattern until we land. Tell him that this is Company business, and that they can check with an FBI agent waiting for us at customs."

The pilot nodded a couple of times. Maguire and Hansen walked back to their seats.

"We'll land before they do, one way or another," Maguire said as he dropped into the seat.

Hansen said nothing.

The Cessna had started to lose altitude, and Hansen swallowed a couple of times, trying to clear his ears. He checked his seat belt and released the seat to its upright position. He always felt uncomfortable flying in small airplanes. He knew that in a crash the size of the airplane wouldn't matter; but for some inexplicable reason, he felt more secure in a big, commercial airplane. Unfortunately, his job at the CIA demanded that he take small planes quite frequently. He always tried to hide his fear from his companions, particularly during a landing. He glanced at his watch; it was 2:55. He thought of the job ahead of them and felt the tension mount inside him.

They had only a few minutes to run to customs and observe Andrea Hendrick and the other Russian passing through. He would have time only to glance at them quickly, to film every movement and to record every sound, for his job would actually start after he had the information recorded. Then he would spend countless hours listening to the voice intonations, analyzing the facial expressions and studying the body language. All this would help him to understand their psychological state, their hidden emotions and stress levels, and perhaps learn something about their intentions. It was a difficult assignment, a job of minute details and guesswork and sometimes a frustrating outcome, because most KGB-trained people could hide their emotions well behind faces as expressionless as those of the dead.

With Andrea it'd be different; he knew her very well. He'd spent many hours debriefing her three years ago. He could still remember vividly when the CIA moved Andrea from the hospital in Washington to the safe house in Virginia, asking him to be her debriefing officer. The CIA had tried to play a game that had failed. They wanted a young debriefing operative for Andrea, with the hope of perhaps getting her interested in him. It had worked before, but Andrea was scared and disoriented, near a breakdown, and perhaps in love with her American target and husband, Greg Elliot.

Hansen had used every possible trick in the business to get Andrea to cooperate, but some crazy sense of loyalty to Greg had prevented her from talking. It wasn't until Maguire had stepped in and threatened Andrea, telling her they'd put Greg in jail for spying, that she had talked.

Her story was unbelievable. She was the daughter of a Russian Army officer who sent her away to an all-American KGB illegals training campus near Moscow. Andrea grew up speaking English as her native language just as well as any American. Then they supplied her with a false background and trained her to live by this history. The KGB had obtained the birth certificate of a girl the same age as the Russian Andrea, a child who had died in Detroit years earlier. The KGB-assigned legend posted her as growing up in Detroit and receiving a computer science degree from the University of Detroit.

Andrea's assignment was one of the most sensitive he could remember. The KGB had sent her to Silicon Valley to recruit an American spy inside the Blue Cube, an ultrasecret satellite control facility located in Sunnyvale, California, the U.S. nerve center for spy satellites.

Fortunately for the CIA, a crazy dude named Carlos Rivas had wrecked the KGB operation, and the Mexican police captured a wounded and dying Andrea in a hangar at the Benito Juarez International Airport. She'd recovered and started to talk about her assignment, but not for very long.

When he had thought that the debriefing was finally progressing, the CIA had stepped in and asked him to close the case. The KGB had offered to trade Andrea for an old, sick CIA spy captured in East Germany. The CIA was hot to bring the old man back and quickly accepted the swap. Hansen recalled his opposition to the trade: it didn't make any sense to him. Andrea was unimportant, compared to the CIA spy. For some reason the KGB had wanted Andrea. He recommended holding the swap until they knew more about her. "Orders are fucking orders," Maguire had told him, taking Andrea with him, and Hansen had never seen her again after that.

The affair didn't end with the spy swap. A West Berlin police car found Andrea's Control's officer, Boris Alexei Grishin, dead with a single shot to the head. His body was in the front seat of a car in a deserted area of the same park where the swap had taken place. CIA analysts concluded that the KGB had executed Boris as an example for his failure in the Blue Cube operation. Hansen recalled the many hours of argument. He didn't agree with the analysis; that was not the KGB's style. They'd have taken Boris back to Moscow, tried him, then sentenced him to death. They'd have made the whole incident very visible, to show punishment for Boris's failure.

The CIA analyst had argued that leaving Boris behind was dishonor enough and a good example. Hansen still hadn't bought the argument. "If the KGB didn't kill Boris, who in hell did?" the analyst had asked. Hansen had shrugged off the question with a noncommittal answer. "That's a question for the operational people," he had said.

Hansen looked out the Cessna window at the high-rises crowding Manhattan. The afternoon was clear and the view was beautiful, but he felt tense and uneasy. His instincts told him that Andrea's return was not simple. She was an insignificant pawn in the high-stakes game of espionage, and the KGB never risked anything without expecting something in return. They were bringing Andrea to New York for a reason. They probably knew that the CIA would identify Andrea immediately and set up a surveillance ring around her. Maybe they were doing a diversion, Hansen thought excitedly.

Now he could see the runways at JFK as the Cessna approached. He took a deep breath. He wasn't looking forward to the hours ahead of him. It was always the same, the long hours that ran into longer days, analyzing small details that could add up to something which he could never verify. There would be twenty-hour days with very little sleep and lots of coffee and junk food, and every time he went through this madness, he promised to quit after he finished the job. He always thought of getting a teaching position at a small college somewhere near a lake. He would have a normal family life, a wife, a couple of children—and lots of fishing. He knew very well that he wasn't cut out for the CIA; he hated the stress and the inhumanity of the job. But he had never quit and he wondered why.

The pilot landed the Cessna smoothly and soon taxied to a gate.

Maguire looked at his watch. "We've got to hurry. They've had the Swissair flight in a holding pattern for the last ten minutes. We don't want to make those KGB bastards suspicious."

Hansen said nothing, trying to keep pace with Maguire's long strides. A man in a dark suit waited for them at the gate and Hansen guessed that he was a FBI agent. The man was in his late forties, of medium build, with dark hair and a stern expression.

"Did the technicians arrive?" Maguire asked, bypassing any introduction.

"They're in, sir," the man replied, leading the way.

They hurried through the gate, along a hallway, and through several doors that the agent opened with a key. Then they faced another long hall that ended in a narrow stairway. They rushed up the stairs, and Hansen was breathless by the time they reached the first floor. The stairs led to another narrow hallway with bare walls and a linoleum floor. There were no other doors or windows and Hansen felt disoriented as the hallway took several turns left and then right. The ceiling was low, as if the floor was sandwiched between two regular floors.

A moment later they stopped in front of a small door. The FBI man opened it without knocking, and they entered a room that looked like a recording studio. Inside it two men stood facing a long console that took up about half the space. Hansen looked around curiously. There were six TV monitors with views of customs. Under the monitors were several signal meters, control knobs, and a joystick. One of the men, wearing earphones, adjusted the knobs under a monitor and moved the joystick. The image on the monitor zoomed in on a customs agent talking to an older man. To the right of the monitors were two video recorders and three high-quality studio audio recorders. The second man loaded a magnetic tape into one of the recorders and both men stopped working and turned to the three new arrivals.

"This is Bud and Gary," the FBI agent said. Bud, short and wiry, wore glasses that looked too big for his face, and Gary, older and balding, was tall and a little on the heavy side. His face was red, as if he had a rash. They both wore T-shirts and tight jeans.

Maguire and Hansen introduced themselves. Then Maguire asked, "When will you be ready?"

"A couple of minutes," Bud said.

Hansen took off his jacket and loosened his tie. The room was hot and the air a little stale. He looked up at the ceiling and saw a small vent that apparently had a fan. I hope we don't suffocate in here, he thought as he placed the jacket on the back of a chair. It was the first time he had seen such a room, but he had heard many rumors about the existence of customs surveillance rooms, which he didn't believe. He felt uncomfortable. He didn't like this, not one bit.

"I want Frank to listen to them live," Maguire told the FBI agent.

The agent nodded, saying nothing.

Maguire stepped close to a monitor and watched the screen for a few seconds. The monitor showed a couple talking to a customs agent. "Have we warned those guys what's going on?" Maguire asked, his eyes on the screen.

The FBI agent glanced at the screen. "We've briefed all seven customs agents. We can't miss."

"Good," Maguire said. "Call Traffic Control and tell them to land the Swissair flight."

Andrea stood in line in the aisle and felt her legs shaking. Soon she would step onto American soil after three and a half years. She never thought she'd be back. The CIA officer who had walked with her during the swap at the entrance of the Glienicker Bridge checkpoint in Berlin had warned her, "If you ever come back and we catch you, you'll spend the rest of your life in jail." Her KGB control agent had ignored her concerns and said that the Center in Moscow had a mission for her in the United States, but had not explained the assignment. She rubbed her forehead, feeling the cold perspiration. The thought of facing a customs agent terrified her. The knot in her stomach tightened and she felt a little nauseated. She had taken two pills just before landing, but they had not helped.

The Boeing was crowded, and it was a few minutes before she stepped into the connecting walkway. She carried a small case and a vinyl tote bag strapped to her shoulder. As she walked, she glanced at Dmitri out of the corner of her eye. His pockmarked face was serious, his eyes alert as his fingers tightened around the handle of his black attaché case. She knew he was tense. He had not been happy with the twenty-minute delayed landing.

They rushed with the crowd through the connecting walkway that ended in a long hallway and walked into a large room that housed the customs agents. Dmitri motioned her to the left and they joined a short line. He stood in front of her. "Let me do the talking," he said.

The line advanced bit by bit and Andrea glanced around warily. The customs agents asked many questions, studied passports and papers, and occasionally asked to look inside handbags and suitcases. She knew that they had diplomatic passports, but the CIA could have warned them that she was a KGB agent. She tried to keep the thought at bay, but it kept coming back.

The customs agent asked a young couple with a child some questions. Then he waved them on and turned to Dmitri. "Papers, please," the agent said.

Dmitri handed him the passports.

The agent opened the passports and studied them. He raised his head briefly and eyed Dmitri, then Andrea. "What's your assignment at the Soviet Mission?" he asked.

"Cultural attaché," Dmitri said.

"Have you ever been in the United States?"

"No, sir."

"Do you know the regulations?"

"Yes, sir. The Foreign Ministry briefed us."

The customs agent gave the passport another glance and passed it back to Dmitri. He kept Andrea's; his eyes remained on her. Dmitri didn't move, as if waiting for the agent to give him the second passport.

"Would you step in front of me?" the customs agent said to Andrea.

She moved slowly as Dmitri stepped aside, barely leaving any room for her on the small counter. The customs agent looked at Dmitri and said, "Please step back. I don't need you any longer."

Dmitri glared at the agent, but said nothing.

"State your name," the agent said.

Andrea cleared her throat. "Valeri Lisenko," she answered.

"Age?"

"Thirty-two."

"Married?"

"Single."

"Are you sure?"

"I . . . said single."

"Where do you live?"

"I don't understand."

"Place of permanent residence in the Soviet Union."

"Oh! I live in Moscow."

"Moscow, where?"

"127 Volgogradskiy prospekt . . . apartment 618."

"How long have you lived there?"

"Three . . . five years."

"What's your assignment in the Soviet Mission?"

"Linguistics specialist."

"What languages?"

"English, French, and Spanish."

"Spanish?"

"Yes. . . ."

"You're fluent in English. You don't have an accent. Where did you learn English?"

"At the Moscow Institute of Linguistics." She paused to rub her forehead. "I have a PhD in English literature."

The agent lowered his eyes to the passport as if checking something. He flipped a couple of pages and then read the first page again. "Where are you going to stay in New York?"

"I understand that I will stay at the Soviet Mission's building. I . . . really don't know the address."

"Do you know the regulations?"

Andrea nodded. "The Foreign Ministry briefed us extensively on that. We . . . I know."

"Good." The customs agent gave the passport back to Andrea, and she prepared to leave.

"Wait a moment, I haven't finished yet."

Andrea stopped abruptly.

"Have you ever been in the United States?"

Andrea shook her head. "No, sir . . ."

"Are you sure?"

Andrea felt her hands shaking and grabbed the handle of the tote bag to hide the trembling. The pain in her stomach was fierce, and she felt like vomiting. She took a deep breath, trying to calm the wild beating of her heart. "Yes, sir," she said, "this is my first time . . . here."

The Customs agent seemed to hesitate, his face serious. "You can go now."

Andrea rushed to Dmitri and they both headed for the exit doors. She hurried to keep up with him.

"They know," Andrea whispered.

The wind swept through the Golden Gate and along the bay. Greg Elliot took his eyes from the main sail to look up at the sunny, cloudless sky. The wind was steady, and he was sailing at the right angle of attack. In front of him the reddish structure of the Golden Gate Bridge spanned the entrance of San Francisco Bay. He glanced at the tall towers holding the steel cables that suspended the mile-and-a-half structure. It was a different view of the bridge. He was at ocean level and had to look up to see it. For a moment he imagined that the bridge was a gigantic gate that guarded the path to the world oceans—and distant countries. Abruptly his eyes darted away from the bridge and looked over at Alcatraz. The old structure was the picture of loneliness and abandonment. What a contrast with the dozens of fluttering white sails that dotted the ocean around the island, he thought.

Greg took a deep breath of the clean, salt air. He tugged at the life vest that he wore over his sweatshirt and pulled a San Francisco 49ers cap down on his long, curly blond hair. As he pushed his sunglasses up on his nose, he tightened his grip on the steering wheel. He felt strong and in command. A year of exercising had trimmed his weight and toned his muscles. Over thirty-five, he had no fear of entering his forties. He was settled and felt no anxiety about the future. He would always be a loner and had learned to accept it.

A noise from the cabin caught his attention. Ron Temple stepped into the cockpit carrying two beers and two plastic-wrapped sandwiches. Greg moved to help Ron with the beers, keeping one hand on the steering wheel.

Ron dropped his tall, wiry frame next to Greg's seat. "Turkey or ham?" he asked as he pushed his windblown hair off his face.

"Turkey," Greg said.

Ron passed him a sandwich, then concentrated on unwrapping his own. They were sailing Ron's brand-new Sabre 42 yacht, which he had bought barely a month ago to celebrate the great year his advertising company in Silicon Valley had had. Ron had surprised Greg when he'd asked him to sail the new Sabre, his third boat in less than three years. When Greg asked about it, Ron had told Greg that it was easier to change boats than wives. At least he didn't have to pay alimony to his old boats.

Greg chewed on his sandwich and sipped a cold beer. "Beautiful afternoon," he said.

"We don't have enough of these," Ron said, his mouth full.

"Thanks for inviting me."

"Not at all." Ron smiled. "But this is not just a pleasure trip. You noticed that I invited no girls." His smile got wider.

Greg became alert but said nothing.

"Well, I wanted to talk with you. I'm worried about you."

"Worried? Why?"

"To tell the truth, I think you've come a long way since your troubles with the spy—"

"Not 'the spy.' *Andrea*."

"Okay . . . whatever you want to call her. I'm also happy that you quit that shitty job at the Blue Cube. They're another spy nest, anyway. But . . ."

"But what . . . ?"

"Your consulting business is doing okay. You're making a living in Silicon Valley."

"Then?"

"But your social life is the pits."

Greg straightened up. "Ron, my social life is *my* business. I'm happy now."

"Don't believe you, buddy. You haven't had a goddamned girlfriend since Andrea left." He shrugged. "I don't even know if you've been laid in the last three years. And now with this AIDS business, I'm sure you don't dare."

Greg shook his head. "Ron, my personal life is my own. You're intruding."

It was Ron's time to get serious. "Greg, I don't have a brother and your brother's dead. So we're the closest we'll ever get to being brothers."

"I appreciate that, Ron."

"I know. I'm concerned about you. You look like a walking zombie. The sadness shows all over you."

"You're wrong. I'm happy now. I like my work—I enjoy it."

"I believe that's the only thing that keeps you going."

"You're wrong again."

Ron moved close to Greg, resting the sandwich on the seat next to him. He put a hand on Greg's shoulder. "Look, buddy, you have to cut your losses. I'd love to see you find someone. Being happy . . . talking about the future. But the first thing that you have to do is to cut off your past—"

"I've done that."

"You *haven't*. You're still married to *Andrea*."

Greg lowered his head.

Ron went on, "I have a lawyer friend. He's one of the few honest lawyers I've ever known. He'll help you get divorced."

Greg took a deep breath. He hadn't given any thought to a divorce; he'd never felt he had to. "It's very difficult to get divorced from someone whose whereabouts you don't even know," he said.

"The lawyer and the courts will take care of that problem. It doesn't matter where she is."

"I'll give it some thought."

"I want you to do it. This is your brother asking you."

"We'll see." Greg picked up the beer can next to him and took a long sip. He gazed off into the distance, beyond the Golden Gate.

CHAPTER 3

They walked across customs as Andrea tried to calm her nerves. Her nausea had eased a bit, but she was still shaking. She wished she could take another pill. Dmitri had not said a word, the look on his face inscrutable, as they walked toward the exit of the International Section.

A driver from the Soviet Mission approached Dmitri and identified himself. He spoke to Dmitri with such deference that Andrea guessed the driver was KGB and that Dmitri was very high in the KGB ranks. She followed both men as they threaded their way through the busy lobby. As they walked, Andrea looked around curiously. Passengers hurried in all directions, some wearing fancy clothes and carrying expensive luggage with little wheels; others in blue jeans, T-shirts, and sneakers, toting only a shoulder bag. The contrast amazed her. They didn't have to worry about their luggage as her control agent in Vienna had sent her luggage by diplomatic courier to the Soviet Mission, and she guessed that Vienna had also sent Dmitri's luggage by courier, a service reserved only for those in the upper echelons of the Foreign Ministry—or the KGB.

The limo was parked by the main entrance of the International Arrival building with another uniformed driver guarding the car. Dmitri and Andrea climbed in the back as both drivers sat in the front. The limo's ample, luxurious interior, with its leather seats, telephone, small TV set, and refrigerator that probably served as a bar, surprised Andrea. The dark-tinted glass provided privacy, and small slide curtains completely isolated the passengers from the outside world. Andrea didn't like the thought that the KGB transported people in such luxury and privacy.

As the driver headed for the exit, Andrea relaxed in her seat, still trying to calm herself. She felt much better now; the pain in her stomach had disappeared. She glanced at Dmitri. He'd taken the seat next to the window on the driver's side and was carefully watching the traffic behind them. Andrea couldn't read the steely look in his eyes.

"How far are we from the Soviet Mission?" She asked to break the tension.

Dmitri waved a hand to quiet her. "I believe they're following us," he said, his eyes still on the traffic.

"I don't understand."

"I saw some suspicious faces in the customs area," he answered.

"It doesn't make any sense, Dmitri. They knew we were coming. They know where we're going."

"The CIA has put an obvious tail on us until we reach the Soviet Mission," Dmitri said, looking at her. "They want us to know they are watching."

Andrea felt her tension return. She didn't understand how she could accomplish any mission for the KGB if the CIA was already aware of them. Besides, she didn't even know what her mission was in New York. She was going to ask Dmitri, but he was again monitoring the traffic.

The traffic got busier. It was late afternoon, and Andrea guessed that it was the rush-hour traffic in New York. To calm her anxiety, she concentrated on reading the traffic signs on the expressway.

The steadily moving traffic was quite a contrast to the crawling mass of vehicles hardly inching along on the other side of the expressway. Andrea could now see, in the distance, New York's high-rises. The sight of the huge structures made her aware that she was approaching one of the largest cities in the world. She had seen pictures of New York before, but the actual view of the city was breathtaking. A sense of excitement ran through her. She had never thought she would be back in the United States.

The ride along Third Avenue was rough and dangerous. Cars dashed all around them, blowing their horns aggressively, speeding through changing traffic lights. Andrea turned away from the window to look at Dmitri. The Russian had said only a few words during the trip, completely absorbed in surveying the traffic. "Are we very far from the Mission, comrade?" she asked.

"A few minutes."

"Is this your first time?" she asked, trying to start a conversation.

"You don't need to know."

She lowered her eyes to the floor. "I'm sorry . . . I still don't know what my mission is here."

"The rezident will let you know in time. Asking questions is not the right way to start, comrade Lisenko."

Andrea hesitated, not knowing what to say.

"I want to remind you that the Center still has you on probation," Dmitri added. "The Center will consider final any misbehavior or failure on your part. We will return you to Moscow immediately and the Center will assign you to a clerk post in Lesozavodsk."

Andrea nodded slowly, needing no further explanation. She had heard rumors about Lesozavodsk, a small town near the Chinese border. The Sixth Department, in charge of China, Vietnam, Korea, and Cambodia, kept dozens of small intelligence posts in towns close to the Chinese border. The living conditions were terrible, and the work was tedious and unimportant. Lesozavodsk was the worst of all the posts. The First Chief Directorate used job assignments there to punish a field agent's failures or to get rid of out-of-favor officers who represented a political risk for the high ranks in the KGB.

"I won't fail, comrade," Andrea said.

The car turned left, and they faced a short block with very little traffic and a few vehicles parked on one side of the street. Andrea looked around curiously at the buildings and the people on the sidewalk, and guessed they were close to the Mission. She noticed a cream-colored, ten-story building that took most of one side of the block. The driver took a sharp turn and drove down a narrow ramp adjacent to the building, the limo barely clearing the turns. They entered a spacious garage with about a dozen parked cars, drove to the far end, and parked next to two other limos. Dmitri got out and Andrea stepped out behind him.

A double door led to a small room and two elevators. Dmitri

pushed the call button and waited silently. The walls were bare and badly in need of paint, and the rug worn and stained. One of the elevators opened, and they stepped in. The two Russians had stayed in the garage. Dmitri pressed the fifth floor button and the elevator started to move. Keeping her eyes down, Andrea rested the carry-on bag on the floor.

"We're going to the living quarters," Dmitri said. "You'll share a room with another comrade."

"What about my work?" Andrea ventured to ask.

"Tomorrow morning you'll go to a training class. It'll take about three days. Then you'll start working."

She wanted to ask about her assignment, but refrained; Dmitri's warning was still clear in her mind. "Good," she said.

The elevator stopped and they stepped out into the small lobby, where a man in his early fifties sat behind a desk. Andrea recalled a similar arrangement in Vienna, where the Rezidence Internal Security kept a watch officer in the front lobby of the dorm floor. His job was to watch everybody and report any misbehavior to the KGB. The arrangement was such that nobody could walk out without the officer noticing. Dmitri strolled toward the desk, and Andrea followed him at a prudent distance.

"I'm Dmitri Kotov."

The short, stocky man rearranged his weight and sat up straight in the chair. "They notified me of your arrival, comrade," he said. A copy of *Pravda*, neatly folded, lay on the desk. "We've assigned room 517 to comrade Lisenko," he added, looking at Andrea.

Andrea nodded, noting the same tone of deference that the limo driver had used at the airport. Her curiosity about Dmitri increased.

"Room 517 is in the wing to your right," the man said. "All the way to the end," he added, lowering his eyes to the newspaper in front of him.

Dmitri and Andrea walked along the hallway. The place had the same rundown appearance as the small room downstairs. The walls and ceiling were painted a faint yellow and the carpet was cheap and worn. Low-watt light bulbs without shades hung from the ceiling. She had been in the place for less than one minute and already she disliked it.

The door to the room was unlocked, and they walked in without knocking. The small, windowless room's walls were painted the same yellow as the hallway. Pictures of Lenin and Gorbachev seemed to stare at each other from opposite walls. Two single beds and two small, four-drawer chests barely left space for a chair and a small walking area between the beds. The bed on the left was made, and a few personal items sat on the chest next to it. The other bed had a stained mattress with a folded blanket and sheet in the middle, next to a pillow. Andrea rested the tote bag and carry-on bag on the bed and turned to Dmitri. "When should I be ready tomorrow?"

"We'll send a clerk for you at 8 a.m." He glanced around the room as if inspecting it. "If you need any help, ask the comrade at the front desk."

Dmitri left without another word, leaving Andrea standing in the middle of the room not knowing what to do. She wondered with whom she was sharing the room. At least she would have somebody to talk to. She walked to the chest next to her bed and opened the top drawer. Some of the clothes she had packed and sent through diplomatic courier in Vienna had already been unpacked and put in the drawers. Slowly she arranged some of the clothes to make room for her other things. As she unpacked, she recalled the time she arrived in Silicon Valley as an Illegal. What a contrast! The motel room had been so spacious, and with so many comforts. Now she realized why so many people volunteered for the Illegals program back in Moscow; they would live like Americans.

After arranging all her clothes inside the drawers, she made the bed and tried the mattress. It was very stiff, and she sighed in relief. Soft beds were bad for her back. However, she wasn't happy that the room's only light came from a single bulb hanging from the ceiling. She'd have preferred a bedside lamp to read by at night, but regulations forbade such lamps. In Vienna, she had managed to hide a small reading light that she attached to books, but those were also illegal, and she had thrown it away before she packed for her trip to New York. Now she'd have to buy another one so she could read during the long, sleepless nights. The doctor in Moscow had said she would soon regain her normal sleep patterns but after three years it had not happened. She had grown used to the insomnia. It gave her a lot of time to think.

The door to the room opened suddenly and a woman walked in. "Oh!" she said. "I didn't think you would be in." She was in her mid-thirties, a little on the heavy side, with short, reddish hair and a very friendly face. "I'm Sylvia Guriev," she said with a smile. "I guess you're my new roommate."

Andrea nodded and returned the smile. "I'm Valeri Lisenko. Nice to meet you, comrade."

Sylvia waved a hand. "Drop the 'comrade' formality. Call me Sylvia. Hopefully, we're going to be very good friends."

"Thanks, Sylvia."

"Did you have a good trip? Where did you come from, Moscow?" Sylvia asked, sitting on her bed.

Andrea sat on her bed, too. "The flight was good. But I don't like long trips. I came from. . . ." She stopped in midsentence, recalling the warning she had had in Vienna before departing. She must not volunteer information to anyone in the Mission, her case officer had said. "I'm sorry, comrade . . . Sylvia, but I'm not supposed to volunteer any information," she added.

"I understand, Valeri. Don't worry, I'm used to the regulations. Don't like them, but I obey them."

Andrea crossed her legs on the bed. "How long have you been in New York? How do you like it?"

"My duty tour is for three years. I've been here a year already." Her eyes brightened. "I love the city. Great place, wonderful stores. What about you?"

Andrea shook her head slowly. "I don't know yet."

"They haven't told you?"

"No."

"Strange."

"I know that I will work as a translator for the Mission, but that's all."

"That's a good job. You must know several languages. Your English is very good."

"I also know French and Spanish. What do you do here?"

"I supervise the typing pool and sometimes provide backup

services for the couriers between the Mission and the Secretariat at the United Nations. It's a busy job. We're always behind schedule."

"I'll probably use your services," Andrea said.

"You will. Everybody else does." She gave a small, malicious smile. "I'll give you special priority for being my roommate."

"Thanks, Sylvia, but I'd prefer no special treatment."

Sylvia's smile got wider. "You soon will be asking me for that. Our service is terrible. I never have enough people to catch up with the workload."

Andrea didn't comment. She felt tired and had an empty sensation in her stomach. "I'm sorry, Sylvia, I must sleep a little. I'm very tired and must be up before eight tomorrow. My briefing is very early. I want to be rested for my first day."

"I know," Sylvia said. "Tomorrow, they'll teach you what you can't do in New York. Where not to go. Where not to shop. What not to read. To whom not to talk. They'll practically tell you where to breathe. . . ." Her malicious smile came back. "But you shouldn't worry. After they're done, I'll give you my personal survival briefing. I know how to bend every one of those rules so you can live it up a little in New York. . . ."

The pain in Andrea's stomach came back. She didn't know what to say; a feeling of danger overcame her. "Could you tell me where the bathroom is?" she said. "I'm feeling sick. . . ."

Dmitri, still carrying the attaché case, walked along the hallway and approached a closed door. He stopped in front of it and pressed a small buzzer which sounded on the other side, and a small peephole opened. An inquiring eye stared at him for a few seconds. "I'm Dmitri Kotov."

Three dead bolts snapped open and the door opened halfway, revealing a corpulent man. "The comrade rezident is waiting for you," the man said in heavily accented English.

Dmitri walked past him without answering. The door led to a small room with a metal desk, a chair, and a couch against one of the walls. He headed for another closed door in the wall opposite the first one. Next to the door was a water fountain topped by a five-gallon bottle. Dmitri opened the door without knocking and walked in.

"Welcome, Colonel Kotov," the white-haired older man said, walking around a massive wooden desk. He was wearing an expensive-looking Western suit, his hand extended for a handshake.

"Let's dispose of formalities, comrade," Dmitri said, pumping the man's hand. In person, the rezident looked older than his early sixties, Dmitri thought as he took in the bony face and sunken eyes behind the rimless glasses. He was a man past his retirement age, and certainly not the best choice to head the KGB in the Soviet Mission.

Dmitri had read Vladimir Ignatiev's dossier before he left the First Chief Directorate headquarters in Moscow. Over forty years in the KGB, Ignatiev was a political man who had managed to survive many purges. After World War II, he had joined the Ministry of State Security, MGB, right after his return from the German front. His ascendance in the Ministry's ranks was swift, taking the right side during the power struggle between Beria and Khrushchev. Ignatiev was among the group at the MGB who apparently had given Khrushchev the winning hand over Beria. He became a high-ranking officer of the newly created KGB and a close, behind-the-scenes political adviser to Khrushchev.

Ignatiev's greatest accomplishment on record was as one of the advisers who masterminded Eisenhower's political embarrassment during the U2 spy plane incident. They let Eisenhower publicly deny the incident and then produced Francis Gary Powers, the pilot of the U2. Powers didn't have the courage to commit suicide, as the CIA had instructed him, after his plane had been shot down by a Soviet SA-2 missile.

The dossier also credited Ignatiev for the swap of the Soviet spy Rudolf Abel for Gary Powers on the Glienicker Bridge in Berlin—a swap that greatly favored the KGB, according to the report.

Dmitri understood Ignatiev's latest assignment as rezident to the Mission. It was a last gift that he had probably managed to get from his contacts in the Politburo, keeping the post for a couple of years until he had procured a good supply of American goods. Then the Center would call him back for retirement and send him into oblivion. Ignatiev was already a Colonel in the KGB, a rank that would entitle him to a dacha on the outskirts of Moscow and yearly vacations at the exclusive mountain resorts on the Caucasus.

Ignatiev motioned Dmitri to a chair. Dmitri let his tired body sink down in the comfortable armchair as his eyes studied the room for a moment. The furniture and the carpet looked expensive. Two of the wood-paneled walls displayed large oil portraits of Lenin and Gorbachev. A Soviet flag stood on a pedastal behind the desk. Dmitri noticed the expensive Persian rug in the middle of the room and the glass and carved-wood cabinet to his left, stocked with exotic liquors. For a moment, he fought to control a feeling of rage against this decadent display of luxury. But an inner voice warned him not to say anything, for his mission could be in jeopardy if Ignatiev failed to cooperate fully.

"Nice office, comrade," he said, toning down his irony.

"It mitigates the duress of the job," Ignatiev said, a brief smile touching the corners of his mouth. He sat down. "The Center has directed me to support you in any way that you ask. . . ." He paused as if planning his next words. "I haven't seen a request like that in years. You must be up to something important. . . ." He let the words hang in the air.

Dmitri said nothing. He rested the briefcase on his lap and aligned the combination lock, then opened it and pulled out a sealed envelope. "Comrade Geidar Aligev sends you this special message with instructions," Dmitri said, handing it to him.

At the mention of Aligev's name, Deputy Premier of the First Chief Directorate, Ignatiev's eyes became icy and alert. Dmitri noticed the change and was pleased. He had gained the right attention from the rezident.

Ignatiev tore off the seal, ripped open the envelope, and took out a piece of paper. After adjusting his glasses on the bridge of his nose, he read the message. A moment later, he leveled his eyes on Dmitri. "The Deputy Premier is ordering me to put at your command the ten best KGB operatives we have in the rezidence."

Dmitri nodded. "I have their names already."

"You have done your homework, comrade," Ignatiev said in a

tone that Dmitri couldn't read.

"I'll move those men out of the Mission," Dmitri said. "Some of them might come back, depending on what happens," he added. He proceeded to recite ten names, and Ignatiev scribbled them on a piece of paper.

"One of them is also my best technician," Ignatiev said, gazing down at the paper in front of him.

"I also want three of your best safe houses in the area," Dmitri added. "One in Manhattan, one in Long Island, and one in New Jersey."

"You'll be served."

"The houses must have had very little activity in the last three years. I don't want compromised places."

"We have such places saved for occasions like this. I guarantee you, the safe houses are clean."

Dmitri nodded, satisfied. He wouldn't have settled for less. Besides, he already knew which houses he wanted. Aligev had pulled some strings in Moscow and had provided him with the addresses. But he would let Ignatiev provide some places first to test the rezident's intentions.

The old Russian stood up from his chair and walked to the wall. He stopped in front of Gorbachev's portrait and pushed the heavy picture aside, uncovering a safe. "I have a group of safe houses here directly under my control," he said, turning the lock.

After taking a small notebook from inside the safe, Ignatiev walked back to his desk, sat down, opened the notebook, and read the addresses of five safe houses. Dmitri listened in silence. Three of them were the ones he wanted.

"Very good, comrade," Dmitri said. "I want Hoboken in New Jersey, Garden City in Long Island, and 111th Street in Manhattan. I want any activity related to those places canceled immediately." He stood up from his chair.

"Do you want the addresses?" Ignatiev asked.

"I already know the addresses, comrade," Dmitri said.

Ignatiev arched one eyebrow and looked at Dmitri over the rim of his glasses.

Dmitri paused in the middle of the room, turning to the rezident. "I want the ten men in a secure room at the Mission tomorrow morning at 8 a.m. I want to start working immediately."

Moments later, Dmitri walked along a hallway toward the Mission's living quarters. He couldn't be more pleased with how everything was falling into place. The rezident would provide the support to execute his assignment. The CIA had already recognized Andrea and was on her trail, and by using her he would flush Greg Elliot out. Greg Elliot had killed a KGB comrade and he would pay for it.

CHAPTER 4

When Andrea awoke the next morning, she was surprised that she had slept more than she normally did. Maybe the long trip had exhausted her to the point where her insomnia had given in to her tired body. Relieved that she had gotten some rest, she found that she had another problem. She couldn't exercise because of the lack of space. She liked to start the morning with aerobics, a habit she had kept since her training days back at the Illegals campus in Moscow. Also, the doctor in Moscow had recommended that she do the exercises as a way to release tension.

But the bathroom provided enough room and privacy for her to exercise. There was no music to give her rhythm; but she had learned to play the music inside her head, a habit that she now enjoyed even when not exercising.

After she had worked out and showered, a clerk from the mission came for her. A young man with a quick and courteous smile, he was probably the son of some influential high-ranking functionary back at the Foreign Ministry in Moscow. He only spoke a few words, saying that he was to take her to the briefing room on the third floor. He did not mention anything about breakfast, and Andrea didn't bring up the subject.

The hallways on the second floor were the same as the ones on the dorm floor. Andrea was now convinced that the whole building was rundown, and that the Mission spent little money on maintenance. For a moment the contrast with her experience in California flashed through her mind. There the buildings had been new and so comfortable that work had been a pleasure. But at the Mission, the Foreign Ministry and the KGB shared expenses that definitely didn't take into consideration the comfort of the people assigned to foreign duty. Andrea sighed. She'd have to make the best of it.

After going through several doors manned by Internal Security, they walked across a large room that had a stockpile of folding chairs stacked against a wall. As she followed the clerk, Andrea glimpsed several bulletin boards crowded with all kinds of meeting notices and Communist slogans. The clerk stopped in front of a door at the far end of the room and asked Andrea to wait. He knocked and then walked in, reappearing a few seconds later to ask her to follow him.

The room was small and windowless, like her own room, and looked like a small classroom. There were about ten rows of gray metal chairs facing a desk and a blackboard. Andrea looked around, wondering where the windows in the Mission were. They probably belonged only to a privilege few. She could hear traffic and concluded that they were close to the outside of the building.

The clerk left the room silently, and Andrea walked to the front row, where a woman in her late forties sat behind a desk.

"May I sit?" Andrea asked.

The woman nodded without raising her eyes from the folder of papers she was reading. She closed the folder. "Welcome, comrade," she said in a coarse, masculine-sounding voice.

"Good morning, comrade," Andrea said timidly.

The woman stood up from the chair and walked around the desk. "I'm comrade Svetlana Serov, your instructor."

"Valeri Lisenko," Andrea's eyes shifted from the tall, hefty face to her muscular arms. The woman reminded her of a wrestling instructor she had had at the Illegals campus. The instructor had been brutal and enjoyed beating the students. Andrea had had only one wrestling match with her, but her bruises had lasted for weeks. Svetlana Serov, the same size as the instructor, had the same vicious expression.

Svetlana leaned against the desk and crossed her arms in front of her chest, staring down at Andrea. "Well, comrade Lisenko, your dossier says you're a linguistics expert, and that we must assign you to the Linguistics Department," she said in fluent but accented English.

Andrea nodded.

"English, French, and Spanish," Svetlana said, as if talking to herself. "That's a good command of languages."

Andrea noticed a touch of admiration in Svetlana's tone.

"You'll start working tomorrow. But before that, you must become familiar with the rules of the Mission. You must obey them without question, for we will punish any violation severely. Do you understand?"

"I do," Andrea said.

"Good." Svetlana turned around and picked up a piece of mimeographed paper from the desk, passing it to Andrea. "These are the main rules you must obey. In essence, they tell you to work obediently, not to talk to strangers, to avoid security risks. Also, that you must keep your eyes open and report anything that is not normal—even the most insignificant detail." Her laugh was more like a grunt. "Sometimes small details lead to big things."

"What about New York?" Andrea asked.

Svetlana frowned. "You all ask the same question. You're not allowed to go out alone, only in groups, with comrades from the Mission. You have a list of stores where you can shop. Never shop in expensive imperialist stores or in Russian émigré stores." Her voice became even coarser. Andrea wondered how she could shop in an expensive store if she didn't have any money.

"I warn you never to visit an American movie theater and not to buy imperialist magazines or CIA brainwashing books." She smiled now. "We have a movie theater on the second floor of the Mission. We show the latest movies from the Soviet Union every Saturday night."

"I'm looking forward to seeing them," Andrea said unenthusiastically. She recalled the same arrangement in Vienna; the movies were terrible and very old.

"On Wednesday nights," Svetlana went on, "we have a Gathering Night at the Mission. Attendance is obligatory. We'll hear the latest news from Moscow, and we'll invite distinguished comrades from our UN Delegation."

"I won't miss the Gatherings. What about my job?"

"The Mission will pay you one hundred dollars per month for your services. This salary includes room and board. You can use the money for buying some clothes at the stores we have listed, or save the money in our own bank on the first floor. We pay good interest—three percent."

Svetlana walked back to her chair and sat down heavily. She pulled a cigarette from a pack on her desk and lit it. Then blew a stream of smoke toward the ceiling. Andrea recognized the American brand; she had seen it in California.

"Once in a while, we'll rent your services to the Secretariat at the United Nations," Svetlana said. "When paid, you must bring back your uncashed check to the Mission. Your salary will still be the same. Your contribution will help to pay additional expenses to keep the Mission in good standing." She paused to wait for the sound of a police siren to fade out. The noise made Andrea nervous.

"During your brief stays at the Secretariat, you must not fraternize with foreigners—unless we ask you to."

"I have medical problems," Andrea said. "I will need help to get some prescriptions."

"We have an excellent general internist. Also, we have a nurse." She paused to take another drag on the cigarette. "I have already sent the internist your medical record that came with your dossier. She will see you this afternoon."

Andrea relaxed. At least she would have some medical attention. Since her condition was improving, she didn't want to go back to the terrible problems she had after she left the clinic in Moscow.

Svetlana took the folder from the desk, slid it under her huge arm, and stood up. After tossing the cigarette on the floor and stepping on it, she walked up to Andrea. "Let's go," she motioned Andrea to stand up. "I'll give you a tour of the Mission. I'll show you the cafeteria first. You'll be eating your meals there. Then I'll take you to your place of work."

As Andrea walked beside Svetlana, the Russian instructor looked even bigger and Andrea had to hurry to catch up with the massive woman. Svetlana's agility surprised her.

Svetlana turned to Andrea, smiled, and said, "Breakfast time is almost gone, comrade. Are you hungry?"

"I'm not," Andrea said, telling the truth.

Frank Hansen removed the heavy headphones from his head

and rested them on the table in front of him. Then he rubbed his ears to ease the numbness in them. For the last seven hours, he had been listening nonstop to the tape recording up to the point where Andrea's words had started to lose any meaning for him. Hansens' chair faced two large folding tables that held all types of electronic equipment. He had two 25-inch TV monitors wired to two video players and an editing console. He also had a high-fidelity audio system with a tape player and a connection to a voice stress analyzer and a graph machine. Hansen looked at the table and shook his head. The place was so littered with pieces of paper, notes, pictures, leftover food, and empty styrofoam cups half-filled with cold coffee that it looked as if he had been working there for a month. This was one of those nights that he dreaded so much and that gave him a bad case of heartburn. He leaned back against the chair, closing his eyes. The vision of a clear lake with a backdrop of mountains appeared in his mind. "Someday," he said. "Nothing else but fishing. I'll love every second of it."

After Andrea and the Russian named Dmitri left the customs area, he and Maguire had taken a van to Manhattan with all the video and sound tapes recorded by the FBI technicians. Maguire had also asked an FBI team to trail the Russians' limo to make sure they were going to the Mission building on 67th Street. "You can never trust those bastards," Maguire had said to the FBI people when they said that it probably didn't make any sense to tail them.

Maguire had set up a safe-house operation in Manhattan on the ground floor of a bankrupt garment company on 29th Street, between seventh and eighth Avenues, in the heart of New York's garment district. It had been empty for quite some time, and the FBI often used the facilities for covert operations. Maguire liked it immediately because he could easily move in and out the cars and vans of the FBI task force he had requested to start a surveillance effort on the Mission.

Hansen stood up from the chair and walked a few steps to stretch his legs. He was alone. Tiredly, he looked around, mentally comparing the rundown and almost empty place with the fresh, crisp, beautiful Moose Lake he had left back in Canada. I must be crazy, he thought as he stopped facing a blackboard. He had scribbled on it many notes relating to his analysis of Andrea's voice stress. He had also taped on the blackboard four large pictures of Andrea's face, showing expressions that he found intriguing. Maguire had also taped up an enlarged picture of Dmitri's face, saying that they had to learn every detail of it and that the Russian's arrival with Andrea was not coincidental.

Walking around a communications van parked next to the tables, Hansen stepped into a small bathroom against one of the walls. He stood in front of the only urinal left in one piece and relieved himself. The room smelled of stale urine and was in deplorable condition. He had complained to Maguire, but the CIA man had said that Langley would not approve hiring a cleaning service for the safe house. After some hesitation, Hansen stopped in front of a dirty washbasin and turned on the faucet. He let the water run until its rusty color disappeared, slid his glasses into a shirt pocket, then splashed cold water on his face. The water felt good and gave him a lift. He then unwrapped a few inches of toilet paper from a roll next to the washbasin and dried his face. He gazed at his face in the shattered mirror of the medicine cabinet atop the basin. He was glad that the glass was not in one piece; he looked sick.

The noise of the electric motor rolling up the metal door at the entrance to the building caught his attention. He rushed out of the bathroom and walked toward the Ford minivan that drove in. The sign painted on the van's side read, "MANHATTAN GARMENT CO."

Maguire parked the minivan next to the communications van and climbed out, slamming the door behind him. "Morning, pal," he greeted Hansen.

"Good morning."

"I have some breakfast here," Maguire said. "Also, I bought a couple of folding beds. At least we don't have to sleep on the seats of this fucking van anymore."

Hansen helped Maguire set the beds up near the wall in a corner. After arranging some racks with old clothes around the beds to give them some privacy, Hansen strolled back to the tables, where Maguire had tossed a box of donuts and two cups of coffee. "We could've selected a better safe house," Hansen said to Maguire, taking a bite out of a donut. "The CIA has a lot of first-class places all over this area."

Maguire shook his head and chewed on his donut. "In four hours we're gonna have an army of FBI guys crawling all over this place. We'd call too much attention in a safe house." He glanced at his watch and added, "We've got a liaison FBI agent assigned to work with us. He's an espionage specialist and a tough cookie, but a good man. I've worked with him before. He'll be here in an hour."

Maguire and Max Taylor, the FBI special agent, sat facing the blackboard. Hansen stood with his back to the blackboard, a few pieces of paper in his hand. Max Taylor had arrived a few minutes earlier, and Maguire wasted no time in introducing him to Hansen. Taylor was a strong-framed man in his early fifties, with short, well-groomed black hair and alert eyes. Maguire had filled Hansen in on Taylor's background. He had a law degree from Notre Dame and had had a distinguished football career that ended because of a badly injured knee, leaving him with a slight limp. He joined the FBI when the Bureau had expanded its counterespionage activities, sending recruiters to many American colleges. Taylor rose rapidly in the ranks as his reputation for tenacity and attention to detail became well-known. It earned him the nickname "Bulldog" Taylor.

Maguire had also told Hansen about two cases they had worked on together in New York and Washington. At the beginning of their first assignment Maguire had felt that he was locking horns with Taylor constantly, but after they had worked together for several weeks, he really liked the man and they had become good friends. So when Maguire needed an FBI liaison officer for this case, he had asked Langley to pull some strings with the Bureau so they would give him Taylor. As Maguire told him about Taylor, Hansen managed to hide his increasing misery. He not only would have to deal with Maguire, but also with Bulldog Taylor. He couldn't believe his bad luck; he'd have to use all his knowledge of human behavior to deal with the two bullies.

Hansen listened as the two men talked about the case. Then Taylor turned in his chair to face Hansen, eyed him for a moment, and then demanded a review of all the information. Hansen looked down at his notes and said, "There are three major stress inflections in Andrea's conversation. Two of them are related to her personal life, one related to her assignment." He turned to the blackboard and pointed to three chart strips taped to the board. They looked like electrocardiogram charts, showing a high frequency plot that peaked in the middle of the paper. "The voice stress analyzer," Hansen went on, "tells me that she was under extreme duress here."

"What were the questions?" Taylor asked.

"The first one was whether she was married." He looked down at the paper. "She answered: 'Single.' Then the customs officer asked again, and she said: 'I . . . said single.' " He pointed to the first chart. "Her stress level went up fivefold here."

"She's still hot for Greg Elliott," Maguire said.

"I wouldn't bet on that," Hansen said. "But she certainly has a sensitive nerve there."

"What about the second question?" Taylor pursued.

"The customs officer asked her what her assignment in the Soviet Mission was, and she answered: 'Linguistics specialist.' " Hansen adjusted his glasses, looking down at the papers again. "She had another high stress point here, but not like the first one. I played the videotape many times. From her facial expressions and eye movements, I can almost say for sure that she's still in the dark about what she's supposed to do."

"How can you tell that?" Taylor asked.

"I can't tell you for sure. It's only a gut feeling. But her face wasn't telling a big lie there. There's just some confusion."

"I can't believe those guys haven't given her a mission yet," Maguire said. "Hell, this is really interesting, isn't it?"

Taylor turned to Maguire. "Y'know what this means? They want to use her as a *lastochki.*"

"A Swallow?" Hansen said. "Don't believe it. Andrea's IQ is too high for her to accept a prostitute's job."

"Maybe the KGB didn't give her a choice," Taylor pursued.

"But the KGB must've told her something," Hansen said.

"The KGB wants to use her to set up a honey trap for some horny diplomat at the United Nations," Taylor said. "She was very successful in California."

Maguire shook his head. "I don't believe so. In a sense, she failed there. The KGB wouldn't give her a second chance unless she's indispensable for the job they have in mind. This is something else, and we don't know what they're up to. What was the third stress point?" he asked.

"The third point was when the officer asked her if she had previously visited the United States. The stress level of her voice here is almost as high as the one on the first question."

"I don't believe that's relevant," Maguire said. "Hell, I'd be as nervous as she was if I were in her shoes, trying to sneak back into the U.S. She's a proven spy whose ass has been swapped once. And now the KGB is bringing her back into the spotlight again."

"Agree," Taylor said.

Maguire got up from his chair and walked to the blackboard. He kept his eyes on the charts as if reading them. "The first two conclusions are interesting. She still cares for Greg Elliot, and she doesn't know yet what in hell she's gonna do here."

Hansen walked to the table, poured half a glass of Perrier into a styrofoam cup, and took a drink. "We could get an answer to the second question by just watching what she does during the next few days. I don't know what to do with the first conclusion."

"We'll have three FBI surveillance teams available this afternoon," Taylor said, "six men on each team. They'll be here at three."

"Three teams ain't enough," Maguire said. "I want to keep a tab on the Russian, too."

"We don't have anything on him yet," Taylor said.

"We don't, either," Maguire said. "The guy's clean. That worries me. Clean guys are rookies, or very good KGB operatives. And the KGB never packs two rookies on the same trip."

"I'll ask for a backup team. Two teams on each one should be enough. Jesus! One hour with you guys and you're wrecking my budget already!"

"Don't complain. You're gonna have fun with this one," Maguire said, reaching for a bottle of Scotch. "Well, it's time to celebrate with a drink."

Hansen shook his head. "I'm sorry, Chuck, my stomach can't take Scotch now. I'll join you with a Perrier."

"Your choice, buddy," Maguire said, passing a cup to Taylor. Then he raised his cup and said, "To spying. It makes life more interesting."

Taylor drained his drink almost as fast as Maguire did. Hansen sipped his Perrier, watching both men. The KGB won't have a chance with these two guys, he thought, glancing back at the blackboard and the pictures taped there. He sipped again as the vision of Andrea's and Dmitri's faces on the videotape came back to him. He still didn't believe that the KGB had sent Andrea back for a simple mission. It was too risky and appeared to be a dumb mistake—and the KGB never made dumb mistakes.

Maguire again poured half a glass of Scotch for Taylor and for himself. "Y'know," he said, turning to Hansen, "ever since this damn thing started, I've had an idea running around in my head, and it makes more sense every time I think of it."

Hansen saw the look in Maguire's eyes and became alert. He had seen the look before, and it spelled trouble.

"Rather than wait for those pricks to start working on their assignment, we should try to get in touch with Andrea and see if we can pump something out of her."

"That's very risky," Hansen said. "They could discover our attempt and cancel their mission. Then we'd never know what they had in mind."

"That's a risk we have to take," Maguire said. "But if we succeed, we might have a direct channel back to the whole damn thing from the beginning."

Hansen realized that he was wasting his time fighting Maguire's idea. He needed to know more. "How do you intend to contact Andrea?" he asked, not daring to guess the answer.

Maguire grinned. "I bet you know."

"I don't want to guess. Tell me."

"Hell, it's very easy."

"I don't think so."

"You're wrong."

"It's crazy," Hansen said.

"Oh, no! I want you to get your ass on a plane to California tonight. I'm almost sure that our friend Greg Elliot would be very happy to know that his wife is back."

"Chuck, this is crazy!" Hansen protested.

"No it's not."

"We don't even know were to find Greg. As far as we know, he could have moved away."

CHAPTER 5

Greg Elliot slowed down the Ford Tempo and steered into the steep driveway. Slowly, he parked next to his small Alfa Romeo. Every time he came from work, he felt guilty parking his brand-new Tempo next to the little Alfa. He felt like a traitor who had abandoned an old friend for the sake of a better appearance. His new job as a consultant sometimes demanded that he take clients out for business lunches and the small blue Alfa convertible was not the proper transportation for that. But that rationalization still couldn't mitigate the feeling of guilt he had when he drove into the garage. To ease his conscience, he always drove the Alfa on weekends—particularly when he visited Napa Valley.

After picking up a stack of mail from the mailbox, he walked up the flight of wooden stairs to the front door. He had returned to his hillside house in Los Altos Hills later than usual, stopping for a quick dinner at a local health food restaurant that had recently opened. It was Wednesday night, and normally he'd have had dinner at home cooked by his cleaning lady, Martha; but she had taken three weeks' vacation to visit some relatives in Mexico. Martha came only once a week, but throughout the years she had become a one-night-a-week mother to him. Greg had never complained about Martha's added role, feeling that he was getting more than he was paying for. It was only her second week off, and already he couldn't wait for her to come back.

He closed the door, and headed for the kitchen. He dropped the mail on the kitchen table, then untied his tie and took off his jacket, draping it over a chair. One of the things he disliked most about his consulting job was that he had to dress up when he was interviewing potential customers.

After taking a beer from the refrigerator, he slid open the glass door to the porch and stood in the middle of the doorway, looking into the distance. It was early evening and Silicon Valley's glitter had started to intensify.

He took a couple of sips of beer and walked back into the kitchen, stopping in front of a small desk by the refrigerator. He pushed the REWIND button of the answering machine, then pressed PLAY. He had one phone message.

"Hi, buddy, it's Ron. I haven't heard from you since Sunday. Working your ass off . . . that's too bad. I called my friend the lawyer, and he told me that you haven't called him. What's happening? I thought we'd agreed you'd call him. Don't be chicken—you need a break. Call me before Friday. I have a couple of girls lined up for this weekend. We'll have fun. See you."

Greg rewound the tape. One thing he liked about Ron was that his friend never gave up on him, but he had to admit that sometimes he had been close to losing his patience with Ron. He took the stack of mail, stepped onto the weathered porch, sat in a reclining chair, and took his shoes off, dropping them on the floor. After another long drink of the beer, he rested the can on the floor, turning his attention to the mail. There were a few bills and a couple of computer magazines, but nothing else. He dropped the mail on the floor as his eyes roamed over the valley. Then he looked beyond, into the open sky.

He wondered if one day he'd receive a postcard from a distant place, saying, "I'm okay."

Hansen stepped out of the shower, dropped the large towel on the bathroom counter, and with a smaller towel, wiped the fogged mirror until he could see his face. All he needed now was a shave and he would become human again. He had arrived at San Francisco International on an American red-eye flight that had left Newark early in the evening. After the plane landed, he barely had enough energy to rent a room at the Hilton right at the airport's entrance. Then, as soon as he stepped into the room, he dropped his carry-on bag, took his clothes off, and collapsed into bed, sleeping for seven hours.

As he shaved, Hansen recalled some of the details he had read in Greg Elliot's dossier more than three years ago. He had never met Greg personally, for the CIA assigned him to debrief Andrea right after they moved her to a safe house in Virginia. Greg had already left for California at the CIA's insistence. At the time, Greg was a loner who had no family except for a retarded brother. His father had abandoned his mother after he learned that she had a hereditary gene that could produce retarded children. Then Greg's mother, feeling guilty, had abandoned Greg and his brother when they were young. What followed was a succession of foster homes for both brothers, with Greg acting as both father and mother to his brother. Greg had hardly any friends and was very shy with women, always avoiding the possibility of a relationship that could lead to a family.

Hansen understood well what followed. The KGB probably learned about Greg's background and vulnerability. Then they sent Andrea Hendrick as an Illegal to seduce him and gain access to the ultrasecret Blue Cube installation where Greg worked as a programmer. Greg fell into the trap easily, falling in love with Andrea. But his world soon shattered when he learned that Andrea was a KGB spy.

Hansen stepped out of the bathroom and got dressed in the same suit that Maguire had given him in Canada, but he wore a fresh shirt that he had bought on his way to Newark International Airport. His stomach was empty, so he ordered from room service: a tuna sandwich, a salad, and a bottle of Perrier. This was his second day of eating sandwiches, and he was starting to hate the damn things.

Hansen pulled a piece of paper from a pocket in his jacket and sat on the edge of the bed next to the phone. Before he'd left the safe house in Manhattan, Maguire had called the FBI agent who was tailing Greg Elliot and asked for Greg's phone number. It was unlisted, but the FBI agent had pulled some strings and got hold of it. The agent had also said that Greg would probably be at home on Wednesday night. Hansen adjusted his glasses, read the number, and dialed, wondering what Greg would say when he asked to see him.

The phone rang for a few seconds. Hansen was starting to think that perhaps Greg was out when he heard the voice at the other end.

"Hello," Greg said.
"Greg Elliot?"
"Yes, who's calling?"
"My name is Frank Hansen. I'm calling from the Hilton at the San Francisco Airport." He paused, not knowing yet what the best approach was. "I'm from the East Coast, and I came here to see you. It's very important."
"I'm sorry, I don't know you. Can you tell me what you want?"
"Can't tell you on the phone. I must see you personally."
A few seconds of silence followed. "What company do you work for?" Greg asked, sounding tense.
"I work for the government . . . in Washington."
"CIA?"
The question surprised Hansen; he didn't answer immediately.
"I'm not interested in talking to you," Greg added without waiting for an answer.
"I must see you. It's very important—"
"I don't want to talk to you guys," Greg interrupted angrily.
Hansen sighed. Fighting with Greg on the phone was the wrong way to start his assignment. "Listen, please . . . I came all the way here to see you, and I'm not going to return until we talk. This assignment is as unpleasant for me as it is for you. But I *must* meet with you."
Another few seconds of silence followed, and Hansen thought that Greg was going to hang up.
"Can you tell me on the phone?" Greg insisted.
"No, I can't. It concerns your past."
"I don't care about the past any longer."
"Maybe not, but I must talk to you."
"Okay. We better get it over with. Do you have my address?"
"Yes, I do. See you in about an hour."
Hansen hung up slowly, cursing Maguire for sending him to California. He had sensed Greg's tension and felt sorry for the man. It had probably taken Greg a long time to accept Andrea's deception. Now Hansen was coming to California to stir up some of those old feelings again. A knock on the door interrupted his thoughts, and he went to answer it. It was probably room service with his food and the Perrier. As he faced the young service

clerk, he realized that he had lost his appetite.

Greg glanced at his watch and grimaced. An hour and half since the man named Frank Hansen had called, and he still couldn't guess what the CIA wanted from him. At first he had thought that something had happened to Andrea and that the CIA wanted to notify him, but it didn't take him too long to realize that that was highly unlikely. Andrea had gone back to Russia, and the CIA couldn't care less what happened to her. Then, if not to tell him about Andrea, what else did they want from him now, he wondered, pacing the living room furiously. Perhaps the CIA had decided to reopen the Blue Cube case and wanted to ask him a few questions, he concluded. The idea of recalling those painful events appealed to him even less. It had taken years to put the whole thing behind him and he would not welcome any attempt to bring it back again.

He stopped pacing and walked into the kitchen, standing in front of the glass door that led to the porch. He had heard a car engine and thought that Hansen had already arrived, but no car pulled into the driveway. He went back to the living room, promising himself not to worry and to keep his cool. Whatever the CIA man had in mind was part of the past, and better left buried.

The door chime sounded and he walked slowly to the door. He pulled it open and found a man with a friendly face. "I'm Frank Hansen, I apologize for being late. My directions weren't too good—I got lost."

Serves you right, Greg thought as he shook hands with the man. "Greg Elliot," he said dryly. "Please come in."

"Nice house," Hansen said, walking in. "But I have to admit that I don't know if I could live in a house perched on a steep hill and supported by stilts." A smile spread on his face, making Greg feel at ease. At least the CIA hasn't sent a bully to talk to me, he thought.

"I had the same feeling when I moved in," Greg said, leading the way to the living room. "Particularly because this is earthquake country." He turned his head to look at Hansen. "But time makes you accept things . . . so it doesn't bother me anymore."

They entered the living room and Greg motioned Hansen to the couch. Hansen sat down and placed on the floor a carry-on bag he had brought with him. Greg wondered why Hansen had carried it into the house; he could have left it in the car.

"Do you want to drink something?" Greg asked.

"I'll have a Perrier, if you have one."

"What about a Calistoga? It's bottled here in California."

Hansen shrugged. "Fine. You guys have only California stuff here, huh?"

Greg smiled. "Only with wine. This is wine country. We're very choosy; we buy local brands." He walked to the kitchen, and a moment later, returned with a bottle of Calistoga mineral water, an empty glass, and a glass of white wine. "I'll have a glass of wine," he said. "I'm gonna need it." He passed the Calistoga and the empty glass to Hansen.

Hansen drank half of the water, taking his time. Greg, sitting in an armchair facing the couch, kept his eyes riveted on Hansen. "Well, let's get to the point," Greg said after taking a sip of wine. "You guys don't pay courtesy visits unless something's up."

Hansen nodded, putting the glass on a table next to him. "I work for the CIA, but I'm not a spy as you might define the word. I have a degree in psychology, and I specialize in debriefing defectors."

At the word *defector*, Greg felt the tension mounting inside him. He was sure now that Hansen's visit had to do with Andrea.

"You don't know me," Hansen went on, "but I know you very well."

"So much for privacy," Greg said.

Hansen shook his head. "Not in the way you think. We haven't been spying on you. I was Andrea's debriefer until we swapped her in Berlin. . . . I know Andrea very well. . . . I've heard a lot about you."

Greg lowered his head. "I don't know if I want to talk about Andrea."

"I understand your position, but we don't have any other choice at the moment."

"I'm sorry. . . . I don't want to."

"I said we don't have any other choice."

"What do you want?"

"I'll tell you in a minute. You have a VHS video cassette recorder around here?" He reached for the bag and pulled out a videotape case. "I have something I want to show you first."

Greg stood up and Hansen followed him. They stopped in front of the TV set and a video cassette recorder on a cart next to the fireplace. "You can use this one," Greg said tensely.

Hansen knelt on the floor. After some hesitation, he turned the power on and slid the video cassette inside the machine. He fumbled with the buttons for a moment, then stopped. "I'm sorry. It's your machine. Help me play the tape."

Greg crouched next to Hansen, turned the TV set on, and pressed a couple of buttons on the video recorder. A series of numbers and code words flashed on the TV screen.

"We'll see the image soon," Hansen said, still on his knees.

Greg got to his feet and stood in front of the TV. He had no idea of what he was about to see.

The image of a uniformed man appeared on the screen. Greg didn't recognize the uniform. The man was not a police officer; he looked like a guard. Then the camera moved, focusing on the face of a woman with a child. No sound accompanied the scene.

The woman had a passport in her hand and passed it to the uniformed man. Greg realized that the man was a customs agent. The woman left, and a tall man with an unfriendly look and a pockmarked complexion walked in front of the camera. The man talked with the customs agent, but still there was no sound. Then the man left and another woman walked into camera range. Greg could not believe his eyes. The woman was Andrea.

He stepped away from the TV as his eyes focused on her face. Andrea looked different, perhaps thinner and darker-complected. Her hair was also darker and shorter—but it was Andrea, and he was astounded.

The sound on the TV came on and the customs agent said, "State your name."

"Valeri Lisenko."

"Age?"

"Thirty-two."

"Married?"

"Single."

"Are you sure?"
"I . . . said single."
"Where do you live?"
"I don't understand."
"Place of permanent residence in the Soviet Union."
"Oh! I live in Moscow."
The tape went silent again, and Greg stood there, watching the image with his mouth open. Slowly he rubbed his forehead as if to verify that Andrea's image was not a vision. "Where did you film that tape?" he asked, his eyes still on the TV set.
Hansen stopped the video cassette machine and ejected the tape. Taking his time, he returned the tape to the case, stood, and dropped the case back into the bag. "We filmed it at JFK two days ago."
"I don't believe it. She'd never come back. They'd never let her. . . ."
Hansen sat on the couch and reached for the Calistoga. He poured the rest of the bottle into the glass and took a long drink.
Greg was still standing in the middle of the room as if rooted to the floor. "There must be a mistake."
"You can bet this house that she's back," Hansen answered convincingly. "We were as surprised as you. She's living in New York."
"New York," Greg mumbled.
"Yes. She's using a new identity. Valeri Lisenko, a linguistics specialist assigned to the Soviet Mission at the UN."
"It doesn't make any sense," Greg said, walking back to his armchair and sitting down abruptly. "The KGB knows that you guys have a detailed dossier on Andrea. They'd get caught, trying to sneak her through JFK."
Hansen nodded. "We're asking ourselves the same question. But we don't believe the KGB's wasting their time. They brought Andrea back for a purpose, and we want to find out what it is."
Greg reached for the glass of wine and drank, then rested the glass on the coffee table. Andrea's return was unbelievable. She looked different, nervous, and tense. But the KGB hadn't killed her. Thank God! Hansen's revelation suddenly dawned on him. The CIA would not have sent a man all the way to California just to tell him about Andrea. The CIA wanted something in return.

"Why are you telling me all about this?" he asked, frowning.

Hansen arranged his glasses, looked at the Calistoga bottle, then raised his eyes to Greg. "We need your help to understand what's happening."

"What kind of help?"

"Langley wants to know what Andrea is doing here."

"Probably trying to screw somebody for a few secrets. That's her official job at the KGB. Isn't it?"

Hansen shook his head. "We don't believe so. The KGB is not dumb enough to use her the same way twice."

"Then your guess is as good as mine."

"You're right."

"What do you want from me?"

"We want you to contact Andrea to find out what she is up to."

"God! You're crazy," Greg said. "You think I'm going to jump in a plane, go to New York, ask Andrea what she's doing there, and she's going to tell me? You're dreaming. . . ." He stood up from the armchair and started to pace in the middle of the living room.

Hansen waited a few seconds, then said, "This will require a major operation on our part. It's kind of turning the tables after what she did to you. We want you to convince her to cooperate with us. She has no other future here. . . ."

"Jesus Christ! You're crazier than I thought!"

"This is a very serious request," Hansen said.

Greg stopped pacing, turned to Hansen, and threw his arms up in the air. "Great! You come here to tell me that I should become a spy and do to Andrea the same dishonest thing that she did to me. . . . You're wasting your time."

"No, we're not. You're her legal husband, and we believe that she could still be in love with you."

"I don't care about her anymore."

"I don't believe you."

"Well, you're wrong. I buried her and my feelings for her a long time ago."

Hansen got up from the couch. "Look, Greg, this is as difficult for me as it is for you. I dreaded this assignment because I knew the confusion and pain I'd cause you. But I must do my job. We want you, and I believe that you should help us. It'd be best for you . . . and for Andrea."

"Thanks for the advice, but no again."

"Well, the CIA's convinced that Andrea is vulnerable. Also, they're very worried about her return. She has worked in very sensitive areas in other places. The KGB is bringing her back as if nothing happened. They know that the CIA isn't dumb. They have a purpose in mind." He reached down for the bag and rested it on the couch, preparing to leave. "The CIA will go after Andrea one way or another. They believe that you're their best bet. You could influence Andrea . . . and talk her into cooperating with them. But if you don't do it, they'll get a young, good-looking agent to go after her—and the CIA will do the screwing. . . . I don't think that you want that."

Greg looked down at the floor. He had had a very bad taste in his mouth when Andrea was in the hospital and he was dealing with the CIA back in Washington. He didn't trust the bastards. He took a deep breath, exhaling slowly. What could he do? "I'm sorry," he said. "Perhaps you're right, but I can't see myself doing to Andrea what she did to me."

"You won't be able to control that outcome. Somebody's going to do it. The question is what's best for you and for Andrea."

Greg bit his lip. Hansen was making it very difficult, but his decision was final. "Look, Hansen, I believe that you've been honest with me, but my decision is final. I won't get involved."

Hansen dipped a hand into a pocket in his jacket and produced a piece of paper, passing it to Greg. "You need a few days to think it over. I didn't expect a decision now. I'm returning to New York tonight. In a couple of days, call me at this number and let me know what you want to do."

"That's fair enough," Greg said, pocketing the paper.

Hansen seemed to hesitate, then said, "Maybe this will help you settle this affair for good. I know that broken hearts take a long time to heal . . . more than we're led to believe sometimes." He smiled, and Greg felt at ease with him for the first time.

They walked to the foyer and Hansen extended a hand to Greg. As they shook hands, Hansen said, "I still wouldn't like to live in a house perched on stilts." Then he walked out the door and was gone.

* * *

The passenger traffic at San Francisco International was light at night. A few people waited, sitting in the empty rows of chairs facing United Airlines gate 49. Flight 245 was leaving for Newark International in ten minutes. The United clerk had already started to board the passengers.

Standing in front of a closed newspaper stand, a stocky man glanced briefly at the people boarding the plane. He wore casual clothes: jeans, plaid shirt, jogging shoes, and a Yankees cap—the kind of clothes any relaxed traveler would wear.

The United employee closed the door to the connecting walkway, and in a few minutes the plane started to move away from the gate. The man then walked casually to a nearby phone, dropped a coin into the slot, and dialed a local number.

"Hello," a voice said.

"Could you tell me the time?" the man said.

"Sorry, I don't have a watch here," the voice said.

The man nodded, satisfied, then said, "Hansen just left. I want to send a message to comrade Dmitri. I also have a package for him."

"Go ahead," the voice said.

CHAPTER 6

From behind the mountains, the orange ball rose in the sky. Greg squinted at the sudden onrush of light and looked away. He glanced around him as if noticing his surroundings for the first time. Wrapped in a blanket, he was huddled on the floor of the porch against the wall, his chest against his doubled-up legs. Two bottles of wine sat next to him, one empty, the other barely touched. He tried to move but his legs were stiff. He didn't remember how long he had been sitting there; he had lost all sense of time.

After Hansen left, he had paced the living room until the walls, the ceiling, and the floor started to spin. He then stopped pacing and considered going for a ride, but he wasn't sure he could drive. The next choice was going to sleep. But how could he go to sleep with such an emotional storm inside him? He had opted for a blanket, two bottles of wine, and a glass. At least the loneliness of the porch and the alcohol would be a good company for his misery.

He had thought that everything was behind him after those three long years. He had led himself to believe that Andrea was living a happy life someplace in Russia, that she had found her own identity and perhaps a family. But deep inside, he had known that all his thinking was a mere illusion and that the KGB had punished Andrea for her failure, either by sending her to jail or by killing her. Then Hansen came and broke the news. Andrea was back—and she was still a spy.

Greg sighed. He had also thought that he didn't care anymore, that his life had finally settled down. How wrong he had been.

He got to his feet, walking a few steps to restore the circulation in his legs. He dropped the blanket on a reclining chair and went into the kitchen. A shower and a pot of coffee would help to clear his mind.

The Alfa's engine coughed a couple of times and then stopped. Greg turned the ignition again, and the small sports car came to life. He waited a few seconds, then pulled out of the garage.

After a shower and a couple of cups of coffee, he had felt more animated. Then he made a phone call, canceling a business appointment he had made for that afternoon. Being a software consultant gave him some flexibility in his schedule, and he appreciated his work more than ever.

The traffic heading for San Francisco was light and Greg enjoyed the ride. The noon-time sun was high in the sky and the day was bright. Fifty minutes later, he drove past the Golden Gate and headed north. Another hour and he'd be in Napa Valley.

This was his first visit in four months. The thought made him feel guilty as he recalled his promise to visit Rancho Caliente every month. The road narrowed, threading along vineyards that followed the curve of the mountains. Greg took a deep breath. The fresh air and the sight of the vineyards always gave him a lift—but they couldn't take the pain out of his heart.

He drove past a small bridge over a creek, then faced a grove of oaks embracing a Tudor house atop a small cliff. Greg steered toward an open plateau that served as a parking lot. Only two cars were parked and Greg was glad. He wasn't in the mood to see a lot of people.

Greg went up to the house and rang the bell. "What a surprise," the old lady said opening the door, then moved forward to embrace him.

"You look wonderful, Madame Suzanne." Greg gave her a gentle hug. "So good to see you."

They stepped back to look at each other. She looked in remarkably good health in spite of her eighty years, Greg thought. She still had those vivacious eyes that never stopped smiling at him.

"You're slimmer than you were the last time I saw you," Madame Suzanne said.

"I'm working hard at it. I'm sorry I haven't visited you in four months. I don't want to give you any excuses. I've been neglectful."

"Don't mention it. You're always welcome here, no matter how much time there is between visits."

Greg nodded. "I know. Thanks."

Madame Suzanne clung to his arm and they walked slowly into a room with two large windows overlooking the cliff and the creek. "How's everything?" he asked, helping her into an armchair.

"Well, things could be better. I can't complain about the vineyards. Business is booming. But the home for retarded children is not doing well."

"What's happening?" Greg asked, pulling up a chair.

"It's very difficult to get outside help. This place is too remote, and there are not many skilled people willing to move down here on a full-time basis."

"I'm sorry to hear that. I wish I could help. . . . I owe you so much."

Madame Suzanne waved a hand. "Don't worry. You did help us a lot. I'll manage somehow."

They talked for about half an hour. Then Greg grew impatient, hardly keeping up with the conversation. He stood up and said, "I must return to the valley soon. I'd like to visit my brother's grave before I return."

"Say a prayer for John in my name," she said.

The dirt road inched its way along a steep mountain, through a vineyard, and then leveled off to a small, flat piece of land that composed the old graveyard that overlooked a few hills with rolling vineyards. The hills ended abruptly in a backdrop of high mountains that were already hiding the sun. The air was fresh and a little chilly. Greg walked the last stretch of road and took a few more steps. Breathing hard, he stopped in front of a wooden cross with a small brass plaque that read, "John C. Elliot."

Slowly he crouched in front of the grave and stared silently at the cross and the plaque. His brother had died a little over three years ago on the same night he had learned the truth about Andrea. When he thought that life had finally smiled at him, destiny put him through the loss of his brother and the truth about a terrible lie. Andrea had never been Andrea.

Greg sat on the ground and crossed his legs, his eyes still on the cross and on his brother's name. John had never said a word and his mind never developed beyond that of a three-year-old child; but he always felt that he could talk to John. His brother always listened to him. Now John was dead, but it made no difference to him. He still could talk to John.

"I'm happy to visit you, John," he said, wiping a tear off his cheek. "You won't believe what I have to tell you. . . ."

Sometime later Greg got up from the ground, shivering. The sky had turned dark, blurring the mountains and the vineyards around him. He didn't know how long he had been sitting there or talking to his brother, but he knew that he had to go. He had a phone call to make.

Dmitri finished encoding the lengthy report, and then folded the four pages into a heavy manila envelope. He sat at a small desk in his ample bedroom in the west wing of the Mission. Next to him on the desk was his personal one-time pad that the Deputy Premier of the First Directorate, Geidar Aligev, had given to him. Dmitri still remembered the excitement he'd felt when Aligev had given him the personal cipher, saying that the Deputy Premier himself would control the matching copy. This was an honor that Dmitri was certain only very few people had shared with Aligev. It was also an indication of the importance of his mission and the great consequences he'd suffer if he failed. He still could recall Aligev's warning: "You must not fail."

This was Dmitri's first report to Aligev. All he had to do now was seal the envelope with melted wax and then drop the envelope into the next diplomatic pouch out of the Mission. He had scribbled the destination code on the top right corner. This special code would take the sealed envelope directly to Aligev's desk.

Dmitri poured the hot wax on the surface of the envelope, pressed it with the sealing stamp he had brought from Moscow, and slid the envelope into another, larger one. He was satisfied. He had reported to Aligev that everything was progressing as they had planned.

After storing the one-time pad and the seal in a safe next to his bed, he got dressed in a short-sleeved shirt and an old worn-out pair of pants. He walked out of the room, happy with the accommodations. The rezident had made available a spacious bedroom in a wing of the building reserved only for very high functionaries of the Foreign Ministry. The well-furnished rooms had private bathrooms and were much more comfortable than the shabby ones he had seen on the lower floors of the building. Still, his room was not as pleasant as his Moscow apartment—one of the things he missed most when he traveled on assignment.

Dropping the envelope at the Mission's communications center was routine, requiring that he sign a master logbook. The officer on duty, after recognizing the special code directing the envelope to the office of the First Chief Directorate, guaranteed him that a special courier would deliver the envelope within five working days.

From the communications center Dmitri took a special elevator that stopped only in the basement of the Mission. The elevator was unmanned and required a special key to operate. The rezident had recommended that he use it only when he wanted to leave the building unnoticed. Dmitri had called Internal Security, arranging for his exit. He had an important meeting to attend in one of the safe houses and didn't want to risk an FBI tail.

The elevator door opened and Dmitri walked into a small room where a man was sitting on a chair next to a closed door. There was a table with a TV monitor and a phone. Dmitri walked toward the man.

"You must wait here, comrade," the man said, pulling white overalls from a box under the table. He passed the overalls to Dmitri. "Wear them," the man added, his eyes on the monitor.

Dmitri got dressed noticing the logo on the back: Quebec Janitorial Services.

Minutes passed. Dmitri grew impatient. The room was hot and the overalls added to his discomfort. He kept his eyes on the TV monitor, which showed a view of the underground garage of the Mission. A few cars drove by the camera, but the van was not in sight.

"Sometimes it takes a few minutes," the man said apologetically.

Soon a van came into camera range. As the vehicle advanced

slowly, the man said, "Get ready, comrade."

Dmitri stepped close to the door.

"Now," the man said.

Dmitri opened the door and stepped into the garage. The van was still moving slowly. The same logo as the one on Dmitri's overalls was printed on the side of the van. Dmitri reached for the rear door, pulled it open, and climbed inside. He sat on a small seat against the wall of the van, hidden from the outside.

The van accelerated and Dmitri grabbed the seat to keep his balance. He was sitting sideways, sandwiched between two metal shelves full of boxes and plastic bottles. Several mops, brooms, and metal buckets and three large plastic bags stuffed with rags were on the floor. A very strong odor of disinfectant inside the van made him want to sneeze and Dmitri rubbed his nose.

The van paused at the exit of the garage, joining the street traffic a few seconds later. Dmitri leaned hard against the back of the seat so that no one could see him from outside the van. The driver was a Russian Illegal planted in Canada with a Russian wife, also an Illegal. They had lived in Quebec for over twenty years, and the KGB had ordered them to move to New York to open the janitorial business which would be used as a front for their courier services to the Mission. The rezident had assured Dmitri that the man was trustworthy and an expert courier. Dmitri still recalled the rezident's proud tone as he described the great success the KGB had had with the Illegal program.

They drove for about an hour, making several sudden changes of direction, then entered an underground garage. The van stopped long enough to let Dmitri jump out. He walked up two levels to a black Buick parked in space 72.

Dmitri went to the only window in the room, moved the blinds a couple of inches, and glanced down at the street. He was in the safe house on the fifth floor of a rundown apartment building on 111th Street in Manhattan, a block from Park Avenue. At first he disliked the place and thought he'd ask the rezident for another safe house. But after he drove around the block a few times, he changed his mind. The area was a true picture of Imperialist America—filled with unpainted, dilapidated buildings splashed with graffiti that exhorted revolution and freedom for the Puerto Rican people. He couldn't believe the garbage dumped on the streets—a flock of hungry pigeons scavenged for survival. The streets were swarming with people—loud people—talking non-stop and listening to blaring radios. He stepped back from the window satisfied. It would be easy to move in and out of the safe house without causing any suspicion. Nobody would care about them.

He walked to the next room, where they had set up the operations center. Dmitri guessed that the small room adjacent to the kitchen had been the dining room. He had ordered a table, four chairs, and some electronic gear he needed.

A man was crouched on the floor at one end of the room, busily setting up some of the electronic equipment. "I approve of the safe house, comrade Grigori," Dmitri said, sitting on a chair in front of the table.

Grigori nodded, his attention still on the cables he was connecting. "We haven't used this one for three years," he said in a heavy Russian accent.

Dmitri turned his attention to an envelope on the table. "I fetched it from the dead drop this morning," Grigori said. "Special courier from California." He walked to the table, pulled out a chair, and sat down facing Dmitri.

Grigori was a KGB veteran with over fifteen years of overseas assignments. Dmitri recalled Grigori's dossier; the small, thin man with slightly Asiatic features specialized in electronic surveillance. The dossier claimed that Grigori was one of the best KGB operatives who worked for Department Fourteen, which supplied all the technical tools for clandestine operations. But Grigori's skills were not confined to electronic devices; he was also a specialist in poisons and assassination devices, skills that Dmitri thought might prove handy as an option.

Dmitri looked at the envelope and felt tempted to open it. He knew what information was inside, but first he wanted to make certain that Grigori had taken care of his orders.

"What about the other comrades?" Dmitri asked.

"I've assigned them just as you ordered," Grigori said. "Three men in Hoboken, three in Long Island. The other three will stay here."

"Good," Dmitri said. "I don't want any operative to go back to the Mission."

"They all used the special procedure for leaving the Mission. I didn't want to compromise the safe houses," Grigori said.

"You must set up living conditions in all three houses. They must live there until we're done."

"How long are we going to stay underground?"

"I don't know," Dmitri said, not wanting to commit to any particular time frame. It would raise false expectations that could lead to moral problems or mistakes. "You'll live here until we complete our mission—no matter how long it takes."

Grigori nodded.

"What about Hansen?" Dmitri asked.

"After he arrived from California, he rented a room at the Grand Hyatt on 42nd Street. I have three men covering him—"

"Remember, if he's alone, you can follow him. But not if he's with another CIA operative or Maguire. I don't want to arouse suspicion yet."

Grigori nodded once more.

"Hansen is an inexperienced operative. He wouldn't notice a tail," Dmitri added to clarify his point.

"I gave the instructions to our men," Grigori said. "Do you want to hear the tape?" he asked, looking at the envelope.

Dmitri stood up from the chair. "Go ahead." He walked over to a cupboard above a formica counter in the kitchen and pulled the door open, instantly smelling the strong odor of roach killer. "Thanks for stocking the kitchen, comrade," he said, eyeing the six bottles of vodka neatly arrayed inside.

He strolled back to the table and sat down with a bottle and a glass in front of him. Grigori brought him a pair of headphones connected to a long cable. Dmitri put on the headphones and poured himself half a glass of vodka. Grigori tore open the envelope and produced an audio cassette; he slid it into a player, put on another set of headphones, and pushed the PLAY button. After adjusting the volume, he walked back to the table and poured himself a drink.

The first thing that Dmitri heard was the ringing of a phone, then a voice saying, "Hello."

Another voice replied, "Mr. Greg Elliot?"

"Yes, who's calling?"

"My name is Frank Hansen. I'm here at the Hilton at San Francisco Airport." A pause followed. "I'm from the East Coast, and I came here to see you. It's very important."

Dmitri leaned back and relaxed as he listened to the conversation, sipping vodka, sometimes smiling.

After the conversation ended, a long pause ensued, followed by the sound of a door chime, a few footsteps, and a door opening. Dmitri leaned forward, resting his elbows on the table and toying with the empty glass. The conversation seemed to revive.

"I'm Frank Hansen. I apologize for being late. My directions weren't too good. I got lost."

A voice that Dmitri recognized from the phone said, "Greg Elliot. Please, come in."

For the next hour, Dmitri listened to the cassette three times. He couldn't be more satisfied.

"Congratulate our comrades in San Francisco for the excellent job done," Dmitri said to Grigori. "I'll make sure the Center knows about it."

Grigori nodded and Dmitri noticed the gleam of satisfaction in the Russian's eyes.

"I'll make sure San Francisco knows," Grigori said.

"Also, tell them to unplug the phone and the listening devices they've installed in Elliot's house."

Grigori frowned as if not understanding.

"We know all that we wanted to know, comrade," Dmitri said. "We don't want to risk the FBI sweeping the place and finding surveillance devices. They'd learn about us too soon."

"I understand," Grigori said, still looking less than happy.

Dmitri stood up, grabbed the vodka bottle and his glass, and walked around the table. He poured a few fingers into Grigori's glass, then raised his own.

"Everything is happening faster than I had anticipated, comrade," Dmitri said. "Let's make a toast to great success."

They both drank.

CHAPTER 7

The airline clerk pushed the wheelchair slowly, maneuvering past the gate door and into the entrance to the connecting walkway and airplane. The large young man in the wheelchair had a cast on his left leg from his knee to his toes. Two young women walked behind the clerk, carrying several bags, tennis rackets, and a small case. They all boarded the plane.

Lucky man, Greg thought, watching the two women talking and smiling at the young man. As Greg moved in his seat, he wondered how the man broke his leg. It wasn't the skiing season yet. But Greg was sure he'd be fine and walking in no time. He still felt a tightening in his chest, though. Wheelchairs reminded him of his brother John. That was the only motion his brother ever knew: John had never walked—not a single step.

Going through life depending on others to be able to move around was not the right way to live. But for John it was even worse; he never knew what life was about. The pain increased in Greg's chest and he looked away from the gate. After all this time and he still couldn't stop thinking about his brother.

The airline employee started to call the passengers for boarding in a monotonous voice. "Flight 411. Destination Newark. Rows 17 to 32." Greg rose from his seat, and as he walked onto the plane, he thought about his trip to Napa Valley. It had helped calm the emotional storm within him. He had needed to talk to someone before making a decision. And who else better than his brother? John had been a good listener, and he had always told John all his secrets, even the most intimate ones. He had sometimes seen some life in John's eyes—the kind of understanding that only a brother could give to another brother.

He had called Hansen the moment he arrived at his house

from Rancho Caliente. When he told Hansen about his decision, the CIA agent sounded pleased and told him he was doing the right thing. Greg didn't like Hansen's tone and retorted: "For me, or for the CIA?" Hansen hadn't answered for a few seconds, and Greg had noticed the tension in that silence. Finally, Hansen had said that they didn't talk like that on the phone and added that he had a paid room under the name of Tom Smith at the Grand Hyatt on 42nd Street. Greg recalled the rage he had felt when Hansen had told him about the room: Hansen had reserved the room in advance; the bastard had known he was coming.

Andrea read the paragraph again and made a few corrections with a pencil. She then leaned back on the hard chair, resting the pencil next to the notepad. She had been translating the lengthy document from Russian into English. Her supervisor had asked for an English version of the Foreign Ministry position paper on the use of chemical weapons in the Iran-Iraq war. The paper was lengthy, and it strongly condemned Iraq for using chemical warfare against Iran.

At first she read the paper with interest, thinking that the Foreign Ministry genuinely wanted to put an end to chemical warfare. Then, as the rhetoric of the document escalated in favor of Iran, she lost interest. The Ministry accused Iraq of repeatedly killing Iranian soldiers and civilians, unscrupulously violating the Geneva Protocol of 1925. But the paper didn't state that the Soviet Union had sold mustard gas and nerve gas to Iran and Iraq at the beginning of the war.

Andrea's thoughts went back to the KGB colonel she'd met in Geneva a year before. The colonel had drunk a little too much and had tried to seduce her, boasting of his expertise as a salesman. He had claimed that he'd sold chemical weapons to both sides in the Iran-Iraq war. With a smirk on his face, the colonel had said that the side which won would be their ally; the side which lost would not be there to complain; and either way, the KGB couldn't lose. Andrea hadn't liked the colonel's reply and had remarked that selling to both sides of a war was immoral. The colonel had looked at her, narrowed his eyes, and replied that she had a lot to learn. Then he had added reflectively that wars had no moral side—they had only winners and losers. Having lost his patience the colonel pulled rank, asking her to sleep with him. Andrea had refused and later denounced him to Internal Security for talking too much. A few days after that, the Center had called the colonel back to Moscow and Andrea had never heard of him again. It was the first time she'd appreciated Internal Security.

Andrea toyed with the pencil for a few seconds, her eyes roaming over the desk and the small cubicle. This was her second day working as a translator, on the third floor of the Mission: they had assigned her to the small department of ten translators, all women, and a tough-looking male supervisor. The department, a large room partitioned into a maze of cubicles, crowded the eastern corner of the building. The cubicles, the furniture, and the walls were all painted gray, and the place had a stark look. There were no pictures on the walls, and gray plywood planks sealed a row of windows that overlooked the street. She had been on the job for only two days, and already she couldn't stand the environment. In a sense they had put her in a jail, the worst of all jails—one that imprisoned her mind.

After rereading the English translation of the paper, she got up from the chair. Her supervisor had said he wanted the paper translated and typed by the next day at 8 a.m. Andrea glanced at her watch: she had only a couple of hours to get the document typed.

The typing department was on the second floor, so Andrea walked briskly down the stairs. The doctor in Moscow had ordered her to exercise, and avoiding elevators was a beginning. Then she had to walk to the other end of the building to get to the department. They should give a medal to the planner who'd decided to locate the typing pool so far from the translators, she thought. She entered an open room with about a dozen typing stations. A clerk behind a desk faced the door.

"I have an urgent request, comrade," Andrea said to the young man, who was staring at her.

"Fill out this form," the clerk said, pulling a piece of paper from a tray in front of him.

Andrea looked at it. "I don't have a pen."

"Bring one next time," the man said, taking a pen out of a

drawer and passing it to her.

The paper was a form with a long list of questions not relevant to the typing job. Andrea answered them, then filled in the requested date and time. She passed the paper and the pen back to the clerk. "Sorry, I must have this typed by 5 p.m. today," she said.

The clerk eyed the paper, then looked up at her. "You don't understand, comrade," he said as if on the edge of losing his patience. "Turnaround time for typing is five days. You're lucky if you get it in ten. Are you new?"

Andrea nodded. "My supervisor asked me to have this translated and typed by 8 a.m. tomorrow."

"Translation thinks it owns the typing pool," the clerk said, "always asking for impossible dates."

"I *must* have it."

The clerk shook his head slowly. "Talk to the typing supervisor. I can't help you."

Andrea sighed. "Okay. Where can I find her?"

"Back there," the clerk said, pointing to the other end of the room. "Last cubicle," he added.

Andrea walked past the open room, thinking about Sylvia's words the first time they met: I'll give you special priority for being my roommate. How right she was.

Sylvia welcomed her with a big smile. "I knew you'd see me soon," she said.

"I'm sorry."

"Don't let it bother you," Sylvia said. "Everybody at the Mission wants my favors sooner or later." She sounded flirtatious.

"I didn't expect to be here so soon," Andrea said. "I need something typed by tomorrow 8 a.m."

"How many pages?"

"Ten."

"It'll take four hours to get it done."

"Four hours?"

"People don't type too fast here," Sylvia grinned. "As the Americans would say, they take their own sweet time."

Andrea glanced at her watch. "Can you finish by seven?"

Sylvia nodded. "I think so."

Andrea passed the form and her papers to Sylvia. "May I

come back around then?" she asked.

"Tell you what," Sylvia said, putting an arm around Andrea's shoulder. "Come around five. We'll go for a walk."

"A walk?"

"To Central Park."

"That's forbidden."

"I told you not to worry. I have ways to bend the rules. I'll show you a couple of tricks."

Andrea hesitated. She didn't want to do something illegal. "Sorry, comrade. I don't want to get into trouble."

"C'mon. You think I'm going to get you in trouble? I'd never do that."

Andrea rubbed her forehead, suddenly feeling hot. "Sorry, I can't do it."

Sylvia turned serious. "You want your job typed by seven?"

Andrea nodded.

"Then come back at five. You won't be sorry. Believe me." She smiled again.

"Okay. You win. But I still don't like it."

Sylvia watched Andrea leave the room. She waited a few seconds more and then walked back to her desk, reached for the phone, dialed a number.

A voice answered in Russian.

"We're going for a walk at five," she said. "Central Park."

"Very good, comrade," the voice said. "Keep me posted."

"I will, comrade Dmitri," Sylvia said, hanging up.

Greg stepped out of the taxi. The driver rushed to the rear of the vehicle and opened the trunk. He grabbed the suitcase and the carry-on bag, dropping them on the sidewalk. They were parked in front of the 42nd Street entrance of the Grand Hyatt.

The taxi drove away and Greg glanced around at the busy street. Every time he visited New York he reaffirmed his love for California. It seemed to him that he had stepped into another world—a world of cars, concrete, and rushing people.

Curiously, he studied the front of the hotel and the revolving doors that constantly ushered people into and out of the Hyatt. Greg liked the second floor, cantilevering over the sidewalk, with its glass windows and glass roof overlooking 42nd Street. The setting reminded him of a greenhouse, one with people sitting inside, warm and comfortable, looking out at people freezing their asses on the street. Good arrangement, he thought.

He walked into the hotel, and his amazement brought him to a halt. The lobby was an atrium packed with bubbling fountains, fancy sculptures, luxurious lounges, and an array of expensive boutiques. It took him a few moments to find the check-in counter. Then he asked for the reservation under the name of Tom Smith. He signed the registration card, using the address of a client he had in Phoenix.

"Your room's on the fifth floor," the clerk told him, passing a key. "Need help to carry your luggage?" she added.

"No, thanks," Greg said. "I'll manage."

The room was spacious and plush, with a cream-colored carpet, a queen-sized bed with an expensive bedspread, and fancy furniture. The bastards were certainly spending money on him. He unpacked, hung up his clothes, and arranged his toiletries on the bathroom counter. Then he undressed, washed his face, and collapsed into bed. He had not slept well for the last couple of days, thinking of Andrea and all that was happening to him. The KGB had forced Andrea into his life; then the CIA and the KGB had taken her away. The CIA had never asked him for his opinion. They hadn't cared. He recalled a similar situation from the past. An adoption agency had separated him from John, sending his brother to a care center for retarded children because nobody had wanted to adopt John. Nobody had cared. He had cried and had refused to eat for days until they brought John back to him. Then they had moved from one foster home to another until he was old enough to work and take care of his brother. He had promised himself never to leave his brother. John was all he had.

As for Andrea, he had thought that she was already part of his past, that perhaps his friend Ron was right: he should divorce her and start a new life. Then, suddenly, everything had changed—Andrea was back and the CIA wanted him to contact her. Andrea's return raised a lot of questions. Was the KGB forcing Andrea to be a spy? Had they brainwashed her? Did she want to be free? Still, he didn't know why he had agreed to get involved in this crazy plan. He didn't know if he loved Andrea or wanted to see her one more time and then walk away. Perhaps that's what he needed—to prove to himself that Andrea didn't matter any more.

"That's why I'm here," he said aloud. "To find out the truth."

Andrea, trembling, felt her palms turn cold and clammy as she spotted Sylvia waiting at the front of the Mission, talking animatedly with the two security men at the door. What would happen if they asked her where she was going, Andrea wondered, now feeling pain in her stomach. She'd have to let Sylvia answer that question, she repeated to herself, to build up some confidence.

"You're punctual," Sylvia said, glancing at her watch.

"I like to be punctual."

"I signed you on the register," Sylvia said. She glanced at the register book. "I told them we're going to buy some feminine necessities at the store on Third Avenue." She winked.

Andrea winced, not having to fake cramps. "Thanks, comrade," she said.

They left the building and headed for Third Avenue. As they walked, Andrea looked around. It was the first time she'd had a chance to walk on the New York streets. Looking up at the Mission, Andrea realized that she hadn't noticed the iron bars covering the windows of the first two floors when she had first seen the building. Nor had she remembered seeing the small police booth at the corner of the street. As they passed it, a police officer, tall and square-shouldered, stood next to it. Andrea avoided the policeman's stare. She didn't expect to find a policeman standing on the sidewalk. "Are we under arrest at the Mission?" she asked Sylvia.

Sylvia smiled. "Oh, no. He's here to protect us."

"I don't understand."

"Well, people might want to harm us. The police would scare them away."

"I see," Andrea said, still not understanding.

There was a string of stores around the corner of 67th Street and Third Avenue. Andrea stopped in front of every window, glancing at the items on display. There was a drug and cosmetic store, a nail salon, and a women's store, Fashions Unlimited. Her eyes lingered on the dresses.

"We must hurry up," Sylvia said, pulling her by the arm. "We don't have time for window shopping."

"Sorry," Andrea said, embarrassed.

Around the corner the buildings were residential. Small trees dotted the street. Also, colorful marquees and fancy ironwork covered the windows and main entrances of the buildings. The ornamental ironwork seemed quite different from the jail-like iron bars at the Mission. As they went on, they began to hurry.

"How far is Central Park?" Andrea asked.

"Only four blocks," Sylvia said, short of breath.

"Do you go there often?" Andrea asked.

"Sometimes."

"If we get caught, we'll be in trouble," Andrea said.

"No time to worry about that now."

The light at the corner was green, and they waited for the crossing sign. Next to them a young woman also waited, jogging in place and rotating her head to stretch the muscles of her neck. Andrea watched the fast-paced traffic on Fifth Avenue. There was something different about the cars in New York. Compared to the cars she had seen in California they were bigger, not so new-looking, more aggressive, and always in a rush. The light changed to green and Sylvia rushed across the street. Andrea hurried behind her as the woman jogger passed them.

They walked by a street that cut across the park, into a narrow path leading to an area with trees, bushes, and shrubs. The contrast with the city just a few steps away was startling. "How big is the park?" she asked.

"Big enough for us," Sylvia said.

"I like it," Andrea said, glancing around.

"It's a nice break from the monotony of the Mission."

"Why they don't allow us to come here?"

Sylvia shrugged. "I don't know. Maybe they're afraid the Americans are going to corrupt us." She glanced at her watch and added, "We have ten minutes."

"It doesn't make any sense."

"There are a lot of things that don't make any sense. But we must obey them, or they'll send us back."

"Do you miss the Soviet Union?" Andrea asked.

"Sometimes," Sylvia said.

"You just told me that you obey the rules to avoid being sent back."

Sylvia shook her head. "I obey rules because I don't have any other choice." She looked around. "I like New York. . . . I live better here, in spite of the restrictions. But I learned a long time ago that I must conform . . . and obey."

Andrea said nothing.

The path cut through a playground and they stopped to watch a few children playing. Andrea saw a bench and turned to Sylvia. "Do you want to sit?"

"No, it's nicer to walk."

"Okay," Andrea said, watching a little boy swinging back and forth in a swing. The child gave a little scream of delight each time his mother pushed him.

"What about you?" Sylvia said, her eyes on the playground. "Do you miss the Soviet Union?"

An inner voice told Andrea to give Sylvia a safe "Yes" answer, but she felt troubled. Sylvia had been honest with her, and the least she could do was to tell her the truth—or at least part of it.

In truth, she didn't know very much about the Soviet Union. The KGB had raised her in an Illegals training campus near Moscow. She'd grown up mimicking the American way of living, speaking English as her native language. She never left the campus, but grew up impersonating the life of another Andrea Hendrick, one who had died in Ann Arbor, Michigan, at the age of three. For years she dreamed of a father, an American father, a mechanical engineer working in Detroit. She also had a mother, not a real one, but a mother.

Time after time she had fantasized that she was the real Andrea with a real father and real mother: Bill and Peggy Hendrick. She wondered about them. Did they miss their daughter? How happy would they be if they knew that they had another daughter—a fake one, but a daughter? She always wanted to know how they'd look: Old? Gray-haired? How did they live? What was their house like? What was the real Andrea's room like?

Sometimes she wondered what would happen if she showed up one day and said, "I'm your other Andrea. I know all about you. I've lived all my life being your daughter. I think like her. I feel like her. I love you; I'm not dead." Would the Hendricks accept her as their daughter? Would they love her?

But all this was a fantasy. The truth was that her real family had abandoned her, giving her away to the Illegals program, and that her family never bothered to come to see her. No, she was sure she didn't miss the Soviet Union; she had no reason to.

"Well, I'm still waiting for an answer," Sylvia said.

"Sorry . . . I miss the Soviet Union," she paused. "It's our country. . . ."

"Do you want to go back?"

"I want to do a good job here first," Andrea said. "But to be honest with you, I'm in no hurry to return. It doesn't mean that much to me."

"I don't understand. Why?"

Andrea looked away, avoiding Sylvia's eyes. She couldn't tell Sylvia about the Illegals campus. It was against the rules. "I'm sorry, comrade," she said. "I can't tell you."

"Let's walk," Sylvia said.

They strolled along a path that cut through trees and crossed a wider paved path. The ground was flat and covered with grass and patches of bare rocks. Nearby, a few roofs formed a cluster of small buildings. "What's that, over there?" Andrea asked, pointing.

"It's a children's zoo," Sylvia replied.

"I'd like to visit it one day."

"There are other great places in the park we can see, too. We must visit them little by little. We'll get caught if we stay here too long."

Andrea walked a few steps ahead of Sylvia and reaching a fork in the path, didn't know which way to go. She looked around. To her right were a bench, a garbage can, and a telephone booth. An old man in ragged clothes sat on the bench, a hat pulled down on his forehead and a newspaper folded in his lap. He wasn't reading; he was looking at her. She walked past the bench and stopped in front of the telephone, staring at it blankly. Her return to the United States had unleashed emotions that she had thought were buried. Now she was discovering that she did not have control; that she still cared for her past; and that the ghosts of two lives were still struggling inside her for dominance.

Sylvia walked over to her, stopping next to the phone. "Are you going to make a call?" Sylvia asked, an unreadable expression on her face.

Andrea rubbed her forehead and found it cold. "Oh, no!" she said. "I was just curious to find a telephone here," she added, wondering if Greg Elliot still had the same telephone number in California.

CHAPTER 8

The phone rang, and Greg, slowly turning in bed, reached for the receiver. He squinted at the digital clock on the bedside table. It was six-thirty in the morning. He had asked the operator at the hotel to call him at seven. So who was calling him now?

"Hello," he said, sounding sleepy.

"Good morning," the voice said.

Greg recognized Hansen's voice. "Isn't it too early?" he asked.

"We've got a lot of work ahead of us," Hansen said. "I'll pick you up in your room in thirty minutes. Dress casually."

"What about breakfast?"

"We'll eat something on our way."

"Should I pack?"

"Not yet. You'll stay here for a few days. No more questions," Hansen said, hanging up.

Greg turned in bed a couple times, fighting the desire to sleep. Then he sat on the edge of the bed, staring at the clock. It took him a few seconds to realize why his body refused to wake up. It was 3:30 a.m. California time.

He showered and shaved and did some calisthenics before dressing. The activity helped him to clear his mind. The only thing missing was a cup of coffee.

He heard a knock at the door and strolled across the room. Hansen was a punctual man; it was seven sharp.

"Let's go," Hansen said without any preamble. He was wearing jeans, a T-shirt, and a pair of jogging shoes.

"Am I casual enough?" Greg asked.

"You're okay."

A moment later they entered the elevator, and Hansen pushed

the second-floor button. "I thought we were going out," Greg said.

"We are, but we don't want to use the lobby. You never know."

"What do you mean?"

"Somebody could be waiting for us down there. We'll leave through a back door."

"Oh! I forgot. We're in the spy business."

Hansen frowned. "This is not a game. We have to follow directions."

"I'm sorry."

Forty-third Street was busy, and Greg looked around at the rush-hour traffic. They walked briskly, heading for the corner. "We'll take the subway," Hansen said without looking at Greg. "Walk fast," he added.

Descending the long stairway, they joined a small crowd rushing down to the subway tracks. Greg tried to stay close to Hansen, for he had no idea what to do if he lost him. Hansen already had two tokens in his hand by the time he reached the turnstile. As a few people rushed into a train, Greg realized how foreign the subway seemed. The last time he'd ridden a subway train was over ten years ago. The cars were old and still covered with graffiti. Hansen started to run as he said, "Let's get into this one. Hurry up!" Greg ran behind him.

After switching trains several times, Greg was completely disoriented. He had been lost even before leaving the first train. Who said that this isn't a game? he thought as he followed Hansen. Then, when he least expected it, Hansen took a short flight of stairs and walked into a narrow street.

"I hope we don't have to do this every time we leave the hotel," Greg said.

"This is too important for us not to take all possible precautions," Hansen said.

Hansen stopped in front of a car parked mid-block and urged Greg to get in. "We've got only a few minutes to lose them, if they're following us on foot," Hansen said, turning on the ignition.

"Do you really think the KGB could be following us?" Greg asked.

"I wouldn't discount it," Hansen said, driving.

Greg turned halfway in his seat. "This is ridiculous. Why would the KGB follow us?"

Hansen glanced at him. "Look, Greg. This isn't easy for me, either. We're going to a safe house. CIA regulations call for taking these precautions that look kind of silly. But our agents have sometimes compromised safe houses by not following this routine. I know it's a pain in the ass, but we must follow the rules."

"Aha! It's not the KGB. It's the CIA that's forcing us to do this stuff."

"Well, in a sense, both are forcing us. This is the way the game's supposed to be played. Period."

They drove in silence for a few minutes, Hansen taking so many turns that it seemed to Greg they must be going in circles. The traffic was heavy; cars, trucks, buses, aggressive taxi drivers blowing their horns, all jamming the streets, inching ahead. Greg figured they were now in the garment district because of some of the signs: Schwartz Garment Imports; Goldsmith Imports—Leather and Furs. All the signs had the word *Imports*. Nothing was from the U.S. anymore.

When Hansen came to a stop, Greg read the worn-out sign atop the metal door: "MANHATTAN GARMENT CO." Hansen reached for the remote control and pressed a button. The door started to roll up. "This is it?" Greg asked.

Hansen nodded. "We borrowed the place from the FBI. It's only temporary until we finish this job." He drove slowly through the narrow door, along a tunnel-like entrance flanked by bare brick walls. Soon the car circled an open space and parked next to a van displaying the same logo as the one on the door.

A tall, heavy-set man walked toward them. Hansen introduced him as Chuck Maguire, a CIA senior operative. "Maguire is in charge of this operation," Hansen said. "I report to him."

"Nobody reports to anybody," Maguire said. "We're all part of the same team."

"I've heard the same words back in Silicon Valley," Greg said. "They don't mean anything. There's always a boss."

Maguire smiled. "I like you. We met once briefly, back when Andrea was in the hospital."

"I'm sorry, I don't remember you. But you might be right.

You look familiar to me."

"Greg must be hungry," Hansen said. "We didn't have time to stop for breakfast."

"I have some donuts and coffee," Maguire said. "But first let me show Greg his bed."

"What?" Greg said.

"You haven't told him?" Maguire said, turning to Hansen.

"I thought that it'd be better if we told him here," Hansen said with a look on his face that Greg interpreted as an apology.

Maguire turned to Greg. "We believe that it's less risky for you if you stay here in the safe house. It's not the Hyatt, but it's safer."

"I left all my clothes back there. . . ." Greg said.

"They'll be here this afternoon," Maguire said. "It's easier to get a suitcase and a carry-on bag out of the hotel unnoticed than it is to get you out with your luggage."

"You think that the KGB is tracking me?" Greg said.

"You can bet your ass they are," Maguire said.

The donuts were stale, the coffee lukewarm, the small bed uncomfortable, and the bathroom unmentionable. The place was a dump. Greg sat at a folding table, struggling to keep his anger under control. He hadn't expected such a set-up. What would happen if he had to live there for several weeks? He wasn't sure he'd be able to stand it, and the two CIA spies even less. He had made a terrible mistake. He should never have gotten involved. Not even for Andrea. . . . he stopped in the middle of his thought. Perhaps for Andrea.

He was curious about the electronic equipment in the room and the blackboard with many small notes. He couldn't take his eyes away from the enlarged pictures taped to the blackboard. The Russian's pockmarked face looked ugly, tough, intimidating. Andrea's face was quite different—she looked scared, fragile, as if she were sick. He still could remember her eyes the first time they met. They were the first thing he'd noticed when they met at the bookstore in Cupertino. He had loved their bright, expressive warmth and they had seemed to smile at him. "I'm Andrea Hendrick, glad to meet you," had been her first words. He remembered behaving awkwardly, feeling embarrassed for days. He hadn't know at the time that with those initial words, Andrea had trapped him into a deadly game—a game that he considered already settled. How wrong he had been. Nothing was settled. Andrea was back.

Hansen came to the table with a fresh pot of coffee. "This will help you," he said, filling Greg's cup.

"Thanks," Greg said.

Maguire came out of the bathroom and stood near Hansen. "You're right," he said. "The place is a dump." He pulled a chair and sat across the table, facing Greg. "We've got a lot of homework to do," he told him.

"I don't understand why there's so much fuss about Andrea. She's just a small fish among those sharks," Greg said, taking a sip of the hot coffee.

"We can't give you all the details," Maguire answered, sounding uptight. "Let's say that Langley is very interested in her."

Greg glared at Maguire. "You just gave me the bullshit line that we're part of a team. Well, unless you tell me all the facts, I'm not gonna be part of this team."

Maguire frowned. "I'm not getting this right, son. Wanna quit?"

"Don't call me son. I'm committed, but only if you guys are straight with me. Too much to ask?"

"He's right," Hansen said.

"Don't tell me what's right. I've got to deal with orders from Langley," Maguire said.

"Sorry, Maguire," Hansen said. "I never heard you had a reputation for following orders."

"Listen," Greg said. "I don't want to start a fight." He looked around. "I'm stuck in this shitty place with you guys. I have secret clearance from the time I worked at the Blue Cube. But if you don't tell me what's going on, I won't cooperate. I'll get my ass on a plane back to California this afternoon."

Maguire waved both hands. "Okay . . . okay . . . I've got a revolt on my hands and we haven't even started the hard work yet." He stood up and walked to the blackboard. "But listen, you guys, if this fails because you don't follow my instructions, I'm going to crunch your nuts and leave you maimed for the rest of your lives. Have I made myself clear? I'm going to put my thirty years with the Company at stake here."

"It's a deal," Greg said, feeling better.

Maguire walked to a small file cabinet that seemed to be made of thick metal, like a safe. Greg watched him. There was a roughness in Maguire that Greg couldn't associate with a desk and office work. Maguire seemed to require action, danger. Greg wondered about his age: mid-fifties, he guessed. Greg didn't understand what Maguire had liked about the CIA to spend thirty years doing the same job. There was a limit, even if you really enjoyed a job. In Silicon Valley nobody stayed in a job more than three years; five years was a record. Different worlds—both crazy.

After several turns of a combination lock, Maguire pulled a thick folder from a drawer and walked back to the table. He dropped the folder in front of Greg. "This is a copy of Andrea's dossier back at the CIA. Read it. You're gonna learn a few things about her. You might not like it. . . . Well, what the hell, you're into this already." He paused. Then, as if having second thoughts, he added, "Let me give you a brief summary to get you into the right mood." He walked around the table and dropped his big frame into the chair. Taking a sip of the coffee, he grimaced. "This damn stuff's cold."

Greg glanced at the folder. It had a **TOP SECRET** stamp on the cover and a CIA emblem. In the lower right corner was a series of digits and code letters that made no sense to him. The thought of reading Andrea's dossier chilled him. And that damn Maguire wasn't making it any easier. How many new things would he learn about Andrea, he wondered, not sure whether he really wanted to know.

Maguire took another sip of coffee, gave the cup an angry glance, and put it down brusquely. "After we swapped Andrea in Berlin," he said, "our channels told us that the KGB took her to a mental clinic in Moscow, the kinda place that screws your brain up. Our analysts back in Langley concluded that it was the end of Andrea. The KGB was punishing her for failing and for the killing of her control agent, Boris Alexei Grishin." He paused. "The KGB blamed us for Boris's death and wanted to make an example of Andrea, accusing her of cooperating with the CIA."

Greg suddenly felt hot. He lowered his hands from the table, clasping them together in his lap. "I didn't know that Boris was dead," he said, trying to sound convincing. "Who . . . do you think killed him?"

Maguire looked at him hard, and Greg sustained the stare. "Our analysts believe that the KGB did it, wanting to make it look like a CIA killing," Maguire said.

"You believe that?" Greg asked.

Maguire frowned. "I'm not gonna worry about the bastard's death. It's possible that he blew his own brains out, when he realized his failure. . . . nobody knows. . . . there could be some other scenarios. . . ." He glanced at Greg now with a look that Greg couldn't read. Greg lowered his eyes, pretending to look at the dossier.

"What happened to Andrea?" Greg asked.

"Well, a few months later we were routinely checking some field information from Cuba and saw a picture of a KGB colonel we'd been tracking." He smiled. "Guess who was standing next to the colonel?"

"Andrea?"

"Fuck! We couldn't believe it. From a KGB death clinic to Cuba! The picture stirred up a lot of interest in Langley, and we asked our people in Cuba to keep tabs on Andrea. Then we learned she was using a different name." He smiled again. "Those guys have a good supply of them."

Greg's interest was aroused. Andrea's survival of the KGB mental clinic had been his main worry when she went back to Moscow. Nightmares of Andrea mentally deranged tormented him for months after he returned to California. "What happened after Cuba?"

"That's the tricky part," Maguire said. "We would never have guessed it. The KGB assigned her to Vienna, where then she often worked with the translators supporting the Russian negotiation team at the Soviet-American arms control talks in Geneva. This move got Langley very interested. We're sailing in dangerous waters over there, and Andrea's track record wasn't good enough for that type of assignment—"

Hansen joined them with a fresh pot of coffee, pouring some for Greg and Maguire.

"Please continue," Greg urged Maguire.

"I don't have to tell you how important Geneva is for us.

There's a lot going on there. Andrea must be aware of a lot of things related to the arms control talks—critical information."

"Yes," Greg said.

"Well, it doesn't make any sense."

"What do you mean?"

"Hell! If she knows so much and is so vulnerable. . . . We even know her bra size . . . excuse me. . . ." He seemed embarrassed. "What in hell is she doing here? Why did the KGB bring her back? This is a fucking puzzle. . . ."

"Do you have more information about her stay in Cuba?"

Maguire's face turned serious. "It's all in the dossier. . . . You can read it. . . ."

Greg didn't like the change in expression. "What is it?" he asked.

Maguire stood up and paced around the table, stopping in front of Andrea's picture. He looked at it for a moment, then turned and said to Greg, "The news from Cuba was that the KGB assigned Andrea to be the mistress of a high-ranking officer of the DGI, the Cuban intelligence service."

Silence followed. Greg, feeling the anguish, raised a hand and rubbed his forehead. It was something he had never considered.

Andrea felt her heart beating uncontrollably and the nauseating sensation was back. She had taken two pills before she had left her room, but they had not helped, at least not yet. The messenger had asked her to meet the Mission rezident immediately. The face of the young man was unfriendly and businesslike. When she asked him what the reason was, he said, "I don't know, comrade. I only deliver messages. I don't need to know why."

Worries crowded Andrea's head, pressing her self-control to the limit. Perhaps someone had seen them in Central Park, and the rezident now wanted to send her back to Moscow. They had warned her severely: no mistakes, no disobedience. Follow the rules. But if not the Central Park walk, what else? Maybe Sylvia had induced her to break the rules to test her. They did that kind of thing on a routine basis to test discipline. Whatever it was, she couldn't change it now, she kept repeating to herself, trying to calm down.

She stopped in front of the door and knocked timidly. She heard steps, and a voice say, "Come in."

The small room, with bare walls and floor, held a table and four chairs. The white-haired man, standing facing the door, leaning against the table, his arms folded against his chest was old and dressed in an elegant gray suit. His bony face had a serious expression, and he didn't look angry. Andrea took a deep breath, trying to control her anxiety.

"Vladimir Ignatiev," the man said, extending his bony hand.

Andrea shook hands with him, worried that the rezident would notice her moist palm. "Valeri Lisenko," she said her voice low.

"Please sit down, comrade Lisenko." Ignatiev pointed to a chair. A large manila envelope was on the table in front of it.

"Thanks, comrade rezident." She sat down, keeping her eyes on Ignatiev and ignoring the envelope.

He walked to the other end, sat down slowly, leaned forward, and rested his arms on the table. "You probably wonder why I have called you," he said, a smile at the corner of his lips.

Andrea nodded, feeling more at ease. Ignatiev didn't seem angry or ready to recall her. But you never knew, she repeated to herself, keeping up her guard.

"You've been living in the Mission for a few days already," Ignatiev said. "How do you like New York?"

"I haven't seen that much yet, comrade."

"You will . . . but remember, this is an imperialist city. They're the enemy."

Andrea nodded agreeably.

"I want to make sure that we set the record straight here," Ignatiev went on. "You work for the Mission, but you report to the KGB . . . to me. Your first job, the only important one, is to execute whatever assignment we give you. Is that clear?"

"Yes."

"Good. Some comrades go around doing other assignments or are too busy buying capitalist goods. They forget about the duties they're expected to perform." He arranged his glasses, as if to look at her better. "We return to Moscow those who forfeit their obligations to the Center. Then Moscow will reassign them to posts in border towns, posts they will dread for the rest of their lives. . . ." He let the words hang in the air.

"I won't deceive you, comrade rezident," Andrea said, trying to sound convincing.

"I have your first assignment here," Ignatiev said, pointing at the envelope. "It's very important that you succeed."

Andrea looked at the envelope.

"Inside, there is the dossier of Ramon Ibarra del Rio, a high-ranking functionary of the Costa Rican Mission to the UN. He's old, very rich, spoiled, and very weak where young women are concerned. But he has many connections with the Costa Rican government. He's a close friend of the President of Costa Rica, Oscar Arias Sanchez. This friendship keeps Ibarra del Rio very well informed about the efforts of the Arias plan for peace in Central America. Our friends in Nicaragua will be very happy, and very obligated to us, if we give them firsthand information on what's happening with the Arias plan."

Andrea took a deep breath. She had worried for nothing. The rezident wanted to give her an assignment. She was falling apart for no reason. She had to control her thoughts. She couldn't continue like this, worrying about everything.

"When should I start working on this assignment, comrade?" she asked.

"Your stay in Cuba and your fluent Spanish will be a plus," Ignatiev went on, ignoring Andrea's question. "Those bureaucrats in Costa Rica like to flirt with Communist countries. We'll serve them well." He smiled.

"I don't know how to start," Andrea said.

"Read the dossier first," Ignatiev said with a frown, as if annoyed by her statement. "Ramon Ibarra del Rio frequents the Secretariat at the United Nations. We've assigned you to work there three days a week, on loan. Mondays, Wednesdays, and Fridays. You must find a way to get close to him—be available."

"Do I need an introduction?"

"We're taking care of that detail. There is a reception at the Costa Rican Mission next Saturday night. We've included your name on the guest list. You must meet Ibarra del Rio there. It won't be difficult—he's always looking for young acquaintances. Have a drink with him. Flirt. Look easy. He'll do the rest."

The thought of having to sleep with Ibarra del Rio crossed

Andrea's mind. She wanted to ask about it but decided to avoid the issue. The rezident had not ordered her to have sex with the Costa Rican, but he had implied it. Maybe she could get away without having to, she told herself, knowing it was wishful thinking.

The rezident stood up with difficulty and walked around the table, motioning Andrea to rise. "I must go. Other duties require my presence. You must read the dossier here and then return it to the Internal Security comrade outside. We don't let these things out of this area. In a couple of days, I'll give you a list of questions we want Ibarra del Rio to answer. The Second Department is working on them now."

Andrea walked with him to the door. Ignatiev opened it and paused, turning to Andrea. "This is an important assignment. It's critical for us and for our allies. Don't spoil it doing silly things, comrade. Nobody's allowed to go to Central Park. It's very dangerous there. . . ."

CHAPTER 9

The driver moved the car a few feet more and stopped again, cursing in Russian, shaking his head in frustration. "Today's the worst I've seen in a long time," he said. He was following a slow-moving line of vehicles that circled the plaza to unload people at the entrance of the Secretariat. Andrea glanced curiously out the window. She and six other people were passengers in the four-door Ford which served as one of the shuttles between the Soviet Mission and the Secretariat. It was shortly before midmorning, and her first day at the United Nations. She fingered the hem of the dress, as she thought back to that morning.

She had gotten up early and after completing her morning ritual, had spread on the bed her only two dresses, which weren't too presentable. She had not shopped for new clothes since they hadn't paid her at the Mission, and she had no cash.

After trying on the dresses a couple of times, she had been frustrated. She had struggled with a small mirror, but in the dim light the dresses had looked as bad on her as they had on the bed. The activity finally had awakened Sylvia. She had looked at Andrea sleepily and offered to lend her a dress so she could get some sleep. Andrea had thanked Sylvia, promising she'd take good care of the dress. Sylvia told her not to worry, that it was only a dress. Then Sylvia had buried her head under the pillow, leaving Andrea to wait three more hours alone until she had to leave.

The car moved again, and Andrea shifted her eyes away from the Dag Hammarskjold Library to the imposing, 39-story Secretariat building. The striking, glass-and-marble structure impressed her even after she'd seen pictures of it at the Mission. This time she couldn't restrain her excitement. At least three times a week, she would be working in the huge building, meeting people from other countries, away from the Mission's sterile environment. It was a welcome break for her, even if the real purpose of her assignment had nothing to do with her job at the Secretariat.

The driver pulled ahead and they stopped in front of the entrance. Andrea could see the lobby of the General Assembly building, overlooking the Secretariat plaza through a huge glass window, as well as the famous domed roof that covered the Assembly Hall, where the General Assembly met.

"Hurry up!" The Russian driver shouted as the passengers rushed to get out.

Andrea stepped into the bright morning light and squinted as she looked up at the impressive building. In the distance she could hear the loud horn of a ship. She took a deep breath, feeling the breeze coming from the East River. "Move on, comrade," someone said behind her, giving her a slight shove. She started to walk, clutching the envelope her supervisor had given her before she'd left the Mission building. Inside was the name of the person to contact and the directions to the office located on the twentieth floor. Andrea began to rush, joining a small crowd.

In the lobby of the building, Andrea threaded her way to the elevator area. Then, after a few minutes, she took one to the twentieth floor.

Once there, she stepped aside and pulled the instructions from the envelope, reading them again. Left corridor, turn right at the first intersection, ask for Carmen Fuentes de Lopez at the Economic Commission for Latin America. She repeated the name to herself several times.

Andrea strolled along the corridor, looking around, walking past people who smiled at her and courteously said good morning. The courtesy, the smiling faces, and the well-kept hallways decorated with Latin American artwork contrasted with the Mission's stark hallways. No wonder the people at the Mission never smiled!

After asking for directions, she finally stopped in front of a door with the sign "ECONOMIC COMMISSION FOR LATIN AMERICA." Andrea knocked, then stepped in, facing a spacious lobby, a desk, and a secretary.

"Good morning," Andrea said. "My name is Valeri Lisenko. I have an appointment with Carmen Fuentes de Lopez."

"One moment please," the woman said, dialing an extension in a small switchboard in front of her. "Ms. Lisenko is here to see you," the woman said. "Okay," she added, hanging up. "Ms. Fuentes de Lopez will see you in a minute," she said, looking up at Andrea. "Please take a seat." Andrea nodded a thank you and walked over to the couch.

As Andrea waited, her mind was flooded with memories of another lobby where she had waited three years ago in California. At that time she was applying for a job at Popular Software. Both situations were so different—and yet so similar.

In California she had been Andrea Hendrick, the American, the computer expert educated in Detroit. Now she was Valeri Lisenko, the Russian, the linguistics expert. In both cases the Office had given her an identity and a profession and had ordered her to lie in order to serve a cause she wasn't sure she believed in anymore. She had not found her real identity yet, and she wondered when she would and what kind of person she would be. She had been someone else ever since she could remember. The instructors were always telling her how the other person would feel, act, live, and talk—that other person who existed only in her mind. The instructors had put words in her mouth, had seeded memories that had never existed, had asked her to have feelings and love for people she'd never met.

How long will this continue? she used to ask herself, always promising that one day she'd find the answer. But then they always gave her another assignment, never asking her if she wanted to stop, always ordering her, telling her what to do, what to feel. Her thoughts made her tremble inwardly and she felt like screaming. She opened her eyes, looking around and seeing nothing, and felt the scream exploding in her chest. Hold it back! Don't scream, the doctor in Moscow had told her; if you start screaming, you might never stop. Control yourself. *Control. Control . . .*

"Are you feeling okay?" somebody asked.

Andrea blinked a few times, focusing her vision on the face in front of her. "Sorry. . . ." she mumbled. "I've been sick for the last few days," she lied—another lie.

"Do you want a glass of water?" the face asked her again.

"Please. I must take a pill."

The face disappeared, coming back in a few seconds, and a hand gave her a paper cup filled with water. "Thank you," Andrea said, taking the pill. "I'll be fine in a minute."

"Take your time," the woman said.

In a few moments Andrea felt better. Then the woman introduced herself as Carmen Fuentes de Lopez. Andrea shook hands with her, still feeling a little disoriented. Carmen smiled at her and said, "Do you feel better?"

Andrea managed a smile.

"Okay. Let's go to my office."

In the spacious room with a large window overlooking the East River, Andrea studied the woman in front of her. She was feeling better—the pill had worked its miracle. "I'm sorry," Andrea said, still embarrassed. "I've been sick for the last three weeks, but the doctor told me I'm okay now, that I only need a little more time." She smiled timidly. "I guess that I'm almost okay."

"You look much better," Carmen said. A petite woman in her early fifties, she wore a conservative suit that couldn't hide her large bust. Carmen's large, expressive eyes dominated the other features of her small dark-complected face. Her very short hair was cut almost mannishly and her facial contours were distinctively Latino-American. Her fluent English was slightly Spanish-accented. Andrea studied the few diplomas on the wall that bore Carmen's name. They were from the University of Caracas in Venezuela. One of the diplomas stated that Carmen had a PhD in economics.

"Well, at last we're going to have some help," Carmen said. "We've been waiting for a translator for over five weeks. It's very difficult to get someone qualified to translate Spanish, Russian, and English." She smiled and Andrea instantly liked her.

"I'll be happy to help, Ms. Fuentes," Andrea said.

"Please, call me Carmensita. Everybody does. I promise I'll call you Valeri. We're all a big family here and want you to feel at home." She smiled. "What's the United Nations, if not a big family of all the countries of the world?"

Andrea nodded, repeating the name in her mind. "I will, Carmensita," she ventured to say.

Carmen opened a folder and looked down at some papers. Then she looked up at Andrea. "I have the papers from the Soviet Mission," she said. "You will work here three days a week and two days at the Mission. Your salary will be four hundred dollars a week. We would have preferred to have you on a full-time basis, but your supervisor at the Mission said that they needed you there badly."

"I'll do my best to help," Andrea said, thinking of the four hundred dollars she would earn. But her supervisor at the Mission had already made it clear that the money belonged to the Soviet Mission and that she must give them the check uncashed.

"What will my work be?" Andrea asked.

Carmen leaned back in her chair. "We deal primarily with Latin America's economic development. You don't know it, but we Latinos are starving for good economic advice to develop our countries. That's the only way to further improve our chances for independence and raise the standard of living of our people. Economic power . . . that's the aim for us these days—pure economic power. We must translate innumerable papers from English to Spanish, passing on all the knowledge that this great country has. We also want to study some of the Socialist economies and make them available to Latin Americans. Who knows, we might be able to learn something from them, too."

"Sounds interesting," Andrea said.

"That's not all. Once in a while we'll need to help other Latin-American Missions with the translation of documents. They're short of manpower, too."

Andrea nodded. "No problem," she said. "Maybe someday we will have computers that can do all that work," she added.

Carmen shook her head. "Our problem would be the same. Then we'd be short of money to buy the computers." She frowned. "Our problem at the United Nations is not a problem of people or computers. It's a problem of not having enough money. We're always short of cash."

"How many translators are in the department?" Andrea asked.

"You're the fourth one, and we need as many more. You're going to be very busy."

"I don't mind."

"Good." Carmen stood up, walked around the desk, and said, "I'll show you your office."

"My *office*?"

"Sure, we give people privacy to do their work."

They walked past the lobby into a small corridor lined with doors. Each had a nameplate; Andrea counted them. The last door to the left of the corridor was open, and they walked into a room containing a desk, a chair, an empty bookcase, and a typewriter on a typing table.

"This will be your office," Carmen said. "I'll ask our secretary to bring you up to date on the building, the bathrooms, the cafeteria, and the medical center." She waved a hand in the air. "The food in the cafeteria is very good. You can order quite a few things from other countries. Some of them are great! I prefer Latin-American food, of course!"

After a handshake and a wish of good luck, Carmen left.

Andrea stood in the middle of the room for a few seconds. The room had no outside window, and she felt disappointed. She'd have loved to see New York from here, but she couldn't complain. There were plenty of places in the building to see the city, and that was not all—she was not in the Mission. That in itself was an improvement.

She sat behind her desk, opening the drawers, searching inside. Most of the drawers were empty, but a few had half-used pads, pencils, and loose paper clips. She collected the items and put them inside the top drawer, then rocked the chair back and forth a few times. It was much more comfortable than the one she had in the Mission. Not surprising, she said to herself.

She was ready to go to the secretary to ask for work when her eyes rested on the phone on the desk. Until that moment, she had not realized she had a phone. A small sticker on the base of the phone read, "Dial 9 first."

Andrea lifted the receiver, raised it to her ear, and heard the dial tone. She put it back on the receiver and stared at it for a few seconds. She couldn't believe she had a phone available to her. She was free to call anywhere. Could she? she wondered.

Slowly, as if the phone were fragile, she lifted the receiver again, dialing 9. A second tone followed, giving her an outside line. Then she dialed, pausing between numbers, struggling to keep dialing and not to hang up. She still remembered the phone number: four-one-five-five-five-five-four-three-two-eight. . . . She heard the ringing, and her heart started to hammer. Then a click followed and a voice said: *I'm sorry, I'm not available right now, but if you want to leave a message, please. . . .* She hung up abruptly, slamming the receiver back in the cradle. She clasped both hands together, unable to control the shaking. It was the first time she had heard Greg Elliot's voice in three years.

"Oh God!" she moaned.

Greg paced furiously inside the small room. Outside the covered window, he could hear the never-ending street traffic. The noise was unnerving him, Greg thought as he tried to control his anxiety. But the real reason for his tension wasn't the five hours he had been waiting in the small apartment on the second floor of a building on 51st Street. He was about to get a look at Andrea. Andrea in person, just a few feet away from him, no videotapes, no pictures—the real Andrea—and he still couldn't believe it!

The long week had been frustrating and when Greg had complained to Hansen, the CIA agent had said that was the way the spy business was, not like a Ludlum novel or a James Bond movie. Not beautiful women dressed in sexy negligees, waiting for you in bed; not breathtaking action in the Swiss Alps with hordes of KGBs chasing you on skis. Spying was only work, Hansen added, and monotonous, at that. It was a job of small details, channels, contacts, friendships, enemies, and lots of guesswork. If you were a good guesser, you could be a good spy, Hansen had said. Greg shook his head and amended that statement. If you were a good liar, you were a good spy. Hansen had not commented on his remark; he'd just walked away. But Greg had seen in Hansen's eyes before he left that he'd agreed with Greg. That was the first time that Greg had really liked Hansen.

Greg had done nothing during the week except watch the FBI people's comings and goings. They always talked to Maguire, and a few times with Hansen. There was no question that Maguire was in charge. So Greg had been right when he'd said there was always a boss. Hansen seemed to accept that fact, and he stayed in the background, giving opinions when asked, or when he thought that something was important. In a sense, Greg's sympathy for Hansen had increased during this past week. He could see that Hansen felt the same way he did—like an outsider.

On Thursday, another FBI guy had arrived, a tough cookie like Maguire. Hansen had said he was known as Bulldog Taylor. Taylor had spent innumerable hours arguing with Maguire and Greg had thought they were fighting, but Hansen had said they were planning. Greg had remarked that they should quit their jobs and move to Silicon Valley. That was the way some companies did their planning there.

Late that same evening, Maguire and Taylor had told him that they needed direct identification of Andrea before continuing. Greg had protested, saying he had seen Andrea's pictures, but Taylor said that the KGB could fool anyone. Greg didn't know how else he could identify Andrea, so he had asked Taylor if he could ask Andrea if she really was Andrea. Taylor frowned and said that Greg didn't have to get so cute. Taylor wanted Greg to look at her from a distance, then say that he was fuckin' sure she was Andrea.

Greg had agreed. The thought of seeing her had excited him. He didn't know how the FBI was going to do it, but it didn't matter.

The plan was simple. They had told him that Andrea worked at the United Nations three times a week, and that she commuted in the Mission's shuttle. The FBI had tracked the shuttle's route every day. They would hold the car for a few minutes with some kind of excuse and would let him take a close look at Andrea with a special telescope. He would be able to see her as if she were within reach. "You'll feel that you can almost touch her," Taylor had said. I wish I could, Greg had mused.

His thoughts were interrupted by the opening of the door. Hansen and another man entered as Greg turned to them. "Well, it's almost time," Hansen said.

The technician carried a metal tripod and a black tubular case. Hansen introduced him as Bill. The technician walked to the window and using a pocket knife cut a circle about ten inches in diameter in the window shade. He then set the tripod and opened the case, pulling out a telescope.

The technician screwed the telescope atop the tripod, made a few adjustments, glanced at the street for a few minutes, and then turned to Greg. "Lemme show you how to use this baby," he said. "First, watch out and don't kick the tripod. That'd waste our effort."

"I'll be careful," Greg said as he stepped closer.

He practiced for about thirty minutes. Hansen glanced at his watch all the time, not saying a word, making Greg nervous. He could see the people about a block away, as if they were in front of him. He wondered how Andrea would look.

The technician pulled a walkie-talkie from the case and said, "We're ready."

"Good," a voice said amid a burst of static.

"How much time do we have?" Greg asked, feeling tense.

"Ten minutes," Hansen said, looking equally nervous.

Another round of static broke out in the walkie-talkie, and a voice said, "They're about five minutes early. Be ready."

Greg took a deep breath.

"Don't kick the tripod," the technician said. "Don't touch the telescope. Just look."

Greg inched his head to the instrument. The street traffic whizzed by. It blurred, almost making him dizzy. He wondered how in hell they would stop the Russian car in that spot. His question was answered a second later.

The line of cars slowed down a bit, and another car, with an old man driving, pulled out of its parking place. The car cut in front of a large van and they crashed abruptly, stopping the traffic. The old man looked as if he might be hurt, and the driver of the van climbed down, rushing over to the window of the old man's car. They talked. Horns started to sound, and the line of vehicles came to a halt.

Greg looked to his left. The third car in the line was a Ford, and the driver seemed angry. Greg looked to the right of the driver. There were three people in the front seat. Greg's heart missed a beat. The person next to the window was a woman—*Andrea*.

She opened the door and stepped out of the car. The driver shouted at her as if telling her to return to the car, but she ignored him. Greg looked at her face. She was thinner, but the eyes were the same—Oh God! He studied her face, her nose, her lips. She seemed to be almost within his reach. "It's her," he whispered. "I'm sure of it. . . ."

Andrea walked a few steps, then returned to the car. After hesitating for a moment, she climbed back in and closed the door. Greg kept his eyes on her, avidly looking for details—anything that would help him, any expression, a furtive glance, a smile. But Andrea's face was serious, her eyes lifeless, without the spark that he remembered so well.

Several people helped the old man move the car to the curb, and the traffic moved again. Andrea's car moved with it. Greg kept looking through the telescope as if hoping that the car would pass in front of him again. Slowly he pulled away from the instrument. "There's no question," he said. "That was Andrea."

"Very good," Hansen said, "because tomorrow we're going to send her a message that you want to see her."

Greg bit his lip, still feeling his heart beating fast, his head filled with her image. He was going to say something, but the words wouldn't come out.

CHAPTER 10

The valet approached the limo and opened the door, standing next to the vehicle with a courteous demeanor that surprised Andrea. He wore white gloves and a red cutaway tailcoat with shiny gold buttons and French cuffs. The man's top hat and the fancy ruffle covering the front of his shirt caught Andrea's attention. She smiled at the young man, glancing at his attire, not knowing if she should thank him for opening the door.

"These Latinos are piss-poor, but they like to act fancy," the heavy-set man sitting next to Andrea said in Russian.

Andrea ignored the comment, climbed out the vehicle, and said, "Thank you, sir."

She waited on the sidewalk for the other people to step out. They were in front of the Costa Rican Mission to the United Nations. The tall, well-kept building was in the middle of an exclusive district. Andrea recognized the area; she was on 43rd Street, a couple of blocks away from the United Nations. Quite different from the block where the Soviet Mission was, Andrea thought. There was no garbage in the street—no police booth.

More limos pulled behind them, and women clad in expensive gowns and men wearing elegant tuxedos stepped out. It was the first time she had seen such a display of elegance and also the first time that she had worn such an expensive gown. To her surprise, the Mission had a wardrobe department in charge of providing good clothes for people attending social events at the United Nations. Her long black evening gown had a low-cut front and stand-up collar. She looked wonderful in it, with its puffed lace sleeves, tucked shoulders, and V-shaped waistline with button front. Lace gloves and a beaded shoulder bag topped off the ensemble.

The technicians at the Mission had tailored the gown, warning her many times to take good care of it, making sure she returned it by the next morning, eight o'clock sharp. She had wondered why they wanted the gown so early; surely nobody was going to use it at that hour. When she had asked, the technician had said those were the rules. Always the rules. As she dressed, she recalled a children's story she had read years ago at the Illegals campus in Moscow. It took her a few minutes to remember the name of the story. Finally, it came to mind: "Cinderella." At that moment she had fantasized herself as a Cinderella spy, wondering when the real prince would come to try the glass shoe on her foot.

She didn't know the other three Russians attending the Costa Rican reception, but from the conversation inside the limo, she concluded that the two good-looking young men, and the older, heavy man knew each other. The older man seemed to be a senior member of the Soviet Mission. Andrea was sure that the two men were KGB. She wondered what female targets they had in mind, for they were groomed like movie actors, wearing a liberal amount of expensive-smelling cologne. She was glad to be out of the limo, for the strong scent had nauseated her. She hoped the cologne would have the same effect on their female targets . . . it'd serve them right. No man smelled like that in America.

Andrea walked amid a group of people under a marquee and inside a fancy lobby with glass chandeliers and well-tended greenery. Young men, attendants, directed them to a cluster of elevators. A small group of people waited in front of them, chatting casually with an ease that unnerved her, in languages she didn't recognize. One of the side effects she still had from her stay at the clinic in Moscow was the fear of crowds and strangers. She had taken two pills before she'd left the Mission. Perhaps I should've taken two extra, she thought, struggling with the sudden urge to leave the room. *Control. Control.* She repeated the words inside her mind; she had to maintain control.

The elevator door opened and they all rushed inside. The Russians stood next to her. Fortunately, the elevator ride was brief, ending on the fifth floor. They exited into a hallway leading to a double door. A sign announced, "WELCOME TO COSTA RICA."

She joined a line that slowly moved in front of four men standing to the side of the door. They shook hands with every one of the people in the line. The older Russian took the lead, followed by the two young Russians, with Andrea last. The first person welcoming the guests was a tall, distinguished, white-haired man wearing a white tuxedo with a red sash. Ramon Ibarra del Rio, she repeated a couple of times, trying to recall some of the details from his dossier. Ibarra del Rio, of pure Spanish descent, wealthy landlord of one of the biggest cattle estates in the Province of Guanacaste on the Pacific coast. His family bloodline dated back to the early Spanish period of the 1700s. He was second-in-command at the Mission, a man of powerful political friends, astute, generous with money—a man of many mistresses.

Andrea felt her hands tremble as she approached Ibarra del Rio. She was glad that her gloves hid the moistness of her palms. She stopped in front of Ibarra del Rio, and the older Russian introduced her. "Valeri Lisenko, a new addition to our linguistics section."

Ibarra del Rio extended a hand. "Welcome to the United Nations community. Glad to meet you."

"*El placer es mio, señor* Ibarra del Rio," Andrea said in Spanish.

"Oh! *Habla Español*," Ibarra del Rio said, looking surprised.

Andrea managed to give Ibarra del Rio a flirtatious smile and said, "*Español es uno de mis idiomas favoritos.*"

Still holding her hand, Ibarra del Rio bowed his head in a greeting. "I'd love to practice Spanish with you sometime this evening," he said, switching to English.

His intense eyes studied her with interest. The dossier had said that he was nearing seventy, but to Andrea he looked at least ten years younger. The strong lines of his face were accentuated by his angular cheeks, strong jaw, and skin weathered by the sun. Andrea recalled seeing pictures of similarly moustached faces in old books. But there was something about him that unsettled her. Perhaps it was the intensity in his eyes, or his suave savoir-faire. Whatever it was, her instincts told her that Ibarra del Rio was not an easy catch, that he was dangerous.

"Let's move," the old Russian said.

Andrea said to Ibarra del Rio, "So would I. See you later." She followed the other three Russians into a large room. Soon the two young Russians disappeared amid the crowd. They had probably seen their target women, Andrea thought. She stayed near the old Russian for a few more minutes, talking some nonsense about decadence in the West. Then, after excusing herself to get some food, she walked to the far end of the room, where a large buffet was displayed. As she waited in line facing the buffet, she felt happy for the first time. She was alone.

About half the food was new to her; she guessed they were Costa Rican specialties. The line moved slowly, and she eavesdropped on the conversation of a couple in front of her. They were from Peru and spoke Spanish. He was short and had a big belly that made his tuxedo look too tight. She was dark-complected and tall, with a very fancy hairdo that made her look even taller. They talked about a resolution they wanted to bring to the General Assembly to help poor, starving people in Latin America. Andrea studied them. They didn't seem to be Communists, but they certainly sounded like them.

The food looked delicious, and she chose some vegetables, carrots, tomatoes, pineapple, a few slices of roast beef, and some bread. She carried her plate as she moved around the room, talking with a few people. Most of the conversations were uninteresting—even boring.

An hour later, a Latin band started to play music which she enjoyed. Several couples danced in front of the band and when a man asked her to dance, she refused. Andrea watched the dancing for a few minutes, but then the band started to play a loud, fast-paced Latin song with words she couldn't understand. She walked away from the band, trying to find a quiet corner and perhaps a chair.

"I haven't seen you dancing, Valeri," a voice said behind her.

She turned around and saw the smiling Ibarra del Rio. "I'm not a good dancer," she said. "I've never tried Latin music."

"Would you like to?" he asked.

Andrea lowered her eyes, "I'm sorry. I'd prefer to talk. Do you mind?"

"Not at all. I always enjoy a good conversation. Where did you learn Spanish?"

"Moscow University."

"Any other languages? Your English is flawless."

She smiled at him. "Thank you. For some reason, I learn foreign languages easily. I'm fluent in French, too."

"Very impressive," Ibarra del Rio said, caressing the tip of his mustache. "How long have you been in the Soviet Mission? I don't recall seeing you before."

"Only a couple of weeks."

He smiled and Andrea noticed his even white teeth. "New York is a great city," he said.

"I haven't seen that much yet."

"Perhaps I could show you around a little," he said, hesitating, "unless there's a jealous husband at the Mission."

Andrea shook her head. "I'm divorced. Y'know, the Foreign Service demands long assignments away from home," she looked away.

"I understand," Ibarra del Rio said. "I'm a widower myself. I miss female companionship."

"I'm sorry," Andrea said as the band started to play a loud tune again, and Andrea rubbed her forehead.

"Are you okay?" Ibarra del Rio said.

"Just a slight headache. I haven't been feeling well these days."

He reached for her arm and gently motioned for her to walk with him. "Let's go to a quieter place. That'll help."

She let him guide her out of the room, feeling his hand on her arm, more like a caress than a grip. They walked through a double door into a small circular room. "This is our art gallery," he said.

A string of paintings ran along the walls and a farm cart stood in the middle, decorated in a way that she had never seen before. Ibarra del Rio headed for the center of the room, stopping in front of the cart. "This is an oxcart," he said. "It's a tradition in our country to decorate oxcarts."

The cart had hundreds of intricate geometric designs, bright, colorful combinations that covered its sides, wheels, and practically every square inch. The wheel designs started at its axle, growing in complexity as they progressed to the perimeter. Diamond shapes, flower shapes, and intricate patterns were repeated over and over. "It's fantastic!" Andrea said. "Hand-painted?"

"Yes. All hand-painted."

"How do your people learn to do this?"

"One generation teaches the next one," he said proudly.

Andrea walked around the oxcart, studying the designs. She stopped again next to him. "This art must be a national treasure," she said.

Ibarra del Rio sighed. "Yes, but unfortunately the younger generation isn't learning it from their parents. They don't want to learn—or don't have the patience to do it any longer."

Andrea noticed a slight touch of sadness in his eyes. For the first time she felt a liking for him. "I'm sorry to hear that," she said. "Your country has been in the spotlight these days," she added.

Ibarra del Rio nodded, "We've been in the headlines."

"I hope the Arias plan works," Andrea said.

"We're more hopeful than ever," Ibarra del Rio said. "The purpose of the Arias plan is to change the focus of the struggle for democracy from the battlefield to the political arena." He paused as a slight smile curved his lips. "We Latin Americans only know of dictatorial governments and strong men in charge."

"Except for your country," Andrea said, recalling the information in the dossier.

"We've had some struggles, too," he said. "The key to peace in Central America is a cease-fire in El Salvador and Nicaragua."

"I agree."

"But a cease-fire would only be a start. Peace talks, human rights, and free elections must follow."

A waiter making his rounds through the reception rooms passed by them and Ibarra del Rio snapped his fingers, catching the waiter's attention. The waiter, carrying glasses of champagne on a tray, stopped in front of them. Ibarra del Rio picked up two glasses, passing one to Andrea. "Drink this," he said. "It'll help your headache."

Andrea took a tiny sip, barely wetting her throat. She wasn't sure she could drink alcohol with her medication. Ibarra del Rio drank half of his glass and looked at Andrea intensely. "Do you work at the Soviet Mission full-time?" he asked.

"I'm on assignment at the Secretariat," she said, rotating the champagne glass in her hand nervously. "Three days a week; Mondays, Wednesdays, and Fridays."

"Where?" he asked.

"At the Economic Commission for Latin America."

"Ah! my good friend, Carmensita Fuentes de Lopez," he said, looking pleased. "Carmensita is one of our best assets in the Latin American section at the United Nations."

"I like her," Andrea said. "But it's hard for me to call her Carmensita."

"You must," he said, draining his glass. "Everybody else does. You don't want to be the only one who doesn't."

"I'll try."

Ibarra del Rio turned serious. "I'm sorry," he said. "Your company is very charming, but I must leave you. I'm one of the hosts tonight and should carry out my duty. We want to gain support for the Arias plan among some very important guests here." He smiled at her, looking into her eyes. "We must practice Spanish some other time."

"It'd be my pleasure," Andrea said.

He walked a couple of steps and hesitated, turning to her. "I'm sure that Carmensita won't object if I stop one day and take you out for lunch," he paused, then added. "Let's call it improving relations with a super-power."

Andrea smiled engagingly. "I'll be waiting."

Ibarra del Rio disappeared through the door, leaving her alone, drink in hand. She looked around, looking for a place to rest the glass. She didn't want to drink the champagne; she was afraid it'd make her headache worse.

Another waiter walked past her and she gave him her glass. The young man offered her another drink, but she refused and asked for the location of the bathroom.

It was at the end of a short hallway. Once inside, she noticed the beautiful carpet. She never had seen carpet inside a bathroom. The wallpaper was colorful, with long, trumpet-shaped flowers in shades of purple. As she waited in a short line, she asked the woman in front of her what the flowers were. The woman told her that they were orchids, the national flower of

Costa Rica, and gave her a look that said, You don't know that! Andrea lowered her eyes, pretending to ignore her.

The line advanced and she opened her purse, looking for a pill. To her right was a long vanity counter with four basins and a mirror. Several women were fixing their dresses and combing their hair. Andrea saw that they all wore expensive jewelry and wondered if they also had a wardrobe department in their respective missions. How many Cinderellas were there? Maybe some of them were spies, too.

She felt good about having fulfilled her assignment. She wasn't looking forward to having lunch with Ibarra del Rio, but at least she had contacted him. Those were her instructions. She'd have to fill out a report back at the Mission for the rezident who had wanted to know every detail of the encounter. In a sense, Ibarra del Rio was not the kind of aggressive person the dossier had described. There was no question that he was interested in her, but he was smooth, polished, and very subtle. From the dossier, Andrea had thought that Ibarra del Rio would ask her to go to bed with him right away and had dreaded the question. But he had not even been fresh with her.

Andrea stepped in front of a washbasin and turned the cold-water handle, letting the water run for a moment. A pill in hand, she cupped water into the other hand. She was ready to take the pill when a voice next to her said, "Need a glass?"

She turned. Another woman was using the adjacent washbasin. "Thanks, I could use one," Andrea said.

The woman opened her purse, slipped a hand inside, and pulled out a collapsible plastic cup. "I use it to brush my teeth," she said, smiling. "I could never go anyplace without a toothbrush and this cup," she added.

Andrea pulled the cup open and poured water in it, then dropped the pill into her mouth and drank the water. "Thank you," she said. "I have a headache. This will help." She collapsed the cup and passed it back to the woman. The young woman wore a provocative gown with a low-cut décolletage that displayed a swelling cleavage, and her shoulders were bare. The diamond choker around her neck shone as intensely as did her matching earrings.

"It's a beautiful necklace," Andrea said.

"Thank you," the woman said. "I like your gown."

If only you knew that it doesn't belong to me, Andrea thought. "Thank you," she said.

"Are you American?" the woman said.

"Valeri Lisenko, Russian Mission," she said, extending a hand.

"Andrea Hendrick," the woman said, shaking hands. "American Mission."

Andrea opened her eyes. "Sorry. I don't understand," she said, puzzled.

The woman smiled. "You don't need to explain. I understand your surprise very well." She looked to her side. They were momentarily alone. "I have a message for you."

Andrea's eyes widened, "Pardon me?"

The woman stepped closer to her, near her ear. "I said I have a message for you . . . Beggar."

Andrea stepped back. Beggar. She hadn't heard that word for three years. God! She couldn't believe it. "Are you talking to the right person?"

The woman nodded. "We don't have much time. There's a New York Public Library. Corner of Second Avenue and 67th Street. You can't miss it. There's a sign that says, 'Power is Knowledge.' Pauper will wait for you there this Wednesday at 5 p.m. If you miss, try Friday, same time." She stepped back, looking at Andrea from head to toe. "You look beautiful, Miss Lisenko." Then she turned around and left the room.

Andrea watched the woman disappear. She couldn't believe it. She had used the same words to contact Greg through the computers and the bulletin board three years ago! Could it be possible that Greg was trying to contact her now? Using the same names? But Greg couldn't have known she was in New York, let alone at a reception at the Costa Rican Mission. It didn't seem possible. There must've been a mistake. But the woman had used her American name in the introduction—Andrea Hendrick! The woman knew who she was talking to, no question about that! And she had used "Beggar" and "Pauper." It *had* to be Greg Elliot!

She opened her purse again and popped the lid of the pill container. She tapped another pill into her hand, opened the faucet, and dropped the pill into her mouth. She felt like running out of the room, leaving the reception, and running until she couldn't move any longer. She felt as if she was losing her mind. *Control*, an inner voice whispered inside her head.

Greg Elliot wanted to see her. How could it be possible?

Was the message real?

The metal door started to roll up, making a grinding sound that annoyed Greg. He jumped from his bed and walked toward the middle of the room. He had been lying in bed with his eyes open for the last two hours. He felt as if the place was closing in on him, and his patience was running out.

The car moved slowly, stopping in the middle of the ample safe house. The headlights went out and the engine died. Hansen stepped out.

"Well?" Greg said, not hiding his impatience.

Hansen raised a hand, forming an okay sign with his index finger and thumb. "We gave her the message. She was shocked, but she believed it. Success, my friend—complete success."

"Don't call me friend," Greg said.

Hansen frowned. "What's the matter?" he said. "You got a bug up your ass?"

"Sorry," Greg said. "I'm uptight. This place drives me crazy . . . and this business with Andrea is maddening." He paused. "Tell me what happened."

Hansen closed the car door and walked over to the table in the center of the room. Greg followed him. A tall FBI man assigned to protect Greg watched from a distance.

Hansen pulled out a chair and sat down. "Y'know," he said. "No matter how much planning you do, these things are unpredictable most of the time."

"What do you mean?" Greg asked, taking a deep breath and slowly letting the air out of his lungs. He looked down, pulled out a chair, and dropped wearily into it.

Hansen leaned forward on the chair, looking Greg in the eye. "You've got to ease off. Drain your emotions. This is only the beginning."

"I forgot I'm talking with a psychologist."

"Sorry, I can't offer psychiatric help. I sometimes feel as screwed up as you are now. But I deal with it—or I put it in the back of my mind."

Greg played with his fingers for a moment as Hansen waited in silence. Perhaps Hansen was right, Greg thought. He was not dealing with the issue. He was there because he wanted to see Andrea—and he wanted to put his life back together. It had been three years, and the emotions had not yet settled. He had to keep going on. He had no other choice.

"What happened?" he asked, looking down at the table.

Hansen leaned back. "Well, we made all kind of plans to approach Andrea. We rehearsed and rehearsed. Then we sent four agents to the Costa Rican Mission. All had memorized the same script. One invited Andrea to dance, but she refused. Another offered her food, but she said she'd had some already and walked away. One of the women failed to arouse her interest in a conversation about evening gowns. Then the last one improvised and finally approached Andrea in the bathroom. She just happened to have a collapsible plastic cup. Andrea wanted to take a pill and needed a glass of water."

"A pill?"

"She said she had a headache, but our agent said that the pill didn't look like aspirin. It was a prescription capsule."

"I have the feeling, looking at the pictures we have, that she's sick," Greg said.

"We're pursuing that. After all, she spent time in one of those KGB clinics in Moscow."

"What did she say?"

"She was shocked. We used the words *beggar* and *pauper*. We hoped they'd give her some confidence that the message was coming from you."

Greg nodded. "She used the same words to approach me in California. How ironic!"

"Not your fault."

"I know."

"What's the next move?"

"You're supposed to meet her at a public library a few blocks from the Soviet Mission."

"You think she'll go?"

Hansen bit his lips for a moment, then said. "Don't know. It depends—"

"On what?"

"Her."

"I still don't understand. This spy business is too much for me."

"It's not the spy business. It's people's behavior and feelings." He smiled. "That's why the CIA hires guys like me."

"Well . . . ?"

"It'll depend on how much she wants to see you. The whole thing is risky. If she gets caught, she'll be in trouble with the KGB thugs. Or . . . she could interpret the message as a KGB trap to test her. Those bastards do that kind of thing all the time." Hansen paused, then added, "If she wants to see you badly, she'll take the risk."

Dmitri heard footsteps coming up the stairs and rose from the armchair. Instinctively he checked to make sure that he had his Tokarev pistol in the holster under his arm. It made him feel secure.

He was expecting Grigori, but he never trusted any movement outside the safe house. The steps stopped in front of the door and the sound of a key sliding into the lock followed. Dmitri relaxed—only Grigori had a key. Grigori walked in, looking happy. Dmitri didn't need to ask him. He already knew the answer.

"They contacted her," Grigori said.

"I knew it," Dmitri said. "Do you know where?"

Grigori shook his head. "We couldn't hear. But it doesn't matter, comrade. We have an iron circle around her. No matter where she goes, we'll be there."

"Very good, comrade."

CHAPTER 11

One hour past midnight, Andrea, the old heavy-set Russian, and the two young men waited in front of the Costa Rican Mission for the limo. The old Russian seemed a little off-balance and uncoordinated, mumbling some of his words as if he had a knot in his tongue. Andrea guessed that he'd had a few too many drinks. The two young men looked exhilarated and were all smiles. When the limo pulled up and they got in, Andrea picked up a few words they said in Russian and concluded that they had been successful in their assignments; the women had been an easy catch.

Traffic was light and it took the limo only a few minutes to reach the underground parking garage of the Soviet Mission. Andrea had been silent most of the trip. She still couldn't believe the incident in the bathroom.

"Well, comrade, can we call the night a success?" the old Russian asked, giving Andrea a malicious look.

"I don't understand what you mean, comrade," Andrea said.

"The rezident wouldn't have put you on the guest list unless he'd given you an assignment. Did he?" He gave Andrea a friendly punch with his elbow. "C'mon, you can trust me."

"I wonder what the rezident would say if he knew that you've had too much to drink," Andrea said, giving the Russian an unfriendly glower.

The Russian raised a hand and adjusted his bow tie. "Nobody can tell," he said. "Getting drunk's part of my job." He smiled at Andrea and she smelled the alcohol on his breath.

"You seem to have had more drinks than the ones you needed to look drunk, comrade."

The Russian looked at her, and the look in his eyes puzzled

Andrea. "You never know, comrade Lisenko. With time it takes an extra effort to look real. People learn to know you. It's very hard to fool them."

"I don't understand, comrade," Andrea said.

"You will . . . give yourself a little more time."

They left the limo and took the elevators to the dorm floor of the Mission. Andrea was happy that she didn't have the company of the men any longer. She tiptoed her way into the bedroom, trying not to awaken Sylvia. Then she took her dress off, placing it carefully on the bed, and after putting on a robe, she walked out of the room toward the bathroom. She didn't feel like sleeping; she wanted to be alone.

The hallways were semidark, with only small night lights, and the bathroom was even darker. Andrea sat on a toilet, locking the door of the stall and resting her head on her hands. The place was dark and she felt it was smaller than ever.

A big question was in her mind. Should she believe the woman and think that Greg wanted to see her? Or was it a KGB trap to test her? The KGB knew about Beggar and Pauper. She had reported the names many times during her mission in California and back in Moscow, after the swap. But it was possible that the CIA had recognized her and told Greg and that he wanted to see her. The thought sent a ripple of excitement through her. She felt confused. Did she want to see Greg? What could that possibly accomplish? They had no future.

She closed her eyes, recalling moments with Greg: the days she lived with him in his house; the trip to Napa Valley to meet his brother, John; the wild trip to Reno and the wedding. She had not thought of those things for quite some time. But Greg was the only past she had besides her life at the Illegals campus. The memories were there, and the realization scared her.

She rubbed her face, gently pressing her eyes. The light pressure felt good and relaxed her a little. The doctor had recommended it for moments of tension. She wished she could talk to the doctor now. Perhaps he'd know the answer.

Andrea stood up and walked out of the stall. She didn't know how long she'd been sitting there. She stretched her arms, feeling her muscles ache. She had not arrived at a conclusion and was now taking the easy way out—postponing any decision. It was already early Sunday morning. She had four days to think about it. Should she go to the library or not?

Geidar Aligev, Deputy Premier of the First Chief Directorate, pulled on the leash and said, "Easy." The huge German shepherd slowed his pace and Aligev caught his breath. He was walking along a path that cut through a small forest and climbed a gentle hill behind his dacha. It was early morning and the sun had climbed high enough to warm the chilled air. Aligev loved the walk. It was the only good thing that his KGB doctor had ever prescribed.

At a bend in the path, the German shepherd stopped and pricked up his ears, listening to a noise in the forest. Aligev pulled the leash tight, afraid the dog would start chasing some wild animal. "Go on," he said. The dog looked back, wagged his tail, and continued walking. Behind Aligev, two young Russians wearing military uniforms walked in silence. They kept a prudent distance from Aligev, as if to give some privacy to the Deputy Premier, but Aligev was always aware of them. These men, a bodyguard and a communications man, were a necessity for anyone of Aligev's rank. Their presence was the only thing he hated during the walks. They were a reminder that the spy business was a full-time job, even when he took a three-day vacation at his dacha.

The path grew steeper, and Aligev had to stop to catch his breath. When he had joined the KGB he had climbed the same path without stopping even once. Now he had to stop at least four times. He wondered when he would have to retire and live on his KGB pension.

The persistent beeper of a phone caught his attention and he turned to the communications man. He was not supposed to receive calls unless there was something important.

The man talked on a portable phone for a moment, then hung up and walked over to Aligev. "The front gate called, comrade," he said. "A courier is bringing you an important package."

Aligev shook his head. That was the end of his walk.

The KGB servant turned a couple of burning logs with a poker and the flames sparkled briskly, gaining strength. She glanced at Aligev, looking for approval. Aligev nodded and she left the room, closing the door behind her. Aligev got up from behind his desk and walked to the wall on his right. The spacious study was wood-paneled and expensively furnished. Aligev faced two pictures on the wall. In one of the pictures, he was standing next to the Prime Minister, addressing a small crowd. The second picture showed a young man in military fatigues. Aligev liked the second picture most; it brought him memories of a real war.

He pulled down both frames at the same time and an electric sound followed. In a few seconds the wood panel moved up, uncovering a large safe. Aligev wasted no time in opening the safe, pulling out a metal box.

Back at his desk, he took a small black book from the box and ripped open a sealed envelope the courier had delivered to him. The code numbers on the envelope told him that the message was from Dmitri, and he was eager to read the report. All he needed to do was decipher the message.

An hour later, Aligev had deciphered the message and read it twice. He couldn't have been more satisfied. Dmitri's report stated that everything was progressing as planned.

After dropping Dmitri's message in the fire, Aligev walked back to his desk. He had to send the coded message to Havana right away. Then he'd have to make a phone call and update the Prime Minister himself.

Late Monday the FBI reported that Andrea had gone to work at the Secretariat, appearing normal. If she was distressed, she'd managed to hide it very well. Greg read the report a few times and felt his tension build. To calm down he did some exercises that afternoon in the safe house. That was the only good thing about it. He could jog around the room and do some push-ups with plenty of space to spare. But he still hated the place.

Tuesday morning he slept late. His FBI bodyguard was quiet, for once, not making the usual noise preparing coffee and fixing breakfast. Greg thanked him for being so quiet, hoping that the compliment would encourage him to continue that pattern.

After lunch Maguire called a meeting to rehearse the events at the library the next day. Greg couldn't wait to get it over with, one way or another. He hadn't felt so much stress since his days at school. He was experiencing the same feeling as when he'd prepared for finals. The only difference was that this time, he'd get either an A or an F. There were no other grades.

They sat around the table, Greg on one side, Hansen next to him, and Maguire and Taylor on the opposite side. Taylor had pinned two blueprints on the blackboard, showing the floor plans of the library. Greg wondered what excuse Taylor had used to get hold of the prints.

Maguire passed a folder to each participant, asking them to open it to the first page. "There're two scenarios here," he said, glancing at the folder in front of him. "Taylor and I worked on them," he added, looking up at the faces around the table.

"Let's review the approach first," Taylor said. "I have two teams covering all the streets around the block where the library's located. A third team will be available two blocks away."

"How many men in each team?" Maguire asked.

"Three," Taylor said.

"What about the Mission?" Hansen asked.

"I have an observation post watching every side of the building. Also a backup team in two cars, waiting to go into action, if required."

"She'll come on foot," Maguire said.

"Probably," Hansen said, "but though there's still the possibility that she could leave work early and show up in a taxi."

"I have another team at the Secretariat. We'll know every step she takes there."

Greg watched in silence, still not understanding the need for such elaborate preparations. "Maybe I'm not familiar with this business," he said. "But I don't understand why we need such a complicated arrangement. Wouldn't it be easier if I wait with a couple of FBI guys at the library—alone?"

Maguire and Taylor gave him a glance that Greg interpreted to mean, "Leave the technical work to us, fella." Greg ignored them and added, "If Andrea realizes what's going on, she might never go to the library."

Hansen touched his arm to get his attention. "Look, Greg,

there's a possibility that Andrea has informed the KGB about the message. All these preparations aren't only to keep an eye on Andrea and the KGB. They're also to protect you."

Now the damn thing's more complicated, Greg thought. "Are you telling me *I'm* at risk?"

Hansen glanced at Maguire, as if asking permission to say something. Then he turned to Greg. "We must cover all the angles—"

"Look, fella," Maguire said, "I ain't gonna bullshit you. The KGB might have a hard-on for you. We definitely don't want them to fuck you."

"You guys are a little paranoid," Greg said, shaking his head.

"When you have thirty years dealing with those bastards, you know they're capable of anything," Maguire said.

"Let's keep going," Taylor urged.

"The two scenarios?" Hansen asked.

Maguire looked down at the folder as if needing to read the information again. "Max and I agree that Andrea could go two ways. One: she's curious and wants to talk to Greg at least once." He looked up at Greg. "Then it's up to you to get her interested in seeing you again."

Gerg nodded in silence, not knowing what he was going to tell Andrea, or what she'd say.

"In this case," Maguire went on, "we have to set up a communications protocol to pass messages for meetings."

"I don't understand," Greg said.

Taylor pulled a matchbox from one of his pockets, searching a couple of pockets before he found his cigarettes. After lighting a cigarette, he said, "We need to know what's easy for Andrea. Can she make phone calls safely? Does she read any papers? Does she frequent any little shops around the Mission or at the UN? We need to know her routine."

Gerg nodded.

Taylor took a drag, fanning the smoke in front of him. "Once we have that information, we can come up with a communication skim to set up future meetings."

"Future meetings!" Greg said. "How long is this thing gonna last?"

"It depends," Maguire said.

"On what?" Greg said.

"Andrea," Maguire said. "She might decide to cooperate with us for months—"

Greg felt Maguire's words like a blow. He hadn't given any thought to the whole thing beyond the first meeting. The CIA wanted to recruit Andrea to spy for them. It was not just a single debriefing, as he had thought. God! The bastards didn't care *what* happened to her. They'd put Andrea in danger with the KGB. If she was caught, the KGB would take her back to Moscow and punish her—perhaps a permanent stay at a KGB mental clinic, or even a firing squad. Christ, he *couldn't* be a party to that. He *wouldn't*.

He stood up, pushing back his chair and walking around the table to face Maguire. "I don't want to be responsible for risking Andrea's life," he said.

Maguire opened his eyes wide, surprised. "What?"

"You heard me. Unless you promise me that we won't use Andrea to spy on the KGB, I'm gonna get into the first plane leaving for California this afternoon."

Maguire waved a hand in the air. "Calm down, son."

"Don't call me son."

"Okay. First, it's not your choice whether Andrea becomes a spy or not. It's her choice."

"I'm the guy who's going to ask her, aren't I?"

Maguire nodded. "Yes, you're right. But don't take the blame for her decision."

Greg was now pacing back and forth. "So, are you telling me that if I know someone wants to blow his brains out and asks me for a gun, I shouldn't feel guilty if I give him one?"

Hansen stood up and walked around the table, stopping in front of Greg. "Look, Greg, I'm sorry if we didn't make it clear to you. Perhaps it was my fault. We must face reality. Andrea's a spy—a KGB spy—and she's in danger right now. Not with the KGB, but with us. If we catch her doing something wrong, we'll put her in jail."

"I understand," Greg said, "but I'm not involved."

"You *are* involved, like it or not."

Greg took a deep breath—he was getting nowhere. He realized he'd never convince them not to use Andrea. He should've known better. They were as ruthless as the other side. They didn't care for him or for Andrea. Why should they?

"I know what you're thinking," Hansen said. "You must understand that this is a war. It's unfortunate, but we must go on with it. They don't give us any other choice."

"It's not my war," Greg said. "I don't want any part of it."

"You're wrong," Hansen said. "We are all involved one way or another. C'mon, let's sit down." He rested his arm on Greg's shoulder, motioning him back to the table.

Greg sat down, looking up at Maguire. "The only way I'm going to agree to continue is if you give me your word that Andrea will not spy on the KGB for more than six months. Then I want you to arrange for her to defect."

Maguire looked at Taylor, then at Hansen, then back at Taylor. The FBI agent nodded in agreement. "Okay," Maguire said. "You realize that it has to be Andrea's decision. We'll offer her the option of defecting in six months. If she wants it, we'll help. If not, we can't force her. That'd be kidnaping."

"I understand," Greg said. "There's another point I want to make. I'm sure I don't want to be involved during all that time. I'll be at the first couple of meetings, but later someone else has to take over. I don't want to wreck my life. I have something personal to settle with Andrea. After that, I don't want any more to do with it.

"That could be a problem," Hansen said. "Andrea might not want to see anybody but you. If that's the case, we might have to arrange to have you fly once a month from California to meet her."

Greg shook his head. "My decision's firm. I don't want to be a spy for you or anybody else. If Andrea doesn't want somebody else, that's your problem."

Hansen was going to say something, but Maguire interrupted him. "Okay—fair enough. We agree. You'll decide when to stop."

Greg understood Maguire's intentions. The CIA agent was counting on Greg not wanting to stop seeing Andrea. The bastard's wrong, Greg said to himself, reaffirming his decision not to get involved.

"We still have a lot of ground to cover," Taylor said, stubbing out his cigarette in a styrofoam cup. "It's very important that you set up the next meeting with her before she leaves the library," he added, looking at Greg. He smiled and added, "Some inexperienced people forget about that, breaking the link of communication."

"I won't forget," Greg said.

Taylor lit another cigarette. "We've set the next meeting with her at Central Park, at the children's playground, one week from Wednesday. You have to tell Andrea that we need two hours of her time. We'll take her to a safe house to talk to Hansen and a disarmament expert. We want to know what she knows from Geneva."

"What if she can't make Central Park?" Greg asked, more calmly.

"Then the backup meeting will be on Friday, same time. We don't want to repeat ourselves or establish regular patterns, but Central Park'd be safe for at least one more meeting."

"Routine makes these operations fall apart. People become overconfident and make mistakes," Maguire said.

"In time, we'll arrange a safe place convenient for Andrea—a safe house in an apartment close by," Hansen said. "But we can't do that until she tells us what's easiest for her."

"Still, we haven't talked about the second scenario," Maguire said. "What happens if Andrea wants to defect on her first meeting? Are we ready to take her or not?"

"I don't see why not," Hansen said.

Greg leaned back in his chair. He had not given any thought to the possibility that Andrea wanted to defect. Jesus Christ! It could be real. She might be ready to do it. Perhaps that was the reason she had agreed to return to the U.S. What should he do? The CIA would take Andrea for months, perhaps years, give her a new identity. She wouldn't be able to stay with him, for the KGB would know right away. But even if he had the choice, he didn't know if he wanted to start over with her again. Yet she was still his legal wife. . . .

"Greg . . . Greg. . . ." Hansen said. "Are you with us?"

"Sorry," Greg said.

"We're not ready to take Andrea on the spot," Maguire said. "It takes a lot of preparations. Logistics. Political and legal stuff."

"Legal?" Greg asked.

"Yeah. Andrea has a diplomatic passport. We have to do our legal homework before taking her. Get her a lawyer. Even prepare her for the emotional stress."

"Then what should I do if she tells me she wants to defect?" Greg asked.

"Tell her that it'll take about two months to get ready. That we'll take her for sure, but we need time," Maguire said.

"What if she can't take the stress during that time?" Greg pursued.

"She must," Maguire said, frowning. "She has no choice." He stood up and walked over to the blackboard, looking at the blueprints of the library for a few seconds. Then he turned around and returned to the table, reaching for a pitcher of water and pouring some into a plastic glass. He took a drink, then looked at Greg. "You have to study the blueprints until you know them by heart. We'll walk you around inside the library so you're on familiar ground, and we'll rehearse the plans for any contingencies. That's important."

Maguire stopped talking and a long silence followed. Greg could hear the street traffic: a car blowing its horn impatiently, a truck engine revving up.

"There's still a loose end that worries me," Maguire said, his face stern. "The Russian named Dmitri Kotov. We haven't seen him since he landed at JFK and went into the Mission. The KGB doesn't send its people to the Soviet Mission for a vacation. They go to a mountain resort at the Caucasus or some other fuckin' place. We don't have any records on him. We don't know who he is. We don't know whether he's still in the Mission or whether he's gone underground. I don't like it . . . it smells like trouble to me." He paused. "I bet my paycheck that he's a KGB. Also, that he's related to Andrea somehow."

"How do you know that?" Greg asked.

"I don't. It's only a gut feeling. But when my guts're telling me something, it means that my brain ain't working right. Yeah . . . I don't like it. Not a fucking bit!"

CHAPTER 12

The morning trip to the Secretariat was the same as the previous ones: traffic jams, sudden stops, and Russian curses from the driver. It was already routine, except that it was Wednesday morning. She had not slept well the night before because of a terrible nightmare. In the dream, she was in an unknown place, an old town with narrow, twisting streets flanked by houses that looked as if they were from another century. There were a lot of people in the town who walked around carrying packages whose contents she couldn't guess.

None of the people talked, and worse, they seemed to ignore her, or at least didn't answer her questions when she asked for directions. The more she walked around, the more lost she became. She realized there was no sound in her dream and not even any color. Everything was grayish, lifeless.

Perhaps I was dead, Andrea thought, recalling the details of the houses and the people and the streets. The people were poor, wearing ragged clothes. She recalled a moment when she thought she'd found the exit to the town, but she had only one guess she could use. If she chose incorrectly, she'd stay there for life. If she chose the right gate, she'd be free forever. She recalled that she didn't make a choice, afraid she'd lose and would have to stay in the town forever. If she saved her only chance, she'd always have the hope inside her, for she was sure that one day she would want to leave that world—a world similar to the one where Pauper lived. She realized now that in the dream she wore ragged clothes like the other people and that she was a beggar, like them.

If I only knew which way to go, Andrea said to herself, looking out the window, ignoring the busy activity around her. One guess. That was the only thing she had left.

"Comrade Lisenko . . ." the voice said.

She realized that the driver was talking to her. "Oh! Sorry," she said.

"If you don't get out of the car, I'll take you back to the Mission," he said, frowning.

"Sorry," she said again as she stepped out of the car, following the people heading for the main doors.

By the time she reached the elevators, she had talked herself into deciding by noon. That'd be the final moment. Either she was going to believe the message and go to the library, or she'd ignore the whole thing. In any event, she'd have to struggle with a major question, and that had nothing to do with the message or the meeting. It was a question that had been on her mind for the last three years, and she had postponed the answer until now. Did she ever want to see Greg Elliot again?

The elevator door closed and Andrea took a deep breath. She had decided to make a decision and to stick to it, no matter what. She'd know by noon.

Greg was ready by ten o'clock. Maguire had said that an FBI car would pick him up about eleven. When asked why so early, Maguire had said they needed a lot of time in order to avoid suspicion. Greg had then asked how they could avoid suspicion if the FBI had an army of people around the place. Maguire had answered that the FBI people were professional and would blend in with the environment. Like trees or garbage dumps? Greg had asked in a heavily ironic tone. Maguire had given him a furious glance and walked away. Greg had been happy. He had spoiled the CIA man's morning—a great way to start the day.

At ten to eleven, the metal door of the safe house rolled up and a car came in. Greg was anxious. He had approached the point of no return. Once in the library, everything would be in motion. He wouldn't be able to control events anymore or even walk away from them.

The car stopped in the middle of the room, and Greg walked slowly, almost nonchalantly, toward the vehicle. Maguire had insisted that he wear casual clothes; blue jeans, sneakers, and a T-shirt. Taylor stepped out. He wore casual clothes, too, and a baseball cap.

"Morning," Taylor said to Greg. "Ready?"

Greg nodded. "Anytime."

"Get inside," Taylor said. "I need to tell Maguire something." He walked to the end of the room, where Maguire stood, watching them. Greg realized for the first time that Taylor limped slightly.

After talking with Maguire for a few seconds, Taylor came back and climbed into the front seat. "We'll have to drive for a while before getting to the library," he said to Greg without looking at him.

"I know the game," Greg answered.

Taylor nodded to the driver to leave, and a few moments later they joined the busy traffic on 29th Street. Greg looked out the window without paying attention to the world outside. His mind was in another place. He wished he could talk to his brother John now.

The trip to the library took three hours instead of the fifteen minutes Greg figured it normally took. The FBI man had driven all around Manhattan, and to his surprise, forced him to switch cars once. If they could cut out all this routine, Greg was sure the FBI would save a lot of money on gas bills.

"We're here," Taylor said, looking at him.

"I don't see the library," Greg said. They were parked in the middle of a residential block with old apartment buildings and lots of cars.

"You want to walk through the front door?" Taylor asked impatiently. "Follow me." He stepped out of the car, urging Greg to move fast. They walked into one of the buildings and stepped down a stairway toward the basement. Greg heard the FBI car driving away.

The stairway led to a hall that smelled of rotten wood. Taylor led the way, walking fast for his limp, with Greg hurrying to keep pace with him. They stopped in front of another door and Taylor took a key out of his pocket. The door hinges squeaked as Taylor opened it. They faced another stairway, this time going up. "What's this?" Greg asked.

"Shut up," Taylor said, sounding uptight.

The new stairway was narrow and felt unstable. They climbed the stairs and soon faced another door with a broken lock and only one hinge. Taylor struggled to pull it open. "Son-of-a-bitch!" he cursed. The door led to a small backyard between the tall buildings. There was an overgrowth of weeds everywhere. Greg shook his head at the sight of a stained mattress and a broken-down couch with bare springs. A TV with a smashed tube sat on the couch. It seemed that someone had dropped it from above. "Watch your step," Taylor said. "There are nails and broken glass everywhere."

"Thanks for the warning," Greg said, looking down.

They walked around a huge pile of putrid garbage in green plastic bags stacked against a wooden fence. Taylor stopped in front of a hole in the fence and turned to Greg. "We can walk through here and right into the library yard."

Bending down, Greg stepped through the hole and onto the library's concrete patio. He wondered what the people in the neighborhood would say if they saw them sneaking through the fence. They'd probably call the police, he concluded, and then the FBI would stop the police from making any fuss. These guys have probably covered all the bases, he thought.

The back door to the library was open and Greg was happy to step into a clean, well-organized room. Neatly stacked shelves of old books were against the walls and the room resembled a storeroom.

"Lemme show you the place," Taylor said. "We have three of our people inside the library already, pretending they're reading," He paused, then added, "One of them is a woman, just in case we need help."

Greg glanced at his watch and grimaced. He still had two and half hours of waiting. "May I see the bathroom first?" he said. "I feel kind of sick."

Taylor glanced at Greg out of the corner of his eye. "Have the jitters, huh?" He smiled. "I kinda had them when I first started in this business. You'll be fine, don't worry."

A new pain shot through Greg's stomach. "I've got to hurry," he said.

* * *

Andrea sat in front of her food tray, staring blankly into space. She had barely touched her lunch. How could she eat? All around her, the cafeteria annex steamed with activity—people searching for tables to eat at, and others, finished, hurriedly walking to the exit door. She could hear people talking animatedly in all kinds of accents. Some of them laughed, some gestured, and some just read newspapers or books. Most seemed happy and trouble-free.

She had missed her self-imposed deadline and had not made a decision yet. For one reason or another, she had postponed the whole thing from one hour to the next. She had promised herself many times that morning that noontime would be the moment. But it was twelve-ten and still she couldn't decide. Well, what's the excuse, Andrea? Need another hour? Then another? Her mind was at an impasse, and she didn't know how to break it. A short walk . . . that's what she needed. Of course! She glanced at her watch. She still had about twenty minutes before her lunch hour was over.

Encouraged by the thought, she returned her lunch tray. "That's what I need," she said in loud voice, leaving the cafeteria. After a pause to orient herself, she walked along the waterfront, past the Conference Building and the General Assembly Building. She recalled seeing a nice track of garden and trees running alongside the river—enough space to be alone.

The strong breeze ruffled her hair and the well-manicured grass felt soft under her feet. In the distance she could see a bridge. She tried to remember its name, but none came to mind. The bridge crossed an island that she hadn't realized was there. A passenger liner sailed under the bridge and she wished she were on the boat, going someplace far away.

She had already broken the rules by not informing Internal Security of the approach and the message at the reception. She hadn't realized that until a day later. If she were to report the incident now, she'd be in trouble.

"You must report any suspicious incidents immediately," the Internal Security man had said the second day she arrived. "You must avoid contact with outside people unless we order otherwise. Watch out for suspicious people trying to get information from you. Report any conversation you hear. You must . . . *you must.* Those are the rules. *You must obey them without question!"*

The damn rules!

She had lived all her life following rules, worrying that she must conform, doing what they wanted in spite of her own thoughts. They had programmed her to follow rules, not to think for herself but to be a servant . . . a docile servant.

What would happen if she didn't go? Would she miss Greg? Would he never come back? What would happen if she *did* go? Would the KGB be there waiting for her, saying *You broke the rules. We got you?* Was it the KGB who sent the message? Would they come to her and say, *You broke the rules, you didn't report the incident?* What would Greg think if he were there waiting for her and she didn't show up? Would he care enough to give it another try?

Oh, God, she thought, so many questions, and no rules to answer them.

She stopped at the edge of the park, facing the river. The water was flat, moving slowly downstream. The memory of another river came back—the river that she had crossed to start her first mission in America which had brought her to this place in her life. She wished she could swim back.

She felt chilled and folded her arms against her chest, trying to warm herself. Her stomach ached and her hands were shaky and cold. She broke into a sweat.

All her struggling boiled down to one question, one that she had not dared to ask herself even once. But she had to answer it before she could make a decision.

Did she care enough for Greg to take the risk?

Grigori searched his pockets until he found the pack of Wrigley's chewing gum. He hated the damn stuff when the flavor was gone. After spitting the old gum into the wrapping paper, he slid a fresh piece into his mouth, chewing avidly. What a difference! He wished that the Soviet Union had gum like that. Maybe one day he could steal the information to manufacture the product. Look how many Russian kids would benefit from his effort.

They'd love it! A little bit imperialist, but what the hell; he loved it, too. He'd volunteer to do it on his spare time, with no additional cost to the KGB or the Soviet government. But first, the big shots would have to commit to building a factory and giving him a free lifetime supply of chewing gum. A real bargain.

Standing in front of the Conference Building, facing the East River, he could see Andrea walking alone in the distance. One of his men had radioed him, informing him that Andrea had left the cafeteria annex and that she was walking along the river toward the garden. Perhaps this is it, Grigori had said to himself. He rushed out of the van parked in a Bulgarian diplomatic spot in the three-level garage under the Secretariat building. Andrea had never taken a walk after lunch, a change from her usual pattern.

Grigori's wary eyes scanned the ground around her. If Andrea was walking to a secret rendezvous, she wouldn't have a chance. He had two observation posts with telescopes and 35 mm cameras posted atop two tall buildings north of the UN complex. The posts covered anything that moved down there in the gardens. He also had four men covering the ground on foot, circling Andrea wherever she moved. He could do nothing but wait—and chew fresh gum.

Greg stared blankly at the book in front of him without looking at the words. Every line seemed blurred, without meaning. He still felt shooting pains across his stomach. He glanced at his watch and sighed. He wished it were already five o'clock. Then it'd be over. He was sitting at a small table in a far corner of the main room in the library, next to a wall and a door that led to a private room. Taylor had arranged for him to take Andrea to the room for the meeting. "She might not want to see you in public," Taylor had said. "The sight of other people usually terrorizes them the first time," he added. Greg wondered how many times Taylor had been involved in secret meetings with spies. The bastard seemed to be fully at ease, enjoying every moment.

Greg raised his head and looked around. There were not that many people in the place: a few young readers glancing at newspapers, an old man looking at a sports magazine. To his right, some other people were browsing through books on the shelves.

He thought maybe they were FBI. He glanced at the library's main entrance. For a moment he imagined Andrea walking in and pictured himself trying to stay cool, not showing his emotions. Hansen had advised him to say casually, "Hello, I haven't seen you in a while." He had tried the line a hundred times inside his head, and it always sounded artificial, void of any feeling. Perhaps he should say, "Hello, Andrea. It's been a long time. I've missed you." But that would give away his feelings immediately. He didn't know what she'd say to that. Maybe, "I've missed you too, Greg."

Perhaps it was better to leave personal emotions aside and get right to the point. That'd probably be Taylor's approach—no feelings. It would probably sound like this: "Well, Andrea, I want you to spy for me now. I almost did it for you once, so it's your turn to pay me back. I want you to work for the CIA."

Jesus! How in hell could he say that? After so much struggling with what Andrea had done to him in California. How could he talk to Andrea without any feelings? How could he ask her to risk her life? A noise behind him interrupted his thoughts. He turned to see Taylor waving at him from the half-open door. Greg stood up and walked over to him, stepping inside the room.

"I just got news that Andrea has left the Secretariat in the first shuttle to the Mission."

"I don't understand," Greg said.

Taylor shook his head. "She usually leaves in the third shuttle car at five o'clock. This time she left in the first, at four-thirty. Something's different."

"I see."

"You don't seem too enthusiastic. Are you?"

"Sorry . . . I'm still nervous."

"She's gonna do something. She might be here in thirty minutes. That's why she's left early."

"Thirty minutes," Greg mumbled.

Taylor nodded.

Andrea told the driver that the Mission had called her, asking her to be there by 5 p.m. The Russian driver didn't seem too happy about having to pack an extra passenger, but he drove her to the Mission. She had judged correctly that the driver would never disobey a Mission's order.

The trip was fast, and Andrea felt her heart's rapid beating. She had taken a double dose of pills to control her anxiety. The thought that perhaps Greg Elliot was nearby had been in her mind all afternoon. She recalled the first time they met at the bookstore in Cupertino. Was the fact that Greg wanted to see her in a library a coincidence? She hadn't realized it until that moment. *Perhaps.*

A line of cars crawled slowly into the underground garage. The driver followed the line until the second level, where he turned right and parked in an empty spot.

Andrea looked at her watch. It was four-fifty. She shook her head as if she had just remembered something. "I forgot," she said. "My roommate wanted some feminine stuff."

The driver gave her an indifferent look, as if saying, it's not my business. Andrea walked back up on the concrete ramp, looking for the main entrance to the garage. She stepped onto the sidewalk of the busy street.

She walked around the corner of Third Avenue and 67th Street, rushing to get out of sight of the Mission. She had thirty minutes before her normal arrival time. That was the extra time she needed to see Greg.

Once on Third Avenue, she walked down a block, stopping in front of a flower shop, and pretended to admire some roses. An idea had been going through her head all afternoon. It was a crazy idea, and she had rejected it a dozen times. There was a way for her to find out if the message was real or if it was a KGB trap. The idea was not completely foolproof, but it might work.

She recalled seeing a phone on her walk to Central Park with Sylvia. She didn't have that much time left, but she had to be cautious. There was too much at stake.

By the time she reached the phone, she had a handful of coins. She lifted the receiver, dropped a coin in the slot, and dialed a number. The operator interrupted, and she dropped in more coins. The ringing started and she thought that her heart was going to burst inside her chest.

After a clicking sound, a voice said, "I'm sorry, I'm not available right now, but if you want to leave a message, please do it after the beep. Thank you."

She hung up slowly, realizing that she had not proven anything with the call. Greg might just not be at home, or he might be in the house, not answering the phone. Andrea shivered at the thought; she'd have to take the risk and meet him, if she ever wanted to see Greg Elliot again.

Andrea turned around, looking at the street in front of her. The library was a few blocks away. She could walk there in less than five minutes. She could see Greg in that much time. All she had to do was go.

CHAPTER 13

Greg glanced at his watch. Five o'clock. Andrea would be showing up any moment. He shifted his weight in the hard chair. He wondered how people could sit still and read for a long time. He looked at the door. Where was she? He lowered his eyes to the book, trying to concentrate on the words; maybe time would pass more quickly that way. The book was about economics, a subject he didn't even like.

Moments later he realized that he was staring at the door again and looked around, embarrassed. Taylor was probably mad at him. He was not a good actor. He'd never make a good spy. It was very hard to look casual when he was a nervous wreck inside. One good thing was that his stomach was feeling better—no more pain. Out of the corner of his eye he saw the silhouette of a woman walking in the door and fought the impulse to look in that direction. He waited a few seconds, then glanced casually around the room until his eyes stopped at the front of the library. The woman was not Andrea. Holding a small child by the hand, she walked over to the front counter and started to talk with one of the clerks. Greg leaned forward in the chair, took a deep breath, and looked down at the book. He had to start reading. That was the only way to kill time—and keep his sanity.

The FBI special agent Lopez lowered his binoculars and glanced at his watch. "Shit," he said. "I can't leave now, and I'm pissing in my pants." Lopez stood next to a window overlooking the block where the library stood. He had been watching for the last two hours. His job was to keep an eye on the block and radio Taylor when Andrea showed up.

I've got to quit drinking so much coffee, he said to himself, looking angrily at the thermos on the floor beside him. He hated having to stand for hours, doing nothing but watching through a peephole in a window. One of these days he was going to ask for a transfer to Miami. He'd love to join the guys over there, fighting drug pushers. The stories he had heard back at the department made the action in *Miami Vice* look like a Saturday-morning kids' program. "One of these days . . ." he muttered, raising his binoculars again.

A couple of cars drove by, but Lopez paid little attention to them. He was expecting somebody on foot, unless the spy came by taxi. He considered running to the bathroom for a quick stop when he saw a woman walking along the sidewalk from the opposite direction of the one he had expected. But it made no difference to him.

Lopez inched the binoculars to his right and adjusted the focus to take a closer look at the woman's face. A moment later he was sure the woman was his target. She was heading for the library. Lopez lowered the binoculars and grabbed a small walkie-talkie, pressing the call button.

"What's up?" a voice said amid a burst of static.

"This is blue," Lopez said. "She's approaching."

"Good. Keep an eye on her," the voice said.

Lopez rested the walkie-talkie on the window frame and raised his binoculars again. The woman had stopped in front of the library entrance, glancing around her as if she were looking for someone. She hesitantly took a step forward, then stepped back.

"C'mon, lady, hurry up. Get your ass inside," Lopez said, "because I'm gonna piss in my pants."

He saw Andrea walk through the door and pause for a moment. Then she made her way closer to the front counter, where she stopped. Greg fought the impulse to stand up and go to her. "Stay where you are," Taylor had said. "Don't move. That'll scare her. Let her walk around a little." What if she panicked and left the library without talking to him? Greg thought in anguish.

Andrea moved casually, pausing in front of a rotating wire rack displaying paperbacks. She's doing better than me, Greg thought, his eyes on her. She looked at the books for a few seconds, then moved on to a long shelf with a sign that read, "Bestsellers." She started to browse through the books, once in a while glancing around.

Look in this direction, Greg thought, flipping a couple of pages of his book without looking down. Andrea drifted to another shelf. He couldn't stand the tension anymore and stood up. He'd have to walk in front of Andrea to get to the shelves across the room.

Their eyes met for the first time, and Greg's heart went wild. He nodded at her in recognition. She lowered her head. Greg continued walking until he stopped between two shelves. He pretended to browse. He could see her in the background.

A man walked across the room and Andrea turned her back to him. Don't get scared, Greg pleaded silently. Again he fought the impulse to approach her directly.

Andrea walked around the room, went into a row of shelves, got to the end, then entered Greg's row of shelves, stopping a couple of feet away from him. "Hi!" Greg said, not knowing what else to say.

"Hi!" she said. "You look good."

"You too," he answered.

She smiled timidly. "Not so good."

"I'm glad to see you," Greg said.

"How did you know I was back?"

"Somebody told me."

"You surprised me with your message."

"I wanted to talk to you . . . to see you again."

She looked around. "This is very dangerous."

"I know. Do you want to step into a small room in the back? We'll be out of sight."

She shook her head twice. "No, please . . . it'd only make things worse."

"Okay—whatever you want. We're safe here."

"I have only a few minutes."

"I want to have more time to talk to you. Can we arrange it?"

"I don't know." She looked around again, and Greg saw the fear in her eyes.

"Please, don't be scared. If something goes wrong, I'll know right away."

"Okay," she said. "What do you want to talk about?"

Greg took a few seconds to answer. "About us," he said. "About the future . . ."

"There's no future," she said.

"There's always a future."

"You might be right. But I can't see mine very clearly now." She picked up a book from the shelf, opened it, and pretended to read.

Greg swallowed hard; time was running out. "I want to talk with you without being under pressure. Two hours—"

"I don't know if I can spare that much time," she said, her eyes on the book.

"Please, I'll make sure you're safe. We have so much to talk about . . . so much to decide."

Andrea looked into his eyes. Greg saw that hers were brimming with tears. "We had a good time," she said. "I have no regrets. But I don't know if it makes sense for me to see you. I could be in a lot of trouble if they catch me."

Greg shook his head. "I want to see you again. I'm not giving up. I've been worrying about you for three years. I thought they'd killed you. Now you're here next to me. *Alive.*"

Andrea's face lit up a little with a brief smile. "You're persistent."

He nodded.

"It's very difficult for me to have private time. They control my life."

"I know," he said. "But there's always a way."

She smiled again, more broadly this time. "You're right. There's always a way."

"I want to see you next week," he said. "Central Park, the children's zoo. Four o'clock. If you miss it, please let's try Friday. Same place."

"I cannot guarantee any of those times," she said. "I'll do my best."

"We'll manage. When you approach me at the park, if I have a newspaper folded in my hands, everything's okay. If my hands are empty, don't stop, keep going."

She nodded. "I must go. . . ."

"One more thing," he said, rushing his words. "Please think

about what's the easiest way to get messages to you. Can you make phone calls? Do you read newspapers? Anything would help."

"I'll think about it. Let you know next time. Sorry, I must go."

Greg stepped close to her and touched her hand gently. Andrea didn't move. "I've missed you," he said.

Andrea's lips parted to say something, but then she closed them abruptly. Sliding the book back onto the shelf, she turned around and walked to the end of the row of shelves. A moment later she walked out of the library.

Greg watched her from a distance.

"You were great! Really great," Maguire said to Greg, reaching for the bottle of Scotch. He poured some into a plastic glass and passed it to Taylor. Then he poured half a glass for himself. He was about to pour some into a third glass when Hansen said, "Not for me, thanks."

"What about you?" Maguire asked Greg.

Greg shook his head. "I don't drink Scotch."

They were sitting around the table at the safe house in the garment district. It had taken them two hours to drive back, and Maguire had called a short meeting to review events and draw some conclusions. Greg had been silent during the trip. He could still feel the touch of Andrea's hand and see her eyes at the brink of tears. He remembered her brief smile.

"What's the matter with you?" Maguire asked, looking at Greg. "You look as if you've just come back from a funeral."

Greg started to answer him, but shook his head instead.

Hansen waved a hand at Maguire. "Leave Greg alone. I know how he feels."

"It's okay," Greg said, looking at Hansen. "Maguire's right. I do feel as if I just came back from a funeral."

Maguire took a long drink from his glass. "There ain't any funeral. You did a great job. I'm proud of you."

"Thanks," Greg said. "But that won't help, either. I feel guilty, trying to make a spy out of Andrea. I'm putting her in danger."

"She's in danger without your involvement," Taylor said.

"Anybody associated with the KGB is in danger," he added.

"I know that," Greg said. "But I can't help my feelings right now."

"There's another way to look at it," Hansen said. "You could be helping Andrea get rid of her ties with the KGB."

"I know that too," Greg said.

"Then?" Maguire said.

"I can't help but feel guilty," Greg said.

"Okay. Okay," Taylor said. "Have it your way. But please don't jump off the roof. This thing is off to a great start." He drained his glass and poured himself another.

Andrea rushed along the hallway. She was five minutes late. With all the excitement and all her worries, she had forgotten that on Wednesday nights she had Gatherings at the Mission. Sylvia had strongly advised her that she should enroll in them, for they made points with the Internal Security people. The Gatherings were small weekly meetings that the Internal Security of the Mission offered to make people aware of New York City's evil nature. This was Andrea's second meeting, and she was already in trouble, for the Internal Security instructor demanded perfect punctuality.

She knocked on the door and walked inside the small classroom. Twenty people were already there. The instructor, an older man with a tough-looking stare, was already setting up a slide projector to show the news of the week. Andrea tiptoed to the fourth row and sat next to Sylvia. The instructor interrupted his work and turned to Andrea. "Well, comrade, could you tell me why are you late?" he said. "Punctuality is the first attribute of a good Communist," he added, without waiting for the answer.

Andrea gasped for air; the fast walk and the nervousness had left her short of breath. She lowered her head. "I'm sorry, comrade—"

Sylvia raised a hand and said, "Sorry to interrupt, comrade. It's my fault. I forgot to tell you about comrade Lisenko's message. She had a very important assignment at the Secretariat this afternoon. She called, telling me she was going to be late to the Gathering. She asked me to inform you." She paused, then added, "The assignment was of utmost urgency." She emphasized the words to imply that there was more to it, but she couldn't say what.

The instructor glared at Andrea first, then at Sylvia; then he lowered his eyes and continued to work with the slide projector.

Andrea took a deep breath and turned to Sylvia. "Thanks for saving my life," she whispered.

Sylvia smiled. "This excuse always works. I've used it myself. You owe me one."

The instructor turned the light off. The projector showed a newspaper clip, reporting the rape of an old woman by two teenagers, one black and one white, who had broken into the old woman's apartment, forcing her to give them twenty-five dollars in cash. Then they raped her. A neighbor had seen the kids breaking into the apartment and called the police. When the boys came out, the police got them after a brief chase. "Look what this imperialist city's doing to its young people!" the instructor shouted. "The city makes them hungry and crazy, forcing them to steal and rape to survive. It doesn't matter if they're white or black. . . ."

Andrea leaned back in the metal chair, taking her eyes from the screen. She wondered what rape had to do with hunger. The two boys were criminals, and the authorities should put them in jail for life. Then her thoughts shifted to Sylvia. She was grateful to Sylvia for coming up with an excuse. She now had to come up with an excuse for Sylvia for later when they returned to the dorm. Sylvia would surely want to know why she was late.

The semidarkness helped Andrea to calm down. The screen and the instructor's voice now seemed distant, and she barely paid any attention. The meeting with Greg came into her mind. She still couldn't believe it.

Greg had seemed eager to see her. He'd lost weight and looked in good shape. Three years . . . it seemed like a distant dream that had never happened. She had dreamed many times of meeting him again, but in her dreams the KGB always separated them by force. She would dream that she was screaming and calling for Greg. She wondered if the same thing would happen in real life. What Greg wanted was still not clear. He had said he wanted to talk. Talk about what? Did he want her to defect?

The word *defector* terrified her. She could never do it. She had heard horror stories about the KGB chasing defectors and executing them: a shot behind the ear. The brain blown into pieces. Sometimes the KGB took them back to Moscow, tried them, and then executed them. Once, there was a rumor on the campus that the KGB had recaptured a very important defector and then thrown him alive into a furnace, which smelled of burnt flesh for weeks.

Perhaps she should not see Greg anymore. It was too risky and they had no future. But how could she not go, knowing that he was there waiting for her? *My God, I'm going mad. Yes, mad.* She rubbed her forehead; it was cold and moist. The room suddenly turned bright. Startled, Andrea jumped involuntarily at the sudden change and squinted in the light.

"Let's talk about security measures we must take when we walk in the street," the instructor said, turning off the projector.

Andrea closed and opened her burning eyes. She realized that she could not meet Greg next Wednesday at four. She couldn't be late to the Gathering again. She struggled with the thought. Greg would be waiting for her in vain. He might think that she didn't want to see him. She had to get a message to him. But how?

Dmitri rushed the last few steps out of the subway. He walked briskly along the dark and poorly illuminated street. The buildings stood silent, abandoned, and dark, the windows and the doors sealed with cinder blocks and concrete. Somebody had sprayed "Freedom for Puerto Rico" on the front of one of the buildings. Maybe a revolution will start here soon, he thought.

The block ended in a small commercial area. A few people walked around, and a small group stood on the corner, speaking in Spanish. One of them had a radio at full volume, but nobody seemed to pay any attention to the loud music. Dmitri walked around the group and headed for a block of stores. He saw Grigori standing in front of one of the windows and stopped next to him. The window displayed pictures of saints and about twenty small religious statues of saints. One of the figures was an old man in rags, walking on crutches. Two dogs were licking the man's leg wounds. Dmitri looked up at the window sign—"Santeria."

"These people really believe in this stuff, huh?" Grigori said.

"They don't have any other choice," Dmitri said. "They see in this the solution to all their problems."

"Wishful thinking," Grigori said.

"What happened?"

Grigori took a wad of chewing gum out of his mouth, pressed it into a small ball, and tossed it into the street. "She met Greg Elliot at the library on 67th Street."

"Hum! We were right."

"Yeah."

"Did you send somebody inside?"

Grigori shook his head. "I decided not to."

"Why?"

"The place was infested with FBI."

"Good decision. We don't want to take any risks now."

"What's next?"

"They'd probably meet again to set up protocol."

"Any ideas?"

"I bet they'll meet in Central Park or at the library again. Those are the only convenient places around."

"We must act before they set up an apartment. Then it'd be too dangerous."

"I'll be ready."

Dmitri started to walk away, but Grigori raised a hand, asking him to wait. "There's something else," he said.

"Tell me."

"I figured out that they wouldn't take Greg Elliot through the front door. I put two teams on the block behind the library and I was right. Two FBI cars picked them up after the meeting." He paused. "One of the cars was careless. We followed them. They have a safe house in the garment district. 29th Street."

"Great job, comrade."

"We know now where they are. I'll put a surveillance team on them immediately." Grigori looked at the figures of saints inside the window and shook his head. "Hey, I still don't know how these people can believe in this shit."

CHAPTER 14

The phone rang, making Andrea jump in her seat. She stared at the phone for a few seconds, wondering who could be calling her. Then she picked up the receiver and said, "Hello, Valeri Lisenko."

"Hello, Valeri," the voice said. "It's me, Ramon Ibarra del Rio."

"Oh! What a surprise."

"I want to invite you for lunch," he said. "My lunch hour is free today, so I hoped that perhaps you could join me."

"It sounds wonderful, but I must check with Carmensita first. I don't want to be late."

"You don't need to. I called Carmensita already. She'll let you go for one hour. We'll meet at the cafeteria annex. I have an important meeting this afternoon. I can't be late."

Andrea was glad that Ibarra del Rio couldn't leave the UN. A short lunch wouldn't hurt, and the rezident would be happy. "I'll meet you down there," she said.

"Wonderful. Let's say this is a warm-up for a formal dinner. I know excellent Latin American places in New York."

"It sounds like an interesting offer," she said.

"Ten minutes?"

"Yes."

"See you." He hung up.

Andrea returned the receiver to the cradle. Ibarra del Rio had made his first move. She wondered what she would do if he wanted to have an affair with her. She would have to stall him for as long as possible. She didn't know if she could carry on the assignment. They had forced her once to do the same thing, and she had dreaded every minute of it. She still remembered the words of her case officer: "You've got no choice, comrade. You go to Havana and execute your mission, or we'll send you back to a clinic for the rest of your life."

The clinic. How could she ignore the warning? They drove her to the edge of madness: the constant taking of pills, then the shots and disorientation, the nausea and vomiting, the nightmares, and finally the desire to give up and die. At the end, that was the only thought in her mind. She constantly heard the word inside her head, as if someone else were whispering it . . . *death . . . death.* She screamed for hours. They would come to throw her naked into a cold shower. She'd awaken, sitting on the floor, wet and shivering, with vomit all over her. Then they'd tie her to the bed and give her more injections, and she'd feel worse.

Andrea stood up from behind the desk, reaching for her purse. She had let her thoughts run away, bringing her to the edge of another anxiety attack. She pulled the pill container from inside her purse and walked out of the office to the water fountain. She had to take two pills right away. The meeting with Greg had made things more difficult. She was sure that the KGB wouldn't accept any excuses. She had a job to do, and the rezident wanted results. She was headed for a dead end.

Ramon Ibarra del Rio waved and smiled at her from a distance as Andrea strode across the room, skirting the tables and the people walking with trays in their hands.

The table was next to a large window overlooking the East River. "What a beautiful day," she said, looking out at the bright, clean sky.

"It's a shame we have to stay indoors on a day like this," he said.

Andrea studied Ibarra del Rio. Everything about him suggested wealth. He had on a three-piece striped blue suit with a silk handkerchief in the breast pocket. Then she noticed that he wore no jewelry except a watch she thought might be a Rolex. The well-manicured hands, the perfect haircut, the well-trimmed mustache, the distinguished air, and the self-confidence of his gestures indicated he was smooth, well educated, and successful.

"Please, sit down," Ibarra del Rio said, standing up.

"Don't stand, please," she said, surprised.

He helped her with the chair, as if they were in a very expensive restaurant, and she nodded a thank you.

"We have wonderful specials today," he said. "Some of them are from Latin America. May I suggest something?" he added.

She nodded again. "I'm in the mood for something different."

The lunch took longer than she had anticipated and the food pleasantly surprised her. Andrea made a mental note to try the same selection again when she lunched there alone. Ibarra del Rio was courteous and very helpful. After a cup of espresso, he said they still had some time left and suggested a short walk in the *Jardin de las Rosas.* Andrea had heard about the place, but had never visited it. They had prize-winning roses there, he informed her.

They strolled along a path through the rose garden. The well-manicured shrubs made a colorful display. A few people walked along the paths, some admiring the roses, others taking pictures. Children ran playfully around the pathways.

"I love this garden," Andrea said.

"This place used to be a rundown area with slaughterhouses and a railroad barge landing," Ibarra del Rio said. "It took many tons of topsoil to make it a garden."

"I can't believe it."

He nodded. "It was just a matter of money and good will."

"I don't understand," Andrea said.

"Sometimes good will alone is not enough to accomplish something. You need the money."

"I agree with you. But some people have the money and don't do anything good with it," she said.

"There are a lot of people like that in Latin America."

Andrea looked up at him again. "You have money," she said. "Do you have the good will to share it?"

Ibarra del Rio took a few seconds to answer. "I belong to a very old family in Costa Rica. Some of my relatives still think that they own the land and the people on it. I grew up thinking like them. Then I started to travel and saw that the rest of the world is not like that. I don't share their views now. I share my wealth. That's why I'm here at the UN."

"Do you go to Costa Rica frequently?" she asked.

"Not when the UN is in session. I miss it."

"Any children?"

He lowered his head, "I never had time for them. I regret it now. As I grow older, I realize more and more how lonely I am."

"A man of your social status must have many offers of companionship," she said.

"I do. But they're not free." He was quiet for a moment. "What about you?" he asked.

Andrea shrugged. "In a sense, I'm a loner too," she said, smiling at him. "But I don't have your money. In my country nobody has money."

"Do you miss companionship?"

"Sometimes."

"I'd like to help during your stay in New York," he said.

Andrea took a moment to answer, stopping to admire a bed of red roses. She didn't know what to say that would not encourage him. "It's very difficult for me to have a social life in New York. The Mission has very strict rules about that kind of thing."

"I know, but you're not at the Mission all the time. We could arrange something." He smiled. "I bet we can arrange a few evenings, too."

"Let me think about it," she said. "I don't want to get in trouble."

"That's fair enough," he said, glancing at his watch. "I must go now. I'll walk you back."

"Thanks for lunch and the walk."

"My pleasure. I'll call you next week, okay?"

Andrea nodded.

Maguire adjusted the temperature control switch on the air conditioning unit. Perhaps it was psychological, but he had been in Florida less than an hour and he felt hot already. It was as if the heat were creeping through the pores of his skin, boiling the blood inside him. It wasn't even summer. He could never retire to this damn place.

He was happy about one thing though: the ride had been superb. He loved those Budget specials, where you could rent a

Continental at bargain daily rates. His per diem expense account at the CIA took care of that luxury, even though the auditors at Langley frowned every time he rented one. Another Continental—huh! Maguire knew the words by heart. They didn't bother him as much as they had at the beginning. He only responded with the same line that he was sure would spoil the auditor's day. Hey, we've got to show class sometimes.

This trip was Maguire's last hope. He was at a dead end, and that had made him frustrated to the point of trying desperate solutions. He glanced down at the map on the seat next to him and looked up at the road signs. Sarasota was a few miles south, and the trip shouldn't be a big thing for the Lincoln.

The paved road ended in front of him, and Maguire looked again at the note scribbled on a piece of paper on his lap. "The second street on the right," Maguire said to himself. There were no street signs, and he cursed in silence. He drove past a dirt road he thought could be the first street, then turned right on another dirt road marked "Beachway St." He drove through a small residential area, past square houses with flat roofs. After driving for three blocks, he turned right again. The last house on the left, he recalled.

The house was at the end of the short block with about half a dozen houses. They all looked alike: square and painted yellow, with flat roofs and double screen doors. The grass in front of the house was yellow and pocked by patches of bare ground and weeds. He parked in front of the house and stepped out of the car. What a place to spend the rest of your life, Maguire thought as he pushed the doorbell. He couldn't hear any bell inside, so he knocked on the aluminum frame of the screen and waited a few seconds. Nobody answered.

He looked around and knocked again, still getting no answer. Then he heard a lawn mower going at the back of the house. "The fool's cutting the lawn," Maguire said to himself.

He walked around the house and stopped, looking at an old man in green Bermuda shorts and white T-shirt. The old man was pulling a rope tied to the handle of a lawn mower. He used the rope to move the lawn mower up and down the slope, cutting the grass.

Maguire walked up to the white-haired man and said, "You're

gonna have a heart attack doin' that. You're fuckin' crazy!"

The man smiled at Maguire and pulled the rope up, dragging the lawn mower over to the edge of the slope. He wiped the sweat off his forehead and turned the engine off. He turned to Maguire with a big smile on his tanned face. "Chuck Maguire," he said. "Jesus Christ! What brings you around here?" They shook hands. "Hope you ain't lost."

"You insane?" Maguire said. "Seventy years old and doin' this shit. If you want to kill yourself, get in bed with a young chick and let her fuck you to death. Not this way. C'mon, Jack, you never were that crazy."

Jack motioned Maguire toward the house. "Too damn expensive. I can't afford to pay someone for cutting the weeds. Besides, it keeps me in good shape." He was short, with hairy arms and hair showing above the neck of his T-shirt.

"How's retirement?" Maguire said, turning serious.

"It stinks. I miss Langley."

"It's been three years."

"You don't forget forty-five years of doing intelligence work in three years."

"Sometimes I wanna forget my years, and I'm not retired yet," Maguire laughed.

"Beer?"

"I'd love one," Maguire said, looking around. "This place feels hot all year round."

Jack wiped his forehead, using the front of his T-shirt. "It's not bad now. I like fall the best."

They went to the back of the house. Jack motioned Maguire to sit in an aluminum chair by a round patio table. "I'll be back with the beer," he said, walking into the house.

Maguire took off his jacket, pulled off his tie, and rolled up the sleeves of his shirt. "I should've brought a Florida outfit with me," he said.

Jack came back with a six-pack and two glasses. He offered a glass to Maguire, who shook his head and said, "I like it better in the can."

After taking a drink, Jack asked, "What's new at Langley?"

"No change," Maguire said. "Chasing our tails, as usual."

Jack smiled. "You should have been there in the good old

days," he said. "We didn't have all that technical paraphernalia they have now. No spy satellites. No computers. No pattern recognition. Only the good old stuff, a field agent worth his weight in gold." He paused to take another sip. "Y'know, a guy with a photographic memory was king at the time."

He smiled again. "You had the fuckin' tool inside your head. A glance and that was it; you'd remember it for the rest of your life—no film, no developing. Nowadays it's different. They send the spy satellite over the country, then they take pictures and make them into ones-and-zeros, computer language. I always wondered how in hell they could trust something that talks only in ones and zeros. Then they need an army of computers and photo interpreters to make any sense out of it. Two levels of interpretation to get some intelligence out of it. Then, by the time the stuff gets to an analyst's desk, the data is all changed and highly unreliable."

"You must remember some good-looking women, huh?" Maguire grinned.

"Some," he said, sipping from his beer, "and some good asses, too. What brings you round here?" he added. "Never knew you paid social visits."

Maguire drained his beer, crushed the aluminum can, and rested it on the floor next to his chair. "Another beer."

Jack passed him another can and opened one for himself.

"I'm at a dead end," Maguire said. "You're right. This fuckin' technology ain't helping me. We've got the most sophisticated computers in the world. The largest and best data banks. Millions of pictures of people. The best pattern-matching programs. But I can't find a face in all that mountain of ones and zeros." He reached for his jacket, searched the inside of the vest pocket, and pulled out an envelope.

Jack leaned forward, resting the beer on the table. Maguire passed him the envelope.

"I have to find out about him. I'm stuck. If I don't know all about this guy, he's gonna fuck me." He paused. "Y'know that nobody fucks Maguire."

Jack didn't comment. He opened the envelope and looked at the two photographs. "Need my glasses," he said, standing up. "I'll be back."

Maguire watched him go into the house and then come back with a pair of rimless glasses in hand. After putting the glasses on, Jack glanced at the pictures again. "Russian?" he asked.

"Yeah," Maguire said, encouraged.

"How recent are these pictures?"

"About three weeks."

"He looks older here."

"You're kidding me. You know him?"

"I think so."

"From where?"

"Beirut. You remember the Russian diplomat incident back in 1985?"

Maguire scratched the back of his head. "Yeah. The Islamic Revolutionary Brigades got out of hand and kidnaped a Russian diplomat."

"Yeah. The same one. Then what happened?"

"The rumor was that the Russians sent a KGB Wet Squad to free the diplomat. . . ."

"Go on. See, you have a good memory, too."

"Those fuckers belonged to a special assassination group controlled directly from Moscow. Tough cookies."

"When they got into Beirut," Jack said. "they stormed several strongholds hiding relatives of the leaders of the brigades. They kidnaped a brother of one of the leaders of the radical Muslims. The rumor was that the KGB mutilated the brother, castrated him, and sent his nuts in a small box together with a message: Free the diplomat or we'll send you the rest of the family, piece by piece." He laughed. "Those suckers got the message and freed the diplomat, no conditions asked."

"What does Dmitri have to do with that?" Maguire asked, holding down his excitement.

"I went to Israel on a special assignment at the end of that year. Mossad showed me a picture. Five Russians. Guess who was the leader of the squad."

"That's why we couldn't find him at Langley."

Jack smiled again. "See, your fuckin' computers don't have the data. You're fucked, too."

"What was his name?"

"Colonel Aleksei K. Yazov, a tough son-of-a-bitch. He solved the crisis in four days. We've been fucking around with hostages for ages and done nothin'. Maybe we should hire him, too, huh?"

"You ain't funny, Jack. But maybe you're right."

"I'll tell you, the Russian impressed Mossad. And those Israelis aren't easily impressed."

Maguire got to his feet. "I need to make a phone call."

"In the kitchen. We've got phones even in this part of the country."

Maguire walked to the back door, which led into a small kitchen with a formica counter and a row of pine cabinets. There were at least two days' worth of dirty dishes in the sink. A toaster containing two stale slices of bread sat next to the sink. "I told Jack to get a wife before he retired," Maguire muttered as he stepped in front of a wall phone.

Maguire heard the number ringing; then a dial tone followed and he redialed. The relay station was rerouting the call to the safe house in Manhattan. The phone rang for a few minutes. He was ready to try another number when a voice answered, "Hansen."

"It's Maguire. Where in hell were you?"

"Taking a leak. I had to run to get the phone."

"We've got problems. Big problems."

"What?"

"My friend remembered the face. I told you he would. Beirut, '85. He saw it in a file that Mossad showed him."

"Jesus!"

"Call Langley. Ask them to get in touch with Mossad. I want a copy of the file. The Russian diplomat kidnaping in 1985. Tell Langley this is urgent."

"No problem. I'll call them right away," Hansen answered.

"This is bigger than we thought. This guy's not a yo-yo. Something big's going on, and we're out in the cold."

CHAPTER 15

Greg watched Hansen hang up, then dial again and talk about a file, Mossad, and Beirut. He wondered what they had to do with Andrea. He had heard the phone ring, but Taylor had told him not to answer it. They had almost lost the call because Hansen was in the bathroom. Now Hansen's concerned look told Greg something was wrong. He waited until Hansen finished, then asked, "What's happening? You look upset about something."

Hansen walked over to the blackboard and stared at Dmitri's picture for a moment, then walked back to Greg and leaned against the edge of the table. "Maguire went to see a friend who has a photographic memory," he said. "The guy practically remembers everything he's ever seen."

"I don't understand," Greg said.

"We know nothing about Dmitri. The computers at Langley didn't produce anything on him. Maguire was upset with the lack of information. He thinks Dmitri's connected with Andrea."

"Maybe they're not."

"Maguire feels strongly that they are. So he went to Florida to visit this friend who worked for the CIA for many years. Maguire's friend remembered the face. It was a Wet Squad incident in Beirut—"

"Wet Squad?"

"Sorry. Wet Squads are special KGB assassination teams controlled directly by KGB Central. They're special people, tough, ruthless, and very skilled at killing. Their job is to eliminate people, important people opposing Moscow policies. Dmitri was the head of a Wet Squad that went to Beirut. Mossad has a file on the incident and Maguire wants to see it."

Greg pulled up a chair and sat down. He couldn't believe his ears. The Russian traveling with Andrea was a highly trained assassin. Greg was ready to say something when Hansen waved a hand, stopping him.

"I know that this is hard for you to believe, but this new information changes the situation with Andrea. Something very serious is going on and we don't know what it is. We have to be very careful."

"Do you think Andrea is involved in some plan?"

Hansen shrugged. "I don't know. Maybe. But she's too obvious and too junior to work with Dmitri."

"Is she in any danger?"

Hansen looked at the floor for a moment and answered slowly. "Maybe. The KGB would not hesitate to waste her if they could get something they wanted in return."

Greg got up, pushing his chair back roughly. "You're telling me that the KGB could kill Andrea?"

Hansen shook his head. "I don't mean that."

"That's what I heard. Waste. That's killing, isn't it?"

"We don't know what waste could mean here."

"I don't care *what* it means. The only truth is that Andrea's in danger!"

"What I'm trying to tell you is that based on the information we have, something else is going on." He paused. "We don't like it."

"Jesus! You sound like a goddamned lawyer. You guys are more concerned about what's going on than you are about a person's safety."

"Greg, don't be so emotional."

"I'm not emotional!"

"You are!"

Greg glared at Hansen.

"Look," Hansen said. "If the KGB wanted to kill Andrea, they'd have done it back in Moscow. They didn't need to bring her here to do that. They're using her for something we don't know about. Now we know there's a high-ranking, trained killer with her. This guy wants something, and he wants to use Andrea to get it."

"I could come up with another guess," Greg said. "This KGB guy could kill Andrea here and blame somebody else for it. That's a perfect trap."

"Too simple," Hansen said.

"Not to me."

"It must be related to the Secretariat. They've sent Andrea to work there three days a week."

"The FBI came up with nothing there," Greg said.

"Still, there's a lot going on there. Andrea's working for the Economic Commission for Latin America. Those guys have connections all over the continent." Hansen smiled. "Who knows, maybe it's something related to Nicaragua."

Greg knew he was getting nowhere. Hansen wasn't concerned about Andrea. Why should he be? Andrea was another Russian spy, KGB—the enemy. He had not looked at her that way. It was true that the KGB had sent Andrea to California to seduce him and then turn him into a spy, but the plan had failed, and Andrea had saved his life at the risk of her own. She got shot saving him; otherwise he'd be dead by now. He owed her.

Greg pulled out the chair and sat down again, his shoulders hunched forward, his eyes on the floor. "You know," he said, "Andrea saved my life."

"That gave her a lot of points with us," Hansen said.

Greg nodded. "It also makes me feel obligated to her. I believe that's why I'm here. In a way, I want to pay her back."

"You're doing that right now."

"I don't feel I'm doing enough."

"We've just started. You'll have time to do more."

"Maybe. But I don't feel that way right now. She's in danger, and it frustrates the hell out of me that I can't do something."

Hansen stepped close to him and said, "These operations take patience. They must progress slowly, one small step at time. We can't rush or we'll make mistakes. In this game, one mistake and you're out; the enemy wins."

Greg took a deep breath. He didn't care about any game. He'd let the CIA and the KGB play each other. He cared about Andrea and about helping her. He had to think more about the whole thing. He didn't know what to do, but he had to do something. One thing he was sure of now; he couldn't keep going like this for many more weeks. Andrea was in danger. "Fine. Your game," he said to Hansen.

Andrea pulled up the back zipper of Sylvia's gown and Sylvia thanked her, then turned around, trying to see herself in the small mirror Andrea held in her hand. "You look beautiful," Andrea said.

Sylvia giggled. "You're being generous. But it could be worse."

"I still don't know why you don't use one of the gowns from the Mission's wardrobe," Andrea said.

Sylvia frowned. "Are you serious? Half the Foreign Service has worn those gowns—" She stopped abruptly. "Sorry. I'm tired of wearing them. People have names for them, reception names: Brazilian reception, Mexican reception. And the tailors have made so many alterations that they look used no matter how often they are dry-cleaned." She turned sideways to look at the gown. "What do you think, huh?" The rose-colored evening dress had a raised waist with a bow and rose trim. The skirt was asymmetrical, creating a cascading effect, and the square neckline was edged with a ruffle.

"You'll be the sensation of the reception," Andrea said.

"I'll settle for less," Sylvia said. "This gown cost me three months' salary, even though I bought it at a second-rate store. They even had a fire sale." Sylvia gave Andrea a malicious look. "Who knows, I might seduce the Foreign Minister himself. If all the other women at the reception are wearing gowns from the Mission's wardrobe, I'll be the most elegant."

"Is he married?"

"Unfortunately, he is. And he'll be staying only a day in Glen Cove. He's on his way to Washington to talk with the U.S. Secretary of State. Y'know, they're hustling a long-range nuclear weapons pact."

"Have you seen him before?"

"It's the first time. I'm lucky they selected me to attend the reception. Internal Security wants us to mingle with the foreign guests and fish for valuable information." Sylvia curtsied, bending her knees, and waved a hand in the air as if she were meeting royalty. "Well, Mr. Foreign Minister Eduard Shevardnadze, I'm Sylvia Guriev, executive comrade in charge of the typing pool at the Mission," she laughed. "Glad to meet you. I promise I'll give you top priority if you ever send a letter for typing." She giggled.

"Tell me about Glen Cove. I didn't know we had an estate on Long Island."

"Maybe I'll bring the ghost with me to tell you the story," Sylvia grinned.

"I don't understand."

"There's a legend about the ghosts of the original owners still haunting the house."

"I don't believe in ghosts."

"Maybe you should," Sylvia said. "The Soviet Union bought Glen Cove in 1948. The house was put up for sale after the owners committed suicide. The story is that a very rich man built the house for his young bride, a small castle with gardens, sculptures, fountains, and a pool. Then, for some reason, they both committed suicide. A servant found their bodies in bed, naked, hugging each other. They had taken arsenic."

Andrea lowered her head. "How sad."

"They must have loved each other madly," Sylvia commented.

"They had love and money. Why did they commit suicide?"

Sylvia shrugged. "Nobody knows. They took the secret with them." She paused. "Perhaps they thought that the only way to preserve their love was to die together. That way their souls would have eternal life."

Andrea looked away. Two words stuck in her mind: love and death.

The courier brought the file from Langley, and Maguire and Hansen read it avidly. It was Monday afternoon, and tension had grown as the second meeting approached. Greg watched them talking and gesturing. Maguire looked and pointed at pictures while Hansen took notes. Greg sat in a folding chair with his feet crossed on another chair as he read a paperback Hansen had bought him. He had loved spy thrillers. But after being involved with Hansen and Maguire, he didn't want to read the stuff any longer, so Hansen had recommended Elmore Leonard's books.

Now he was reading *Bandits,* about an ex-con who worked in a funeral parlor, an ex-nun with a very rich father, and an ex-cop turned bartender—-all three trying to pull a job on the Nicaraguan Contras by stealing five million dollars. Greg laughed to himself. Maybe they should work for the CIA, Greg thought, putting down the book. He stood and walked to the table where Maguire and Hansen discussed the file.

"Anything new?" Greg asked.

"There's very little of value here," Maguire said. "A couple of pictures at the airport, then them climbing into a Mercedes. One week later, three more pictures at the airport, leaving." He sounded frustrated.

"How many of them?" Greg asked.

"Five," Hansen said. "Dmitri is in every one."

"Can't ignore their success," Maguire said. "Those guys solved the kidnaping in a week," he smiled. "And left behind a castrated Arab."

Greg thought for a moment. "I can't believe there's no more information."

"Mossad's report states only the facts," Maguire said. "The quick action of the Wet Squad impressed Mossad. It was very professional."

"Do you think Dmitri is part of a Wet Squad here in New York?" Greg asked.

Maguire looked down at the pictures spread before him. "Hansen doesn't think so, and I agree. We believe Dmitri's on special assignment."

"Why?"

"Dmitri came through JFK with Andrea," Hansen said. "Diplomatic passport, very visible. Then he went underground. We haven't seen him doing any of the cover work that the Mission usually gives its KGB people, the type of work Andrea's doing at the Secretariat. Andrea's visible and Dmitri isn't. Very strange, isn't it?"

"Maybe Andrea has seen him," Greg said.

"We were talking about that," Maguire said. "We need more information, and perhaps Andrea's the solution. But we must be careful. We don't want to scare her and spoil the whole thing."

"I want your meeting with Andrea Wednesday to be just friendly," Hansen said. "Two old friends getting reacquainted. Nothing risky or threatening to her."

"So you want me to start seducing her right away," Greg said.

"I don't mean it that way," Hansen say.

"I'd prefer for you to say it openly," Greg said.

Hansen frowned at Greg. "All that I'm saying is that it's not a good idea to start asking questions immediately. You must reestablish a friendship first; put her at ease. Then you can start with the questions."

Greg realized he was jumping on Hansen again. "Sorry," he said, "I'm very sensitive about this whole issue of spying. Besides, the waiting in this place drives me nuts." He looked at Maguire and added, "After Wednesday I want to go back to California for a few days. I need to take care of a few things there. It'd be a nice break."

"We can arrange the trip," Maguire said.

"I want to call my answering machine now," Greg said. "I haven't checked my messages in days."

"Help him," Maguire said to Hansen.

Hansen got up and signaled Greg to follow him to the communications van. "We'll use one of our relay phones to call your house. Nobody can trace the call back to us."

They climbed into the van and stopped in front of a console holding three phones. Hansen lifted a receiver, dialed a couple of times, and passed it to Greg. "You can dial your number now."

Greg dialed and waited until the initial message finished. Then he entered the code number for his messages. The machine said, "You have four messages. Please press P to listen to the last one."

Greg pressed the letter P. "Hello, it's Ron. Where in hell are you? I've called you twice. Are you hiding from me? I'll only forgive you if you're in Hawaii with a blonde and she's fucking your brains out. Please call me."

Greg smiled, then pressed the letter D to discard the message and the letter P for the next one. "It's me. I can't make it Wednesday." Greg recognized Andrea's voice. He pressed the letter D and hung up the phone. He wouldn't be seeing Andrea until Friday. Five more days. The wait would drive him mad.

"What happened?" Hansen asked.

"Andrea left me a message. She won't be able to make it Wednesday," he paused, then added, "I hate this waiting."

He never did listen to the other two messages.

The black Mercedes slowed and cruised through the circular driveway bordering a huge water fountain. The driver stopped the Mercedes facing the front door of the Spanish villa and General Alejandro Carreras climbed out of the vehicle. Carreras, a tall, stocky man in his late fifties, wore olive-green fatigues, polished black combat boots, and a cap. He also wore a pistol belt strapped to his waist. Carreras' face was angular, with a strong jaw and a beard down to his chest. From a distance he resembled Fidel Castro—his associates always pointed it out to him, and he never denied it. Carreras was a general in the DGI, the Cuban intelligence service: he held a position of power and control over the lives of many people, and he had many enemies.

The villa sat on a stretch of land north of Havana, an exclusive area facing a sandy beach and the ocean. Abandoned by a rich family at the beginning of the Cuban revolution, the villa stood dilapidated for many years until Carreras discovered it. Then he restored the house with first-class materials brought from Mexico and Spain. Carreras loved the house, but his problems with his mulatto wife ruined his enjoyment of it.

A servant opened the door and said, "She's drunk again, señor."

"Nothing new," Carreras said, walking past the servant. He strode along the ample foyer with its polished marble floor, headed for the large, circular staircase that led to an arch on the second floor. He climbed the stairs briskly, followed by the servant.

At the top of the stairs, Carreras turned to the servant. "Wait here."

Carreras pushed open the doors and walked into a large bedroom with a ceramic tile floor, floral drapes, and a brass bed. The naked woman in the bed lay with her head in a pool of vomit. She turned her head around at the sound of the boots on the floor. "You're . . . back. . . ."

Carreras shook his head. "You're damned drunk again!" He glanced at the empty bottles of Chivas Regal on the nightstand. He walked over to the table and, with a sweeping movement of his arm, knocked the bottles to the floor.

The woman pushed herself halfway up in bed and shouted, "*Animal! Cabrón.*"

Carreras looked at her contemptuously. In her early thirties, she was gaunt, her dark Afro unkempt and soaked in vomit. This creature seemed quite different from the beautiful young mulatto he'd met years earlier on one of his trips to the countryside. Gloria's voracity for sex and pleasure had captivated him, and he'd married her. Her blend of Spanish and Negro blood had promised him the realization of his fantasies. But Gloria couldn't take the pressure, the loneliness during his long overseas trips, the lack of attention—or his mistresses.

She stared at him with glassy eyes. "You don't love me anymore." She opened her legs slightly. "You don't screw me anymore. Only your mistresses. I've had it with them." She looked at his holster. "Maybe I should start fucking your gun. He'll always be hard for me."

Carreras shook his head again. "You're a fucking mess. When you fuck my gun, I hope you pull the trigger. It'll give you a hell of an orgasm." He turned around, calling the servant, who stopped at the bedroom door. "Drag her into a shower," Carreras said. "I've got too many things on my mind to deal with her now."

He left the room as the servant walked over to the bed. He heard Gloria screaming, then cursing him. "Damn drunk," Carreras muttered.

In his study, Carreras walked to the double window overlooking the ocean and watched the waves pounding against the beach. He was disturbed as he thought about the courier who had delivered the pouch to the house, breaking the agreed-upon protocol. At first he was angry; then he thought that perhaps the message was very urgent. He turned around and looked at the massive desk in the center of the room. The pouch lay there unopened. He walked over and ripped the seal off the pouch,

Inside was another sealed envelope, unmarked, as called for in the agreement. He tore open the envelope and pulled out a piece of paper. There were no signatures on the paper, but the first and last code words of the message told him that it was legitimate.

He read the message twice, memorizing the instructions. He couldn't believe that Aligev himself had sent the message. If Castro ever found out that he was a KGB agent, he'd have him shot. He tossed the crunched paper and envelope into the stone fireplace, poured lighter fluid over them, and lit them. The fire lasted only a few moments, the message almost instantly in ashes. He couldn't believe Aligev's instructions but he had to obey them. He had no other choice.

CHAPTER 16

Tuesday and Wednesday went very slowly. By Thursday he had stopped counting the days and started counting the hours. It was madness at its worst. He had never known that waiting could drive him crazy. Hansen had brought him more Elmore Leonard books, but they didn't help. Nothing could help him now. Only the meeting, seeing Andrea, or getting into a plane heading for California.

He had not told Hansen that maybe it was better for him to stop seeing Andrea after the Friday meeting and to return to California. He was afraid Hansen would use what he knew of psychology to talk him into staying in New York. He was not even sure Hansen had not manipulated him from the beginning.

Friday morning an army of FBI men arrived very early, and Greg found himself the focus of all their attention. Two agents who specialized in disguises were probably hired by the FBI directly from Universal Studios, Greg told Hansen as the two agents outfitted him as a vagrant. Then two other technicians wired him with a transmitter and a receiver. A minuscule earphone was attached to the back of his ear so that he could hear instructions at any time. Then a small microphone was attached inside the lapel of his ragged suit. He needed only to lower his head and talk. The FBI'd be listening at the other end.

Then, with all that paraphernalia, another FBI special agent started to coach him on body language and how to look like a real vagrant. Greg wondered if the FBI man had actually studied vagrants in the street. The last lesson in the crash course on spying was signaling with a newspaper to let Andrea know that everything was okay.

Then Hansen took over, telling him what to tell Andrea and

what not to tell her—also, how to handle the car and the apartment that the FBI had set up a few blocks from Central Park to give them privacy.

Greg felt uncomfortable with the arrangement and asked Hansen if they had one-way mirrors and video cameras and hidden microphones. Hansen didn't answer. Greg was irritated and promised Hansen that the meeting would be strictly platonic. Hansen finally gave him a hard stare, telling him to shut up and take the coaching seriously. Greg's anger increased. He told Hansen that he couldn't take all this Hollywood stuff seriously. Hansen retorted that if Greg wanted to play around, that was fine, but his life could be at stake. Greg said nothing. Hansen's words pushed him into a deeper depression.

He should never have left California. Perhaps his friend Ron was right. He should've been in Hawaii with a blonde.

At noon they had a light lunch, sandwiches and Coke. Greg wasn't hungry and barely touched his food. Taylor had made fun of him, saying, "Have the jitters again, huh?" Greg ignored the comment and concentrated on what he was going to say to Andrea when they met. This time he'd be asking her to go to an apartment, and she might panic and say no. He needed to be convincing. Hansen had suggested a couple of lines, and he'd rehearsed them in his mind. Still, they weren't his words, and that made him uneasy.

The metal door of the safe house rolled up at twelve-thirty, and three cars and a van joined the street traffic. Greg was riding in the middle car with Hansen next to him. Taylor had said it'd take about two hours to get to Central Park. The game was always the same. Greg sighed in desperation. He wondered how they could keep doing it for thirty years. He almost suggested that they come up with an honor protocol with the KGB. A you-don't-follow-me-I-don't-follow-you-and-we'll-save-a-lot-of-time agreement.

As the driver hustled with the busy traffic around them, Greg mentally went over the plan for the meeting. They would drop him on Central Park West and 67th Street. Then he'd walk across the park toward a children's zoo near the corner of Fifth

Avenue and 65th Street. Several FBI special agents would be tailing him to protect him in case of trouble. After the initial contact he would ask Andrea to go with him to a more private place. He would emphasize security as the reason for the request. An FBI car would pick him up on the transverse road of Central Park; the one connecting with West 66th Street. At the apartment he'd talk with Andrea for about an hour. Hansen had advised setting up the next meeting first; then he'd given Greg a list of questions he'd like answered. The questions were mainly about her stay in Havana and her job as a translator in Geneva. Hansen had also said that Greg shouldn't press for answers, to let Andrea feel comfortable with him first. Greg then asked if he could get his personal questions out of the way first, and Hansen had agreed.

They switched cars once, and Greg wondered what people would say when they saw a vagrant rushing from one car to another in the company of well-dressed people. In California, nobody would care. In New York, who knew what the reaction would be? Soon the driver slowed down and told him to get out."

As Greg opened the door to step out, he could hear Hansen saying, "Good luck." He didn't look back as the FBI driver sped away.

He looked around to familiarize himself with the place. He stood at the corner of 67th Street and Central Park West and when the traffic light changed to red, Greg rushed across the street toward Central Park. He tried to remember some of the body language the FBI had taught him, but he was embarrassed to try it. He just walked fast, the newspaper under his arm.

"Do you read me?" a voice whispered behind his ear.

"I can hear you," he said into the lapel of his suit.

"Good, keep in touch," the voice said.

The FBI had shown him pictures and a videotape of his route to the children's zoo, but the place was still foreign to him. He stopped a couple of times before he walked into the park. Everybody on the sidewalk seemed to stare at him. What's the problem. he asked himself? Hadn't these people ever seen a vagrant in New York? He wished he were in California. Nobody'd be staring at him.

He walked past a circular parking area packed with cars, then across a wider paved road and into a narrow track. He recalled the track from the videotape. A few people were strolling along casually; a couple of them sped by him on bicycles. Others, clad in colorful sweatsuits, jogged or ran. In a sense, the place was not very different from a California park, and he guessed that the same type of people went to the parks—health freaks.

The road wound its way through trees and bushes, and he looked around, feeling more private. He tried his vagrant walk and some of the body language. He even scratched his armpit a couple of times, but he was too embarrassed to scratch his crotch in public, as the FBI men had suggested.

After crossing another wide road and then a few short paths, he found a bench in a small clearing in the trees. An old woman sat there holding a small dog by a leash. The dog looked well groomed and had a pink collar. He approached the bench and sat down next to the lady. She looked him over from head to toe. "Beautiful day ma'am, isn't it?" he said.

The dog came close to him and started to smell his leg. The woman pulled the dog back and replied, "Nice day, sir."

"Do you have the time, ma'am?" he asked, trying his best to use the tired, hungry tone that the FBI specialist had suggested.

The woman looked at her watch, stood up from the bench, said, "Three thirty-five," and walked away with the dog.

Greg refrained from glancing at his own watch. They had warned him that bums don't wear watches. Mentally, he counted to one hundred and then stood up. He could see in the distance the blue roofs of the children's zoo. Andrea would be there in thirty minutes.

"Who was that?" the voice whispered behind his ear.

Greg lowered his head. "It was nothing—an old lady with a dog."

"Be careful," the voice said. "Don't talk to strangers. You never know."

Greg shook his head. Yeah, perhaps the dog was KGB, he said to himself.

Andrea glanced at her watch. Oh, God! It was three-thirty

already. All day she'd tried to think of a way to get to Central Park to meet Greg, and had finally come up with a plan to pretend she was sick, and leave work early. There were no Mission shuttles until four o'clock, so she had decided to take a taxi instead. Laying the groundwork for her plan, she had hinted that morning to one of the secretaries that she was feeling sick. Actually, she didn't have to fake it much, for she had cold sweats and shaky hands. The secretary had been very sympathetic and even offered help. Andrea had thanked her and said that she'd let her know.

She had skipped lunch and stayed in her office. With so much tension, she had lost her appetite. During the afternoon, she did very little work but pretended she was busy to avoid suspicion. Now it was time to leave if she wanted to be at Central Park by four. She got up from the chair, walking around the desk. Carmensita was out for the afternoon at a meeting somewhere. Andrea was happy she didn't have to lie to her. She walked over to a departmental secretary, a woman from Peru, and said, "Sorry, I can't stay any longer. I called the Mission Internist and he wants to see me right away. I'm on medication, and he's worried that something might be wrong with me."

"No problem. Hope you feel good soon." the secretary said, and went on typing.

Andrea couldn't believe how easily the secretary had dismissed her. At the Mission there would have been a dozen questions first, then a form from the internist excusing her, and finally a request that she be back to work the next day, no matter how sick she was feeling.

Purse in hand, she went out to the elevators. She still couldn't believe that she'd be seeing Greg in just thirty minutes!

There was a short line of cabs to one side of the Secretariat building, and she had no problem getting one. She ordered the driver to go to the Plaza Hotel at 57th Street. She'd decided to walk the few blocks to the children's zoo. Glancing at her watch again, she decided that she would stay with Greg until five forty-five. Two hours was a lot of time and she couldn't wait to see him again.

Greg scratched his armpit, then the back of his head. He was getting good at it, but he had not tried scratching his crotch yet. He was still too embarrassed. The children's zoo steamed with activity as hordes of small children played, watched, and petted the little animals. Greg walked slowly, trying not to get too close to the children. Several mothers had given him dirty looks when he had smiled at a little girl near him.

He found a bench away from the throng and sat down, took off his shoe, and scratched his foot. That was an effective scratch, the FBI agent had told him. He was absentmindedly glancing around when the voice behind his ear said, "She just took a taxi. She should be in your area in thirty minutes."

Greg looked down and said, "I read you. Keep me informed."

He slid the shoe back on, crossed his leg, and started to replay the words he'd say to Andrea. Suddenly he found he didn't really know what to say to her. Let the words flow out of you, Hansen had said when Greg had told him of his problem. For the first time, Greg wished Hansen were there to help him. He had started to like the bastard.

A man who looked like a bum sat next to him on the bench. A baseball cap pulled down to his eyes hid the forehead of his dirty, unshaven face. His toes protruded through worn-out tennis shoes that at one time had been white, and he wore no socks.

"Smoke?" the man asked.

Greg shook his head. "Don't have any."

"What about some dough?" the man persisted.

"I'm broke. What about you? Have some?" Greg said, building up some courage.

The man smiled; two of his front teeth were missing. "If I had some, I wouldn't be askin' you."

Greg got up from the bench, and the man did the same. When Greg started to walk, the man walked next to him. Greg turned to him, frowning. "Look, buddy. I've had a bad day. I don't need company. Bug off."

The man stopped walking. "You don't need to be rude, brother. Have it your way."

Greg strolled casually in front of the animal cages. His eyes were not on the animals but on the faces of the children. The voice behind his ear spoke again, "She just got out of the taxi.

She's at the Plaza Hotel. She'll be coming through the south gate of the park. Good luck!"

"Thanks," Greg muttered into his lapel. He started to walk toward the south entrance of the zoo, searching for Andrea, holding the folded newspaper in his hand. He had to make the newspaper visible to Andrea, he told himself. Jesus! She'd be here in five minutes.

Andrea paid the driver and ran into the park. She wanted to be inside as soon as possible. For some reason, she felt more secure inside the park. The thought that the KGB could have men posted on high buildings watching her with binoculars terrified her. She could hardly come up with an excuse for her early departure from the Secretariat, much less, the walk in Central Park.

As she walked, she struggled to find the words she'd say to Greg. Their meeting at the library had been brief, with no time to talk. Now they'd have almost two hours, and she had so many things to tell him. They had three years to catch up on. They had their future to talk about. That was the hardest part of all: the future. What should she do? Keep seeing him or say good-bye and walk away? Would she go with him if he asked her to? She wasn't ready yet, but who knew? They had done crazy things together in the past.

The sign said "Children's Zoo," and Andrea quickened her pace. Greg was there someplace, waiting for her. She still couldn't believe it. It was a dream come true. She hoped she'd never wake up.

Greg nervously twisted the newspaper in his hands, but he stopped when he realized what he was doing. He didn't want to tear the paper in two and confuse Andrea with the signal. From where he stood, he could see the path that brought people to the zoo from the south end of the park. He could also see the massive gray stone building that according to the videotapes was the former Arsenal Building. Andrea would have to walk past it before she got to the children's zoo.

Greg stretched his neck to scan the faces of a group of people coming from that direction. He didn't see Andrea, so he moved over to watch another group behind the first. This time, to his surprise, Andrea was walking in front of the group. She was also turning her head as if searching for someone.

Greg fought the impulse to run and meet her. Instead, he kept his eyes on her, waiting to see in which direction she was heading. Andrea walked to the right, slowing down. Then she stopped in front of one of the cages, next to a group of children. Greg decided to approach her immediately. He didn't want to waste any time.

Andrea looked at him a couple of times before she recognized him. Greg scratched his head with the rolled-up newspaper to make the coded signal evident, and she nodded in response. He turned around, heading for a remote spot that he had selected beforehand. "I have visual contact," he whispered into his lapel. "We're going to meet now."

"I read you," the voice said.

He stopped next to some bushes, under a tree. The shaded place was difficult to see from a distance. Andrea walked toward him, stopping a few feet away.

"You look like a pauper," she said.

"Sorry. I didn't want to compromise you. You look very nice."

She smiled uncertainly. "I'm a nervous wreck—worse than the first time we met."

"I'm nervous, too. I'm not good at this stuff."

"What do you want to do?"

"How long do we have?"

"I must be back by five forty-five."

He looked around, then at her. "I have a place, and a car to take us there."

"Who's helping you?" she said. Greg noticed the apprehensive look in her eyes.

"Trust me," he rushed. "Everything's gonna be okay."

"I'm afraid they'll follow me," she said. "I'll be in terrible trouble!"

"That's why I want a private place. Follow me slowly. When we reach the transverse road, a car will stop and we're going to climb in. The driver will take us to a place nearby. We'll be safe there." He started to walk and Andrea followed him.

They went down a small dirt slope and stopped next to the road. The traffic was heavy and Greg cursed their bad luck. He looked away when he noticed that some of the drivers were staring at them. Then a black sedan came to a stop. Greg recognized the FBI driver who had taken him to the park earlier. He grabbed Andrea by the arm and both of them ran to the car. Pulling the rear door open, he helped Andrea in, then climbed in after her. The car took off.

Greg lost his balance and fell against the back seat. "Easy," he said to the driver. "You don't want to kill us."

The cars in front of them slowed them down. The driver cursed and hit the brakes. Greg looked at Andrea beside him. She was ashen, shaking badly, her hands clasped as if to stop their tremor. She stared at him, her eyes wide.

He couldn't bear the tension any longer. He pulled her against him in a tight embrace. Andrea started to cry and he cried too. "I've missed you," he mumbled between sobs.

"I've missed you, too," she said, still crying.

"Oh, God!" he said.

He felt her body trembling and tightened the embrace. She responded by doing the same. His cheek was against hers, and he could feel her tears running down her face. "Pauper and Beggar are together again," he said.

"Yes," she said.

"Remember what we did in Reno?" he asked. "It was crazy, but we never regretted it."

She nodded.

"I still remember the old man's words. '*Greg, do you take this woman to be your lawfully-wedded wife, and do you promise before this witness to love her, comfort her, honor and keep her, in sickness and in health, and forsaking all others, keep thee only unto her?*' "

"I remember them, too," she whispered in his ear.

He released her gently and wiped the tears from her face. Then he looked outside the car. They had stopped at a light. It was a crazy idea, but he had to do it. It was now or never, he told himself, grabbing Andrea's hand.

The light changed as he yanked the handle of the door. He

CHAPTER 17

Maguire couldn't believe the words coming out of the walkie-talkie. He shouted a couple of orders into the device and glanced at Hansen sitting next to him in the car. "Jesus Christ! All hell's broken loose. Greg got crazy and jumped out of the car with Andrea!"

"I was afraid that'd happen," Hansen said.

"You thought about this guy running away and never told me?" Maguire said, glaring at him.

"Sorry. It just crossed my mind this morning. Greg was very uptight."

"Not uptight. He's got a big bug up his ass. If the KGB grabs them first, they're in for real trouble."

"He just blew Andrea's cover."

"Not if we get our hands on them within the next hour," Maguire said. "One hour is all we have." He turned to the FBI driver. "Get me Taylor on the radio."

The FBI driver reached for the mike and said, "Get me red." Then he passed the mike to Maguire.

"This is red," the voice said.

"It's Maguire. What's happening? We only have one hour to recoup this fuckin' mess, huh?"

"They just went down into the subway. We have a man on foot after them. We've asked for train schedules in the area."

"Send a couple of men to every bridge and tunnel around here. We don't want them to leave Manhattan."

"It'll cost me an army to seal off Manhattan."

"It's gonna cost you more if they leave the area," Maguire snapped back.

"Right."

"We still have radio contact with him, don't we?"

"We can hear some noises."

"I want to talk to him."

"You're wasting your time," Hansen said. "He's in a panic by now. He'd trust nobody."

"I've got to try," Maguire insisted.

Hansen extended his hand. "Let me try. Maybe I can put some sense into him."

Maguire passed the mike to Hansen and said, "You better be convincing. Otherwise he's headed for a lot of trouble."

The voice on the car radio said, "You're connected. Go ahead."

Hansen cleared his throat. "Greg . . . Greg . . . this is Hansen. Please, talk to me. . . ."

Greg and Andrea crossed Central Park West and ran down the subway stairs. He kept pulling her by the hand, afraid that she might slip away. Greg constantly looked over his shoulder to see if the FBI man was following them. He couldn't see anyone, and that gave him some confidence. He looked around to orient himself.

There were short lines in front of the token booths and he considered going there, but they'd lose critical time. Instead, he ran toward the gates leading to the train platforms. Two teenagers at the turnstiles had tokens in their hands and were ready to drop them in the slot when Greg said, "We're in a big hurry. I'll give you five dollars for the tokens right now."

The two teenagers looked at each other. "Give us the money first," one of them said.

Greg pulled out his wallet and passed a five-dollar bill to them, glad he had some money with him. He got the tokens in return. Soon he and Andrea ran onto the platform to get on a waiting train. He didn't care where the train was going. He only cared about getting away from there.

"I'm out of breath," Andrea said as they stepped into the southbound train.

"Me too," he answered her, leaning against the window and keeping his eyes on the station entrance.

The train started to move as Greg took a deep breath and sat down next to Andrea. They were moving, but not out of trouble yet. He saw an FBI man jump the turnstile, dash along the platform, and try to get onto the train. But the train had gained too much speed for him to catch up. The man stood at the end of the platform, looking miserable. Greg saw him pull out a walkie–talkie.

"We've got to get out of here as soon as the train stops," Greg told Andrea.

She nodded, still breathing heavily.

Hansen's voice came through to him weakly amid a burst of static. He'd forgotten about the receiver and earphone behind his ear. Without answering, he pulled the wire from the back of his neck and tore the mike wire from his lapel. Andrea opened her eyes in surprise. Then he took off his ragged jacket with the electronic equipment inside, bundled up the jacket, and dropped it on the floor between his legs.

"We've just burnt our bridges," he said to her.

They got off the train at 59th Street and followed a small crowd that rushed onto a double stairway. Greg and Andrea mingled with them, trying to make it difficult for somebody to see them from a distance. Greg saw that they were at Columbus Circle. Soon they rushed onto another platform. A train was ready to leave, and they ran the last few steps to get into it. He didn't have any idea where the train was heading, but they had to keep moving.

The next stop was Times Square, 42nd Street. They walked next to a group of people heading for the exit. Greg asked Andrea to walk behind him as he looked around, searching for FBI people. There was a possibility that the police had been alerted and were watching for Andrea and a man who looked like a vagrant.

A policeman rushed in the other direction toward the entrance. Greg held his breath, looking away as the man went past. The officer was in a hurry, but he didn't seem to be searching for anyone in particular. Greg was glad he'd left behind the ragged jacket that had been part of his disguise. He didn't look so bad in a short-sleeved shirt. As they reached the sidewalk, he turned to Andrea and said, "We're almost free."

She smiled at him.

Times Square teemed with activity, and Greg wasted no time in joining the crowds walking along Broadway. He'd been there once and remembered the Lincoln Tunnel. They had to get a taxi as soon as possible.

A cab pulled over a few yards in front of them and a couple stepped out. Greg and Andrea dashed toward the vehicle as another man, carrying a raincoat over his arm, also rushed for it.

Greg turned to the man. "We've got an emergency, sir. Please, let us have the taxi."

The short, balding man shook his head. "I got here first."

"No, you didn't," Greg said.

The man started to get into the taxi, and Greg grabbed him by the arm.

"Don't touch me," the man said in a threatening tone.

"My wife's very sick. I need to take her to a hospital," Greg said.

The man looked at Andrea. "You don't look sick to me."

"Hey, guys, make up your minds, huh?" the taxi driver said. "I'm fuckin' losing money not moving."

The man glared at Greg. "Fuck you," he said, walking away.

"My pleasure," Greg said, climbing inside the car. He turned to the driver. "I'll pay you double if you get us through the Lincoln Tunnel in less than fifteen minutes."

"You've got a deal, buddy."

Greg pulled the curtain, covering the single window in the room. He turned around to look at Andrea. She sat on the edge of the bed, her shoulders hunched, her arms folded together against her stomach, her eyes staring at the floor.

"We'll be safe here for one night," he said.

Andrea smiled at him timidly. "I'm scared."

"I am, too," he said, walking to her. The small room had only a single bed, a small bedside table scarred with cigarette burns, and a lamp secured with screws. There was no TV set or telephone. "Sorry about this place," he said.

"It's okay," she said.

After the taxi driver raced through the Lincoln Tunnel, Greg had asked him to take the first exit and drop them off a few blocks into Union City. Then they had walked about a mile south to Hoboken and had asked for directions to the nearest place where they could catch a bus to Newark. On the bus they had traveled separately so that passengers would not remember their being together. In Newark, they had left the bus on the outskirts of the city and walked for about a mile until they had found the small motel. He had asked Andrea to stay out of sight and had walked into the small, rundown office. He had rented a room under a false name, paid cash, and then spirited Andrea into the room. Now Greg struggled with the next course of action. He was afraid to go to the airport to take a plane for California. The FBI would probably be waiting for him at one airport or another.

"What are we going to do?" she asked.

"I don't know yet. We need time to organize our thoughts," he paused. "We need money. I don't want to use my credit cards. They'll get us right away."

He stepped close to her, caressing her hair. "Don't worry—we'll manage. The important thing is that we're together—and that you're free."

Andrea smiled at him timidly, "I'm shivering. I need to take my pills." She got up from the bed and reached for her purse on the bed. Opening it, she pulled a small container and tapped out two pills.

"What are the pills for?" he asked.

"After I left the clinic in Moscow, the doctor prescribed them. They control my anxiety."

"The bastards took you to a mental clinic?"

She nodded. "At first I dreamt of you every night. Then I had terrible nightmares." She paused. "Then there were hallucinations. I lost all sense of reality. I thought you wanted to kill me. . . . I was going mad."

Greg paced back and forth. "We should never have swapped you. I thought you would be happy there."

Andrea rubbed her eyes. "I'm happy now." She went into the small bathroom and took the pills, then came back, folding her arms against her chest. "I'm still shivering."

"We'll get a doctor to see you as soon as we get to California." He paused, then added, "We need a lawyer, too."

"I don't understand."

"We need to know your legal status in the U.S. I want to protect you, not just from the KGB, but also from the FBI and the CIA."

"How're we going to get to California?"

"By bus or by train, but we need cash." He sat down on the bed next to her. "I know how to get the money. I have a good friend in California. He'll help us with cash. I'll ask him to get it here by tomorrow." He stood up and walked over to the door.

"Please don't leave me alone," she pleaded.

"I can't take you to the front desk. I'll be back in five minutes."

He stopped at the door and smiled at her, wanting to give her confidence and assurance, but he was far from confident himself. He had taken an impulsive step without being prepared. He had hardly any money, having left most of it in his suitcase back at the safe house, and by now the FBI, the CIA, and probably the KGB were looking for them. He cursed himself for his lack of planning—but all his troubles were worth it. He had Andrea.

California was constantly on his mind. He'd be safe there, and he'd find a secure place to hide Andrea until a lawyer gave them advice. This time wouldn't be like the last time. He wouldn't let the CIA control Andrea and take her away. He'd be with her all the time, and with a lawyer. *A lawyer. That was all they needed now.*

He closed the door and double-checked to make sure that it was locked. Then he walked down the hallway, turned right, and went down one flight. The clerk sitting behind the small counter was an old black man with short, white hair, a beard, and heavy-framed glasses that made his eyes look out of proportion to the rest of his face. He was leaning back in a chair, reading a paperback.

"Have a phone around here?" Greg asked.

The man motioned to his left. He lowered his eyes to the paperback, and Greg didn't move. The man stopped reading and gave Greg another glance.

"I need your address," Greg said.

The man leaned forward, pulled a small piece of stationery from under the counter, and passed it to Greg. The paper had a picture and the address of the motel. The picture looked at least twenty years old. "Thanks."

"No problem, sir," the man said, his eyes still on his book.

The connection for the collect call took only a moment, and Greg sighed in relief when Ron answered the phone. "Where in the hell are you?" Ron demanded.

"Listen," Greg rushed on, "I can't explain now. I'm in a lot of trouble. Don't tell anybody you talked with me. *Nobody.* Is that clear?"

"Uh-oh!" Ron said. "What is it?"

"Just listen to me. I need money—cash. I want you to send me a thousand in cash to this address—"

"Wait a moment, lemme get a pencil. . . ."

Greg gave Ron the address.

"Jesus Christ! What in the fuck're you doing there?"

"I told you not to ask any questions. Send the money to Jack Ackerman . . . remember the name, Jack Ackerman."

"I won't forget."

"Wire it right away. I need it early tomorrow morning."

"I need to go to the bank for cash."

"You're not listening to me. I need the money here early. You've got to send it *now.*"

"Now?"

"Damn it, yes!"

"Okay . . . don't get jumpy. I'll get some cash from the automatic teller at the bank. I don't know if I can get up to a thousand."

"Get as much as possible, but do it now. I'll be calling you when I get to California. Good-bye." He hung up.

When he opened the door to his room, Andrea was on the floor in the middle of the room, curled up in a fetal position, in a pool of vomit. Her eyes blank, she was trembling uncontrollably, breathing in painful gasps.

"Andrea!" Greg shouted, running to her and dropping to his knees. He opened her mouth to make sure she was not choking on her tongue. Andrea looked at him, trying to say something, but only a gasp came from her throat. He lifted her head up and pulled her against his chest. "For Christ's sake, we need a doctor!" he said.

Andrea looked at him and shook her head, then leaned against his chest. He pressed her hard against him, feeling the trembling, not knowing what to do.

"The . . . shower. . . ." she said.

Greg got to his feet, lifted her in his arms, and rushed her to the bathroom. Gently he put her inside the bathtub, cushioning her head with his forearm, trying to make sure she wasn't hurt, holding back a cry of anguish. He stretched his arm and turned the water on, and then switched it to the shower.

The jet of water hit him on the back, making him jump. Then the water hit Andrea in the face and she screamed. "Andrea, please, control yourself. Andrea. . . ." he cried.

She grabbed his hands and her sharp fingernails dug into his palms. Greg winced but said nothing. Andrea started to cry, gasping for air. "Let it go . . . cry . . . cry," he said.

She screamed again, then cried, and he reached forward and hugged her against his chest. "You're safe. You're with me," he said. "I love you . . . you know that . . . I love you. . . ."

He didn't know how long they cried together under the shower. Suddenly he realized that he was also inside the bathtub, soaking wet, with Andrea in his arms. He kissed her face, her tears, her eyes. He tasted the vomit and didn't care, kissing her again and again. Andrea's arms searched for him, and she kissed him back eagerly.

Their hands caressed each other and he felt her trembling, opening her mouth, wanting to get more of his tongue. Greg reached for her blouse and ripped it open, plunging his face down into her breasts, kissing them. Andrea stopped crying. "Oh Greg," she said.

She opened her legs and Greg moved slowly, still kissing her breasts, and pulled up her skirt. The shower sprayed his back now.

Andrea pulled him in, closing her eyes, letting her head rest on the edge of the bathtub. He felt her and thrust in deeper. "I love you," he said.

"I love you, too," she said.

They were naked, lying on the bed, and Andrea slept next to him, using his chest as a pillow. He embraced her, caressing her back softly. He didn't recall their taking their clothes off and tossing them on the floor. The bed was wet and the shower was still running. He didn't care. He had Andrea in his arms. They had made love twice and she had said she loved him.

The room was semidark and he felt drowsy, exhausted by lovemaking. He recalled the first time they'd made love. He couldn't stop thinking of her for days. He couldn't wait until he had her in his arms again. Then came the trip to Reno and the frenzied night. The wedding. It all seemed so long ago, a distant dream that never happened.

Then came the separation and the pain and the loneliness. The days, months, years, guessing and dreaming . . . all that was behind him now. Andrea was with him, and he'd never let her out of his sight again, not for the CIA, not for the FBI. . . not for the KGB.

Andrea was his wife, and he wanted to have her at his side forever. Yes, he was sure, now more than ever. No one would pull them apart. They'd be one person, one life . . . one love. They'd go to California and hire a lawyer.

He kissed her on the forehead, moving her gently toward the side of the bed. He had to turn the shower off; he couldn't let the water run all night. They had to get up very early in the morning and get Andrea out of the room; then he'd have to wait for the money to arrive. After that, they'd go to a train station or a bus terminal. Perhaps they'd take a bus south, then west to California. Once they were there, everything'd be okay. They'd be free.

Slowly he rolled to the side of the bed, trying not to disturb her. He walked to the bathroom and turned off the shower. Then he heard a noise behind him. He thought that Andrea had moved in the bed, but the noise sounded like a door closing. How could that be? Andrea was in bed, sleeping. He turned around and froze, astounded, and saw two shadows in the middle of the room. "Who are you?" he shouted.

Someone walked to the lamp on the nightstand and turned on the light. Greg, standing naked in the bathroom doorway, squinted at the sudden burst of light. Then Andrea screamed.

"Don't do anything foolish, comrade," the taller of the two men said, pulling a gun from inside his jacket.

Greg recognized the pockmarked face. It was Dmitri Kotov.

CHAPTER 18

Andrea screamed again and the second man walked around the bed and slapped her face. "Stop it," he said, as she started to cry.

"Bastard!" Greg shouted, stepping forward. "You have no right—"

Dmitri aimed his gun at Greg's face. "We have every right," he said. "Comrade Lisenko is a defector."

"Leave him alone," Andrea said, still crying. "I'll go with you." She rose from the bed.

"No!" Greg shouted. "You won't go with them. "This is a free country. . . . You're free."

The other Russian shook his head. "Very touching, very touching. We've got a couple of lovebirds here." He looked at Greg first, then at Andrea. He smiled and added, "You guys had fun, did you? Too bad." He dipped a hand inside a pocket and pulled out a piece of chewing gum, opened the wrapper, and slid the gum into his mouth. "Get dressed. We don't have all day," he said to Andrea.

"Let him go," Andrea insisted. "I won't cause any trouble."

Greg shook his head. "I don't want you to go. You'll stay here until the police arrive."

The Russians looked at each other. "I don't think you understand," Dmitri said. "You have no other choice."

"How'd you find us?" Andrea said.

Dmitri walked over to the nightstand, reached for Andrea's purse, and pulled out the pill container. Popping the cap off, he emptied the pills on the bed and looked inside the container. "There's a pill glued on the bottom here," he said. "Comrade Grigori here did an excellent job putting a radio transmitter inside it. We knew where you were every moment."

Greg motioned for his clothes on the floor. He had to get dressed and find a way out. He couldn't let the Russians take Andrea away. Somehow he had to catch someone's attention and get the police there.

"Hold it!" Dmitri said.

"I have to get dressed," Greg said.

"Not with those clothes," Dmitri said. He looked at Grigori and said, "Give him the bag."

Grigori walked over to the front of the room and picked up a blue tote bag from the floor, dropping it in front of Greg. "Look inside," he said.

Greg became alert. It didn't make any sense to let him change clothes unless they wanted to take him, too. He couldn't believe it. They were kidnapping him! Struggling to keep calm, he said, "I want my own clothes."

Dmitri shook his head. "We have clothes for you inside the bag."

"We're wasting time," Grigori said, turning to Andrea. "Hurry up."

"You're upsetting comrade Grigori," Dmitri said to Greg, walking close to him and hitting him on the temple with the barrel of the gun.

Greg lost all the strength in his legs, and pain shot through his head, making the room spin. "Fuck you!" he shouted. He heard Andrea shouting, begging them to stop it. He stepped back to keep his balance. Dmitri pushed him in the chest, and Greg grabbed Dmitri's arm to wrestle him away. Then he threw a punch at Dmitri. He wanted to smash the bastard's face, but the Russian ducked the punch and swung the gun at Greg's head again. Greg winced in pain. Blood spattered his shoulder and ran down his bare chest. The lights went out and the room was plunged into darkness.

Hansen had never seen Maguire so upset. From a distance, sitting in a chair with a cup of coffee in his hand, he watched Maguire pace the spacious room. Maguire's furious steps left no doubt in Hansen's mind that now they were in serious trouble.

All it had taken was an impulsive moment, and everything was lost; the lengthy planning, the careful orchestration of the events—the guessing. Greg had jumped out of the car and disappeared with Andrea. That crazy bastard had destroyed many hours of hard work. But Hansen couldn't blame Greg for it. He should've predicted the irrational factor: Greg was uptight, desperate, and madly in love with Andrea. He should've guessed it. Now it was too late for analysis; the damage was done. Greg and Andrea had disappeared. The plan now was simple: to minimize the damage; to get them back before the KGB found them. If they got to them first, that'd be the end for them—a terrible disaster.

They'd decided to let the FBI do the searching. Maguire then suggested they should return to the safe house. He had to inform Langley. They'd be in constant communication with Taylor, but so far the FBI had no results. Nobody had seen them.

After the first hour passed, Maguire had lost all hope of returning Andrea and pretending nothing had happened. The KGB by now had to be hot on her trail, he had said to Hansen as they arrived at the safe house. Hansen had thought that they still had one or two hours' head start on the KGB, but Maguire hadn't believed it. The KGB was always on the alert. They'd waste no time.

Tired of watching Maguire pace, Hansen stood up and walked over to him, offering a cup of coffee. Maguire shook his head. "A fuckin' drink. That's what I need right now."

"You're going to wear yourself out," Hansen said. "Stop pacing."

"I want to numb my brain," Maguire said. "I want to forget the last two hours. I still can't believe it. I shouldn't have trusted that bastard from California."

"You're going insane." Hansen said. "Calm down."

Maguire glared at Hansen, then stopped pacing. He walked over to the table and pressed the switch of a speaker phone, dialing a direct line. A voice said over the speaker, "Yes, sir?"

"Get Taylor," Maguire said.

A few seconds later another voice said, "Taylor."

"This is Maguire. Anything new?"

"Nothing new. Still looking for them."

"Any ideas?"

"Your guess is as good as mine."

"What about the Mission?" Maguire asked, sitting on the edge of the table.

"I've got an army around 'em. Nothing extraordinary. Everything looks normal."

"Of course! Those bastards won't give us a hint." What about the U.N.?"

"Nothing new there either."

"You ain't too helpful."

"Be my guest. He was your bird," Taylor shot back.

"That ain't funny. I'm pissed off."

"Welcome to the club."

"I don't want to stop searching for them," Maguire said.

"Time's running out fast."

"Call me if something develops, will ya?"

"Wait a minute . . . don't go. We just got a report from a taxi driver. He dropped off a couple in Union City. They were in a hurry and looked like Greg and Andrea. We're sending someone with pictures to have a positive ID."

"Uh! That's all we need. They're already in New Jersey. I bet they're heading for California."

"Yes."

"Did you seal off the airports?"

"It's done. They don't have a chance," Taylor said and hung up.

Andrea saw Greg crumple to the floor. She ran and crouched next to him, shouting at Dmitri, "You killed him!" Greg lay on the floor sideways, bleeding from the head, and Andrea shook him by the shoulders.

Dmitri reached down and grabbed her by the hair, yanking her up. "He's not dead," he said. "I'm ordering you to get dressed or I'll kill him."

Andrea winced. "Don't hurt him anymore," she said, ignoring her own pain. "I'll get dressed."

After picking up her clothes from the floor, she got dressed as best she could pulling on her torn, wet blouse. She then walked to a corner of the room and leaned against the wall, watching Dmitri and the other Russian dress Greg in a jumpsuit they had inside the bag. Greg's body was still inert, but he moaned a few times. Andrea sighed, relieved. Greg was not dead.

Dmitri cleaned the blood from Greg's head with a piece of toilet paper, then pulled him by the arms, and with Grigori's help, stood him upright. Dmitri ordered Andrea to walk in front of them and not to try anything crazy. He'd shoot her at the first sign of any attempt to get someone's attention. Dmitri's steely eyes told Andrea he meant it.

A car with a driver was waiting for them behind the motel. There were no outside lights and Andrea walked slowly, afraid she'd stumble over the garbage and abandoned furniture piled against the walls. Dmitri and Grigori walked holding Greg by the arms, dragging him along, Greg's head hanging limp against his chest. They stopped at the rear of the car and Dmitri opened the trunk. The driver had gotten out of the car and helped them to load Greg into the trunk.

"He's going to suffocate in there!" Andrea protested.

"He wont' be in the trunk for too long," Dmitri said to her. "Get in the back seat."

She climbed in and Dmitri and Grigori sat on either side of her. The driver drove away with the lights off until he was about a block away from the motel.

Andrea watched the motel as they passed it. She and Greg had spent a few hours there, dreaming of a future and a new life. They had discovered each other again and a love that would never die. What fools they were! There was no future and never would be. Dmitri would send her to Russia and they'd punish her for trying to defect. She couldn't understand why they wanted Greg, too. His only fault was that he loved her and had risked everything for her. Perhaps they'd keep him secluded until they took her out of the country. The FBI and the CIA would be looking for them. That was probably the reason. Dmitri wanted a bargaining chip, and Greg was a good one. Poor Greg. She was causing him pain again.

As they sped along, Andrea read the signs: Route 21 North. Passaic 3 miles. She had no idea where they were going, but perhaps she could try to do something to help Greg.

Traffic was light and the driver took the exit a little fast. "Slow down," Dmitri cautioned the driver. About a mile later, the driver pulled into a small parking lot and drove around a brick building, turning off the headlights. A van waited for them there. Dmitri ordered Andrea to stay in the car and she watched the Russians lift Greg out of the trunk and carry him into the back of the van. Greg moved his hands and legs, as if regaining consciousness. She sighed in relief; he was still alive.

Soon the van left and Grigori stood next to the car, watching them drive away. Dmitri went with the van and Andrea wondered why. She noticed the sign on the side of the van, Quebec Janitorial Services.

Grigori climbed into the back of the car and ordered his driver to get started.

"Where're you taking him?" Andrea asked.

The Russian looked at her.

"Where're you taking him?" she insisted.

"You think we're going to tell you, eh?"

"You're not going to harm him, are you?" she demanded.

Grigori looked at Andrea with a steady gaze. "If we wanted him dead, he'd be dead by now."

"I'll do anything you want. Don't hurt him!"

Grigori shook his head slowly. "It won't help, comrade. You're wasting your time."

Andrea was going to ask him where they were taking her, but changed her mind. Grigori would never tell. She eased back in the seat and stared out the window, as they entered a freeway. She read the sign as they rushed by it: George Washington Bridge. Grigori was taking her back to Manhattan.

The traffic got a little busier as they approached the toll gate. Grigori turned to her. "I want you to lie down on the floor of the car. I'll put a blanket over you." He pulled a gun fitted with a silencer from inside his jacket. "One move and I'll splash your brains all over this car. Is that clear?" he added.

Andrea nodded.

"Now," he said, and she hid on the floor.

She didn't know how long she'd been under the blanket, but

at one point she thought she'd suffocate. She hadn't felt like that since the Aeroflot flight to Canada, when she had hid in a special trunk to get into Montreal illegally. Her case officer at the time, Colonel Boris Alexei Grishin, had taken her from the Illegals campus near Moscow and had ordered her to move to Silicon Valley. He had told her to recruit Greg Elliot to spy for the KGB. But a lifetime of training couldn't hide the truth from her. She had found America different, and Greg Elliot was a difficult target. How many things had happened since then! How many things would happen yet?

Grigori pulled the blanket back. "You can sit up now. We're close to the safe house," he said.

She got up. Grigori still had the gun on his lap. The ride on the floor had made her stiff and the seat felt comfortable. She looked out the window, trying to orient herself. It was dark and there were a lot of people on the sidewalks, mostly young people wearing strange clothes, talking in groups, some carrying large radios playing loud music. Most of the signs in the stores were in Spanish. She managed to see a street sign. They were on Lexington Avenue. A building on the corner had all the windows and doors boarded over, walls covered with graffiti in Spanish, a mountain of garbage and junk piled up in the front.

"This is a good picture of America," Grigori said.

"Spanish Harlem?" Andrea said, not expecting any answer.

"Yeah. They're ready for us. Our revolution should start here," he said. "These people should have the opportunity to live with the rich people of the East Side." He smiled. "They'd love it."

"What's going to happen to Greg?" she asked.

"You don't give up."

"You don't have the right."

"We have every right."

"He didn't do anything. I did."

"He helped you, so he's just as guilty."

"He's American."

"It makes no different to us. He's guilty. That's all."

Andrea knew she was getting nowhere. The KGB would do whatever they wanted. The only way to help Greg was to notify the police or the FBI. She didn't know where the KGB was taking Greg. The only clue she had was the van. Quebec Janitorial Services. The name must mean something. She had to tell the FBI, but how? She was also a prisoner, and the KGB would probably take her to Moscow soon. Then there'd be no hope for her or for Greg. They both were as good as dead.

Her mind was racing as she looked out the window. She had to find a way to get away and call the FBI. By now they must be looking for Greg and her all over New York.

She had to escape. It was her last hope.

They brought him food twice, but he refused to eat. Instead, he shouted at them to let him free. The Russian looked at him, shrugged, and walked away, leaving the tray of food in front of him. Greg kicked the tray away and started shouting again. Nobody paid any attention.

They had handcuffed him to a metal ring embedded in a wall. The room resembled a walk-in freezer. Long metal bars running along the walls had steel hooks that he guessed were for hanging meat, but the room was very hot.

Greg rubbed his nose as if to stop the stench that filled his nostrils. He was sitting on the hard floor, barefoot, still wearing the jumpsuit. He didn't recall how he got there or how long he'd been there. He remembered only that the Russian named Dmitri had hit him twice on the head. He had asked several times about Andrea, but they had responded with only silence. Then, after trying many more times, he had finally given up. They'd never tell him. That was part of the game.

The pain on the side of his head was reduced to a lingering ache, and his hair was sticky with dried blood. Still, once in a while, a stab of pain pierced him, as if to remind him of the bad moment at the motel. He should've listened to Maguire. How right he was, not trusting those KGB bastards. Now it was too late for remorse. He had screwed up.

As the door opened, Dmitri walked in with two tough-looking Russians. "I demand that you turn me loose," Greg said to Dmitri. "I'm an American citizen, and you have no right to do this in my country."

A smile flashed across Dmitri's face. "You're in no position to demand anything, comrade," he said.

Greg got up from the floor and stepped as far as his handcuffs would let him. "Fuck you!" he said. "Wait until the FBI gets its hands on you!"

"That's wishful thinking," Dmitri said. "We've got some other plans for you."

"Where's Andrea?"

"She's already on her way to Moscow."

"I don't believe you," Greg said.

"Suit yourself."

"You know the FBI's looking for us."

"They're wasting their time." Dmitri looked at the two men and nodded.

They walked over to Greg and opened the handcuffs, grabbing him by the arms, their grip tight.

Pain shot through his arms. "What're you doing?" he shouted.

"We're going for a short trip," Dmitri said, leading the way.

The door led to a small warehouse that looked like a meat processing plant, with long conveyor belts and carts with metal frames and sharp hooks. It was an abandoned building, with piles of junk against the walls. Greg felt the dust and the dirt under his bare feet. They approached a blue, unmarked van parked near a roll-up metal door. Greg didn't remember having seen it before.

One of the Russians opened the rear door and motioned Greg inside. He obeyed without resistance, and the Russian and Dmitri climbed in behind him. The Russian blindfolded Greg after handcuffing him to a metal ring attached to the wall. The van pulled away from the building, and soon Greg could hear the highway traffic. He took a deep breath, filling his lungs with fresh air. It was a welcome change from the stale air of the freezer. He wondered where they were taking him and where they had taken Andrea. He still couldn't believe that she was already on her way back to Moscow.

They had been traveling for several hours, and he was again in terrible discomfort. He had changed position many times, trying to ease the pain in his body. He sat on the metal floor with his hands pinned close to the wall. A couple of times his legs cramped, but he couldn't relieve them. He could only bite his lip and try to withstand the pain. The Russians next to him had only spoken a few words in Russian, so he couldn't understand what they were saying. He tried to pick up the mood of the conversation based on the intonation of their voices, but he couldn't arrive at any conclusion. The only thing he knew was that they were going some place—very far away.

The road they were traveling had also changed. There were no more highway traffic sounds around him. They left the paved road for a dirt road: he could feel the bumps and hear the dirt hitting the underframe of the van and the fenders. He wondered where they were taking him. It was dark and he was still blindfolded.

The van braked to a halt and the Russians opened the back door and jumped out. Then the driver released the handcuffs and helped Greg step down.

"Watch your step," he heard Dmitri say.

Greg jumped down from the van and almost lost his balance. He felt four pairs of hands steadying him. The air smelled fresh, and he heard a sound that chilled him—the ocean. "Where are we?" he demanded.

"Walk with us," Dmitri said.

Again the hands grabbed his arms, propelling him along a dirt path. He now felt sand under his bare feet. He came to a halt. "I won't walk any more unless you tell me where are we going," he protested.

The grip on his arms tightened, and Dmitri said, "That's a foolish decision, comrade. We could make you unconscious again." He paused, then added, "I don't think you want that."

Greg realized that Dmitri was right, but he couldn't walk to his death without a fight. "If you're gonna kill me, you better do it here. I'm not walking any more."

He heard Dmitri laugh. "If we wanted you dead, we'd have buried you by now. Don't be foolish. Walk."

They pushed him forward, and he started to walk again.

The sand ended and they were now walking on wooden planks. Greg guessed they were on a pier; he could hear the sounds of the surf beneath. "You're not going to tell me anything?" he asked.

"Soon you'll know where you're going. Don't be impatient." Dmitri said.

With difficulty he descended a narrow flight of stairs. The Russians again helped him keep his balance. They sat him in the middle of a boat. Soon he heard an engine running and felt the boat move. Jesus Christ! he said to himself. God only knows where we're heading.

The boat now bobbed gently with its engine and all its lights off. It was very dark, and Dmitri took Greg's blindfold off. He looked around and could see only the dark mass of water and a faint glitter beyond the horizon that he guessed was New York City. The Russian piloting the boat had talked on the radio a few times in a language Greg didn't recognize.

"So this is how you guys do this," Greg said to Dmitri. "A submarine comes along and spirits me back to Russia."

Dmitri looked at Greg with an amused expression. "You Americans watch too many James Bond movies." He laughed. "We use submarines only as a last resort. We have better uses for them."

"Then what?" Greg said.

"Be patient. You'll know soon."

"I want to know *now*."

"Don't start. You've been obedient so far."

Greg cursed softly to himself.

The radio in the boat broke the silence once more. Static and a voice came through, broken by a good deal of static. The Russian spoke into the mike, then turned to Dmitri and said something in Russian.

They all looked toward their right. Greg followed their eyes. A freighter was approaching them.

CHAPTER 19

Maguire stood in the middle of the motel room, watching an army of FBI technicians crawling all over the place. There was no question in his mind that Greg and Andrea had stayed there. The evidence was conclusive. And he was sure the KGB had taken them away. For the last hour, FBI technicians had been looking for bits of information that could be pieced together to form a clear story. Maguire couldn't believe his bad luck; the KGB had Greg. He should've known better.

Taylor had called Maguire around midmorning with the information about a motel in Newark who had phoned the police to notify them of a suspicious finding. The man claimed he'd found the door of the room open when he wanted to deliver a package early in the morning. He said that he was old enough to know when something smelled like trouble. The police had dispatched a patrol car to the motel. The manager was right; Greg and Andrea were in serious trouble.

The items in the room puzzled Maguire. The FBI technicians took pictures without disturbing them. Maguire recognized Greg's street disguise of trousers, shirt, and shoes, but he couldn't find the jacket. Could this mean that the KGB took Greg while he was wearing only the jacket? The clothes were still damp, as if Greg had washed them—even the shoes. It made no sense. How in the hell did they get wet? And there were pills spilled on the bed and the floor. An FBI technician took a few, dropping them in a small plastic bag for the lab analysis. The last item was a chewing gum wrapper: Wrigley's spearmint. He didn't recall Greg or Andrea liking chewing gum. The wrapper must have been dropped by one of the KGB bastards.

Maguire stepped to the side, allowing the FBI photographer to take some wide-angle pictures. As he waited, Hansen walked into the room. "The motel manager is waiting for you," he said.

"What a fuckin' mess," Maguire grunted.

The room behind the registration desk was small and crowded. There was a dented gray metal desk, a chair with a torn vinyl seat, and a battered file cabinet. There was a thick coating of dust on the flat surfaces. Maguire took his eyes from a faded poster of the Bahamas and looked at the motel manager sitting behind the desk. The old man looked haggard and very nervous.

Maguire pulled a cigarette pack from one of his pockets and said, "Smoke?"

The man shook his head. "No, thanks. It took me five years to quit."

Maguire pocketed the pack; he wasn't in the mood for a smoke either. "Do you work here all night?" he asked.

The man nodded. "Yes, sir. I'm the night shift manager."

"You recognized the picture of the man who rented the room last night." Maguire said. "You said there was no woman with him, didn't you?"

The man shook his head. "I'm sure, sir."

"Could this guy sneak in someone without you seeing?"

The old man arranged his heavy-framed glasses to look at Maguire. "It happens all the time, sir. Women are funny, they don't like to be seen when they come here to fuck someone. The man comes to the front desk and asks for a room with a big bed. You see the horny look on his face. One person, no way, this guy ain't foolin' me, but I pretend. Let 'em have some fun. Next day, my cleaning lady picks up condoms all over the room. What's this guy doin', masturbating with condoms? No, sir, he ain't."

"How can they sneak a woman into the room?" Hansen asked.

The man shrugged. "Very easy, through the back door." He pointed to his right. "Our parkin' lot's in the rear. We've got to give our patrons a key to get inside the building."

"What about the package?" Maguire asked.

The man's lips stretched into a little smile. "We don't get

business people here. Hey, I said to myself. Somethin's fishy here. Special delivery—a package from California. For a bum? Nights're long, y'know. I read Agatha Christie. I know when somethin' ain't right." He smiled again. "Then the door was open and I found wet clothes all over the floor, bloodstains, no people—no condoms. I gave the police a buzz."

Andrea pushed away her plate. She had not touched her food. How could she? She reached for a glass of water and took a couple of sips, resting the glass next to the plate. Her stomach ached; she felt as if it had a knot in it, and she wondered how long she could hang on without her pills. Grigori, sitting on a metal stool, a glass of vodka in hand, watched her from the kitchen. Three days had gone by and the Russian had barely spoken a word, freeing her only to eat her meals and use the bathroom. Then he handcuffed her and locked her in a room with no windows and only a bare mattress on the floor. That was the only time she was alone. It was okay to have Grigori watching her when she was eating, but she still couldn't get used to going to the bathroom with the door open and the Russian watching her. When she protested the lack of privacy, the Russian said, "I watch you or you don't go." After a full day of not using the bathroom, she couldn't stand it anymore. Her physical necessity prevailed over her sensitivity.

"Where's Greg?" she asked.

"None of your business," Grigori said.

"He has done nothing wrong," she said.

"He's a CIA spy."

She knew the lines by heart—the same questions, the same answers. She was getting nowhere.

"When is Dmitri coming back?" she tried again.

Grigori took a long sip from the glass and stared at her silently as if to say, Don't you ever get tired of asking questions? Andrea returned the stare, trying to hide her terror.

Grigori put down the glass, hitting the counter hard. He jumped off the stool and walked over to her. "I'm tired of your questions," he said, grabbing her by the arm.

Andrea winced. He dragged her to the door of the room,

hurled her inside, and slammed the door. Andrea lost her balance and landed on her hands and knees. Sitting up, she rubbed her arm to ease the pain. This time she didn't cry. She had promised herself not to cry anymore. There was no more time to feel sorry for Greg or for herself. The only way to free Greg from the KGB was to tell the FBI. She had to find a way to escape before Dmitri came back, and she had to keep control of her emotions.

Maguire looked at the folder in front of him and grimaced. Three frenzied days and hundreds of FBI agents turning over every stone in Manhattan and the western states had produced five typed pages. Greg Elliot and Andrea Hendrick were still missing—and perhaps were already in Moscow.

Taylor, Hansen, and an FBI technician named Dave sat around the table at the safe house in the Garment District. At Langley's insistence, Maguire had called the meeting to review the status of the investigation and to discuss some concerns that his superior had sent him in a coded message.

Taylor looked at the technician. "Why don't you summarize the report so we can go ahead with the conclusions," he said.

The technician, a man in his late forties, heavy, with long sideburns and a nervous twitch in his left eye, looked down at the papers. "Well, sir, the bloodstains match Mr. Elliot's blood type. We don't think he was badly hurt. There wasn't enough blood in the carpet for that."

"Could you clarify that?" Hansen said.

The technician cleared his throat. "There were no gunshot traces in the room, so the blood came from a blow on the subject's head or from a cut with a sharp object."

"A knife?" Maguire said.

The technician nodded. "Yes,—but a knife would've produced much more blood than a blow to the head."

"So they whacked Greg on the head," Maguire said.

"Yeah."

"What else?" Maguire pursued.

The technician loosened his tie. "Well," he said, "we found pubic hair in the bathtub."

Maguire frowned. "Same type?"

"Two different people."

"Aha! That explains the wet clothes," Maguire said.

"Yes, sir."

"They jumped into the shower fully dressed and then started to fuck there, didn't they?"

The technician looked at Maguire, then at Hansen, then at Taylor. "Yes, it seems that they had intercourse in the bathtub."

"They were in a rush, huh?" Maguire grinned. "Can't blame them; three years is a long time."

"What about the pills?" Hansen asked.

"The lab report says that they are a strong tranquilizer. Based on Ms. Hendrick's dossier, the pills are for controlling her anxiety attacks." He paused and looked at Hansen. "She was in a KGB clinic."

"Yes," Hansen said.

"The money?" Maguire asked.

"We traced a collect call from the motel to California," Taylor cut in. "Greg called his friend, Ron Temple, and asked for cash. We think Greg wanted to travel by bus or train to California."

"Any other calls?" Maguire said.

"None that we could trace," Taylor said.

Maguire played with a pencil for a few seconds, staring at the papers in front of him. Then he glanced at Taylor. "Langley wants answers to three questions they consider critical."

"Shoot," Taylor said.

"Well, number one: how in hell did the KGB know about the motel? We were hot on Greg and Andrea's trail and lost them. Those KGB fuckers ain't better than us, but they got there first. The big question is: did Andrea make a sucker out of us and turn Greg in to the KGB?" Maguire looked around to see if anyone would volunteer an answer. Nobody spoke.

"Number two: why does the KGB want Greg Elliot? Not to kill him—otherwise we would've found his body in the motel. The KGB wants Greg alive and well, but for what purpose?

"Number three: who pulled the job?" He paused, then added, "I'm willing to bet my paycheck that Dmitri Kotov did it. But we don't have any fucking proof he was in the motel—only a son-of-a-bitch who chews Wrigley's gum."

He looked around again, but no volunteers came forward with answers. Hell, they were as lost as he was, and it didn't make him feel any better. "Any fucking suggestions?" he asked.

But there were none.

He didn't remember ever feeling so sick. For three long days he was seasick—constantly throwing up, bearing terrible headaches, and suffering from nonstop diarrhea. They had locked him in a cell with no windows and a metal floor, walls, and ceiling. He had only a cot and a latrine that stank like a decomposing corpse. The swaying and bobbing and rolling made him so ill that he couldn't even keep water in his stomach. The mere thought of food make him run for the latrine to vomit. Yet even in the depths of such misery, he couldn't stop thinking of Andrea. The physical pain was nothing compared to the terrible anguish that gripped his heart. He'd had Andrea, and he'd lost her. For a few hours they'd been in paradise, and now all was hell. He blamed himself for doing what he'd done. He'd thought he could fool the KGB and the CIA, but he had been terribly mistaken.

As time passed, he lost hope that the nightmare would end, and he started to have dreams of dying. Then, suddenly, the freighter stopped moving; he heard the noise of cranes and of people shouting. The shouts were too distant and blurred by the background noise for him to understand a word. He was relieved that the ship was not moving anymore; but the grief in his heart was still there, giving him no mercy.

Twice he heard steps outside the cell, but nobody came for him. He thought that maybe the ship would leave soon, but quickly realized he was wrong when he heard the lock of his cell snap open. Using the walls to keep his balance, he stood up and faced the door. A tall, serious-faced black man stood in the doorframe, armed with a submachine gun and wearing military fatigues. "Follow me," he said.

Another armed man, also in fatigues, was waiting outside the cell. They went along a catwalk into a narrow pathway. The black man led the way, with the second man behind him.

Greg squinted at the light bulbs hanging from the low ceiling.

"Where am I going?" he asked, but got no answer.

They stepped onto the foredeck, and he took a deep breath, filling his lungs with the fresh air. What a difference from the latrine and the cell! He looked around. The ship was docked on a rundown pier, facing an electric power plant with four tall smokestacks that poured out long columns of black smoke. An elevated railroad track stretched in front of the power plant, crossing under a long coal conveyor that reached all the way down to the pier. Greg noticed about fifty cars neatly parked in a small lot. It looked as if the ship had just unloaded them. He couldn't determine the make of the cars. It was dusk, and the sky was dark and cloudless. They were at the end of a long bay, where the water was calm and very flat. In the distance, the lights of a city followed the contour of the bay. He had an eerie feeling as he looked at the pier and the power plant; they looked old, as if frozen in time. Yes, he was sure now, he had stepped back in time, at least twenty years. "Where are we?" he asked again.

The black man turned his head and gave him a hostile look, saying nothing.

They reached the opposite side of the ship, where a metal ladder reached down to the water and a gray powerboat waited. The boat, without lights or flags, had a machine gun on the aft deck, and a man stood next to it.

The black man pointed at the ladder with his submachine gun. Greg knew they had taken him out of the ship on the opposite side of the pier so that nobody could see him from the ground. He obeyed silently, grabbing the metal rail with both hands, afraid he'd slip and fall into the water.

As he stepped down, he could see the side of the ship, its hull rusty and badly in need of a paint job. The name of the ship was Sozopol. Greg wasn't sure what the name meant or to which country the ship belonged. He jumped into the boat, grabbing a railing to keep his balance, and the two men followed him. Greg leaned back on the hard seat inside the cabin, rubbing his nose a couple of times as a foul smell coming from the water reached his nostrils. One of the men started the engine and they pulled away.

Soon the ship, the pier, and the power plant were just distant shapes slipping into darkness. Greg watched them from the distance, glad that he would soon be on land. But he didn't understand where they were taking him and for what purpose. He didn't believe he was in Russia, for the trip had not been long enough. He was up north or down south. And if it was south, there were only two countries in which the KGB had control—Cuba or Nicaragua.

In either case he was in serious trouble.

The men in the boat were silent during most of the trip, speaking in Spanish only a couple of times. The boat approached a small pier, and the black man stepped to the foredeck, then jumped to the pier. Once on land, they walked toward a military jeep. Greg was still barefoot and walked with difficulty on the loose gravel. They were in a shallow meadow about half a mile from the ship, an open field with clusters of heavy-topped trees and thick undergrowth. Not far away, there was a highway with very light traffic.

"Are you going to tell me where I am going?" Greg asked the black man again.

"You will know soon," the man said, his accent unrecognizable.

They rode for about an hour, past populated areas with large, square clusters of buildings that looked like apartment complexes. The highway bordered the ocean, which had turned as black as the sky. Only a few trucks, buses, and very old American cars were on the road. Greg saw a few signs exhorting productivity improvements in the factories and agricultural output. He also saw a couple of signs with large portraits of Lenin and Che Guevara. He still didn't know where he was.

The driver of the jeep steered right, turning into a dirt road off the highway. Greg missed the sign next to the exit because the light over the sign was off. He felt disoriented in the dark, but the fresh air had helped him to recover some of his strength. Now he could see a string of yellow lights; a fence? Soon they stopped in front of a gatehouse manned by two armed soldiers who waved them in without asking for papers, as if they knew the people in the jeep.

The military camp stood on flat ground, disappearing into the darkness. Green prefabricated barracks were spaced evenly across the land. There was little activity in the camp; Greg saw a few military vehicles parked in open lots, two large tanks with long guns, and a few military people on foot. He still couldn't understand what he was doing there. He was sure he'd know soon, though; the trip seemed to have come to an end.

The driver parked in front of a small building with a large number 7 painted on the door. The black man jumped out, urging Greg to do the same. They entered the building and stopped in front of a desk where another military man sat.

"He's waiting," the man said, his accent heavy. He nodded at a closed door, and the black man motioned Greg toward it.

Greg hesitated, still not understanding what was happening to him. The KGB had kidnaped him and taken him to a country he guessed was in Latin America. Now he was in a military camp, facing a closed door and ready to meet someone who was waiting for him. None of it made any sense: the kidnaping, the trip in the freighter, and now the camp. He pushed the door open and walked inside, the black man following him.

He faced a small table and two chairs, one of which was occupied by a man in military fatigues and cap. Some papers were arranged on the table in front of him. The man said, "Greg Elliot?"

The man waited for an answer, his face stern. "Where am I?" Greg said. "I'm an American citizen." His dry mouth tasted foul as he struggled to speak.

The man stood up and pulled out a photograph from underneath the papers. He glanced at the picture and then at Greg's face as if to be sure they were the same person. He walked around the table, stepping close to Greg.

Weak and confused, Greg tilted his head and blinked a few times. His vision was blurred and he had difficulty focusing his eyes. The man had a beard and an angular nose and looked a little like Fidel Castro. It couldn't be, Greg thought, it must be a hallucination. Now he was sure he was going mad.

"Are you Greg Elliot?" the man asked again.

Greg nodded and said, "I'm sick."

The man circled Greg as if studying him. Then he picked up another paper, which he started to read silently.

"Who are you?" Greg asked.

The man raised his eyes for a moment, then went on reading, then leaned back in his chair. "I'm General Alejandro Carreras from the DGI," he said in flawless English.

"DGI? I don't understand," Greg said.

"DGI is the Cuban intelligence service."

"I'm in Cuba—right?"

"You've guessed it. And you're in trouble."

Greg rubbed his eyes, feeling ill, on the border of collapsing. "I'm sick," he repeated, "I need a doctor. . . ."

Carreras glanced at the paper. "In the name of the Cuban government and our brothers of the Soviet Union, we're placing you under arrest for the killing of the Soviet citizen Boris Alexei Grishin. You will be summarily tried and punished for the crime."

"What!" Greg said. "Are you serious?"

"Yes. Deadly serious. . . ."

CHAPTER 20

Andrea got up from the mattress and tiptoed to the door. She pressed her ear against it and listened for a few seconds. There was no sound on the other side. Then she tried the door knob, but it didn't turn. What would happen if she pulled it hard? The door didn't seem too strong, and perhaps she could get it open. She grabbed the knob with both hands and was ready to give it a strong pull when a sudden thought stopped her. She would be taking the risk that the noise would awaken Grigori, and then he would handcuff her.

That afternoon, at dinnertime, she had concluded that Dmitri would be coming for her the next day. Grigori had not said a word to warn her, but the way he had behaved and looked at her told her what was about to happen. It was as if he wanted something, but didn't dare ask. Then he had circled around her several times, like a predator ready to jump on its victim. She was sure that Grigori wanted to have sex with her, and the only reason he was so uptight was because he feared what Dmitri would say. Dmitri's arrival would be the end of her hopes to help Greg. She had no idea where Dmitri planned to take her but she assumed it was to the Soviet Union.

The thought of returning to Russia terrified her. The memories of the KGB clinic were still too vivid in her mind. When they had taken her out of the clinic, she promised herself she'd never go back there. At the time she didn't know what the promise meant. This time she was sure, preferring to die rather than to live again through the drugs, the hallucinations, and the nightmares. At the clinic they had killed her mind, leaving her body intact. This time she'd decide her own fate. She'd keep both her body and her mind, and they'd never take her alive.

She stepped back and sat on the floor, crossing her legs, staring at the door. It was early morning, and the room was semidark. She wondered where they had taken Greg, and if he was also thinking of dying. She was now sure she loved him and wished they could die together. Then nobody could keep them apart.

She heard steps approaching, and rushing to the mattress, she pretended she was asleep. The door opened and Grigori stood in the doorway. By now she knew the routine well—a trip to the bathroom, with Grigori keeping watch, enjoying the view of her sitting on the toilet. The bastard didn't even hide the smile on his face.

Pretending to be half-asleep, she got up from the mattress and walked to the bathroom, with Grigori following her.

"I feel very sick," she said, trying to justify a little more time in the bathroom.

Grigori said nothing.

She sat on the toilet and buried her face in her hands, as if the pain was too strong. "I need some water!" she shouted at Grigori, but she got no response.

"Let me know when you're gonna die," Grigori said.

"If I die, Dmitri will kill you," she said.

Grigori's face became serious."

"Oh—my God!" she went on. "The pain is too much."

Grigori walked over to the door of the bathroom. "What do you want?" he asked.

"I need some water and a pill."

"I don't have any more pills. I'll bring the water."

Andrea watched him as he headed for the kitchen at the other side of the apartment. This was the moment, and she had only a few seconds. She tiptoed to the bathroom door, closed it, and locked it. The door wasn't strong enough to stop Grigori, but it'd delay him long enough. She hurried to the other side of the bathroom.

The window was small, and she was not sure if she could open it, but she had to try. This was her last chance. There was no lock on the window, and she pushed up the sash. It stuck halfway up and she pushed harder, moving it a few inches.

Andrea looked over her shoulder; there was still no sign of

Grigori. She slid both hands under the window sash and pushed up with all her strength. It moved a few inches more, enough for her to slide her head through. She looked down. The apartment was on the third floor, but there was a roof one floor below. She considered jumping but hesitated, afraid she'd break an ankle. Grigori would catch up with her if she got hurt. She looked to her left and saw a drainage pipe running all the way down to the roof. If she could reach the pipe, she could slide down safely.

She heard Grigori pounding on the door and shouting. She started to tremble, barely keeping control of her movements. She had to escape to help Greg, she told herself as Grigori tried to break the lock. God! She had only a few seconds left. It was now or never. She had to stop her shaking. *Control . . . control,* she repeated.

Grabbing the window frame with both hands, she slid her head and chest through the window, half-hanging in open space one story up. She looked down and closed her eyes. If she fell, she'd break her neck. She looked at the pipe about twenty inches away and slid one hand out the window, then the other. Her legs were still inside the bathroom. She could still hear Grigori tampering with the lock. He would break into the bathroom at any moment.

One more push was all she needed. She reached the pipe with one hand, searching for a place to grab it, but the pipe was too wide around for only one hand. She needed both hands.

The door broke open and she heard Grigori cursing and rushing for her. She grabbed the pipe with her hands and pulled hard. She slid her legs out as Grigori rushed for her ankles. Her weight helped her swing into the open and out of the window. She tightened her grip on the rusty pipe, but her hold wasn't strong enough and she began to slide. She felt her hands burning as if they were on fire. She grabbed the pipe firmly and screamed. It was her last chance to stop the fall. She held on as hard as she could and felt the slippery blood and the pain from the cuts and torn skin of her hands. She thought of Greg. She had to do it now. She stopped a few feet from the roof.

Slowly she jumped onto the roof and heard shouting above her. Grigori was half out the bathroom window, ordering her to come back. He was trying to get through the window, but was wedged in the narrow space. He cursed a few words in Russian and slid back inside.

Andrea knew she was far from free. Grigori would pursue her. She needed to get off the roof and into the street, and to get some distance from the house. She had a good head start. It'd take a few minutes for Grigori to get around the building.

She ran across the roof toward a small door in a wall facing the far side of the roof. She prayed that the door would be open. The lock was broken and she ran inside and found a narrow stairway leading down to a hallway. A moment later she dashed along a dark hallway but couldn't see the stairs to the street. The place seemed to be an apartment house. The hallway was full of boxes and old furniture, and several children were playing there. She had no idea where she was or how far she was from Grigori and the safe house. She stopped and asked a boy where the exit stairs to the street were. She ran in that direction. At a turn in the hallway, she saw the stairs, a small lobby, and the front door.

She halted at the door and looked at the street. There was still no sign of Grigori. Her chest heaved and she gasped for air. Her stomach hurt and her hands stung badly. Slowly she pushed the door open and stepped out, trying to orient herself. She was almost sure that the safe house was to the right, so she took off to the left.

The next building's doors and windows were boarded up with plywood. A lot behind the building looked like a garbage dump, full of old furniture and dilapidated electric appliances. She cut across the lot, trying to stay out of sight. She hoped Grigori would go into the first building looking for her.

The lot ended in another street next to a lot containing tombstones for sale. She ran past that lot and stopped on the sidewalk to catch her breath. She stood in front of a small shop with about half a dozen motorcycles for sale.

Andrea hesitated, wondering whether she should walk into the shop and ask for help. But what would happen if Grigori discovered her and went inside the shop, too? The people there probably would not protect her. She was ready to run farther down the block, when a huge man walked out of the shop. He wore black leather pants and a leather vest with nothing underneath. Chains adorned his neck and wrists and tattoos covered his upper arms. The man had long hair, a thick mustache, and a small diamond on the side of his nose. His muscular arms gave him the look of a weight lifter. Andrea struggled with the thought of asking for his help.

The man walked over to a motorcycle and climbed on. He was ready to kick the starter when Andrea approached him. "Excuse me, sir," she said. "I'm in desperate need of a ride. Where're you going?"

The man looked at her. "What do you want?"

"I need a ride, please."

"You in trouble?"

Andrea nodded several times, holding back a sob. "Please, I need help . . . please. . . ."

"Okay," the man said. "Jump on. But I'm not responsible if you fall off."

Andrea climbed on the motorcycle, grabbing the man around his chest. He reeked of old sweat, tobacco, and alcohol, but somehow the stench was comforting to her.

"Where're you going?" she asked.

"New Jersey."

Andrea pulled herself harder against the big hulk and closed her eyes. "That suits me fine," she said.

Early in the morning two armed soldiers came for him. He had spent the night in a small cell at the rear of the building. The bunk bed was hard, and throughout the night, he had felt the springs under the mattress. Now his back hurt badly, and he had an empty sensation in his stomach that bordered on pain. He had slept only a few minutes, but his sleeplessness was not due to the pain. He still couldn't believe that the Cubans were going to try him for the killing of Boris Alexei Grishin.

The affair had happened over three years ago, and he had thought that it was all but forgotten. At the time he had had no other choice but to kill Boris. He was desperate then and was going mad. Boris had used Andrea to destroy his life and was not willing to stop blackmailing him. Boris was the one who had suggested the swap at the Glienicker Bridge checkpoint in

Berlin. The message that Boris had sent him was that the Americans desperately wanted the return of a critically ill West German CIA spy. The CIA was hot for a swap, and Boris suggested to Greg that he'd offer to use Andrea as long as he got what he wanted—a back door to the Blue Cube's cipher codes.

Greg recalled the hours of internal struggle when he was in Berlin. Killing Boris was against his principles. He never thought he could actually do it until he had pulled the trigger and saw Boris's head bursting into a mélange of blood, brains, and flesh. Seeing Andrea walk across the bridge was the last straw. All hope, love, and dreams of a future with her were gone. It had taken only a few seconds and the realization came suddenly. He saw nothing else for him. Nothing else mattered after that, not even killing Boris Alexei Grishin.

The two soldiers motioned to him to step into the rear of a van. The vehicle, painted in military colors, looked like a small transport for prisoners with its long wooden bench against one wall and a metal grid separating the back from the front. The two soldiers closed the door and Greg heard them lock it. Then they climbed into the front and drove away. Greg didn't ask them where they were taking him. He was sure they had orders not to tell him.

He tried to find a comfortable position on the bench. The ride was rough and he bounced with the vehicle. Still, there was no comparison between this trip and the one he had taken on the ship. At least now he had plenty of fresh air.

The van started to climb a hill, and at a turn around some trees he saw the gigantic mass of a fortress. He moved to the front of the bench to glance at the fortress through the front window of the van. The road headed directly toward the fortress gate. The driver steered into the entrance, driving over a bridge. As they crossed it, Greg glimpsed a deep, dry moat surrounded by ancient stone walls. The bottom of the moat was covered with a blanket of yellowish weeds, and he guessed that the medieval-looking stronghold was at least two hundred years old.

The driver stopped in front of two armed soldiers posted at the gate and produced some papers. The soldiers waved him in, and the van drove through a tunnel-like entrance into an ample courtyard.

Greg stepped out of the van, escorted by the two military men. They held their submachine guns as a warning that he should not resist. Greg looked around, astounded. The place looked like a prison, with many armed soldiers on patrol.

The tiny registration room had a small, barred window high in the wall. A military man sat behind a table with a large registration book. His stern expression suggested that he thought the new prisoner was going to cause him more work. Greg stood in front of the table, and the two guards stood behind him, still gripping their weapons.

"Name?" the man said.

"Greg Elliot," he said.

"Nationality?"

"American."

The man arched an eyebrow and gave Greg a studied glance. Then he proceeded to write in the register. "Age?" he asked.

"Thirty-five."

The man scribbled again.

"I want to see a lawyer—an American lawyer," Greg said.

The man stopped writing. "The Revolution will assign you a lawyer," he said.

"I don't want your lawyer," Greg said.

"You don't understand—"

"I *do* understand," Greg interrupted. "I want an American lawyer, and I want to notify the people in charge of American affairs in Cuba that I'm here in jail."

The man dropped the pencil and closed the book brusquely. "You're accused of a grave crime, and the Revolution will give you a fair trial."

"I'm here illegally," Greg said. "You have no right to hold me here."

The man smiled. "We have every right. This is our country. We're not American slaves anymore. We're free people. You've committed a crime and you'll pay for it."

Greg shook his head and stepped close to the table. "I don't care about your rights. I want mine."

The man glanced at the soldiers and motioned to them to take Greg away. Greg started to protest, but the soldiers grabbed him by the arms, dragging him out of the room.

The sign on the door read, *Almacen,* which Greg didn't understand. The soldiers pushed him inside and he faced a small storeroom. In the back there were long shelves holding blue clothes, neatly folded, and a double row of shoes. One of the soldiers motioned to him to stand in front of a small counter where an old man in a blue uniform sat in a chair. The man stood up at the sight of the soldiers.

"Ropa para este," the soldier said.

The old man seemed nervous in the presence of the soldiers. He glanced at Greg, estimating his size, then walked to the shelves and picked up a pair of pants and a shirt. The man had a big C printed on the back of his shirt. Greg guessed that he, too, was a prisoner in the fortress. The man tossed the clothes on the counter and said to Greg, *"Desvistate."*

Greg didn't understand the word and didn't move. The man started to act out taking his clothes off, and then Greg understood.

The clothes were a little too big, but they were at least clean—very different from the jumpsuit he was wearing, soaked with vomit and with the latrine smell still on it. The shirt also had a large C printed on the back. Greg shook his head. He was one of them now.

The man dropped a pair of shoes on the counter and Greg tried them on. The shoes were too small, and the man brought a bigger pair, which were worn-out and stained, but much better than walking barefoot.

The next step was a stop in a little room that looked like a barber shop. Greg didn't recall ever having seen such an old barber chair. The floor was littered with hair, and a strong odor of disinfectant filled the room. Another old prisoner was in charge of the shop. He seemed eager to help and motioned Greg to the chair. Greg hesitated and was ready to protest when he saw the two soldiers grabbing their submachine guns. He climbed on the chair, and the old man put a stained apron over him. The soldiers walked out of the room and stood by the door, watching them.

"What're you going to do?" Greg asked, not expecting an answer from the man.

"You don't want to be full of lice. Y'know, *piojoso.*"

"You speak English."

"Poquito," the man said almost in a whisper. He reached for hand clippers and slowly started to cut Greg's hair. The clippers were dull and pulled his hair.

Greg grimaced. "It hurts," he said.

"Sorry—only tool I have."

"Where am I?" Greg asked, glancing at the two soldiers who were talking outside.

"You don't know?"

Greg shook his head and felt his hair being pulled. "Ouch!" he said.

"Sorry."

"Tell me, please."

"This is La Cabaña. A prison."

"Where?"

"Don't understand, *señor?"*

"Where in Cuba?"

"Ah—yes. At the other side of Havana Bay. You can see Havana from here."

"Any way to get a message out of here?" Greg asked.

The man worked on his hair harder and faster, and Greg felt the tension in him. "Sorry, *señor.* Too dangerous. Nobody gets out of here."

"Please, I must send a message to the people in charge of American affairs in Havana."

"No . . . no. Impossible."

The man started to cut the hair around the area where Dmitri had hit him, and Greg grimaced. "That hurts."

"Sorry."

"My name's Greg Elliot. I want to send a message out to the Americans. You've got to help me. Please."

"You're wasting your time."

"I don't understand."

"Nobody gets out of here." The man paused as he walked around the chair to cut the hair on the other side of Greg's head.

The bump on Greg's head was throbbing painfully. Greg felt nauseated; his eyes were bloodshot, and his thoughts whirled inside his head. He was going mad, losing all control. He had to send a message, let somebody know that he was in Havana; that the Communists wanted to try him; that his life was in danger; that the KGB had taken Andrea.

He felt a scream building in his chest, and he grabbed the armrest of the chair, pressing his nails into the wood. He had to convince the man to send out a message. This was his last chance . . . his very last.

"Please," he begged again. "I need your help. You're my last hope."

The man looked at the soldiers, then at Greg, sweeping some hair off his shoulder. "There's only one way out of here, *señor*," he said.

"Which way?"

"It's down to the moat. Once you go there, you never come back walking. They have a firing squad waiting for you . . . and a pine box. . . ."

CHAPTER 21

The man on the motorcycle was skillful and daring, skirting the busy Manhattan traffic, zigzagging his way through the slow-moving mass of vehicles. The quick maneuvering scared Andrea, and she hugged the man harder. Soon he sped along the George Washington Bridge, and the air ruffled Andrea's hair. She dared to open her eyes to look at the city from the height of the bridge. It was a mesmerizing view.

Exiting the bridge, they rode for a few more minutes. Andrea thought they might already be in New Jersey and was happy. There was no way for Grigori to recapture her. He'd never figure out the man on the motorcycle had helped her.

Beyond Willowbrook Shopping Mall she saw a huge parking lot packed with cars. At the center of the lot was a long stretch of seemingly connected buildings. The man took a peripheral road around the parking lot, bypassing several lines of cars inching into the place. Soon the man reached the rear of the shopping center and steered into a short, dead-end street. A few old buildings stood on both sides. Andrea loosened her grip as the man parked the motorcycle in front of a one-story building: it was a bar. At least a dozen motorcycles were parked in front, and Andrea and the man got off the motorcycle.

"Well, thank you for giving me a lift," she said, preparing to leave.

The man grabbed Andrea's arm. "Not so fast, ma'am. How about a drink?" He looked at her as if he were seeing her for the first time.

Andrea winced in pain and started to answer, when the man walked toward the bar and through the door, dragging her along.

"I'm not interested," she said finally.

The man seemed not to hear her and kept ahold of her arm. The smoke-filled room was crowded and at the polished wooden bar, a long line of patrons on stools held drinks and cigarettes. Behind the counter, a large fat man in red suspenders agilely mixed drinks, passing them to a young waitress. The motorcycle man and Andrea walked past the counter, stopping at the end. He made room at the counter for them as the few tables in the center of the room were full. In one corner a couple of long-haired guys in leather outfits studied the selections on an old jukebox.

The motorcycle man snapped his fingers, calling the fat bartender. The chains on his wrist rattled in Andrea's face, and his muscular arm almost touched her. Andrea turned her face away. The bartender looked in their direction and the motorcycle man yelled for a couple of drafts. Andrea wanted to run, but the motorcycle man had his hand on the counter next to her. She wouldn't be able to get very far if he wanted to stop her. Andrea looked around; she had to find a way out.

The bartender approached the counter with two beer mugs. "Great lookin' suspenders, Bruce," the motorcycle man said.

"Nice company," the bartender said, eyeing Andrea.

Both men laughed maliciously.

Andrea started to move away from the counter, but the man grabbed her arm. "Drink your beer," he said.

"I'm not thirsty," she said.

"Maybe you want to drink in private," the man said. "We've got a small room in the back. We can have fun, huh?" He grinned, displaying a set of yellow, rotting teeth.

Andrea shook her head, frowning. "You don't understand. I don't want a drink. I want to leave now."

The man drank half of his beer, slammed the mug on the counter, and wiped the beer off his mustache with the back of his hand. "You're pissin' me off, ma'am."

Andrea swallowed hard, summoning up some courage. "If you don't let me go, I'm going to scream until the police come."

"Don't get bitchy, ma'am. We can talk this over."

"I have to go," she insisted.

"You don't like my company, huh? How come you came with me?"

"Somebody was after me. I had to get away."

"Somebody?"

"Yes."

"You in trouble?"

"God! Now you're listening to me. The FBI was looking for me," she lied.

The man opened his eyes. "What for?"

"I'm a Russian spy."

The man exploded into a laugh and pounded the top of the counter with his open hand. "You a Russian spy," he laughed again, pounding the counter. "Yeah! Nobody's pulled that one on me before. Ma'am, you're . . . ha-ha . . . too much . . . ha-ha. . . ." He stopped laughing suddenly, and grabbed Andrea's beer, glaring at her. "Hey, babe, get your ass out of here. You ain't foolin' me."

Andrea ran out of the bar and stopped in the middle of the street. Her best choice was to walk to the mall and find a public phone. She had to call someone for help. She didn't know if she wanted to call the police or the FBI. They both scared her, and she wasn't sure they'd even believe her. After all, she *was* a Russian spy. She thought again of Greg. Every minute that passed made things worse for him. Who knew where Dmitri had taken him?

She ran to the street and across the parking lot, stopping a few times to catch her breath and ignoring the curious eyes of the people inside the cars. The mall was about a hundred yards from the bar, and she approached the first entrance she saw. People stared at her as she entered the department store. She was panting and poorly dressed, her hair in disarray. She wondered whether someone would call the police; that would solve her problem real fast.

She looked around, disoriented. Waves of people were shopping, oblivious to their surroundings. There were "30% off" and "Sale" signs everywhere. She felt like screaming, telling them she needed help, that the KGB had taken Greg away, that his life was in danger. She bit her lip, killing the scream inside her before it reached her throat. Nobody'd believe her. Her only hope was the FBI. They were already looking for her and Greg. They knew the truth.

A phone . . . where's a phone? she thought frantically, but there were no phones in sight. She stepped into the mall and a wave of shoppers caught up with her, dragging her along. As she walked, she pushed and shoved, elbowing the people around her. Several hands pushed her back and stern eyes glared at her. Others muttered angrily, but she paid no attention. She had to find a phone . . . soon.

She stopped suddenly, turning on her heels. She had caught a glimpse of a phone booth just a few steps away. A young boy licking an ice-cream cone was on the phone. The ice cream was dripping all over him and the booth. Andrea stopped next to the boy and pointed to the phone. The boy ignored Andrea and continued talking. She thought of looking for another phone when the boy slammed the receiver back and glared at her. "You can have it now, ma'am," he said, ice cream all over his mouth.

Andrea picked up the receiver and listened to the dial tone. The phone was sticky, but she didn't care. She was ready to dial the operator to ask for the FBI number when another number came to mind. She could call collect and was sure they'd accept the call at the other end.

She dialed zero, asked to make a collect call, and told the operator the number. After a couple of seconds, a voice said, "Carmensita Fuentes del Rio."

The operator asked for authorization for the collect call. "Who's calling?" Carmensita asked.

"Andrea . . . Valeri Lisenko," Andrea said.

"Sure . . . sure, I accept the call," Carmensita said. "Valeri, where are you?"

Andrea hesitated, not knowing if she was doing the right thing. It was too late now. "Carmensita, please listen to me. I'm in serious trouble—"

"Sorry, I don't understand," Carmensita interrupted.

"Please," Andrea said. "I'm not with the Soviet Mission anymore." She paused. "I'm KGB, and I've defected."

"What!"

"I need your help. The KGB is looking for me. If they get

me, I'll be as good as dead. They've already kidnapped my husband, Greg Elliot." The word *husband* sounded strange to her. She kept talking. "I want to get in touch with the FBI. They must help Greg. I don't know where the KGB have taken him."

"Where are you?"

"I'm in New Jersey . . . a shopping mall. The name is Willowbrook. I don't know the way."

"I know the place. It's in Fairfield. We'll find it."

"Can you get in touch with the FBI?"

"They'll be there right away. Please, stay out of sight. Wait for the FBI at the main entrance. I'll make sure they send someone you know."

Andrea took a deep breath. Carmensita's words were reassuring. "I won't move," she said.

Dmitri fought the impulse to pull out his gun and put a bullet between Grigori's eyes. He couldn't believe Andrea had escaped.

Right after he'd received Grigori's message informing him of the events, he had ordered Grigori to abandon the safe house immediately. He also had told Grigori to meet him at a backup place on an abandoned pier on the New Jersey side of the Hudson River. Dmitri wanted to evaluate the situation and draw up a contingency plan. Andrea had probably gone directly to the FBI, spoiling everything they'd planned. Another thought upset Dmitri: he had to inform Moscow of the escape, a task he wasn't looking forward to. Geidar Aligev would be angry. The Deputy Premier of the First Chief Directorate had made it very clear when he'd handed him the assignment that there could be no mistakes.

"I have all the men out looking for her," Grigori said, a sad look on his face.

Dmitri paced around Grigori, still feeling the urge to shoot him. "We might as well assume she's in the hands of the FBI by now," he said. "The chance of finding her in Manhattan is like finding a needle in a haystack."

"There aren't that many places she could go," Grigori said. "I've got men covering every FBI outpost. We'll know if they have her."

"You know we're risking a summary trial in Moscow," Dmitri said. "Aligev doesn't want to hear we have failed. This is a major operation, and we must control Andrea."

Grigori lowered his head, grimacing. "I know, comrade. I failed you."

They were inside a small warehouse at the end of the pier. There was no electricity in the place. The only light came through holes in the roof and walls. They both had driven inside the building to keep the cars out of sight. The faint light cast shadows on Grigori's face, distorting his features. The bastard already looked dead. He only needed a shot in the back of the head. Again Dmitri struggled with the thought—one muffled shot.

"I'm going to contact the rezident at the Mission," Dmitri said, turning his back to Grigori. "We must have every available man looking for Andrea." He paused and turned his head, looking over his shoulder. "I want you out there, too. I want Andrea back. Is that clear?"

Grigori nodded. "You'll have Andrea," he said, walking toward his car. Dmitri watched him go. He should've shot the bastard. Andrea's escape had jeopardized three years of careful preparation.

Greg, escorted by two soldiers, walked slowly along a corridor, oblivious to the echoing of the steps on the stone floor. The semidark, tunnel-like corridor had a long string of metal doors on both sides and ended in a stone wall with a small window sealed with iron bars. As he walked, Greg recalled a similar setting, the world of the Master Pauper. He couldn't believe he was in that world now—a world of steel doors, stone hallways and walls, iron bars, small windows, darkness and stale air. Only the bats were missing.

He wished he had the spells. He could used them now. Perhaps this was all a dream and soon he'd stop in front of a door and use his magic to get out and be free. Unfortunately, he knew no spells. The KGB had trapped him, Pauper, and they'd never let him go. He could not save Andrea. Pauper and Beggar were lost forever. What an illusion! Their love had lasted only a few hours. He should've known better.

As he walked, he heard noises inside the cells, like people crawling on the floor. He wondered who was inside—probably paupers like him, with no spells and no magic. One of the soldiers told him to halt, then inserted a key into a cell lock and pulled the door open. The old, rusty hinges squeaked. The small cell with stone walls, floor, and ceiling contained a bunk bed with a bare mattress and no blankets or pillow. Greg noticed the hole in the floor in one corner of the cell. The air around it stank like the latrine on the ship. So that was the bathroom. The soldier motioned him inside, and he silently obeyed. The door slammed shut and he was all alone.

He slowly sank down into the bunk bed and glanced around the cell. There was not much to it, just old stones everywhere. He didn't feel like looking into the hole in the floor. The smell told him what was inside. His head still ached and he raised his hand to caress the top of his head. His shaved head felt like sandpaper. He was glad he didn't have a mirror. He didn't want to see his face; he had to look terrible.

The man in the barber shop had refused to send the message, and Greg realized the man was too terrified to help him. Perhaps by word of mouth other prisoners could get the message out. He had told the man his name. No, he thought, that was wishful thinking. Unless he took action, he could not hope for a break. There was nothing he could do at the moment except wait.

He lay down on the mattress and crossed his arms behind his head, using them as pillow. Staring blankly at the ceiling, he thought of Andrea. He had no idea where she was at the moment. Dmitri had said she was on her way to Moscow. Perhaps the Russian had misled him and she was still in the U.S. He wished he knew. He wished her good luck. They both were going to need lots of it.

The steps sounded far away but came nearer. He sat up on the bed, listening carefully. Yes, they were approaching. Greg got up and pressed his ear to the iron door. Two people were coming. The footsteps stopped in front of his cell and he hurried to the bed and sat down. The lock turned and the door squeaked open. A soldier holding a submachine gun stood in the doorway.

The soldier stepped aside to let another man, dressed in military fatigues, walk in. The man was tall, in his late sixties, gaunt, and balding. He had no weapons but was carrying a folder. The soldier closed the door. "I'm Lieutenant Garcia," the man said in accented English. "I'm your lawyer."

Greg stepped back to make room for the man. "Greg Elliot," he said, without extending his hand.

Lieutenant Garcia glanced around as if looking for a place to sit and Greg didn't offer the bed. He had no reason to be polite to the bastard.

"Are you really a lawyer?" Greg asked.

Garcia nodded. "I've been a lawyer all my life," he said proudly.

Greg took a deep breath and got a strong whiff of the smell coming from the hole in the floor. "You're also in the military," he said.

"That's the only way I can defend people."

"I don't understand."

"These people won't let a civil lawyer defend prisoners." He paused, then added. "It's a big risk, because if I don't do what they say, they can courtmartial me, too."

Greg studied Garcia's sagging, sad face and clear but evasive eyes. His expression reminded Greg of an English teacher he'd had in high school. They both wore the same sad look. Perhaps Garcia could help him, he thought. "Are you really going to defend me?" he asked.

Garcia took a few seconds to answer. Finally he stared into Greg's eyes and said, "This is a very difficult case, you know."

"They don't have a case," Greg said. "I'm innocent."

"Everybody says the same thing," Garcia said in a matter-of-fact tone, a trace of a smile at the corner of his mouth.

"I don't care what the other people say. I'm innocent."

Garcia opened the folder and looked inside. "They have pictures of you in Berlin," he said. "They're sure you were there at the time that Boris Alexei Grishin was shot." He dipped a hand into a pocket and pulled out a cigarette pack. "Do you want a smoke?" he said.

Greg shook his head.

"Mind if I smoke?"

"Yes, I do. The cell's too small and it already smells."

Garcia looked at the pack for a moment, then slid it back into the same pocket. "Want to tell me what you were doing in Berlin?" he said.

"I was there because I wanted to see the swapping of Andrea Hendrick," he paused. "She's my wife. I had no other reason."

"Sounds reasonable, but it won't work. They claim that Boris was waiting for you."

"I never saw him alive."

"They don't believe that."

"What happens if the CIA killed him?"

"Good guess," Garcia said. "They believe you're a CIA spy, and that Langley ordered you to kill Boris."

"I'm not a killer," Greg protested.

"Anybody can be a killer," Garcia said, "given the right circumstances."

Greg lowered his head and leaned against the wall, gazing at the floor. He was not making much progress with Garcia. "I don't want to offend you," he said, "but what if I want an outside lawyer?"

Garcia shook his head. "I'm the only choice you've got."

"This is what they call justice."

"Justice has many forms."

"Don't give me that bullshit."

Garcia closed the folder. "The trial is tomorrow."

"They can't wait, huh?" Greg said.

"You'll find out that Cuban military tribunals are very efficient . . . and fast."

"I don't understand."

"The trial will last only a few minutes. They'll find you guilty or innocent, and the sentence will follow immediately."

Greg couldn't believe Garcia's words. They were going to try him for killing Boris! The KGB bastard had absolutely deserved the bullet he got.

"You know they kidnaped me here. They have no legal

grounds."

"It makes no difference. You're here now."

"What are my choices?" he asked.

Garcia cleared his throat and looked at the folder for a moment, as if mentally reviewing the case. "This is a very clear-cut case," he answered. "I've seen them many times in the past. Always the same facts . . . the same results. I advise you to plead guilty—"

"What! Guilty—fuck, no!"

"Calm down. You've got no other choice. You should plead guilty, and I can ask for mercy." He paused. "Perhaps they'll commute your sentence to twenty or thirty years."

Greg stepped back. "Are you serious?"

"Yes, I am. This approach works in about ten percent of the cases."

"What about if I want a trial?"

"They'll find you guilty."

"Then?"

"They'll shoot you the next morning."

CHAPTER 22

Hansen flipped a page of *Time* magazine and glanced at a picture. He then closed the magazine abruptly and tossed it on the table. How could he sit there and read? He should never have agreed to stay in the safe house and wait. There was nothing worse than waiting when he was under stress; it drove him nuts. A drink of water might help.

He got up from the chair and walked over to the small refrigerator, opened it, and pulled out a Perrier. With a quick twist of the cap, he poured half the water into a cup and took a long drink.

He was alone in the safe house. Maguire had left an hour ago to meet Taylor at the main FBI building for a meeting with some high-ranking CIA official from Langley. The events had frustrated everybody, making Maguire and Taylor short-tempered. They all feared the worst for Greg and Andrea. Hansen sighed and took another sip from the cup.

Maguire had asked him to stay next to the phone in case something new developed. The morning had been slow, and the wait was unnerving him. He wished he could do something concrete to help Greg. After all, he was the one who went to California to get Greg involved. He felt sorry for Greg. He should've left him alone.

The phone rang, and he walked around the table to reach it. "Hansen," he said.

"Is Maguire in?" a woman's voice said. "It's urgent."

"He's not available right now," he said. "Who're you?"

"Listen," the voice said urgently. "I work with Maguire. I have to give him a message."

"I'm Maguire's assistant. How did you get this number?"

"No time for explanations," she said. "Tell Maguire that I just received a call from Andrea Hendrick."

"What? Are you serious?"

"I said no questions. Please, tell Maguire that Andrea is free. She just called me from a shopping mall—Willowbrook in Fairfield, New Jersey. She's scared. She claims the KGB kidnaped her husband, Greg Elliot." She paused, then added, "I told Andrea not to move and to wait for somebody she could trust. Maguire must pick her up right away. Andrea might run away to another place. Do it now!" The woman hung up, and Hansen stared at the receiver, astounded. Andrea was free! Jesus Christ! Somebody had to go for her immediately. There was no time to waste.

Without hesitating, he ran to the car. He knew the area; he could be there in twenty minutes. Andrea was free! He couldn't believe it. He turned the ignition and drove to the exit. The door seemed to take forever to roll up. As soon as he could drive under it, he gunned the gas pedal, pressing the remote control to close the door behind him. He headed for the Lincoln Tunnel. Willowbrook was about fifteen miles away.

Speeding through the tunnel and onto the highway, he skirted a few slow-moving vehicles to get into the fast lane. Then he realized he hadn't radioed Maguire with the news. He should have asked for an FBI backup unit. Still, he was the best one to pick up Andrea. She knew him well and would go with him willingly.

Hansen reached for the mike and called the central unit. It took a few seconds for the voice to come over the radio's speaker. "This is Hansen," he said. "I have an urgent message for Maguire." He paused. "I also want a backup unit."

Nagishkin grabbed the steering wheel with both hands, stretching his neck, trying to keep his eyes on the car speeding in front of him. By pure luck he had not lost the car in the heavy Manhattan traffic. Then the light traffic in the Lincoln tunnel had helped him. If he lost Hansen on the highway, he'd be as good as dead. Grigori had ordered him to keep an eye on the safe house in the Garment district. Grigori had said that he should tail Hansen wherever the CIA man went and also that if he lost Hansen even once, it'd be the end of his career and probably his life. Nagishkin knew he was risking his twenty years in the KGB, not to mention the pension he so badly wanted. Worse than that, he didn't want to end up buried in the New Jersey meadowlands with a bullet through his head. He thought of the many Mafia people buried there. He didn't want that kind of company, even in death.

He had seen Hansen driving away from the safe house like a maniac, breaking every law in the book. Something very important must have happened, Nagishkin said to himself.

Once in New Jersey, Nagishkin used the scanner to see if he could intercept any radio contact. To his dismay, he couldn't latch onto Hansen's transmitter. The bastard was probably using a scrambler. One thing he could do was to contact his own people. He had the hunch that Hansen was onto something important, and he had better tell Grigori.

After two tries, he got Grigori on the radio. "What's happening?" Grigori asked.

Nagishkin gave Grigori a quick update, using common language codewords. Hansen was the fish man, and Nagishkin said that Hansen was driving as if his tail were on fire.

"Stick with him," Grigori ordered. "I'm not very far from where you are now. I'll join you right away."

Nagishkin put the mike down and stamped on the gas pedal. Grigori sounded exited and Nagishkin smelled a breakthrough. If they could get Andrea back, he'd be a hero, deserving at least the Medal of Lenin. With so much clout, he would have no trouble securing a nice pension.

Andrea glanced at the entrance of the mall for what seemed to be the one-hundredth time. Inside a store, about fifty yards from the main entrance, behind a few racks of clothes, she pretended she was looking at them. She guessed that she had called Carmensita more than an hour ago. She wondered why it was taking so long for someone to come for her. She had no watch, but she was sure they should've had enough time by now.

A new thought sent a chill of terror through her. What if

Carmensita were a KGB agent? Oh, God! She'd call Dmitri instead of the FBI. Carmensita had hired her from the Soviet Mission. The KGB always boasted that they had many agents at the UN. Could Carmensita be one of them? She had not given any thought to that possibility. What a mistake!

Maybe she should leave the mall immediately and call the FBI from another place. But what if the KGB was already looking for her in the mall? The last thing she wanted was to go into the parking lot alone. They'd grab her and force her into a car in a split second. She started to shake, wishing she had her pills. She couldn't believe they'd capture her again.

Slowly, she walked around the rack of clothes to get a better view of the entrance. The store had no back door, so nobody could surprise her from behind, but it was also impossible for her to escape. The only way out was the front.

There was a mirror near her, and she took a jacket from a hanger and acted as if she was trying it on. She looked different in the jacket; perhaps she should keep trying on things for a few minutes more.

A man walking in a group of people entered the mall. Andrea's eyes rested on him; it was Hansen. He was rushing around as if looking for someone. Andrea was sure he was looking for her. Thank God it was not the KGB. She took the jacket off and walked around the clothes racks, rushing toward the door. She was not sure yet how to approach Hansen. At that moment, he saw her and waved a hand. Andrea gave a sigh of relief; she was in good hands.

"We've got no time to waste," Hansen said. "We'll have a FBI backup unit shortly. Where's Greg?"

Andrea shook her head. "I don't know. They took him away as soon as we left the motel."

"Jesus!" Hansen said, grabbing Andrea by the arm and guiding her toward the exit. "I have a car parked in front," he added. "Let's hurry up."

They ran the last few steps to the car, Hansen's keys in his hand. He opened the door swiftly and let Andrea get in the back. "Stay down," he said. "I don't want anyone to see you."

Andrea obeyed, dropping to the floor of the car. She was trembling, and her stomach hurt more than ever. Breathing hard, and fighting for control, she bit her lips and asked, "Where are we going?"

"Back to New York. The FBI should be here any moment," Hansen said, starting the car. "We'll meet them in the parking lot."

He drove away and Andrea, nauseated, pressed her head against the seat. She clutched the seat with both hands, nails piercing the vinyl. She had to control herself. She had to help Greg. *"Control . . . Control . . ."* she mumbled.

They had been riding for a short time when Hansen braked suddenly, hurling her against the front seat. Andrea screamed. She heard Hansen cursing, then shouting. She pulled herself up from the floor and saw a car in front of them blocking the way. Another car was pulling up from behind, also blocking them in the middle lane of the parking lot.

Hansen put the car into reverse and hit the gas pedal, crashing into the car behind him. The impact thrust Andrea backward. She grabbed the front seat to keep her balance, still not understanding what had happened.

A man rushed to the driver's window as Hansen shifted the car into forward. The man had a gun aimed at Hansen's head. Andrea looked at the man and screamed. She recognized Grigori.

Greg didn't recall ever being in such a pitch-black darkness. Everywhere he looked, he saw nothing. He lay on the bunk bed, his arms crossed behind his head, staring into the darkness. The only relation to physical space he felt was the sensation of being inside the cell and the smell—the terrible, foul smell coming from the hole in the floor.

For some reason he didn't understand, he felt the small cell closing in on him as if at any moment the walls, floor, and ceiling would crush him. He shook his head at the thought. He had to control his emotions and try to keep his sanity intact—at least for the little time he had left.

After Garcia left, they brought him some food—if the sticky, maggot-infested ball of rice could be called food. It was accompanied by something that resembled a potato but tasted completely different. The guard had opened the door of the cell and put the plate and a small plastic cup with water on the floor. The guard then said he had five minutes to eat and kept glancing at a watch he had in his hand. Greg was not hungry but knew he had to eat to keep up his energy. He had had not food for three days. There was not fork or spoon, so he had to eat with his hands. He felt like thowing up when he saw the maggots, but he pushed himself to eat them, closing his eyes and telling himself that they were protein. He still felt the maggots moving in his mouth as he chewed them with the rice.

The potato-shaped thing was bland and needed some salt. Then, after exactly five minutes, the guard grabbed his submachine gun and asked for the plate. Miraculously enough, Greg didn't become ill from the food.

At first he thought he was alone in the tunnel-like corridor, but then he could hear the guard repeating the dinner routine in several other cells. He was able to count the doors opening and closing and the five minute intervals. In one of the cells, a prisoner started to scream and threw the plate at the guard. He shouted in Spanish and sounded as if he was crying.

Greg turned sideways on the bed, being careful to avoid putting pressure on the bump on his head. Andrea came into his mind. He wondered where she was at that moment and if she was thinking of him. For three years he'd worried about her, not knowing if she was dead or alive. Now he knew she still loved him, but he worried about what was going to happen to her. Ironically, he had come full circle again: now it didn't matter anymore. He had no control over his destiny, and Andrea was in the same situation. Maguire and Hansen and the CIA and the FBI with all their power wouldn't be able to do a thing to help either of them.

The sound of footsteps startled him out of his light sleep. To his surprise, a bit of weak light filtered into his cell through the cracks in the door, and he guessed that dawn had arrived. The steps sounded as if five or six military men were marching; their boots struck the floor almost in unison. A voices shouted an order and the steps stopped. Then the shouts started, sounding as if they were coming through a long tunnel. Greg realized that the sounds came from the other prisoners, shouting in Spanish and pounding on their cell doors. The military voice shouted more orders, but the voices in the cells didn't stop.

"*Asesinos . . . criminales . . . pigs . . .*" the voice shouted.

Greg got up weakly, lost his balance, and fell, hitting his head on the wall. Painfully, he tried to pull himself up from the floor by using the wall as a support, but the surface was slick and his hands slipped. He rolled over on his back and stayed quiet for a few moments, breathing fast and biting his lip to avoid screaming in pain. Somebody opened a door. A man shouted and cried, alternately begging and insulting the guards.

He heard more shouting, then a scuffle, as if people were fighting, pushing, and hitting someone. More cries followed. Greg shook as he crawled to the front of the cell and pressed his head against the floor, trying to see something through the small gap at the bottom of the door. But he saw only the floor and a few inches of the cell door across from his.

The noise from the other cells grew louder as the prisoners pounded on the metal doors with their fists. The man's screaming increased, followed by shouts. He heard them walking again—not marching. The man broke into sobbing. The other prisoners continued to shout, calling out a name he didn't understand.

The steps went past his cell, and Greg saw boots and the feet of a man being dragged along. Then came the last pair of boots, those belonging to the commander of the unit.

The muffled voices in the cells started to sing, a song that had the candence of a hymn. Greg didn't understand the words. *Al combate corred, Bayameses, que la patria os comtempla orgullosa; no temais una muerte gloriosa. . . .* Shaking badly, Greg passed his hands over his face and realized that he was crying.

The pounding and singing lasted a few more minutes, then started to diminish. At the end, only a single weak, hoarse voice from the far end of the corridor kept on for a while. Then it faded and stopped, and an eerie silence descended over the place; Greg heard nothing, not a voice, not a movement, as if the men inside the cells held their breaths to minimize any sounds.

Greg didn't understand the reason for the silence. Slowly he turned on his side and used his hands to push himself up to a sitting position against the wall. His eyes were still on the gap under the door, his only window to the outside world. He tried to avoid making any sound. He didn't know why, but he felt compelled to do the same as the other prisoners. Then he thought of calling to them, to ask what was happening, but he didn't. They probably didn't speak English, and the silence overwhelmed him.

He thought of the man the soldiers had dragged out of the cell, wondering where they had taken him. Greg hadn't understood a word of the shouting, begging, and singing. God! What was happening to the other prisoners—and him? How was all of this possible? Was it real? Or was it just a terrible nightmare from which he'd awaken soon?

Rivulets of sweat ran down his forehead and he wiped them off, then touched his face. He had not shaved or bathed in days. Had it been three days? A week? He had lost all sense of time. The days seemed to be an almost uninterrupted stretch of time; he hardly knew when one day ended and the next began, and he was sure he was going mad.

A short succession of shots sounded like a burst of fire. They were spaced far enough apart for him to realize several people were shooting. The shots were far away, but the sound was loud enough to frighten Greg. Silence followed. A moment later he heard a single pistol shot. Greg clasped both hands together to stop his trembling. The shouts in the cells started again and the prisoners pounded on the cell doors. He tried to understand the words, but the prisoners spoke too fast, in a nonstop string of words. Still, Greg understood what had happened; it was clear now. A firing squad had just shot the prisoner. Greg buried his face in his hands and cried.

He didn't know how long he had been sitting on the floor crying when the sound of boots woke him from his stupor. The footsteps stopped in front of his cell. Greg got up, struggling to keep his balance, and managed to sit on the bed. He wiped his face with his hand to take away any trace of tears; he didn't want the bastards to know he'd been crying. His eyes burned and his vision was fuzzy. The cell door opened with a screeching sound and the bright daylight poured in. Greg squinted and made out the silhouette of a soldier standing in the doorway, submachine gun in hand.

"Get out," the soldier said.

Greg didn't move.

"Get out," the soldier said again, pointing his weapon at Greg.

"Where am I going?" Greg asked weakly, his voice strange to his ears.

"Trial," the soldier said.

Slowly, he stood up and walked hesitantly toward the door, as if he were too weak to stand on his feet. The soldier moved aside, making room for him. Three other soldiers waited outside, all armed with submachine guns.

"I don't know if I can walk," Greg said.

"Walk," the solider said with a frown.

As they walked along the corridor, Greg heard the sound of boots hitting the stone floor and thought of the man the soldiers had dragged away early that morning. He wondered if his turn would come and what he would do. There was no sense in fighting at the last moment. The bastards would take him anyway. He then thought of his brother John, wishing he could talk to him. Maybe he'd join John soon.

The windowless room was sparsely furnished with a long table, five wooden chairs, and a metal chair facing the table. Desktop lamps sat on the long table and two spot lights in the ceiling were trained on the metal chair. The stale, humid air made Greg think that they were in the basement of the fortress. One of the soldiers pointed at the metal chair with his submachine gun. Greg sat, glad he didn't have to stand anymore. His legs shook badly and he couldn't hold his weight any longer. The soldiers split in two groups, standing on guard a few feet from him. He looked at the table, the chairs, the lamps, and the room. He couldn't believe that all of this was real. He closed his eyes, hoping to awaken from this nightmare.

The door opened and a man entered whom Greg recognized as Garcia, his lawyer. Garcia walked up to him and nodded in recognition, but Greg stared at him and said nothing. Garcia looked nervous. Perhaps he was worried that they'd sentence him, too.

"They're coming," Garcia said.

CHAPTER 23

The soldiers grabbed their weapons firmly, squared their shoulders, and clicked their heels. Five men in military fatigues entered the room. Silently they walked around the table and stood facing Greg. The man in the middle of the group caught Greg's attention. He recognized the steely eyes and bearded face of the military man who resembled Fidel Castro. Greg tried to remember the man's name but couldn't. He knew only that the man was a general in the Cuban DGI. "Stand up," the general said.

Greg didn't move.

"Stand up," the general said again, scowling.

Garcia reached down and whispered in Greg's ear, "General Carreras wants you to stand."

One of the soldiers stepped forward and shoved the barrel of his submachine gun into Greg's back.

Greg stood up.

Carreras opened a folder and glanced at a piece of paper inside. "State your name."

"Greg Elliot."

"Residence?"

"Los Altos Hills, California."

Carreras raised his eyes for a moment, studying Greg, then looked down at the document again. "You are accused of killing the Soviet citizen Boris Alexei Grishin. The trial is formally open." He glanced at the other men around him and they all sat down.

Greg didn't move. "I'm an American citizen," he said. "The KGB brought me here illegally. I want an American lawyer."

"You won't get very far with this," Garcia said to Greg. "General," he said, looking up at Carreras. "In the name of the

Revolution, I want to plead for mercy for the accused."

Greg glared at Garcia. "You've no right to plead anything for me! I haven't given you any authorization!" He took a small step forward and two of the soldiers rushed to his side, readying their weapons.

Carreras raised a hand, ordering the soldiers to do nothing. "You don't understand," Carreras said.

"Yes, I do," Greg shouted. "This is a set-up. You've no right—"

Carreras struck the table with his fist and shot to his feet. "You Americans still believe you own Cuba. You're wrong. You're in *our* country. We're not slaves anymore. You've committed a crime and you're going to pay for it." He motioned to the two soldiers. They grabbed Greg by the shoulders and pushed him down into the chair.

Carreras glared angrily at Greg for a few seconds, his lips tight, his breath coming in short gasps.

"General, the accused didn't mean to enrage the tribunal," Garcia said quietly. "He's confused. The cell and the surrounding are unfamiliar to him."

"What were you doing in Berlin on the day Boris Alexei Grishin was shot?" asked an older man sitting at one end of the table.

"You might as well find me guilty," Greg said.

"Do you want a trial or not?" Carreras said. "We can still sentence you."

"You call this a trial?" Greg said.

Garcia put his hand on Greg's shoulder, pressing hard. "We want a trial, General." He looked at Greg and added, "Please stay seated."

Greg could hear his own fast breathing. He almost said something when Garcia gripped his shoulder harder.

"Please, answer the question," Garcia said to Greg.

"I went to Berlin to see the swapping of my wife Andrea Hendrick for a CIA spy."

"Your wife?" Carreras said.

Greg noticed the expression of surprise that briefly crossed Carreras' face, as if the information was new to him. "Yes," Greg said. "We got married on a trip to Reno, Nevada."

"Who arranged the swapping?" asked the man at the end of the table.

"Boris did."

"Why did he do that?" asked another man.

Greg looked at the man—the military uniform, the medals on his chest, the stern, almost inhuman expression on his face.

"Boris had sent me a message a month before, telling me he could swap Andrea for an old spy the CIA wanted very badly. He offered to use Andrea for the swap if I agreed to give him the information he wanted."

"What information?" Carreras asked.

Greg took a moment to answer, leaning back in the metal chair. He felt weak, the spotlights making him perspire profusely. The room seemed to be moving. He rubbed his forehead, blinking his eyes a few times. "Listen," he said. "I've committed no crime. If you want to find me guilty, you'll be making a mistake. I'm innocent—"

Garcia interrupted him again, grabbing his shoulder. "We want to continue, general."

"What information? Carreras pursued.

"Boris wanted the Blue Cube cipher codes," Greg said weakly.

"Blue Cube?"

"Yes."

"What's the Blue Cube?"

"I can't tell you."

"Yes, you can."

Garcia shook Greg by the shoulder again. "Please, answer," he said.

Greg took a deep breath, feeling the sweat rolling down his face. "The Blue Cube is a Satellite Control Facility in Sunnyvale, California."

"Did you work there?"

"Yes."

"What type of work?"

"I'm a programmer."

"What kind of satellites?"

"Can't tell you."

Carreras moved forward in his chair and rested his elbows on the table, looking up into Greg's eyes. "Spy satellites?"

"I'm not gonna answer."

"Your choice," Carreras said. "You worked for the Blue Cube, and our intelligence tells us that the Blue Cube controls the spy satellites for the CIA, the same spy satellites that violate Cuban airspace. You work for the CIA, and you're spying on all the free countries of the world—"

"I'm *not* a CIA spy!" Greg shouted.

"Yes, you are," Carreras snarled back.

"For the record," Garcia said. "I want to point out that Mr. Elliot was never a field spy—"

"I said that I've never worked for the CIA in my life. I'm not a CIA spy," Greg said, interrupting Garcia.

"Let's go back to the day when comrade Boris was shot," another man said. "What did you do after Andrea Hendrick crossed the bridge?"

Greg rubbed his eyes and forehead. They were trying to break him down, to make him confess that he'd killed Boris. The trial was a farce—a circus. The bastards were playing with him, trying to crush his spirit, whatever spirit he had left. He felt the urge to stop talking and quit playing their game. They'd find him guilty no matter what he said. He was ready to say, *Fuck you,* when he recalled Garcia's words. Perhaps he could get a life sentence; then he could send a message to the people in charge of the American interests in Havana. Perhaps they could apply diplomatic pressure on the Cubans. Perhaps he could get out of Cuba. *Perhaps.* So many unknowns. His chances of surviving were slim, but he had to try. He had to stay alive. He wanted to get out of there. He had to think of Andrea.

"I walked to an area of the park where Boris was waiting for me," he said slowly, as if thinking out every word before he said it.

"Then you shot him?" the man said.

"Jesus Christ! How many times do I have to tell you that I didn't kill Boris." He returned the man's stare. They had no way of knowing the truth. Nobody did.

"Then what happened?" the man went on.

"I got to the car and found Boris dead . . . shot in the head. I panicked and ran away. I didn't tell anybody. I took a plane for California."

"Why didn't you go to the police?" the man pursued.

"I got scared and fled. I thought the killer might be around."

"Who do you think shot Boris?" the man went on, not giving up.

Greg shook his head. "Don't know, maybe the KGB."

"The KGB had no reason to do it. Boris was successful," Carreras cut in.

Greg shrugged. "Then it was the CIA."

"You're right," Carreras said. "The CIA killed him. But it was you. Boris was a very experienced agent. He'd have put up a fight if he'd seen someone different from the person he was expecting. He saw you coming and never thought the CIA had ordered you to shoot him. You killed him, shot him in the eye. It was cold-blooded murder."

Greg stood up. "You're lying! I've never killed anybody. I'm innocent. This is a farce, a fucking farce."

One of the soldiers rushed over to him and hit him with the submachine gun in the back, near his kidneys. Greg moaned in pain, losing strength in his legs and falling to the floor. "Sons of bitches!" he shouted.

Two more soldiers hurried over to Greg, grabbing his arms and yanking him up. They hit him in the stomach with the butts of their guns. Greg gasped for air.

"That's enough!" Garcia shouted.

The soldiers held Greg down on the chair, their weapons aimed at him. Carreras rose. "We're closing the trial now. We've got enough evidence to reach a conclusion." The five men left the room.

Greg bent forward, trying to catch his breath, the pain in his back fierce. He pressed both hands against his stomach, biting his lips to avoid screaming. He wouldn't let the bastards know he was on the edge of tears.

Garcia started to pace around Greg. "This doesn't look good," he said. "You acted very foolishly. I told you."

"Fuck you, too," Greg said.

Garcia shook his head. "You're a fool."

Maguire jumped out of the car and ran toward a group of FBI agents standing next to Hansen's car. He couldn't believe that the KGB had taken Andrea and Hansen. There were about a dozen police cars barricading the huge parking lot and a small crowd stood behind a yellow ribbon blocking off the place. Maguire walked over to the driver's side of the car and stared at the window without saying a word. The glass had been shattered. Somebody had smashed the window and grabbed the driver. He looked inside the car but didn't see any bloodstains. The KGB had not hurt them, but where in hell had they taken them?

Taylor approached him, looking gloomy. "What happened?" Maguire asked.

Taylor looked at the car, then at Maguire. "A fuck-up of major proportions," he said. "That's what happened." He shook his head. "Hansen should never have come here alone to pick up Andrea. You guys should leave all these psychologists back at Langley. They make lousy spies."

"I'm not in the mood for a post mortem," Maguire said, glaring at Taylor. "Tell me what the fuck happened here."

"Sorry," Taylor said. "I'm in the same state of mind as you are: pissed off."

"Go ahead."

"The FBI backup unit that Hansen asked for got here and found a group of people standing around the car. They checked and found nobody. Some of the witnesses said they came in two cars. Two men. They cut into the front and then the rear of Hansen's vehicle. They had guns, and they forced the driver and a woman into one of the cars, driving away at full speed. They were quick, very quick."

"How did they know?"

"Perhaps they were tailing Hansen."

"It's possible," Maguire said. "You never know with those pricks. Then what happened?"

"The FBI team leader called the highway patrol for help, but it was too late. Nobody saw them."

Maguire took a deep breath, keeping his eyes on the smashed window and thinking of Hansen and Andrea. He could understand why the KGB had taken Andrea, but he had no idea why they had taken Hansen, too. They knew the FBI was vigorously looking for them.

"What do you want to do?" Taylor asked. "We should have a lab report on the car shortly."

Lab reports, Maguire thought; he hated lab reports. All they said was that someone was missing. He didn't need a lab report now. The KGB had taken Hansen, and his life was at risk, the same as Andrea's. He and the FBI had failed miserably. How was it possible? So much preparation, so much technology—fuck technology. That was the problem. They had learned to rely on technology too much and not to trust their gut feelings anymore. They were robots, following computer printouts—not intuition.

"Maguire . . . Maguire . . ." He realized that Taylor was grabbing his arm. "What's the matter? You goin' nuts?"

"Sorry," Maguire said, "my mind ain't here."

"Hansen?"

"Yeah. He didn't belong here."

"Don't tell me you're feeling guilty now, huh?"

"I'm pissed off, but I still feel sorry for Hansen. He should've been fishing at a lake in Canada."

Greg didn't know how long he'd been waiting. The pain in his stomach had disappeared, but his back still hurt badly. The pain started in his kidneys and reached under his rib cage. He was sure he was bleeding internally, but at the moment it was not important.

The soldiers had stepped back, leaving more room for him and Garcia, who was nervous, pacing and smoking.

Greg felt the tension mount. He didn't how long he had to wait or what the tribunal would say. He thought of starting a conversation with Garcia to ease the tension. Time would pass faster that way. "What's happening?" he asked.

"They're deliberating. Soon they'll come back and tell you the verdict." He took a drag on his cigarette, then blew a long stream of smoke toward the ceiling and studied it for a few seconds.

"Have you seen many of these trials?" Greg asked.

Garcia stopped walking. "Too many."

"How many?"

"You want to know?"

"Yes."

"About three hundred."

Greg raised his head. "Three hundred!"

Garcia nodded.

Greg didn't know if he wanted to ask the question, but he did anyway. "How many of the prisoners were shot?"

Garcia scratched his head nervously, then looked at the cigarette. "Are you sure you want to know?"

Greg nodded.

The lawyer looked at the table, then at the ceiling, as if concentrating on remembering the number. "I don't know exactly, perhaps a hundred and eighty. I used to keep count and lose my sleep on the number. Then, one day, I lost count and realized it didn't matter to me anymore. The dead men didn't feel anything. Here I was, going crazy thinking about them." He paused, then added, "Their families don't even know where they're buried—just a pile of dirt in some second-rate cemetery someplace in Havana."

Greg stared at Garcia for a moment. "The bastards are trigger-happy, aren't they?"

"In a revolution, the best enemy is a dead enemy. That's why they're always bloodthirsty," Garcia said. "Lots of people die."

"I could be one of them," Greg said reflectively, still not believing his own words. "You the only lawyer?"

"At the beginning, there were ten of us." Garcia scratched his chin, shifting his eyes to the soldiers, then added, "There are four left. Three were shot with their clients, two are now in a mental hospital, one quit." The cigarette almost burned his fingers and he dropped the butt on the floor, stepping on it. He crouched next to the chair and brought his face close to Greg's ear. "Listen," he said, "you've got to trust me and follow my instructions. It's your only hope."

Greg angled his head down to see into Garcia's eyes. "How can you expect me to trust you? You're one of them."

"In a sense, I became one of them. I'm also your only hope to come out of this alive." He looked at the soldiers again, at the door, then at Greg. "Your only priority is to come out of this *alive*. If they shoot you, that's it. They'll dump you into a hole, shovel dirt on you, and not even mark the place. Nobody would know where you were. Ever."

"That's the way they hide their murders," Greg said. "A fresh pile of dirt, covering a body."

"That's not the point. What I'm telling you is that after they shoot you, it doesn't matter any more. You're finished. No more hope, no more breathing—no more life."

Greg grimaced, struggling with the thought. The image of the dirt piling up on his brother's casket came to mind. He recalled the mountains, and the strange thudding sound of the dirt as it hit the casket. He recalled tossing a handful of dirt into the grave. His brother was lucky. People knew where he was buried—and he had a cross.

Garcia reached for Greg's arm and shook him. "Pay attention to me," he said. "If they find you guilty, they'll shoot you tomorrow morning at dawn. The only recourse we have is to appeal. The revolutionary tribunal will listen to your appeal on the spot. Then they'll make a final vote, and that's it. A life sentence—or a firing squad."

Greg felt his temples throbbing. *A life sentence—or a firing squad.* He didn't know if he could stand spending the rest of his life in a dungeon-like prison, but he definitely didn't want to die. "What do you want me to do?"

"When they come back, they'll tell you the verdict. If you're guilty, I'll appeal. You must confess that you killed Boris. Then I'll plead for mercy."

Greg frowned at Garcia. "You're asking me to confess?"

Garcia nodded.

"Hell, no."

"Sometimes the approach works. I've saved three lives this way, and it didn't matter if they were guilty or not. When they confessed, the tribunal changed their sentence to life."

"I can't do that," Greg said. "I want a fair trial. That's all I'm asking."

"Dead people don't need fair trials."

"I said no."

"Calm down. If they find you guilty, you have nothing to lose pleading guilty. They'll shoot you the next day anyhow."

Greg felt his hands shaking and clasped them together, trying to hide his fright. He fought to hang onto his sanity, whatever was left of it. He couldn't believe they'd find him guilty and shoot him. They had no right to do it. They had not given him a fair trial. It was a farce, a mockery of justice—revolutionary justice. They only had the right because they had the power. The next morning the soldiers would come to his cell and drag him away. The other prisoners would start shouting; then they'd be silent until they heard the firing squad. Then again silence—and one more shot. Yes, the *coup the grace*, in his temple. He would not feel it—because he'd be dead.

"Listen to me," Garcia said, urgently. "They're coming. I can hear their steps. You must trust me. I'm your only hope."

Greg stared at him blankly, as if he had lost control of his vision. Garcia was a vague image in front of him. The two spotlights felt like scorching suns, baking him. Perspiration ran down his face and torso, soaking his shirt under the armpits and around the collar. His entire body itched. He was already dead. They had killed him without shooting a single bullet. They now wanted to complete the murder, to destroy him. Yes, they had killed his soul and broken his spirit. They were already murderers and they even didn't know it. *Murderers! Murderers!* The words echoed inside his head. He needed only to shout them. He opened his mouth but no words came out.

Garcia shook him by the shoulder and said in a whisper, "Trust me . . . please. . . ."

Greg blinked a few times, trying to focus. He knew Garcia's face was next to his because he felt his breath and smelled its heavy cigarette odor. Greg turned his head away and took a few deep breaths, gasping for air, as if suffocating. How could he trust Garcia? He was one of them.

"I trust nobody," he said.

CHAPTER 24

Greg watched the five men. As Carreras led the way, they filed into the room with the kind of ceremonial bearing that gave the moment a solemn air. The bastards had had enough practice, Greg thought, his heart pounding hard. It was so simple, so terribly simple: a *guilty* verdict, a firing squad—and death. They had control of human lives and were playing God, deciding when a man should die.

The men walked around the table and sat; only Carreras stood. "The prisoner must stand up," he had Garcia.

Greg rose slowly, facing the table and the five men. Two soldiers stepped close to him, clutching their weapons. Garcia also stepped close, looking nervous. Greg took a deep breath, tightening his jaw firmly. He was ready for whatever came from them.

The silence in the room was stifling. Finally Carreras glanced at the folder in front of him and said, "The Cuban revolutionary tribunal has reviewed the case against Greg Elliot and finds him guilty. The decision is unanimous and the punishment is death by firing squad."

Greg's legs became weak and he had to concentrate on remaining upright. He had been expecting a guilty verdict, but he still couldn't believe it when it was announced. *Death by firing squad.* They were going to kill him the next morning. Shaking badly, he raised a hand and rubbed his forehead. He opened his mouth to say something when Garcia said, "General, the accused's counsel wants to appeal the death penalty decision."

"Very well," Carreras said, sitting down. "The appeal is opened immediately."

Garcia turned to Greg. "Do you have a statement to make? The appeal is now open."

Greg looked at Garcia as if not understanding. Appeal for what? They'd find him guilty again. Nothing had changed. "What do you want me to say?" he asked Garcia.

Garcia stepped close and whispered into Greg's ear. "We talked about this before. You've got nothing to lose. Please try."

Greg swallowed. What choice did he have? He was as good as dead. His brother John came to mind, and Andrea, too. If he died, he could do nothing for her. The other choice was a life sentence. Garcia looked at him, his eyes wide open, begging. The man was sincere, Greg concluded. *Plead guilty,* the inner voice said. *Plead guilty*. . . . He shook his head, cleared his throat, straightened up, and said, "I plead guilty, sir."

Carreras leaned back in the chair, his eyes gleaming with satisfaction. "Did you kill Boris Alexei Grishin?" he asked.

Greg nodded slowly. "I did kill him, sir."

A brief smile flashed over Carreras' lips. "What else?" he asked.

"I . . . feel sorry I killed him. I didn't mean to."

"Did the CIA order you to do it?" Carreras asked.

Out of the corner of his eye, Greg saw Garcia nod slowly, prompting him to agree. "Yes, they . . . they did," he answered.

"Do you want to say anything else?" Carreras asked, visibly satisfied.

"I don't want to die. I understand now that I didn't have the right to end someone else's life . . . that was a mistake, my mistake. . . ." Greg didn't need to lie this time. He spoke from his heart. No matter what Boris had done to him, he'd no right to kill him. He was not a judge and even less an executioner. Noone should have that much power. He saw that now. "I do not want to die," he went on, "I'm pleading for mercy." The words sounded foreign to Greg, as if someone else were speaking for him.

Garcia looked at Carreras. "Any other questions, general? My client has confessed. He's repented. I beg the tribunal for mercy. Show this American how generous and human the Cuban Revolution is. Give him a lesson he can remember the rest of his life." He paused, catching his breath, then added, "A life sentence would be a good punishment. He'd be paying for his crime every day he spends in jail."

"Enough," Carreras said, waving a hand brusquely. "We can vote for the appeal now," he added, looking at the people sitting around him.

The first man to the right of the table stood up. "Guilty. Firing squad."

"Next," Carreras said.

An older man with heavy-framed glasses said, "Guilty. Life sentence."

Greg took a deep breath and held it without even realizing he was doing so. The tribunal needed a majority vote. At least one of them had changed his mind. There was hope.

The man to the left of Carreras stood up, looked at Greg for a few moments, and then said, "Guilty. Life sentence."

Greg breathed again.

The last man on Carreras' left stood up, frowning. He looked at Greg, then at Carreras. "Guilty. Firing squad," he said as he sat down.

Greg felt his heart miss a beat. Two votes for a life sentence, two for the firing squad. Carreras himself had to break the tie: one vote—one life. Greg raised his eyes and looked into Carreras', returning his stare. The General's steady eyes were icy. The two men looked at each other for a few seconds. Carreras' face was a mask of stone. Not a muscle moved, and no emotion showed. A strange silence took hold of the room. Carreras opened his mouth to speak, but the words didn't reach Greg at first. Then he heard them. "Guilty. Firing squad. . . ."

Andrea felt her legs give out. She was standing next to a wall, her hands tied around a thick drainage pipe. Grigori had tied her that she couldn't sit down; she had to stand or hang by her wrists. From where she was, she could see Hansen tied to a steel beam that served as a support in the middle of the warehouse. She didn't know where they had been taken but knew they were in an abandoned place close to a river. She could sometimes hear foghorns in the distance. She believed they were still in New Jersey for Grigori had not crossed a bridge or gone through a tunnel before they arrived there.

Sitting in a chair about twenty yards from her, Grigori watched them in silence. The other Russian had disappeared in a hurry, as if he were going to look for someone. She guessed the Russian had gone for Dmitri, to inform him of the news. She couldn't believe it yet. The KGB not only had her and Greg, but also Hansen.

The door of the warehouse opened and a car drove in. Andrea looked at the driver in terror. She recognized Dmitri's pockmarked face behind the steering wheel. Grigori rushed to close the door and to welcome Dmitri. They shook hands and Andrea saw their beaming faces. The bastards were euphoric.

Dmitri and Grigori walked over and faced her. "You've caused us a lot of trouble," Dmitri said, letting his anger show.

Andrea returned his stare in silence.

Dmitri stepped closer and, in a swift movement, slapped her face. "This will teach you a lesson, comrade."

The wrenching pain rushed to her head, and her lips started to bleed. "Where's Greg?" she asked.

Dmitri's mouth stretched into a smile. "Still thinking of that killer! Greg will receive his punishment soon."

"What do you mean?" she said. "He hasn't done anything wrong."

"That's for us to decide," Grigori said.

Dmitri glanced at his watch. "We must leave now."

"Leave for where?" Andrea asked, shaking.

Dmitri, without answering, motioned to Grigori with his head. Grigori pulled a small penknife from a pocket, pulled out the blade, and cut the nylon cord that tied her to the pipe.

She rubbed her wrists to restore circulation and leaned against the pipe for support. She winced in pain as Grigori grabbed her arm roughly and pushed her ahead of him, motioning to her to walk toward Dmitri's car. "Where are we going? I don't want to go," Andrea protested, getting no response.

They stopped next to the trunk of the car and Dmitri pulled it open. Grigori tied her hands behind her back and taped her mouth. She could barely breathe. Then both men pushed her into the trunk.

As Dmitri closed the trunk, she heard Grigori say, "Have a

good trip back to Moscow, comrade."

The ride was very rough, with many stops and turns. Sometimes she heard heavy traffic around her, cars braking and engines accelerating. Once she thought she'd suffocate. She tried to control her nerves to avoid panicking. They apparently were not going to kill her right away. Grigori's words kept coming back to her: *Have a good trip back to Moscow, comrade.* Was it possible that Dmitri was taking her to Moscow? She wondered if they were also taking Greg to Moscow. That would be the end for her and for Greg. The KGB would have no mercy with both of them there.

The stop came unexpectedly; then, in a few minutes, the trunk opened and she breathed fresh air again. The car was inside a huge, semidark building that looked like a hangar. Dmitri came over and grabbed her by the arm, pulling her up. "Hurry up."

With difficulty, Andrea stepped out of the trunk, her legs weak and barely able to support her. She was sure they were inside some kind of hangar when she saw a small jet plane near the car. Dmitri pushed her to walk faster and she knew that they would board it.

Dmitri pushed her to the rear section of the luxurious plane and they stopped at a small door leading to a bathroom. He opened the door and shoved her in first. Below the washbasin was a small cabinet that Dmitri opened. Grabbing Andrea by the neck, he forced her to kneel. The back panel of the cabinet was missing, and the opening led to a small compartment big enough for both of them.

After they were inside, Dmitri pulled in the doors of the cabinet and then a false wall hiding them. The room was uncomfortable, but much better than the trunk of the car. A small pilot light above them lit the place. Andrea noticed a few holes in the side walls to circulate the air. At least they would not suffocate.

Sitting on the floor, Dmitri drew a gun fitted with a silencer from his pocket. "One sound and I'll put a bullet in your brain," he said, touching her forehead.

She didn't know how long they would have to wait as she heard someone driving the car away. Then people came in and worked on the plane, apparently fueling it. Soon the plane moved slowly, and she heard the high pitch of jet engines. She guessed that their secret compartment was very close to the tail of the plane. Finally the plane took off and she saw the excitement in Dmitri's eyes.

Andrea widened her eyes, asking Dmitri with them to take the tape off her mouth. Dmitri looked at her for a moment as if deciding what to do. Then he slid the gun back into his pocket and peeled off the tape, some of the skin around her mouth torn in the process. She held back a scream, breathing through her mouth, until she felt calmer. "Where are we going?" she asked.

Dmitri looked at her and smiled, his pockmarked face beaming with satisfaction. "Mexico."

The Russian dragged a chair across the large warehouse and sat down in front of Hansen, staring at him silently. Hansen watched him without moving a muscle. Andrea had called the Russian Grigori, and Hansen didn't recall having heard of him before. He had seen Dmitri loading Andrea into the trunk of the car and feared the worst for her. Grigori had not said a word. He just sat there chewing gum, staring at him. Hansen was sure that Grigori was one of the KGB people who had taken Greg and Andrea from the motel in Newark. He wondered how many other KGB agents the CIA didn't know about.

As well as he could, Hansen pointed at his gag with his hands tied around the steel beam. Grigori smiled as he continued to chew his gum, but he didn't move a muscle.

Hansen kept pointing at the gag until Grigori got up and walked over to him.

"Wanna talk?" Grigori said, a strange look in his eyes.

Hansen nodded a couple of times.

Grigori shrugged and then peeled off the tape. Walking back to the chair, he said, "Well, what's on your mind? I'm listening."

"Where did you take Andrea?" Hansen asked.

Grigori giggled a little, then became serious. "You don't expect me to tell you that. It'd be stupid, huh?"

"Maybe not," Hansen said. "If you help me, I could plead with the FBI so you'd never have to return to Moscow."

Now Grigori laughed. "You fool! You expect me to free you and call the FBI." He laughed again. "You Americans are so naïve."

"All I'm saying is that if you help me, I'll help you to come out of this in a very convenient way. You could be a government witness."

Grigori spat the chewing gum into the palm of his hand, looked at it for a moment, then threw it away and pulled a fresh pack from his pocket. He started to chew another piece. "Good," he said. "What are you saying?" he asked as if he had not heard him.

Hansen hugged the beam to change the position of his body. The tight nylon cord around his wrists had cut off the circulation in his hands, but that was the least of his worries. He knew that Dmitri was taking Andrea out of the country. Every minute counted if he wanted to save her. He had to convince Grigori to free him. "You know Dmitri's taking Andrea away," he said.

Grigori shrugged. "It's none of my business."

"Yes, it *is* your business. He's leaving the country, leaving you behind."

"I know that."

"That's not the point. There's an army of FBI agents looking for you. Dmitri's sacrificing you in order to escape."

"I'm not a lamb," Grigori said, frowning.

Hansen felt a surge of hope. He had to make Grigori angry and suspicious of Dmitri. "Yes, you are. While Dmitri escapes, he has left you behind to watch me and risk having the FBI catch you. That'll give Dmitri time to escape. It'll take the heat off him." He spoke fast, trying to confuse Grigori.

"I know what Dmitri's doing," Grigori said.

"Of course you do. But he didn't tell you somebody had to take the fall. It's typical of these operations. You take the heat, and he gets away free and clear. Then the FBI gets you and they're happy because they got something in return."

Grigori narrowed his eyes, staring at Hansen for a few seconds, as if thinking about what Hansen had just said. Hansen stared back at him, feeling that in the next few seconds Grigori would decide. "Thirty to life," he said. "The rest of your life in a prison, or all the comforts of a government witness. It's your choice."

Grigori stood up and stepped close to Hansen. "The CIA pays well, huh? How much did they pay the other defectors you have?"

Hansen couldn't fathom Grigori's meaning. The icy look in the Russian's eyes warned of danger, but Hansen had to keep trying. "I don't know. We never pay defectors to come over here. They decide that by themselves. We only help them to get settled."

"A new identity and a nice bundle of cash. Sounds good to me," Grigori said, shrugging.

Hansen nodded.

"You give them a house?"

"Yes, and we also give them jobs."

"A car?"

"Yes."

"What about some pussy? Yeah, some American pussy. Do you get 'em laid, too? Is that the way you lure 'em to this imperialist country? Money and pussy? Is that what you're offering me, uh?" He stepped close, jabbing Hansen in the chest. "I want you to know I've been five years in this country. I like your whores. Hey, they're a great fuck. And you know what I like best? When this country becomes communist, the same whores are gonna be fervent communists. They're gonna pour all their anger back at you and people like you who are forcing 'em to be whores. Yeah! I've seen it in other countries. They'll turn militant and work with us to erase all the social injustices your country has been building up for two hundred years."

"Goddamn!" Hansen said, angrily. "I'm offering you a way out! Listen to me, please!"

Grigori threw his hands up in the air. "I don't want to listen to you anymore. If you don't shut up, I'll gag you again. I have a job to do." He turned around and walked back to the chair, staring at Hansen.

Hansen leaned against the steel beam, trying to ease the stress on his hands, sagging his body a little to ease the pain in his legs. Grigori had been playing with him, not giving any thought to his offer. What was going to happen next? What job did Grigori have to do? He was just waiting. But waiting for what?

Minutes passed and Grigori still sat there, glancing at his watch once in a while. Hansen gazed back at him in silence.

Grigori became more nervous and began to frown constantly. He was even chewing his gum at a faster pace, crossing his legs, then uncrossing them. Hansen noticed the change and didn't like it. Something was about to happen. Hansen decided to keep silent and wait. He didn't want to risk making Grigori angry again.

By now Grigori was looking at his watch almost every minute, and Hansen guessed it had been about an hour since Dmitri had taken Andrea. That was it; they wanted to hold him for an hour before they turned him loose.

Grigori stood up and walked over to Hansen. "Time's up," he said.

"Up for what?" Hansen said.

Grigori smiled nervously. "To free you."

Hansen didn't like it. Grigori didn't sound convincing. "Leave me here," he said. "You can go."

"Oh, no, That's not the order I have." He pulled out a gun, then searched in a pocket and produced a small penknife. "I'm gonna cut you free. If you try something funny, I'm gonna blow your brains out."

He cut the nylon cord and Hansen lowered his arms. His hands hurt badly and he moved his fingers to restore the circulation.

"Walk," Grigori said, grabbing him by the arm.

"Where?"

"Up there," Grigori said, nodding toward the end of the building.

They stopped in front of the rear wall facing a small door that Grigori pulled open. The door led to a small, dilapidated pier with many missing planks. A large hole in front of the door revealed the river underneath the pier. One step and he'd fall into the water. "What are you going to do?" Hansen asked.

Grigori stepped behind him, grabbing his shoulder, forcing him to look toward the door and the pier. Hansen saw New York's high-rises across the river. It was getting dark and some lights gleamed in the distance. He felt his legs giving out as the situation became clear to him. Then he felt the hard steel of the gun pressing against the bone behind his right ear. He closed his eyes.

He pictured a stretch of lake opening in front of him: the sparkling water, the white-topped mountains, and the blue sky in the background. He took a deep breath, feeling the fresh, crisp air fill his lungs with the smell of greenery and fresh snow.

"Don't move," Grigori said, pressing the gun harder against his skull.

Hansen closed his eyes even tighter. He thought of an empty johnboat bobbing gently in the lake, and of the fishing gear left inside the boat. He thought of trout swimming in the water.

He thought of nothing else. . . .

CHAPTER 25

Grigori watched Hansen's body fall into the water, and then stared down at it for a few seconds as if in a trance. He had killed many people, but he still hated it. Dmitri had ordered him to kill Hansen, saying Hansen should never have gotten mixed up with Andrea. When Grigori had said he didn't believe Hansen could spoil anything, Dmitri said they didn't know what Andrea had told Hansen during the moments when they were alone in the shopping center. The safe thing to do was to kill Hansen, and that killing was Grigori's job.

It had only taken a split second; the bullet had smashed into Hansen's skull, splashing part of his brain into the air. Grigori shook his head, still looking at the water. He didn't know for how long he could keep doing this. He really hated it.

Slowly he slid the gun back into the holster, closed the door, and walked back to the car. In a few days some poor soul would find the body floating in the river, when it started to decompose and become filled with gases. By then he'd be far away—on the other side of the world. The FBI would never be able to catch him. He was happy with the thought.

After he unlocked the trunk, he lifted out a large tool box, and rested it on the driver's seat. He opened the lid and studied the timer for a moment. He needed only to press a button and the explosives would go off in four hours. He glanced at his watch and pressed the button. He was five minutes ahead of schedule.

As he climbed down, the rust on the metal ladder scratched the palms of his hands and he hoped he wouldn't get tetanus. The boat bobbed gently at the end of the ladder. He looked around, hoping not to see Hansen's body floating nearby.

He sailed away from the pier, steering downstream in the

Hudson River. It'd take him about one hour to get to his destination; then he'd be safe.

The ship, an old Italian freighter badly in need of a paint job, was moored at Pier 72, on the Manhattan side of the river. The next few minutes were the most critical, and Grigori felt the tension building inside of him. There was still enough light for someone to see him boarding the ship who then could call the police or the FBI.

A few yards from the ship, he turned off the engine, walking to the front to stop the boat from colliding with the hull of the freighter. He looked around but didn't see anybody. It was dinnertime, and his contact had assured him the deck would be clear. He tied a rope to a ladder hanging over the side to keep the boat from drifting away. Then he walked back to the middle of the boat and reached down to a valve in the center of the hull. He opened it, and water started to pour in. From the ladder he watched the boat drift away and sink slowly. In a few minutes there would be no trace.

He concentrated on climbing the ladder. Looking up, he saw the shadow of a man waving at him with both hands. His contact was waiting. In two hours they'd be sailing away. He could hardly wait and looked forward to a quiet trip to Italy. His job was getting to him.

Andrea didn't know how long they had been flying. It seemed like a long time, for she was very thirsty and hungry, and her legs ached terribly. Dmitri had said very little during the trip and kept a tight grip on the gun in his lap. On several occasions they had heard people entering the bathroom. Dmitri had raised the gun, pushed the silencer into her mouth, and whispered, "One move and I'll kill you."

The sound of people using the bathroom had made Andrea even more uncomfortable because she needed to go, too. When she told Dmitri, he said, "Piss in your pants. I don't care." She found that she couldn't do it, so she bore the discomfort.

The pressure in her ears told her they were losing altitude. Then she felt the bumpy ride through the lower atmosphere, and the jet engines picking up power for the landing. Andrea was relieved that they would be on the ground soon. She'd be able to rest and organize her thoughts. The lack of sleep made concentrating very difficult. She had a lot to decide. She had to figure out a way to escape and tell the Mexican authorities. As she turned on her side to ease the discomfort in her back, a thought crossed her mind. Perhaps they had brought Greg to Mexico, too, and she would see him. A surge of excitement took hold of her, making her forget about her thirst, her empty stomach, and the other discomforts. She'd give anything to see him. Anything.

After a smooth landing, the plane taxied for about five minutes, then she heard sounds of a door opening and three or four people leaving the plane, talking in Spanish. She wondered who they were. The owner of the plane probably had some connection with Dmitri, or they would not have been in the plane. Dmitri held the gun against her back while the people were deplaning. Finally, they heard the pilots leave, and it was silent once more.

"Let's get out now," Dmitri said.

Andrea crawled underneath the washbasin into the bathroom and hesitated, looking at the toilet for a few seconds. Dmitri pulled her by the arm. "No time for that. Move on."

She followed him off the plane, glancing around. They were at the end of the airfield, near a large hangar. In the distance, she saw a large Boeing 747 taking off. The airfield was semi-dark, and it was difficult to see details. Dmitri grabbed her arm and rushed her. "Hurry up. We don't have all day."

A few yards from the plane, they met a man waiting in an electric luggage carrier and Dmitri motioned her to jump into the rear of the truck. As she climbed on, she saw the small sign on the side door—Cubana de Aviacion. Andrea's hopes were dashed; Dmitri was taking her to Cuba. Once there, they'd be in a Communist country, and there would be no more hope for her or for Greg. In Cuba the KGB could do whatever they pleased, including sending her to Moscow anytime.

As the truck rode along the airfield, she fought the impulse to jump off and try to escape, but the thought of Dmitri's gun stopped her. She was sure Dmitri would not hesitate to kill her if she tried to run. Perhaps that was the best ending for her. Death would bring her peace at last. But then she wouldn't be able to do anything for Greg. She started to shiver. She had not had her pills since Dmitri had emptied the container on the bed at the motel in Newark and had been holding up pretty well except for those moments when she had wished she had the pills. And she desperately needed one now. She felt nauseated and thought she might throw up in the truck. She curled her body, pushing both fists against her stomach, clenching her jaws so that she wouldn't scream. At that moment she felt the warm liquid run down her legs. She had wet her pants.

Greg was sitting on the bunk bed with his legs crossed, leaning against the wall, staring at the darkness in front of him, seeing nothing. He could hear in the distance the sound of a truck entering the main courtyard of the prison. Voices shouted orders in Spanish, and then there was silence. The noises were important to him because they were his only link to the outside world—a world that would end for him the next morning at dawn.

After the appeal the soldiers had brought him back to the cell. Garcia had wished him good luck and eternal peace; Carreras had frowned at him and walked out of the room without saying a word. Greg recalled Garcia's words: *Cuban military tribunals are very efficient and fast.* He had not understood what Garcia meant until the trial. Garcia had been right. Carreras had been fast and efficient. The bastard had had plenty of practice.

Early that evening a guard had brought dinner—the same maggot-infested rice and water and the strange potato. He had refused dinner, telling the guard he wanted a pen and paper.

When asked why, he had told the guard he wanted to write a letter. The guard had given him a strange look that said: you crazy American. After he had finished serving the meals, the guard came over to Greg's cell and shouted, "No paper, no pencil." Greg had then realized he had nobody to write to. He had been thinking of Andrea, hoping that perhaps Garcia would help to deliver a letter to her.

Now as the cell grew darker, and all outside activity ceased, Greg thought he might sleep a little, but after lying there for a long time, he still couldn't sleep.

He had not thought of death before, and now he faced it in a very unexpected way. He had a strange feeling of acceptance, as if it was his destiny to die. There was nothing he could do to avoid it, so he promised himself not to fight the guards in the morning when they came for him. At least he'd show them he had some dignity left.

He closed his eyes and took a deep breath, picturing Napa Valley's rolling mountains with its never-ending vineyards. He'd give anything to be able to visit Madame Suzanne one more time. He had never thought that way before and hadn't appreciated enough whenever he went there to talk to her. He could see now the small trail leading to the cemetery and the old gravestones dotting the bare ground. How good it would be to be buried there with his brother, John. At least he would have a wooden cross, too.

He pictured himself sitting on the ground, staring at the cross. Then he thought of the name on the cross and saw a new name: *Greg Elliot*. He felt a cry rise in his throat, but stopped it. He had promised himself he would not cry—not even once.

John, I haven't talked to you since I left California, he said to himself, hearing his voice inside his head. *I'm sorry about leaving you behind and not saying good-bye. I'm sorry about not sharing my last moments with you. I know that wherever you are, you're listening to me now. I know that you love me.* He paused, holding back a sob. *I know that if it's possible, we'll be together soon. No matter where our remains are, no matter how far the distance, souls have no physical boundaries.*

Nothing can keep us apart; no walls, no steel doors, no hundred-year-old fortresses, no hatred. Nothing. We're brothers, and they can't kill that. I love you, John.

He raised his hand and dried a tear. Perhaps Andrea was with John already; perhaps they were waiting for him. He took a lungful of air, holding his breath for a few moments. Life could not end in death. There had to be something better. He'd know soon.

Once again Greg heard the sound of marching, of boots striking the stone floor. His heart beat fast, and the palms of his hands were wet as he started to shake.

Slowly he got up from the bunk and leaned against the wall. He had not slept a single moment during the night. But no matter how much he had prepared himself through those long hours, he knew he was afraid to die.

The steps got closer and he straightened up against the wall. He would walk under his own power. He would not be dragged out of the cell.

To his surprise, the steps went past his cell and stopped at the end of the corridor. He heard a door opening and then a few shouts. He hadn't known that another man also waited for the firing squad. The heavy footsteps resumed and approached his cell, then stopped. It was his turn.

Somebody opened the door and shouted an order in Spanish. He didn't understand and didn't care. He walked out slowly and a soldier pushed him into the middle of the squad next to a young, barefoot man dressed in rags that barely covered his emaciated body. His head was fleshless and skull-like. Greg looked into his hollow eyes and tried to smile, but grimaced instead. The guards pushed them and the squad marched again along the corridor. Greg lowered his head to his chest and stared at the soldiers' boots, wondering how many other men had looked at the same boots on their way to the firing squad.

The screaming and the pounding on cell doors began. Startled, Greg jumped. He had forgotten about the ritual. There were at least half a dozen prisoners left, shouting and singing in Spanish the same hymn-like song he had heard before. The soldiers scowled at the cell doors. Greg also remembered the other ritual. Soon he would face the firing squad, and it would do its work. Then would come the *coup de grace*—the final shot.

They exited into a courtyard. It was still dark and he couldn't see very far. The guards began to march at a faster pace. Once in a while the guard behind him pushed him and said something in Spanish that sounded like an insult.

The courtyard ended in a small stone fence and the guards started to walk through a door-like opening one by one. A few of them waited for Greg and the other man to reach the door. Greg saw the steep edge of a wall and below it the moat surrounding the fortress.

About fifty yards from the door, an observation tower overlooking the courtyard had a powerful spotlight trained on the entrance to the moat. A long stone stairway led to the bottom. The stairway had no railing on the open side. Greg stepped close to the wall, rubbing his shoulder against the stones, squinting at the spotlight. The man in front of him did the same. For a moment he thought that perhaps it would be better if he jumped from the top of the stairs and broke his neck in the fall. He toyed with the idea for a few more seconds but decided against it. He'd let the bastards do the killing. Why make their jobs easier?

The bottom of the moat was dry and covered with a yellowish blanket of weeds, loose stones, and old garbage. The guards used a small path that they seemed to know well. The spotlight wasn't strong enough there, but a few rays of daylight were already filtering through the sky. They walked in line for about a minute and then stopped. In a small clearing in the moat Greg saw the two poles, about twenty feet apart, standing in front of a sandbag wall. A few yards to the right of the poles were two pinewood coffins, lids removed and propped up against the floor. Greg swallowed hard. Soon he would be in one of those boxes.

Two guards came along and pushed him toward the pole to the right. They grabbed his hands and tied them behind the pole. One of the guards pulled a piece of cloth from a pocket and asked Greg if he wanted a blindfold. Greg shook his head. The man next to him said yes and they blindfolded him. The man, badly shaken, was barely able to stand. A guard walked over to him and punched him in the stomach, saying something in Spanish. The man groaned and yelled back at the guard.

"Leave him alone!" Greg shouted.

The scowling guard walked up to Greg, and slapped his face, then walked away.

The other guards regrouped and started to load their rifles. Speaking in Spanish, they ignored the prisoners. Some of them laughed and others talked very fast. A few of them started to smoke.

Nothing happened for a few minutes, and Greg surmised that the guards were waiting for someone. Then they extinguished their cigarettes and grouped in military formation. Greg realized that two men were walking down the stairs to the moat. One of the men, in a black cassock and clerical collar, wore a large cross on his chest. Greg looked at the other man and recognized the bearded face of General Carreras. The bastard wanted to command the firing squad himself.

The priest walked over to the other prisoner and talked with him for a few seconds. The priest prayed, then raised the cross and put it in front of the man's face for him to kiss. General Carreras talked with the squad, and the men arranged themselves in a single line.

The priest came over to Greg and said, "Do you want to say a prayer, my son?"

Greg looked at the priest. "Are you with them?"

The priest looked at him as if not understanding the question. "Do you want to say a prayer?" he asked again.

"Are you a Communist?" Greg asked.

"I'm with the Lord," the priest said.

"You're here with them, aren't you?"

The priest shook his head. "The Lord is in every place.

That's why I'm here."

Greg leaned against the pole, trying not to fall to the ground. He looked into the priest's eyes. "Save your prayer for them. They're gonna need it more than I will. They're going straight to hell."

The priest opened his eyes wide, but said nothing as he turned around and stepped out of the way. He watched from the distance, cross in hand, moving his lips, praying.

The firing squad, now in place, five soldiers standing straight, looked very tense. General Carreras stepped back a few yards to their left and faced Greg and the other man, studying them with cold, steady eyes, his face totally devoid of emotion. Greg looked at the other man, who was trembling violently and crying silently, his head lowered to his chest.

Greg looked defiantly back at Carreras. He wanted to see the bastard's face as he gave the final order.

"Attention," Carreras shouted.

The soldiers snapped to attention, staring straight ahead.

"Ready!" Carreras shouted again.

The soldiers readied their rifles.

"Aim!"

At that moment Greg realized the soldiers were not aiming at him, but at the other man. The silence grew, then suddenly the man shouted, *"Viva Cuba Libre!"*

"Fire!"

Instinctively Greg closed his eyes, expecting the worst, but he felt no bullets. Instead he heard the rifles discharge and the bullets hitting the man next to him. He opened his eyes and saw the man's body convulse briefly, then sag limply from the pole. The bullets had hit the man mostly in the chest and blood still poured out.

"Criminals!" Greg shouted, losing his last shred of self-control as the tears ran down his face.

General Carreras walked slowly over to the dead man, pulling the pistol from his holster. He moved closer and held the pistol against the man's temple. When he pressed the trigger, the man's head burst open. Greg closed his eyes, wishing he had been first.

He held his breath, trying to stop his crying, trying to think of something else. He wanted to control himself in the last seconds of his life. Andrea. Yes, Andrea. She'd be his last thought.

He heard a flurry of movement and opened his eyes. Two of the soldiers ran to the pole and cut the rope. The inert body fell to the ground, making a strange, hollow sound. The soldiers grabbed the body by the hands and feet and carried it to one of the pine caskets. After dropping the body inside, they rushed back into formation.

"You'll pay for this, you bastards," Greg shouted, but nobody paid any attention to him. He was breathing fast, clenching his jaw. He stared at the firing squad angrily, feeling his heart beat wildly. He would not cry anymore.

Carreras walked over to the soldiers and talked with them a moment. Then the soldiers started to reload their rifles—with the bullets that would end his life. The soldiers took their time, as if enjoying their job.

Greg leaned against the pole, no longer able to stand on his own. His wrists hurt badly as he strained against the rope that bound them. He looked up at the deep blue sky with a few clouds flying high—the last sky of his life, until the end of time.

Carreras ordered the soldiers to stand at attention. In the eerie silence that followed, Carreras stepped to the side and looked at Greg, then at the soldiers.

Greg's eyes were fixed on Carreras. He wanted to see him as he gave the final order.

Carreras said, "Ready!"

Greg held his breath. He did not need to breathe anymore. He thought of Andrea.

Carreras spoke slowly. "Aim!"

"I love you, Andrea," Greg whispered aloud.

"Fire!"

CHAPTER 26

Maguire parked his car a few yards from the fire truck and got out. Half a dozen firemen rolled up fire hoses and cleaned up the mess around them. There were two more fire trucks farther down and eight to ten police cars with their rotating lights still going. All the vehicles were parked around an old, half-burnt pier. At the sight of the ambulance, Maguire increased his pace. Taylor had called him on the radio, asking him to come immediately. When he asked why, Taylor had only said, "Get your ass down here in a hurry. I've got very bad news for you."

He walked past two police officers who were setting up a yellow ribbon cordoning off the area. Then he skirted more hoses and firemen gathering together axes, extension ladders, and other tools. Inside the pier, about a dozen portable spotlights mounted on small metal tripods were aimed at a pile of twisted metal that resembled the chassis of a car. A strong smell of burning rubber filled the air. Maguire grimaced at the sight of the wreck, worrying that Taylor had found somebody dead inside the car. He was walking over to it when he saw Taylor talking to a couple of FBI agents. Taylor walked over to meet him. His face was grim and his limp more noticeable.

"What happened?" Maguire asked.

"A bomb."

"Anybody dead?"

Taylor nodded. Maguire frowned at him. "Who?" he said.

"Hansen."

"Jesus Christ!" Maguire said, shaking his head. "They blew him up in the car, right?"

"Not there," Taylor said, glancing at the wrecked car.

"I don't follow you."

"Nobody was inside the car. When we got here, a fireman noticed bloodstains on a doorframe leading to a pier. The blood splashes were fresh and high enough for us to assume that someone was shot while standing in the doorway." He paused, looking down at the floor. "We called the divers and they went down into the river with flashlights. They found Hansen's body tangled with some rubbish a few yards from the door. The bastards shot him behind the right ear."

Maguire shook his head slowly. "That's the way the KGB does executions."

"Did he have a wife or children?"

"His next of kin is his mother. I believe she's living in Boston. I'll call Langley and get the address and then tell her myself."

Maguire stepped close to the car, studying the wreck for a few moments. "Anything here?" he asked Taylor.

"So far we've got nothing. But it's too early to say. We have to let the technicians do a little more work."

"Why did they blow up the car?" Maguire asked. "I don't get it."

"I don't either." Taylor said, shrugging. "Perhaps they wanted to destroy some evidence."

"Maybe . . . maybe," Maguire said, not sounding convinced. The KGB never did anything that looked simple. They always had a reason, and sometimes that reason was buried in many layers of deception. He wouldn't guess that the KGB was just hiding evidence. "I bet they had something else in mind when they blew up that car," he added. "We have to search every square inch of this place, and then maybe we can piece together a clear story."

"I've got twenty-five technicians doing that," Taylor said.

"What about the surrounding area?" Maguire asked.

"I have ten men on foot questioning everybody around here."

"You're doing the right thing."

Maguire saw two men carrying a long plastic bag on a stretcher. He grabbed Taylor's arm and they walked together toward it.

Maguire reached down and opened a few inches of the bag, revealing Hansen's head. Maguire stared at the pale face for a moment, observing Hansen's strange, painless expression. Maguire deduced that Hansen had been dead for a few hours; his face showed some effects of the water. Maguire recalled the moment he had gone to get Hansen at Moose Lake in British Columbia. He should have let Hansen complete his vacation, Maguire thought, fighting a feeling of guilt. But feeling guilty was not going to help Hansen. All he could do now was to nail the ass of the prick who had pulled the trigger.

Slowly he closed the bag and motioned for the men to move on. Maguire glanced at the men as they approached the ambulance. "Are you sure there are no more bodies in the river?" he asked Taylor.

"That's what the divers tell me," Taylor said. "But we're gonna keep searching until tomorrow morning." Taylor paused, then added, "If they ain't down there, where do you think they are now?"

Maguire said nothing for a few seconds. Then he said, "I don't know, but if the KGB has taken them out of the country already, there is very little we can do to help them. In that case Greg and Andrea are as good as dead."

Andrea grabbed the metal railing and stepped down the ladder to the airfield with Dmitri following her. Haggard and exhausted, Andrea glanced around, squinting. It was close to mid-morning, and in the very bright sunlight she recognized Havana's José Martí International Airport. She had been there many times before, but she never thought she'd be back.

The flight from Mexico City to Havana had been long and tiring. This time they had regular seats and food and use of the bathroom. They only had to hide in a small closet until the plane took off and then walk out casually. A couple of seats at the rear of the plane were reserved for them.

Two men were waiting for them at the door of the terminal. Dressed in short-sleeved shirts, jeans, and dark glasses, they had stern expressions on their faces. Andrea recognized the DGI men, the Cuban Intelligence Service, which she had dealt with before. The ruthless, well-trained agents were docile servants of the KGB.

The men motioned to them to walk around the line facing an immigration counter, past a closed door. They spoke only a few words in Spanish, not hiding their deference to Dmitri's high rank in the KGB.

A black Mercedes waited at the side exit and one of the DGI men rushed ahead and opened the passenger door. Dmitri motioned to Andrea to enter first; then he climbed in. The two Cubans, one the driver, sat in the front. Soon the Mercedes joined the airport traffic.

Andrea watched Dmitri out of the corner of her eye. Now that they were in Havana, all traces of tension were gone from his face. After some hesitation she ventured a question; maybe she would get an answer. "Where are we going?"

Dmitri took his eyes from the window and looked at her. She returned his stare. "You look terrible," he said.

"Am I under arrest?"

Dmitri shook his head, still looking at her. "You don't give up, do you?" he said. "Of course you are. Nothing has changed. You're a defector."

"Where am I going?"

He looked out the window, studying the traffic around them. When Andrea thought he would not say another word, he answered, "You'll be under detention at DGI headquarters in Havana." He paused, then added, "Until we arrange your trip back to Moscow."

Andrea struggled for a moment with her next question before she decided to give it a try. She had nothing to lose. "Where's Greg? Is he in Havana, too?"

Not a muscle of Dmitri's face moved. With his eyes still on the traffic, he said, "I'm tired of your questions. One more word and I'll gag you. Is that clear?"

Andrea nodded slowly.

The DGI headquarters was housed in a complex of buildings

that stretched for several blocks. The buildings, actually luxurious homes, dated back to before the revolution. They had belonged to rich families living in an exclusive neighborhood south of Havana called Miramar. Andrea had visited the place several times during her two-year stay in Havana. She liked the old houses, mostly two-story colonial structures, with large windows framed in ornate ironwork. Manicured gardens with full-topped trees whose names she didn't know; beautiful, slim royal palms; and well-cared-for greenery. From a sample of the houses she visited, she had concluded that rich Cubans had known how to live in luxury. Unfortunately for them, they hadn't known how to safeguard all that wealth. Rich people had been the first ones to leave Cuba when Castro took power, abandoning their homes, even leaving the furniture. The DGI quickly took control of the houses, establishing their headquarters in them and digging tunnels connecting them. It was not hard for Andrea to conclude that the DGI people knew how to live well, too.

Dmitri had said she'd stay in one of the houses now, but she was sure she wouldn't be in the comfortable living quarters. She'd heard rumors of basements full of small cells, and one of those cells was meant for her now. Then another thought crossed her mind. Perhaps Greg was also being held there. If that was the case, she would do her best to find out. She still had some friends in the DGI. Maybe they could help.

The driver paused in front of the gate, and an armed guard approached the window, then waved the car in with one hand.

The house was a two-story structure with long, rectangular windows and a portico with two pairs of columns. The driver steered into the circular driveway and stopped by the front door. Another armed guard rushed to open the door of the Mercedes, and Dmitri and Andrea got out. The Cuban DGI sitting in the passenger seat also left the car, leading the way into the house.

Andrea didn't recall having seen this building before, but the heavy armed guard around the premises told her that the house was a DGI prison. As she entered through the front door, she promised herself to look for Greg right away. She didn't know how she would be able to do that, but she had to give it her best try. Perhaps they were now under the same roof, she thought excitedly.

Dmitri opened the door of the hotel room. He couldn't recall ever being so tired. The spacious room, with a large bed, two nightstands holding lamps, a small refrigerator, and a TV set was a welcome sight. The curtains and carpet seemed new and smelled clean. He walked to the bed and found a suitcase with fresh clothes. All he needed now was a shower and a drink. In the refrigerator he found two bottles of vodka and some caviar. The internal security comrades had taken proper care of him. Grabbing a bottle, he filled a small glass and took a long sip, feeling the drink washing away the dust in his throat. What a long trip! But now he was safe, and his mission was almost complete. Geidar Aligev would be very pleased. Dmitri was sure that a promotion for him was already in Aligev's mind.

He went to the window which overlooked Havana's Vedado District. In the distance was Havana Bay's narrow entrance, with the Morro Castle on its northern side. Dmitri was pleased with the accommodations. He was on the twenty-second floor of the Habana Libre Hotel, which had been the Havana Hilton until Castro took power. The KGB had permanently secured the highest floor, refurbishing every room. The Internal Security Office at the Soviet Embassy in Havana managed the floor, using it for special Soviet visitors. He had used the same room every time he'd stayed in Havana. That was one of the privileges of his rank—an ocean view.

After another glass of vodka, he was in the mood for a shower and some first-class food. He reached for the telephone on the nightstand and dialed slowly, not wanting to make a mistake. A moment later the line started to ring.

"General Carreras," the voice at the other end said.

"This is Dmitri Kotov."

"Welcome back, comrade."

"How's everything?"

"Fine," Carreras replied. "I've carried out the instructions to the last detail."

"Very good, comrade." Dmitri said.

Maguire looked at the wreckage of the car, wondering why the KGB had blown it up. It still didn't make any sense to him. There was nothing to hide except for a few fingerprints. He looked over his shoulder at the two men loading the stretcher with Hansen's body into the ambulance. A thought crossed Maguire's mind, and he wasted no time. He ran toward the ambulance, waving both hands at the men, not wanting them to leave. The men saw him and stopped.

"Sorry," Maguire said, a little short of breath. "How long since he died?"

"When did he die?" the man responded, looking for Maguire's exact meaning.

Maguire looked at the plastic bag. "How many hours has he been dead?"

"Sorry, sir," the same man said. "It's very difficult to determine that without doing forensic work."

"I just want a guess."

The man looked at the bag, then at his partner, then back at Maguire. "Well, we've got a pretty good idea from rigor mortis."

"Yes?"

The man scratched his head, "We think he's been dead for about five or six hours."

"Five hours," Maguire repeated. "That's close enough." He looked at the plastic bag and said, "We'll get the bastard."

He found Taylor standing next to the wreck, watching the FBI technicians combing the charred pieces. "Get a couple of flashlights and come with me."

"What's on your mind?" Taylor said.

"Something important."

"What is it?"

"No time for questions. I want to check something. Where

are the flashlights?"

Taylor asked one of the technicians, and soon they had a couple of flashlights in hand. Maguire headed for the rear of the building, Taylor behind him.

"Slow down," Taylor said. "I can't walk that fast."

They stopped in front of the door where the KGB had killed Hansen. The fire had not reached that section of the structure; the walls and part of the roof were intact. "You told me there was another door around here," Maguire said, sweeping the flashlight beam over the wall, not seeing anything.

"It's a very small door," Taylor said. "Look to your right." He moved the light in that direction.

Maguire saw the small door and started toward it pointing the flashlight ahead of him. Half the size of a regular door, it looked like a small gate to dump stuff into the river rather than to walk through.

"What's behind the door?" Maguire asked.

"Nothing."

"I don't understand."

"I mean, no pier, only the river."

"Did you look carefully?" Maguire asked.

"I had a man take a look. He said that the building ended there. No pier."

Maguire opened the door and crouched on the edge, pointing the beam of the flashlight down. He saw nothing but the Hudson River.

"Be careful," Taylor said. "Don't take a dive."

Grabbing the frame of the door with one hand and holding the flashlight with the other, Maguire leaned forward. He then turned the flashlight in and swept the beam under the building. "Aha—son of a bitch!" he said.

Taylor grabbed Maguire's arm, afraid that the CIA agent would fall into the water. "What're you lookin' at?" he asked. "Be careful, you're gonna drag me down with you."

Maguire pulled back and sat on the edge of the floor, his legs hanging down. "I know how the pricks who killed Hansen escaped. Y'know, it didn't make any sense to me that they blew up the car, unless they wanted to keep us busy searching for clues."

"Then?" Taylor said.

"There's an iron ladder under the floor leading straight to the water. Also, there's enough room for a small boat to sail out of this mess, heading downstream."

"That's fucking sneaky," Taylor said. "The bastards left the building using a small boat."

"I don't think that Andrea and Greg could've made it down the ladder," Maguire said. "But a couple of KGB bastards could."

"Where in hell did they go?"

"I bet they're hiding inside some freighter around here, waiting to sneak out of the country." Maguire got up from the floor, directing the flashlight at Taylor's face. "I also bet the freighter has left in the last couple of hours."

"Get that thing out of my face," Taylor said.

"Sorry." Maguire aimed the beam at the floor. "All we need to do is check with the Maritime Association of the Port of New York," he said. "I want you to check for any freighter that has left the port in the last four hours and was moored no more than one mile from this place."

"We might have to inspect a dozen ships," Taylor said.

"I don't give a fuck what we have to do. I want to get my hands on the bastards who killed Hansen."

They hurried to the front of the building, Taylor struggling to catch up with Maguire's fast strides. They stopped in front of a car and Taylor grabbed the mike, requesting a connection with the communications center.

Maguire tapped Taylor on the shoulder. "Ask for two helicopters. We're gonna need them."

CHAPTER 27

Maguire felt like grabbing the page and pulling it out of the fax machine. The damn thing was taking its time to get through the narrow slot. They were inside an FBI communications van parked in the front of the pier. Taylor stood next to Maguire, also frowning at the machine. It had taken them a few minutes to get through several layers of bureaucracy at the Maritime Association of the Port of New York. At Taylor's insistence the manager on duty had called the home of the department manager in charge of port traffic, asking for permission to pull the information out of the computer. The manager agreed to help as long as he had an FBI request in writing on his desk by the next morning. Taylor had committed to the letter even if he had to type it himself. Then the manager said they'd have a fax in twenty minutes.

The page stopped and Maguire snapped it from the machine. It contained a list of six ships arranged in alphabetical order. Maguire read the names eagerly as Taylor stepped close to do the same.

The first name on the list was a cruise ship scheduled to leave Pier 40 in two hours. The ship's itinerary called for a stop in Miami, then the Caribbean. Maguire shook his head. The KGB wouldn't use that route. Too many people were on board.

The second ship, a cargo vessel under the Panamanian flag, had already left for Jacksonville, Florida. After that stop, the ship was scheduled to sail for Brazil. It had been moored at a pier on the New Jersey side of the Hudson. Maguire raised his eyes to Taylor, "Jacksonville, then Brazil. What do you think?"

Taylor looked at the paper. "I don't know. I can't guess on this one."

"I don't like the stop," Maguire said. "It'd be too risky for the KGB."

"Your guess," Taylor said.

Maguire lowered his eyes to the paper. The next ship shuttled between New York and Atlantic City. The KGB couldn't go very far with that one. He looked at the next one on the list, a freighter heading for Naples, Italy. The ship had left port three hours ago and met all the basic requirements for the KGB to hide in it. The itinerary was a direct one, and the pier where the ship had been moored stood only half a mile from the burnt pier. There was only one problem; the ship was already in international waters.

"Hey, this one fills the bill," Maguire said.

"The bastards are taking a vacation in Naples," Taylor said, frowning.

"We'd better get our asses on this ship," Maguire said excitedly.

"What about the last two on the list?" Taylor asked.

Maguire glanced at the paper. One of the freighters was still moored, scheduled to leave in two hours for Canada, with one stop in Boston. The last one was a small tanker already on its way to Saudi Arabia.

"My gut feeling is that the Italian ship is the right fucking one," Maguire said. "We still can check the freighters to Canada and Brazil if we find nothing in this one." He looked down at the paper. The name of the freighter was the *Mira Taglio*. He folded the paper into his pocket, glaring at Taylor. "Where in hell are the helicopters?"

The two helicopters hovered over the *Mira Taglio*, making a deafening clatter. Maguire looked down, feeling his adrenalin rising. The cargo vessel's engine was idle, and she rocked on the rough ocean. It was still dark and the helicopter's spotlights bounced off the deck as the pilots looked for a place to land.

Maguire and Taylor had flown in the lead helicopter while four heavily armed FBI special agents were crammed into the second one. Maguire didn't know how many KGB people were hiding on the ship, so he wanted to be prepared for the worst. There was still a possibility the KGB had taken Andrea and Greg with them. If that was the case, the situation would be better, but much more complicated. The Russians could use them as hostages to save their necks.

Taylor had also radioed the Coast Guard, asking them to sail a couple of cutters in the vicinity of the freighter. Nobody knew what was going to happen, he had said to Maguire after he finished the call.

As the helicopter approached the deck, Maguire looked down again. The bridge and accommodation quarters were on the aft deck. Two small cranes and a tall mast sat atop a mast house. The ship's deck was poorly lit, and Maguire understood the reason for the helicopter pilot's cautious approach. One mistake and they'd crash with one of the cranes, plunging into the rough ocean. What a way to go!

Taylor looked at Maguire and gave him a thumbs-up as a nervous smile spread over his face. You don't fool me, buddy, Maguire thought, smiling back. You're shitting in your pants, too. The pilot flew level with the upper deck of the ship but a few yards above the water. Hope this guy has some landing experience on carriers, Maguire said to himself, grabbing the side of his seat with both hands.

The pilot had barely touched a large metal hatch facing the bridge when Taylor pulled the door open and jumped out. Maguire followed him, glad they were on solid ground again. A few yards away, the second helicopter approached a space on the deck between a mast and a crane. Maguire glanced at the helicopter touching the deck, then ran behind Taylor. Only one thing was in his mind now: finding the Russians and making them pay for killing Hansen.

A sailor waited for them in a small door on the side of the bridge. His face wasn't friendly, as if the delay of the ship was causing him some inconvenience. "The captain's waiting for you in the wheelhouse," he said in a heavy Italian accent.

As they started to climb the metal ladder, Taylor got close to

Maguire and said, "I'll do the talking. Remember, we're in international waters. The captain's doing this only as a courtesy to us. We had a hard time convincing him to let us aboard. He claims there's nobody there."

"They all say the same thing," Maguire said. "But if we flush a couple of KGBs out of his ship, he's gonna be in a lot of trouble."

"Or somebody else is," Taylor said. "The captain might not have been involved."

The wheelhouse was small and looked crowded. A wheelsman was on guard, steering the ship and staring out a long window overlooking the foredeck and a black ocean. Behind the wheel was a long console holding all kinds of gadgets and instruments, including a radar display and a compass. Maguire shifted his eyes away from the console and glanced at the man standing next to the wheelsman. He was in his late fifties, short but tough-looking. He had on a blue weather-proof coat, jeans, and sneakers. Taylor shook hands with the man and said, "Max Taylor, FBI, special agent." He turned to introduce Maguire. "This is Chuck Maguire, CIA."

The captain turned his head, giving Maguire a short nod, and not making a movement to shake hands with him. Fuck you, Maguire thought, thinking the captain was probably an Italian Socialist. He nodded, too, returning the captain's stare.

"I appreciate your letting us aboard your ship, Captain," Taylor said, emphasizing the last words. "I know we're causing you some inconvenience," he added.

Maguire had never seen Taylor so polite. The bastard must be seasick, he concluded, itching to cut out the bullshit and start searching the ship. The longer it took for them to get going, the easier it was for the Russians to find a good spot to hide. He moved closer to the captain and said, "I want to talk to your crew. How many men to do you have on board?"

The captain looked at Maguire, and then turned to Taylor. "I guarantee my men are not communists. I don't see why you need to talk to them." His accented English was fluent.

"Captain," Taylor said, "if you have people aboard, it is

because somebody has helped them."

"Then I'm sure there's nobody aboard," the captain said.

"Jesus, Captain. We're wasting our goddamn time," Maguire said.

Taylor stepped between the captain and Maguire. "Sorry, Captain, perhaps we could save time by talking to your men."

The captain hesitated, then turned toward the console. He grabbed a phone and shouted a couple of orders in Italian. After slamming the phone down, he gave Maguire an angry look and said to Taylor, "You can talk to my men in the radio room."

A moment later he walked out of the wheelhouse, slamming the metal door behind him.

"That guy has a temper," Maguire said.

"Where is the radio room?" Taylor said.

"Follow me," said the sailor who was their guide.

The radio room was on a level below and to the rear of the wheelhouse facing the stern. A radioman on guard in the room, faced a console full of communications gear. There was a small open space to his right and a table with a chair. Maguire sat on the edge of the table, his eyes on the door. He couldn't wait to talk with the sailors. Taylor pulled a walkie-talkie from his pocket and instructed the FBI special agents to wait on deck. "Keep your eyes open!" he shouted, and then switched off.

The first four men they talked to didn't show any suspicious signs. Most of them were sleepy, or angry because they had been awakened.

"We ain't doin' too good," Maguire said to Taylor, barely controlling his impatience. "Shit! We should start searching this sardine can before the captain changes his mind."

"Let's keep going," Taylor said. "If the KGB people have a good hiding place, you're never gonna find them."

The next man was skinny and short, with heavy-framed glasses, and a two-day beard. Wearing a T-shirt, jeans, and sandals, the man kept his eyes on the floor, avoiding all eye contact. Maguire became alert; the man was hiding something.

"What's your name?" he asked.

"They call me Nick, sir," he said, still looking down.
"What do you do here?" Taylor asked.
"I am the assistant mechanic, sir."
"Hmm," Maguire said, pretending he was thinking of something, trying to scare the bastard.
Nick gave him a quick glance, then lowered his eyes again.
"You scared?" Maguire said, getting right to the point.
"Me? What for?" Nick asked.
"You look scared shitless to me. Yeah, you do," Maguire said.
"No, sir," Nick said with another quick glance.
"You know we're looking for a murderer," Taylor said.
"No," Nick said, shaking his head.
"And, if you're hiding him, you're a fucking accomplice," Maguire added, jumping off the table and moving toward to the sailor.
Nick retreated, stopping when his back reached the wall. He shook his head. "Sorry, I haven't seen anybody."
"I don't believe you, Nicky," Maguire said, moving closer to him. "These pricks we're looking for blew my friend's brains out. Y'know, I'm really pissed off, and if you're lying to me, I'm gonna shoot you in the nuts. You readin' me, Nicky?"
Nick opened his eyes wide and shook his head. Maguire could see the panic in his face. "Life in prison, that's what you'll get if you don't cooperate. You understand? *Lei capisce?"*
Nick nodded several times.
Maguire now was almost breathing in Nick's face. "You sure you saw nothing, huh?"
"Per favore, signore," Nick said, beginning to tremble, then blurted out, "they forced me. It's not my fault."
"Okay . . . okay. . . ." Taylor said, grabbing Maguire's arm and moving him to the side. "I know how these people work. They're sneaky. How many people on board?"
"Uno."
"Just one, huh?"
Nick nodded.

"When did he come in?" Taylor pursued.

"One hour before the ship left port."

"Are you sure there were no others?" Taylor demanded.

"I'm sure, sir. Only one."

Taylor looked at Maguire but said nothing. He then looked at Nick. "Do you know his name?"

"Grigori. That's all I know."

"Pockmarked face? Tall? Mean-looking son of a bitch?" Maguire interrupted.

"No, *signore*, he's skinny. Looks Oriental."

"Good boy." Taylor rested his hand on Nick's shoulder. "Now you're going to tell me where this Grigori's hiding. Right?"

"Sure, *signore*, sure. He's hiding in the bosun's store—"

"Bosun's store?" Taylor interrupted.

"Oh—you no sailor," Nick said.

"Of course."

"It's the place where we store ropes, rigging equipment, paint, lamps—"

"Okay, okay, I got it. Where is it?"

Nick pointed. "Under the forecastle. Y'know, the front of the ship."

Taylor smiled and patted Nick on the shoulder, "Good boy," he said again.

Nick raised his eyes, looking at Taylor, an expression of misery on his face. "What's goin' to happen to me, sir? I've got a wife, eight children. I needed the money. I meant no harm."

"Let's see what happens," Taylor said to Nick. "You've helped us. Maybe we'll let you go if you've told the truth."

Nick nodded several times. "I did, *signore*."

"Stay here," Maguire said. "Don't move."

"Call the captain and inform him," Taylor said to the radioman. "Keep an eye on Nick."

Both men left the room in a hurry, Maguire leading the way and Taylor trying not to lose him. "I'm gonna nail Grigori's ass," Maguire said.

"Remember, we want to get him alive," Taylor said. "He's the only link we have to Greg and Andrea."

They joined the four FBI special agents on deck. The men readied their automatic weapons and headed for the front of the ship. As they went past the helicopters, Maguire waved them to a stop, picking up two flashlights. He gave one to Taylor. "Let's split into two groups. We've got to prevent this prick from escaping inside the ship."

"Okay," Taylor said, assigning two men to Maguire.

The freighter, barely advancing, pitched and rolled on the rough ocean. The men walked with difficulty, projecting the flashlight beams ahead of them. The ship was very dark with a few pilot lights every few yards illuminating the deck.

"The bastard knew very well where to hide," Maguire said to Taylor as they stopped by the forecastle with a metal ladder leading to a small deck. Maguire looked around; he didn't see any door. The entrance to the bosun's store had to be on the top. Before they left, Nick had assured them that there was only one door. If he was still there, the Russian would be trapped.

They climbed the ladder stealthily, not wanting to give Grigori any advantage. Taylor asked two of the men to stay outside, just in case Grigori had already left the bosun's store.

The small deck was empty except for a windlass holding two anchor cables disappearing down through a spurling pipe. The metal floor was wet, and every time the ship's bow pitched, a wave showered the forecastle. Maguire looked at Taylor, cursing the ocean for being so rough. He grabbed the railing, trying to keep his balance. Sweeping the beam of light ahead of him, he saw the hatch leading to the bosun's store. Maguire could hardly restrain his anger. Below the hatch was the bastard who had killed Hansen and had probably pulled the trigger without a second's hesitation. But that was history now. The only thing he could do was to get Grigori and make him pay for his crime. He reached down and pulled the hatch open, pointing the flashlight inside the black hole. He couldn't see a thing.

"Jesus!" he said, turning to Taylor. "It's a fuckin' dungeon down there. Stay here and cover me."

"You're crazy," Taylor shouted as the bow took another dive and a new surge of water splashed them.

"You cover me," Maguire said again. "He has no way out. Stay here." He started down the metal ladder, water rushing over it, wetting the steps. Maguire, his gun in one hand, clutched the railing with his other hand, which was also holding the flashlight. He walked slowly, almost studying every step before he took the next one. The last thing he wanted was to get hit by a bullet. Not that he was afraid to die; he was simply beyond the point of worrying about it. But he wanted to nail the bastard's ass first.

After a few more steps his head was below the deck. He moved the light in a sweeping pattern and could see some of the room. There were many boxes and cans and huge coils of rope secured in compact piles. Some loose cans rolled with each movement of the ship. The room was larger than he had expected. There was plenty of room for Grigori to hide. He pointed the light to the right and suddenly a bullet ricocheted on the steel wall next to him. He had not heard the shot; Grigori was using a pistol with a silencer.

Maguire turned the flashlight off and rushed down the last few steps. At that moment the hull took another dive and he slipped on the last step, hitting the steel floor with his shoulder. "Shit!" he said, trying to hold to his gun. He had lost the flashlight.

Another bullet whizzed by him. This time he had heard a small pop beforehand. He felt a slight kick in his left arm and knew the bullet had hit him. "Fuck you!" he shouted, rolling on the wet floor, looking for refuge in the darkness. As he rolled, he stumbled over the flashlight and grabbed it with his injured arm.

"Maguire . . . Maguire?" he heard Taylor shouting, but he didn't answer, not wanting to let Grigori know where he was.

He crawled a few feet more, as silently as possible, feeling the water under him and timing the bow's movements so he could keep his balance. It was very dark and his eyes had not yet adapted to the lack of light. Grigori had the advantage; he had been in the darkness for a long time.

Maguire's head bumped against a wall and he pulled himself up slowly, not making any sound. He sat on the floor, rested the gun on his lap, and touched his injured arm. The wound, a superficial one, burned a little, and blood trickled down.

He grabbed his gun again and looked around, opening his eyes wide, trying to get a feel for the room. A can of paint came rolling by him and he raised his gun, thinking for a moment that perhaps Grigori was pushing it, but he didn't fire.

A noise to his left made him turn his head. He saw some shapes now, but not very clearly. Gun in hand, he got to his feet. He moved in a bent-over position, his shoulder against the wall for balance. The ship's bow moved up, and he moved a few yards. Then he leaned against the wall, waiting for the steep dive. He was ready to walk a few steps more when he saw a silhouette moving from behind some boxes. The bastard was circling to shoot him in the back.

The bow plunged downward and then up again. Maguire ran to his right and saw Grigori's silhouette, his gun raised. Maguire turned on the flashlight, aiming at the man's face. Grigori hesitated, squinting in the sudden light. Maguire raised his gun and fired, aiming at Grigori's legs. He didn't want to kill the bastard—not yet.

The gunshot resounded inside the metal room, and Grigori bent down, reaching for his right leg. Maguire fired again and put a bullet through Grigori's hand. The Russian dropped the gun and fell to his knees. Maguire ran toward Grigori, keeping the light on him. Grigori raised his head and scrambled for his gun.

"Hold it!" Maguire shouted, still running. "You prick!"

Grabbing the gun from the floor, Grigori turned it toward his face. He pushed the silencer into his mouth, holding the butt with both hands, his finger searching for the trigger.

"Don't do it, don't . . . !" Maguire shouted.

Grigori ignored him.

Maguire stopped, holding his gun and the flashlight with

both hands together. He started to fire, pulling the trigger until he ran out of bullets.

Maguire dropped the gun to the floor and pointed the light at the Russian's face. He was dead. "I couldn't let you kill yourself, prick," Maguire said. "That was the least I could do for Hansen."

Andrea pulled herself up in the bunk bed and leaned against the wall, her back sore from lying there for so many hours. She had to admit that the rest and the food had eased some of her discomfort, but the waiting and the silence were driving her mad. Nobody had said a word to her since she arrived. Perhaps Dmitri had ordered the Cubans not to talk to her.

The first thing they had done when she went down to the basement was to take her to a shower room. The room had been empty except for a tough-looking female guard who seemed to have a permanent scowl. Then the guard had thrown her a change of clothes that looked like a prison uniform and had told her to get dressed. Andrea had asked the woman a couple of questions, but got only angry looks.

The woman guard then had escorted her to a cell and had locked her up. On her way to the cell, Andrea had seen other cells with female inmates and assumed the pavilion was a prison for women. The food had come a few minutes later, and she had hungrily devoured the large plateful of steamy rice, bread, some vegetables, and fried chicken. The food had been bland, but it had felt good in her stomach and had restored some of her energy.

For the next couple of hours after that, she had knelt next to the barred door, watching everybody that went past. She had hoped that she could talk to somebody and ask if the person had heard about an American just recently brought in.

But hours had passed and nobody had paid any attention to her. She then had decided to rest on the bunk bed. Her knees had become swollen and had began to hurt.

Now she heard steps approaching and sat on the edge of the

bed. A military man stopped in front of the cell and slid a key into the lock. Andrea watched him without moving. The soldier opened the door and ordered, "Follow me."

"Where am I going?" she asked as she left the cell.

"Just come with me," the man said dryly.

She walked beside him, noting the pistol in a holster hanging from his waist. He looked relaxed and Andrea held her breath, feeling excited. Perhaps he was taking her to see Greg.

The soldier headed for a door and they faced a stairway leading out of the basement. Perhaps Greg was in another building, she said to her self, still struggling to keep her hope alive.

The stairway led to another hallway, and they walked for about twenty yards. They passed a few people, who ignored them. Going through another door, into a small courtyard surrounded by trees and thick greenery so that nothing beyond the yard could be seen, Andrea saw a jeep, its motor running.

The soldier asked her to climb in the front, and he slid into the back seat, ordering the driver to get moving.

Andrea turned her head, looking over her shoulder. "Are you going to tell me where am I going?"

The soldier hesitated, then said, "General Carreras wants to see you. Stay quiet."

Andrea's heart sank in dismay. General Carreras was the last person she wanted to see.

CHAPTER 28

Greg opened and closed his eyes a few times. He could still feel and see but he felt as if he were coming out of a long sleep. Maybe that's what death was all about—a long, tiring sleep. Slowly he turned his head and looked around. The room and its objects were blurred. He squinted, trying to focus. He lay in a bed, covered with a white sheet up to his neck. A small board kept his left arm straight and steady for the intravenous needle in his vein. His eyes followed the plastic tube and stopped on the intravenous bottle. He was not dead; he was in a hospital bed. Jesus! How could that be? They had shot him. He saw them firing—and felt the bullets.

He tried to move but his whole body ached, especially the muscles around his chest. With his free arm he moved the sheet down, looking for bandages. He saw none. The bullets had not hurt him. Then he moved his legs and felt them; they were okay, too. He was confused. He was sure the firing squad had shot at him. He still remembered General Carreras' voice commanding the squad, then the deafening sound of the rifle shots. That was his last memory: the rifles aimed at him and the faces of the soldiers against their weapon sights. The soldiers' goal had been clear: not to miss their mark—his heart.

His back hurt badly, so he turned a little to ease the discomfort. He realized that his mouth was very dry and foul-tasting. He didn't know how long he had been lying on the bed; but judging by the way he felt, he guessed several days. He touched his face and felt the long whiskers turning into a full beard. He was sure now he had not shaved for at least a week. He probably looked as bad as he felt—a human wreck.

The door opened and he turned his head in that direction.

Garcia walked over to the bed, and looked down at him.

"I'm alive," Greg said weakly.

"I can see that," Garcia said, a pleased expression on his face.

"I don't understand," Greg said. "I saw them shooting at me."

Garcia nodded. "They did."

"But I'm not dead."

A brief smile crossed Garcia's lips. "You're lucky. Very lucky."

"They didn't shoot me, did they?"

Garcia shook his head slowly. "No. They do that sometimes."

"Do what?"

"Well, it's kind of a lesson. They tell you they're going to shoot you. Then they shoot you with somebody else, so you can see the other guy dying. Then the firing squad loads special bullets into the rifles." He paused, looking around. "They're rubber bullets in low-powder cartridges. The bullets hit you hard, but they won't harm you—only knock you out."

"Jesus!" Greg said, opening his eyes. "You mean they wanted to scare me?"

Garcia nodded again. "Not only to scare you, to prove the point that they can kill you any time they want."

Greg rubbed his forehead, narrowing his eyes. Garcia's face was still dim. "You're telling me they only wanted to scare me? My God! I'll never forget this for the rest of my life. How could I? Those bastards!"

"That's not all," Garcia said.

"What?"

"They haven't commuted your death sentence to life. It's only suspended—"

"I don't understand."

"They can come back and put you in front of a firing squad any time."

So that was their game. By keeping the sentence open, they'd play psychological games, driving him mad. "Why am I here?"

he said.

"You had cardiac arrest."

"A heart attack?"

"I wouldn't call it a heart attack, but some people have actually died of a heart attack when the rubber bullets hit them."

Greg looked at Garcia for a few seconds. The lawyer was standing next to the bed, his hands clasped, looking concerned about him. Was Garcia one of them? Greg struggled with the thought. He had not been able to read Garcia. Sometimes he thought that the Cuban really wanted to help him but at other times, Garcia sounded just like the rest of them. "The sons of bitches can kill you one way or another," Greg said, watching Garcia's expression.

"That's the way they play the game. If you play it right, you can stay alive."

"Where am I?" Greg asked.

"In a military hospital north of Havana."

"How long will they keep me here?"

"I don't know. Perhaps a few days, until you've recovered."

"Then?"

Garcia shrugged. "It depends. They could take you back to La Cabaña or to the Boniato prison, over four hundred miles from here." He paused and looked around again. "Sending you to La Cabaña would be a bad sign. They can shoot you there anytime."

Greg closed his eyes; his head had started to ache. The possibilities that Garcia was explaining to him weren't too encouraging. He opened his eyes and stared at him. "What about Boniato?"

"They don't kill people in Boniato . . . at least they don't put them in front of a firing squad and shoot them. But the six-by-four isolation cells there are worse than dying in front of a firing squad."

Greg eyes went blank for a moment; then he blinked a couple times, still staring at Garcia. "Either way is terrible," he said.

"Yes."

"Would you help me, please?" Greg asked.

"There's very little I can do for you now."

"Yes, you can."

"The trial's over. What do you mean?"

"You can send a message to someone telling them I'm here. Perhaps they can help me."

Greg saw Garcia nervously biting his lip. "You don't understand," Garcia said. "I've done all I can do for you."

Greg shook his head. "You can still help me."

"There's nothing else I can do," Garcia said in a tense tone. "And you're a very lucky person."

"You call this lucky?"

"Yes, I do. You could've been the other guy, the one they shot first."

The driver skirted the sparse traffic on Malecón Drive, driving at high speed and darting around slow-moving vehicles. Andrea had not said a word since they left the DGI complex. She was sure the soldiers would not volunteer any other information. As they advanced, she tried to calm down. She had not seen Carreras for over a year and wasn't looking forward to seeing him again.

She wondered what Carreras wanted. He had probably known beforehand that Dmitri was going to detain her at the DGI headquarters. Dmitri would never have put her there without consulting Carreras first, but taking her out of the cell was something else. Dmitri might get very upset, and perhaps she could play Carreras against Dmitri. If Greg was in Cuba, Carreras could arrange a visit to see him. The thought excited her, but not for long. She knew Carreras well, and the Cuban General was as shrewd and as brutal as Dmitri. She wouldn't be able to get anything out of Carreras except what he wanted to tell her. Why did Carreras want to see her? Why was he taking her out of the cell? Andrea leaned back in the seat, closing her eyes for a few seconds, feeling the wind blowing in her face. She was at a complete loss.

Malecón Drive bordered Havana's shoreline, and the driver slowed down at the sign indicating the entrance to the tunnel crossing the bay. Several blocks of old houses, belonging to Spain's colonial times, flanked the last stretch of Malecón before the tunnel. Andrea looked at the houses as they went past them. Castro had launched a major restoration program to save them the first year she had arrived in Cuba, three years ago. The ladders and the piles of construction material in front of the houses showed that the program was still in progress, but the houses still looked dilapidated and ready to collapse. It was the same with her; three years and she was going nowhere. She wondered when she would see the end to all this.

The driver braked to a halt in front of the Spanish villa, and the soldier riding in the back jumped out, motioning to Andrea to do the same. "Wait here," the soldier told the driver.

Slowly Andrea climbed out of the vehicle. As they walked toward the house, she felt that she was losing what little self-control she had built up during the trip. Memories of the two years she had stayed in Havana started to rush into her mind, like a fast succession of images flashing on a screen inside her head. She hated every one of them. She had been at the edge of madness, and now she was in front of the same house, the same man.

The KGB had taken her out of the mental clinic in Moscow and sent her home. A few weeks after her recovery, a KGB officer came to her home and told her she had a choice to make. She could go back to the mental clinic or to Havana to work on an assignment. When she asked about the assignment, the officer said they would tell her in Havana. She accepted Havana, thinking that nothing could be worse than the clinic. A month later she realized she'd guessed wrong. When she arrived in Havana, the KGB rezident told her her assignment was General Carreras.

A servant in military fatigues waited for them at the door. "The General is waiting," he said to the soldier.

The soldier nodded. "We'll be back tomorrow morning."

"Follow me," the servant said dryly. He was young, strong,

and dark-skinned, in a militia uniform with a gun at his waist.

Andrea didn't need any help finding her way; she knew that Carreras was waiting for her where he always waited.

They walked past the marble-floored foyer, the circular stairs, and an arched hallway and went through a door leading to an inside patio with a large swimming pool. The small guest cabin was at the end of the swimming pool, just a few yards from a sandy beach. It was Carreras' favorite refuge—a place for solitude, drinking, and pleasure, he had always told her.

Andrea slowed her pace, trying to summon some courage again. She owed nothing to Carreras; she had nothing to offer him. The KGB could not hurt her more than they already had. In a sense she was free. She took a deep breath, filling her lungs with the ocean air. She had nothing to lose. They had already taken everything from her.

The servant stopped in front of the door, knocking discreetly. "The General is inside," he said in a low voice, as if not wanting anybody else to know.

Andrea reached for the knob and walked in. She knew the cabin well; a living room and kitchen, both small, and furnished with white-painted rattan furniture; then the large bedroom with a terrace overlooking the ocean—and a large bed. Carreras would be waiting for her on the terrace as he always did—half-drunk and in a vicious mood.

To her surprise Carreras stood in the living room, his arms open, a big smile on his face. "What a pleasure, Valeri Lisenko," he said, walking up to her.

Andrea stopped, trying to keep her distance. "I thought I'd never see you again."

"C'mon, Valeri, or should I call you Andrea Hendrick?" He grabbed her by the shoulders and shook her a little in a playful way.

Andrea watched Carreras' eyes. She could always tell what was in his mind by watching his eyes. No matter what expression the rest of his face had, his eyes never lied. Wearing military fatigues, combat boots, and the pistol belt, he looked a little heavier than he had a year earlier, but his resemblance to

Fidel Castro was still astounding. Andrea stepped back and twisted her shoulder to break his grip. Carreras let her go and walked over to a small bar against one of the walls. He opened a cupboard below the counter and pulled out a bottle of Cuban rum. "Do you want the usual?" he asked.

"I don't drink anymore," she said in an unfriendly tone.

Carreras turned his head and looked at her, but said nothing. He poured half a glass for himself and took a sip as he turned around and leaned against the counter. "I heard that you're in a lot of trouble."

Andrea studied his face, still trying to read his eyes. "What do you want?"

"Dmitri's planning to take you to Moscow in a couple of days," he said.

"Dmitri told me."

"Defectors don't get a second chance," Carreras said, looking at his drink.

Andrea walked a few steps, stopping behind the rattan loveseat. She rested both hands against the back of the seat and shifted her weight. "I don't want a second chance. I'm through with them."

A little smile lifted the corner of Carreras' mouth. "That's not a smart way to talk, Valeri. The KGB despises brave defectors. They kill them slowly and very painfully."

"They've already hurt me," she said.

"Not enough, Valeri, not enough. . . ." He started to pace the room, drink in hand, eyeing her.

Andrea watched him. His icy eyes remained on her, the eyes of a predator studying his victim, trying to determine the best moment to attack. "What do you want from me?" she asked again.

"We had very good times together, huh?" he said, still pacing. "I haven't forgotten them."

Andrea tightened her grip on the back of the loveseat to control the shaking in her hands. "For me it was only a job," she said. "They forced me to do it."

He stopped a few feet from her. "I knew what you were

doing. I'm not a fool. The bastards thought they were buying me. But I went along and enjoyed it." He paused, then added, "I believe you did, too."

Andrea shook her head. "You're wrong. I had no other choice. I had to succeed or they'd have killed me." She lowered her head. "I was weak. I was afraid to die and did whatever I had to do to survive. I'm not afraid anymore. I don't care what Dmitri or the KGB have planned for me."

Carreras came up to Andrea and rested a hand over hers. "Valeri . . . Valeri . . . who's talking about dying? We want to live, to enjoy the great things around us . . . to have fun together."

Andrea slid her hand out from under his, glaring at him. "I don't want to live the way you have in mind. I've had enough of you. If you don't tell me what you want, I'll walk out of here. You can't force me to stay."

Carreras drained his glass. "I'm the only one who can help you. I'm your last hope, and you know it."

Andrea became alert and looked into his eyes.

He went on, "I can get you free to go wherever you want to go—"

"I don't believe you," she said.

He frowned. "This is Cuba. They don't own our land yet."

"What can you do for me?"

"I can arrange for you to escape."

They stared at each other for a few seconds. Andrea trembled, without trying to hide it from Carreras any longer. "What do you want in return?"

"I want a night with you."

"I don't believe you," she said, walking to the door. Then she paused and added, "I don't trust you."

"Don't go," Carreras said, raising a hand.

"I've had enough," she said.

"You're a fool."

"You don't understand. I won't sell myself for my freedom."

Carreras laughed. "Everything has a price."

She kept watching his eyes.

"You're making a big mistake," he went on, still laughing.

She opened the door and stepped into the doorway, turning slightly to face him. "There's nothing you can do to have me. You're a bastard, and I hated every moment that I was with you. I'll hate myself for it for the rest of whatever life I have left."

Carreras rested the glass on the cocktail table and pulled an envelope from his pocket. "Before you go," he said, "I want you to read the paper inside. Then you can leave." He tossed the envelope on the loveseat, then turned around and walked over to the bar. Grabbing the bottle of rum, he left and went out onto the terrace overlooking the ocean.

Andrea hesitated, keeping her eyes on the envelope, not understanding Carreras's intentions. What was inside the envelope that could interest her? There was only one way to find out. Still, an inner voice told her not to move, not to do anything; it could be a trap.

Finally, she made her decision. She walked over to the loveseat, picked up the envelope, and opened it. Slowly she unfolded the paper inside. It was a typed letter with the DGI emblem on the top, signed by Carreras himself. She read it a couple of times, not believing her eyes.

The letter was directed to the officer in charge of custody at the Camilo Cienfuegos hospital. It said:

I am herewith authorizing KGB officer Valeri Lisenko to take into her custody the American Greg Elliot.
General Alejandro Carreras.

Andrea felt the room spin around her. She breathed in gasps, trying to control the whirl of emotions inside her. Greg was in Havana, in a nearby hospital. She couldn't believe it! She knew the place well for she had visited the hospital several times to see a doctor there when she was in Cuba. She folded the letter and slid it into the pocket of her skirt. She rubbed her stomach, feeling the pain. Carreras had made an offer. It was up to her now to decide.

She walked slowly to the door of the terrace. Carreras faced the ocean, drink in hand. The strong wind ruffled her hair and she pushed aside strands of it blowing in her face. "You're right," she said, looking at the distant ocean. "There's always a price for everything."

Carreras looked at her avidly. "You can pick up Greg Elliot tomorrow morning."

CHAPTER 29

"Well, I'm glad to see that you're being reasonable." Carreras rested his hand on her shoulder, but she didn't move. "Let's go inside."

Andrea hesitated. There was no guarantee that Carreras would keep his word the next morning. She knew the risk she was taking. But how could she refuse? She had a letter in her pocket that would get Greg out of the hospital. And it was real—she had seen the DGI stationery before. Once she was at the hospital, they'd release Greg to her. Then what? She knew very few places in Cuba. They could chase them and bring them back to jail. Another thought crossed her mind: Why would Carreras do this for one night in bed with her? It might be a trap, but she had to take the risk. She struggled with the decision. One step at a time, she said to herself. And the first step was to get Greg free.

They walked inside the cabin, Carreras still resting his arm around her shoulder. Andrea held her anger inside. The bastard was relishing the thought of the plans he had for her. She had to play for time and find a way out.

Carreras pulled her close to him and looked at her for a few seconds. Their faces were very close, and she felt his breath. "I dreamed of you for weeks after you left," he said, his mouth almost touching hers. "I was crazy for days. They never told me you were gone—"

"I don't believe you," she said, trying to start a conversation and gain some time to organize her thoughts. "You had many women."

"Not like you," he said, pulling her closer.

Andrea put her hands against his chest. "You're a liar."

"I'm telling you the truth," he answered. "You excited me as nobody else ever has. You drove me crazy."

He pulled her hard against him and kissed her. Andrea pushed against his chest with both hands. She felt his lips and beard, his breath, and closed her eyes, thinking of Greg. Andrea managed to pull away from him and Carreras frowned. She saw anger in his eyes. "You've got to give me a few seconds, please. I need a drink."

"Rum?" he said.

"Yes, a full glass."

He smiled. "Like old times, huh?"

She nodded.

Carreras filled two glasses and handed one to her. Carreras raised his and made a toast. "To the good old times."

Andrea raised her drink and took a sip, looking at him over the rim of the glass. The glance lasted only a moment, but she didn't like the gleam in Carreras' eyes. He had something else in mind. And she knew what it was. She was sure the bastard planned to deceive her. After they spent the night together, Carreras would overpower her and take the letter away. He would then kill her, claiming he'd brought her to the house for interrogation and she'd tried to escape. That would be an easy way out for him. She had to escape. But how?

"I'm getting horny," Carreras said. Looking at the bedroom door and motioning to Andrea to follow him. "You know your way around," he said.

They walked into the bedroom, and Andrea turned to him. "Would you bring the rum with you?"

"Oh, I forgot," he said, smiling. "We'll get smashed in bed," he added, with a lewd look in his eyes.

That was not a bad idea, Andrea thought. But she had to get into bed with him for that. Greg came to mind. How would she be able to face him after a night with Carreras? Three years ago it had been different. She had thought that Greg didn't love her anymore. They had told her that hundreds of times at the KGB clinic. For a time she had believed the KGB doctor, but now she knew Greg loved her, always had. She stopped in front of the bed and shook her head. Carreras could change his mind anytime during the night. She had to do something. "Oh God!" she whispered.

Carreras came back with two bottles of rum and the glasses. He rested the bottles on the nightstand, pulling the bedspread to the floor. He started to disrobe unbuttoning his military shirt. Andrea watched him, still not knowing what to do.

"Get undressed," he said abruptly.

She nodded, pulling her dress over her head. Having worn no underwear she stood naked on the other side of the bed.

"Very good," Carreras said. Unbuckling his pistol belt and laying it folded on a dresser near the nightstand. He sat on the bed and took off his boots, then his pants. Andrea was still watching him.

Carreras took off his briefs and rolled on the bed naked. Andrea still hadn't moved. He extended a hand for her to come to him, then pulled himself up in the bed, tucking a pillow under his head. He opened his legs and started to caress his penis. "C'mon, come over here. I can't wait to fuck you." His eyes burned with lust.

Andrea walked slowly around the bed, her eyes fixed on his. He devoured her with his eyes as he increased the strokes on his penis. The bastard was ready.

She stopped at a prudent distance from him on the side of the bed where he had put the two bottles of rum. She still had the glass in her hand. Carreras opened his legs wider. "Come down to me," he said. "I want you to kiss me all over."

Andrea leaned forward, her eyes still on him and Carreras moaned.

In a swift movement, she splashed rum in his face. Carreras screamed, momentarily blinded. "Bitch!" he screamed, rubbing his eyes with both hands. "I'll kill you."

Andrea darted for his gun. She opened the holster and pulled out the pistol, releasing the safety. Holding the pistol with both hands, she waited until Carreras had finished wiping his eyes. "I'll kill you!" he shouted again amidst his curses.

"I don't think you will," she said, still waiting for him to open his eyes.

He dried his face with one of the pillows as he sat halfway up in the bed and blinked a few times. "You bitch!" he shouted. "I'm gonna fuck you first and then put a bullet in your brain!"

Andrea increased the pressure on the trigger, aiming at his chest. She had to kill him. There was no other choice. He stared at her in surprise; then his face changed and he started to laugh. "You bitch," he said. "You'd actually have killed me, wouldn't you?" He laughed harder.

Andrea didn't understand. He should have been scared to death. He was going to die.

He kept laughing. "I knew that you'd try to kill me," he said, rolling out of bed and standing naked in front of her. He took a couple of steps toward her.

Andrea retreated. "Don't move," she said, still not understanding. "I'll kill you."

Carreras shook his head, still chuckling. "Oh no. You won't. You can't shoot me."

"Don't try me."

He moved another step, puffing his chest out. "Okay. I'll tell you. Shoot me here," he pointed to the middle of his chest, "A bullet in my heart. Go ahead. I bet you can't do it."

Andrea increased the grip on the weapon. "If that's what you want," She pulled the trigger and nothing happened.

"The pistol's empty," he said, bursting into laughter. He yanked the weapon from her hand and slapped her across the face. "That'll teach you a lesson. General Carreras trusts no son-of-a-bitch Russian."

Andrea faltered from the stinging pain. He slapped her again, and her lips started to bleed. "I'm gonna fuck you anyway before I kill you."

"You won't get away with this," she mumbled, holding her face. "Dmitri'll kill you."

"Fuck Dmitri, too," he yelled.

She tried to pull back and run for the door, but Carreras grabbed her arm, twisting it behind her back. Andrea winced in pain. He grabbed her hair, pulling her face close to his. "I gave you the letter because I wanted you to fuck me like you did before. We could've had a lot of fun. Now I'll enjoy it by myself."

"Bastard!" she screamed.

He dragged her to the bed and forced her on top of him. She tried to roll to the other side, but he grabbed one of her legs and pulled her back. "Don't be stupid!" he yelled. "We can still have some fun."

"Never!" she shouted. "You'll have to *kill* me first."

"I will," he said, climbing on her, holding her arms, trying to put his legs between hers.

Andrea struggled to get free, but he was too strong for her. She knew that she was losing ground. She wouldn't be able to stop him. She started to scream. His face was next to hers, and she smelled his hot, alcohol-laden breath. He rubbed his body against her, getting hard against her leg, his hand in search of his penis to penetrate her. She screamed again. Carreras kissed her neck and then moved his head down, trying to kiss her breasts. She closed her eyes, still struggling to get free.

The gunshot sounded loud, and she felt his body jerk, then go limp on top of her. A second gunshot rang out, but he didn't move. She opened her eyes, feeling his blood running down her chest. She felt no pain.

A woman was near the bed, a gun in her hand, staring at Carreras blankly. She wore a military uniform. "I killed the bastard," she said, slurring her words. She was drunk.

Andrea recognized Carreras' wife, the mulatto. "Don't shoot any more," she said, trying to push his body off her.

The woman raised the gun and aimed at Andrea. "You're going to die, too."

"No, please," Andrea begged. "He was raping me. I didn't want to go to bed with him."

"I don't believe you," the woman said.

"Look at my face," Andrea said. "He hit me." She pointed at her still-bleeding mouth and reddened cheek.

Slowly Andrea slid out from under Carreras, leaving him face down on the bed. The two shots had taken off the back of his cranium, his brain was split open. Andrea took her eyes away from the sight. She had to convince the woman, keeping her eyes steady on the weapon.

"I need your help," she said. "I have to get out of here. The KGB wants to kill me," she begged. "I have a husband. They want to kill him, too." She walked around the bed, the woman following her every move with the gun.

"He raped me, too. I was only twelve," she added, starting to cry.

"I know how you feel," Andrea said gently.

"No, you don't. He was a bastard." She moved the gun away from Andrea and aimed it at Carreras, as if ready to shoot him again.

Andrea rushed and grabbed her wrist. "Please give me your gun."

The woman looked at Andrea with glassy eyes. "He's dead, isn't he?"

Andrea nodded and the woman loosened her grip on the gun. "Thank you," Andrea said, taking the gun from the woman's hand. "I'm going to need your uniform, too."

The black Mercedes pulled up in front of the service entrance to the hospital. Andrea knew the place well. That was the door she used to get in and out of the hospital whenever she went to see the doctor. Her KGB control officer in Havana had ordered her to use the service door every time. They could be watching the front door, the KGB officer had said. When she had asked who "they" were, the officer had said, the CIA, of course. Andrea had not believed the man but she had obeyed his orders. Now she was glad she had. She knew her way around.

She had found the Mercedes in the garage, and the keys were always in the car. When she had asked Carreras once why he left them there, he boasted that nobody would dare steal the car.

Andrea walked along the hallway of the hospital, trying not to seem too much in a hurry, in the military uniform with the gun strapped to her waist. She had a head start, but she needed to find Greg as soon as possible. Someone undoubtedly would have heard the shots and would find Carreras' body and call the DGI or Dmitri, ending her hope of freeing Greg.

The fourth floor of the hospital was reserved for highranking DGI people and KGB officers. She wanted to avoid asking too many questions and having somebody call security. She would never make it through a routine check. She had to take a gamble and hope she was right.

The elevator opened and she got out on the fourth floor with a nurse who had been in the elevator. Andrea took a few steps, trying to recall the layout of the floor. The doctor's offices were to the left, and a large wing with patients' rooms was on the right. There was a nurses' station to the right of the elevator where several nurses were chatting behind a counter. She decided to pass them without stopping.

As she walked by, a nurse lifted her head and said, "May I help you, comrade?"

Andrea paused and turned her head toward the nurse, frowning. "I'm Major Lisenko," she said in Spanish. "I'm supposed to pick up a prisoner from this floor."

"What's his name?" the nurse asked.

"Greg Elliot."

The nurse stood up, resting her hand on a nearby phone. "I must check with security first."

"I already have," Andrea said, producing the letter from her pocket and flashing it in the nurse's face. "They sent me here."

The nurse didn't move. "I must call," she insisted.

"I'm in a hurry, comrade," Andrea said. "General Carreras is going to be very upset if I don't take the prisoner immediately."

Andrea noticed the hesitation in the woman's eyes after the mention of Carreras's name. "I'll bring you to him," she finally assented.

They walked briskly through a long hallway, past a small counter with two nurses on duty. Andrea was glad the nurse was guiding her. It would have taken her much longer to find Greg's room alone. Soon they headed for a short wing with rooms on both sides. A soldier sat on a chair next to the door of the last room. Andrea felt her heart trip. When they were a few steps closer, the soldier realized they were coming toward him. He stood up, hoisting his submachine gun.

"Major Lisenko, DGI," Andrea said in an authoritative tone.

The soldier straightened up and looked at Andrea, then at the nurse. "What do you want?"

Andrea unfolded the letter and showed it to the soldier. "Did you check with security?"

Andrea nodded. "I did," she lied. "General Carreras wants to interrogate the prisoner immediately. We want to fly him to Moscow tomorrow morning."

The soldier's face relaxed. "I'll help you."

"You both stay here until I take him out. We still need you to stay on guard. It'll be safer for us if it looks as if the prisoner is still here. Understand?" She looked at the soldier and the nurse; they both nodded. Authority works wonders, Andrea thought nervously.

She rearranged the gun in the holster hanging from her waist, preparing herself for anything. Then she reached for the doorknob and walked inside. There was still the possibility that Greg wasn't in this room. A man was asleep. She stepped closer and let out a sigh of relief. It was Greg. She couldn't believe how terrible he looked.

She shook him by the shoulder, and he stirred but didn't seem to wake. She shook him again and this time he opened his eyes, looking at her as if he didn't know her.

"It's me—Andrea," she whispered, holding back a sob.

Greg opened his mouth, but she put her hand on his lips. "Please, don't say a thing. We must hurry. We might still have a chance to get out of here."

She reached for his arm and pulled the intravenous needle out of his arm. Greg winced.

"I love you," she said.

* * *

Dmitri stopped the jeep and jumped out, leaving the engine running. He ran toward the entrance of the house, where the military servant awaited him. "Where is he?" Dmitri asked.

"In the guest cabin, Colonel. I called you as soon as I found him."

"Is the woman still there?"

"I asked her to stay in the room," the servant told him.

They hurried through the house, the servant leading the way. Dmitri was stunned by the events. The servant had phoned him at the hotel with the news. Carreras was dead, and his wife was drunk and incoherent. The servant had said there'd been another woman with Carreras. Dmitri called the DGI headquarters and learned that Carreras had taken Andrea out of her cell. Andrea might be dead, too. "Are you sure there isn't any other body around?" he suggested.

"There's nobody else in the cabin."

"What about outside?"

"I didn't look outside, Colonel."

"I want you to search outside the cabin and on the beach. The other woman could be wounded and in a panic."

The servant nodded.

When they reached the front door, Dmitri again insisted that the servant look for the other woman. He then walked inside. Carreras' body was in the bed in a pool of blood. His wife sat in a chair, naked, staring at the body as if in a trance. Tears ran down her cheeks.

"Who killed him?" Dmitri asked her.

She didn't respond.

Dmitri walked around the bed and stood blocking the woman's view of Carreras' body. He grabbed her by the hair and shook her. "I asked you a question. *Who killed him?*"

The woman opened her eyes and started to cry. "I did . . . I did!"

"Why?"

"He was raping her . . . the same as he did to me. . . ."

"What happened to the other woman?"

"She took my uniform and left."

"Did you hurt her?"

The woman shook her head. "I wanted to shoot her, but she was not guilty. It was all his fault. The bastard. . . ." she cried.

Dmitri let go of the woman's hair and went over to the bed. He stared at Carreras for a moment. He'd have killed the hot-headed Cuban himself if he had known that Carreras had taken Andrea out of her cell to rape her. The bastard didn't know how to follow directions. He looked around for a phone; he was sure Andrea would try to free Greg Elliot.

He dialed the hospital's internal security number. After a few rings, somebody answered.

"This is Colonel Kotov," he said. "I want to talk to Lieutenant Bravo."

"*Un momento,*" the voice said.

"Lieutenant Bravo," a new voice said.

"This is Kotov. Where's Greg Elliot?" Dmitri asked.

"We released him an hour ago. General Carreras sent for him."

"Who took him?"

"I have the release paper here," Bravo said. "One moment, comrade. Yes, General Carreras sent a release notice authorizing Valeri Lisenko to take the *Americano* with her."

"Did they have an escort?"

"We offered one, but she refused."

"I'll call Carreras," Dmitri said, hanging up the phone.

He turned around and looked at Carreras' body. Maybe it was not such a bad thing that he was dead, he thought.

The servant entered the cabin and said, "There's nobody around, Colonel."

"I know." They both walked to the door. "Take care of her," Dmitri said.

The military servant smiled. "It's about time."

By the time Dmitri reached the pool, he heard the shot. He stopped and looked at the clear water. These Cubans don't have the revolution in their hearts, he thought, glancing at the Spanish villa and the blue ocean. They're too close to the

Imperialists.

The servant came out of the house and hurried to meet Dmitri. "All taken care of, Colonel."

"Good job, comrade." Dmitri said. Then he pulled a pistol from inside his jacket and he shot the servant in the chest.

The jeep's motor was still running as Dmitri climbed behind the steering wheel and released the hand brake. There was only one place where Andrea would take Greg Elliot—and he had to get there before they escaped from Cuba.

He shifted into first and gunned the gas pedal. Andrea had an hour of lead time. He had to hurry to catch up with them.

"Damn Carreras!" he said.

CHAPTER 30

Andrea narrowed her eyes, squinting into the darkness ahead. She eased her foot on the gas pedal and kept her eyes on the narrow road. The entrance to the road leading to the house would show up on the right at any moment now, and she didn't want to miss it. Getting lost so close to their destination would be a disaster.

Their trip had taken almost three hours, and the long drive and constant tension had taken its toll on them. Greg sat next to her, exhausted. He also watched the road, not knowing where they were going. He had slept much of the time; at other times he talked incoherently or hugged and kissed her, crying a little. She guessed they had drugged him intravenously. The KGB doctors had used drugs on her when she was in the KGB clinic in Moscow and the bastards were doing the same thing in Cuba.

"Are you sure you know your way?" Greg asked, his eyes still on the road.

"I told you," Andrea said tensely. "I've been here many times."

"Are you sure the house is empty?" he asked.

"You're making me nervous," she answered, her voice tight.

"I'm sorry . . . I don't mean to. I'm a nervous wreck myself."

She looked at him and smiled. "I'm not mad at you. But we have to keep moving. They could be after us right now."

"How far are we from Havana?"

"I don't know exactly. About a hundred and fifty miles. Varadero Beach is in another province."

"I never heard of it."

"It's the most beautiful beach in Cuba. Rich people used to come here before Castro. Then the Revolution took control of the beach and the empty houses the rich people had left behind." She paused, then added, "The KGB controls several of these houses. High-ranking generals use them when they come to Cuba. The bastards like the good life, too."

"Watch out!" Greg said, interrupting her. "A sharp turn's coming up."

Andrea braked and the tires screeched as the Mercedes took the curve on the curb, its side brushing against dense foliage that bordered the road. "The house is half a mile after this turn. That was close," she added nervously.

"Please slow down."

"I will," she said.

"Are you sure the house is empty?" he asked.

"Most of the time. I came here several times to party and meet high-ranking DGI officers. . . ." She paused, then added, "I met General Carreras here." She didn't want to talk about the general. She had not told Greg that the general was dead and that she had been his lover for two years. They would talk about it later, when they were safe, but now was not the right time. She felt an awkward silence in the car for a few moments. She wasn't sure, but she felt that Greg already knew. Trying to break the silence, she said, "The house is next to the beach. A power boat was always ready at the pier." She glanced quickly at Greg's serious face. She went on, "Varadero is only 90 miles off the Florida keys. It's the part of Cuba closest to America."

"I knew it was 90 miles, but didn't know from where."

She gave him a brief smile. "We've got to talk when we're finally free," she said.

Greg nodded. "Sorry, I'm very uptight. I want you to know that I love you, no matter what. Whether we make it or not, I want you to remember that." He paused, then said, "You're my wife."

Andrea held back her tears. Looking down at the dashboard, she said quietly, "I love you, too."

The headlights illuminated an iron gate. Andrea stopped the

car and jumped out to inspect it. A chain and a heavy-duty padlock hung from the gate and meant that nobody was in the house.

Sliding in behind the steering wheel, she told Greg, "Hold onto the dashboard." She pressed the gas pedal and crashed through the gate.

The impact shattered one of the headlights, but they had enough visibility to keep going on the narrow, one-lane road. Palm trees planted thickly on both sides of the road cast dark shadows ahead of them. She heard the sand drumming the fenders and underframe of the car. The house was three hundred yards from the gate; the ocean, the pier, and the boat were only a few more yards beyond the house. She could hardly wait. The open ocean was just a few minutes away, and 90 miles away was America. "We're almost there," she said, not looking at Greg.

Andrea accelerated as she sighted the house. She drove around the arched front, heading for a separate building that served as a garage. She parked behind the building, facing the ocean. "Nobody can see the car from the front road," she said as they got out and hurried to the house. Greg grabbed her hand, which was cold and clammy. "We'll make it," she said.

She guided Greg to a concrete terrace facing the ocean, walking around a few aluminum chairs and tables with folded umbrellas. They saw no lights inside the house, and Andrea felt confident no one was there. She stopped in front of a glass door and tried to open it. Sometimes they left the door open, she recalled, but now it was locked. "We need a large stone," she said to Greg.

He walked to the edge of the terrace and came back carrying a cinder block. "Step aside."

A moment later he had smashed the glass and they'd gone inside. The door led to a dining room and a kitchen. Andrea turned on a light and searched a few drawers until she found a flashlight. She turned off the lights. "Somebody could see us from a distance."

"Where is the boat?" Greg asked.

"The pier's to the right of the terrace, but first we need to get some food and water." She paused, then added, "You need some food now and a cup of strong coffee." She caressed his forehead. "You're cold and sweaty."

"I'm not hungry," he said, sitting down on one of the kitchen chairs. "I can barely walk. I'm so tired."

"The coffee will stimulate you and help to get rid of the drugs."

Pointing the flashlight into the kitchen cabinets, she searched them one by one. There was no food, except for two cans of soup, a half-empty jar of instant coffee, and a stale package of sliced bread. She smelled the bread; it was still good enough to eat. She looked inside the refrigerator, but it was empty. The cans of soup and the bread were all the food they had for their trip.

Andrea poured some water into a metal pan and rested it on the electric stove. "Watch the water boil," she told Greg. "I want to check the boat."

Greg got up from his chair. "Please don't go. I don't want you out of my sight." He stepped closer and pulled her against him.

Andrea embraced him, too, kissing him softly on the lips. "I promise you, I'll never leave you again."

He kissed her hard, and she felt his rough beard. "I'll die before I'll lose you again," he said after the kiss, still hugging her tightly.

She felt his arms tremble from the effort. "You've got to save your strength for our trip," she said. "Perhaps we can do some other things with that much free time on the ocean." She kissed him on the cheek. "We must hurry. Watch the water." She left the room with the flashlight, hoping that the boat was gassed up.

Dmitri released the gas pedal, switched off the headlights, and braked the jeep to a halt. He faced the iron gate leading to the house on the beach. He knew the place well; he had spent many days there with Cuban women: a special treat for the high-ranking KGB comrades when they visited Cuba. He also knew that Andrea had visited the house on assignments, and that the house had a power boat ready for fishing and scuba diving. He was sure that Andrea had the boat on her mind. It was their only way out.

He climbed out of the jeep and inspected the gate. Somebody had crashed through it, sending shattered glass everywhere. No doubt it had been Andrea. He rushed back to the jeep and parked it so that it blocked the exit gate, then turned off the engine and pocketed the key. A high stone fence surrounded the property, so the only way out was the gate or the ocean. The thought made him jump out of the jeep. He would walk the last stretch of road to the house. Andrea had no way of knowing he was coming. They were probably busy getting the boat ready to sail.

Dmitri pulled out his gun and made sure that he had a fresh magazine inside. He slid the gun into the rig under his arm and began to walk fast. He had a big surprise for Andrea and Greg, and he couldn't wait.

Greg and Andrea walked along the long, narrow, wooden pier that ended at the moored boat. Greg carried a small cardboard box with the bread, the soups, a knife, a can opener, and a few empty wine bottles filled with water. Andrea walked in front of him, with the lit flashlight and a couple of blankets. She was right; the coffee had helped him dispel the fog inside his head from the drugs. But he had refused to eat the bread, saving it for the boat.

Andrea had searched the boat and had returned with a big smile on her face. The single-engine cruiser had enough gas to make the 90-mile stretch. It also had a sleeping cabin and a radio they could use to call for help once they were closer to the Florida keys. Greg was worried because they didn't know how to sail, but he thought they would be all right if they followed the compass west. Sooner or later, they'd find ground. He was sure of that.

Andrea reached the boat first and tossed the blankets inside. She turned to Greg to help him with the box and then froze. "Oh God!" she said, an expression of panic on her face.

"What's the matter?" Greg asked. Turning his head, he looked over his shoulder and made out the silhouette of a man standing at the other end of the pier. The man with a gun walked slowly in their direction, and Andrea pointed the flashlight at him.

"Dmitri!" Andrea said.

Dmitri stopped a few yards from Greg. "Turn off that flashlight," he said icily. "Your trip is off."

Greg stood between Dmitri and Andrea, holding the box with the food and water. He didn't know what to do, but he couldn't let the bastard stop them.

"Step to the side, Valeri," Dmitri said to Andrea. "I want to see you."

Andrea moved next to Greg, keeping her hands low, close to her gun. Greg realized what she wanted to do. She was thinking of shooting Dmitri, but there was no way she could shoot him first; the Russian's gun was already aimed at them. "Please, don't try anything foolish," Greg begged Andrea. "He'll kill you."

"Very good," Dmitri said. "I'm glad you're being reasonable." He moved close and stopped again.

Greg looked at Dmitri's face. He hated the bastard.

"Let Greg go, and I'll go with you," Andrea said.

Dmitri smiled. "Very good offer, comrade."

"Fuck no!" Greg shouted. "You've caused us enough trouble. I want to take Andrea with me."

Dmitri looked at Andrea. "The gun. Take your gun out of the holster with your fingertips. Throw it into the water."

Greg saw Andrea hesitating. "Please do it or he'll kill you."

Andrea glanced at Dmitri, then at Greg. She slowly slid the gun out and tossed it into the water.

"Very good, comrade."

"I want you to let Greg go free," she said. "He's suffered

enough. You know he's not CIA. I'll cooperate with you. You've got my word."

"I said no!" Greg protested again. "We'll face whatever is ahead together."

Dmitri walked within a couple of feet of Greg and shook his head. "Very touching. You're in love." He smiled again. "The Center will love this one. A KGB spy in love with an American boy." He laughed again.

Dmitri took his eyes off them for a split second as he laughed and the gun wavered slightly. Greg had been waiting for just that moment. He hurled the box of food at Dmitri, hitting him in the middle of the chest. Caught by surprise, the Russian took a step backward. The bottles crashed on the pier. Greg jumped forward and grabbed Dmitri with both hands, wrestling him for control of the gun. Dmitri twisted his body to loosen Greg's grip, but failed. They lost their balance, slipping and falling on the wet pier.

"The gun! Watch out for the gun!" Andrea shouted, running to help Greg.

The two men rolled around on the pier, trying to grab the weapon. Greg knew he was losing ground. He was weak, while the Russian was very strong. "Run to the boat!" he shouted to Andrea. "I'll hold him down."

With a sudden twist of the wrist, Dmitri freed his hand with the gun and shouted, "I'll kill you!" He hit Greg's head with the barrel of the gun.

Greg felt the pier and the sky disappearing from around him. He struggled not to lose consciousness, shaking his head. "You'll have to kill me, you bastard!" he shouted.

Dmitri had raised the gun to hit him again when Andrea jumped on Dmitri's back and grabbed the gun with both hands. She bit his arm near the wrist and Dmitri screamed.

Greg grabbed Dmitri's hair and yanked him to the side, rolling over him. Andrea lost her balance, rolling with Dmitri. Dmitri fired once, but the bullet went astray. Andrea, tangled up with Dmitri, still had her teeth clamped on his forearm.

Dmitri tried to grab Andrea's hair with his free hand, but

Greg punched him in the face. The Russian fell on his back against the pier and Greg reached for the gun and yanked with all the strength he had left. The gun slipped from the Russian's hand and fell on the pier.

Greg plunged after the gun as Dmitri still struggled with Andrea. Greg got hold of the weapon and whacked Dmitri on the forehead with the butt. Dmitri moaned and kicked Greg in the leg. "I'll kill you, you son of a bitch!" Greg shouted, putting his pain out of his mind.

Dmitri punched Andrea's shoulder and she fell backward. The Russian got to his knees, preparing to stand up; Greg kicked him in the ribs. Dmitri lost his balance, falling off the pier into the water. Greg dropped to his knees, looking down at the darkness under the pier. He saw a black mass moving in the water and fired the gun until the magazine was empty. He then threw the gun where he had last seen Dmitri. He looked down for a few seconds, but saw no movement.

"Let's hurry up," Andrea said, grabbing him by the shoulder.

"Are you okay?"

She didn't answer. "The boat. We've got to get away. Somebody might've heard the shots."

They ran to the boat and Andrea started the engine while Greg untied the rigs. He jumped into the boat and Andrea pulled the throttle. The boat moved forward, leaving the pier behind.

"Do you know your way out of here?" Greg asked, still panting and feeling the pain on the side of his head.

"I do," she said. "But we have no water and no food."

"We're gonna make it or die," he said. "But we're gonna be together."

"That's the way I want it," she answered.

EPILOGUE

Greg squinted at the sun above him. He didn't remember seeing such a hot sun in all his life. The orange ball felt like a furnace at full blast. He was sure they were sailing directly through hell. He raised his hand slowly and rubbed his face, touching his mouth with his fingertips. His lips were swollen and cracked and he couldn't speak without feeling a burning pain. He was so thirsty, and they were surrounded by undrinkable water. Lying in the cabin of the boat, a blanket tucked under his head, he had lost track of how many days they had been adrift without food and water. He only knew that the engine had stopped working early the first morning. And to make the situation worse, the boat's radio had never worked.

At first, they were afraid that a Cuban patrol boat would discover them and take them back to Cuba. Then, as the days passed, they began to worry about staying alive. Without water they couldn't survive. Days later, it didn't matter anymore. They just wanted to be together when they died.

Greg turned on his side and, grabbing a wooden railing, pulled himself up. His legs were weak and barely held his weight. Slowly he walked to the narrow ladder to the boat's sleeping quarters. He hesitated, not knowing if he could walk down it; but he had to. Andrea was down there, and he didn't want to leave her alone for any length of time.

Step by step he made his way down, resting against the side of the ladder to regain some of his strength. His eyes darted to the bunk bed where Andrea lay. He saw her breathing and sighed with relief. She was still alive.

He approached the bed and sat weakly on the edge. When he shook her gently, she opened her eyes.

"How are you doing?" he asked, trying to smile to comfort her, but his cracked lips forced him to stop.

"I'm fine," she said, weakly. "How 'bout you?"

He nodded a few times. "I'm hanging in there. We're gonna make it." Greg touched her forehead. She had a high fever; her eyes were hollow and the skin around them dry and greenish. Still, he said, "You look great."

Andrea smiled.

Greg got to his feet, watching her. Whatever was in the future for them, they'd face it together.

"Where are you going?" she asked, her eyes half-open.

"Back to the cabin," he said. "Who knows? Maybe we'll see a nice cruise ship going to California."

"You can't sail to California from here," she said, smiling weakly.

"We could use the Panama Canal," he said.

She extended her hand. "I want to go up to the cabin with you."

"You'll get seasick," he said.

"I couldn't be any sicker than I am," she answered. "And I'll be with you."

Greg saw the fear in her eyes. Perhaps she didn't want to die alone, Greg thought. "I'll help you."

After he pushed her up the ladder, he gathered enough strength to go up himself. They sat on the floor of the cabin with their arms around each other. Andrea rested her head on his shoulder and sobbed silently for a few seconds.

"Don't cry, please. We're together now, and that's all that

matters."

"Remember Reno," she said.

"Yes."

"Some day we'll go back to the place where we got married."

"I promise you we will," Greg said, his eyes moist. He wiped his tears.

"Hey, you! Anybody there?" a voice shouted. At first Greg believed it was his imagination, but then he heard another shout. "Anybody inside?"

He dragged himself up against the wall of the cabin, leaving Andrea on the floor. He didn't believe his eyes. The large hull of a freighter was next to the boat. He slid halfway through the small window and looked up. About half a dozen sailors were perched on the railing of the freighter's deck. Greg waved at them.

"You in trouble?" one of the sailors said.

Greg nodded, too weak to shout.

A rope ladder went over the side of the freighter, and a man started to climb down. A thought crossed Greg's mind: the freighter could be sailing back to Cuba.

He waited until the man reached the side of the cruiser and jumped to the deck. The man was tall and bare-chested; he had a mustache, and his chest bore a large tattoo of a naked woman. "You look like shit," the man said.

"We're almost dead," Greg answered.

The man shouted for water and medical assistance. Greg couldn't stand any longer and slid to the floor next to Andrea.

He waited until the man walked over to them. "Where's your ship going?" he asked, his eyes riveted on the sailor.

The man looked at him and smiled. "Puerto Rico. Why? Where do you want to go?"

Greg let a long sigh escape from his chest. He hugged

Andrea and felt her crying. He kissed her on the head. "Puerto Rico is fine."

It was more than fine. It was perfect.

ABOUT THE AUTHOR

ARNALDO HERNANDEZ is a Cuban writer exiled in this country for over twenty years. His expertise in computers and experience working for many computer firms in Silicon Valley provide the background for his novels. He currently lives in Los Altos, California.